Praise for
The Gardins of Edin

"The surprises and heart in this fast-paced family drama kept me turning pages late into the night."
—KJ DELL'ANTONIA, *New York Times* bestselling author of *The Chicken Sisters*

"In a clever twist, debut author Rosey Lee plucks four women inspired by the Bible and sets them down in a tension-filled contemporary Black family struggling to find answers to messy and pesky questions. As they sort out relational fireworks, will they figure out how to stay a family and also be their best selves? It's a loving and lovely journey from an exciting, talented new author willing to explore the meaning of family in intriguing ways."
—PATRICIA RAYBON, Christy Award–winning author of the Annalee Spain Mystery series and two critically acclaimed memoirs, *My First White Friend* and *I Told the Mountain to Move*

"Rosey Lee's *The Gardins of Edin* testifies to all that it means to be family. It conveys the passion, heartbreak, faithfulness, and conflict that come with loving the people closest to you. Readers will wish they owned a cottage on the Gardin estate or lived close enough to witness firsthand all the goings-on in Lee's fascinating saga."
—ROBIN W. PEARSON, Christy Award–winning author

"Nothing complicates a family more than a family business. *The Gardins of Edin* by Rosey Lee is a gorgeous debut that freshly examines the painful past of two sisters and their matriarch, their cousin by marriage, and their successful peanut farm. With courage and ambition akin to the casts and epic dramas of Tayari Jones, Lee has written a page-turner of grief and hope."

—MELISSA SCHOLES YOUNG, author of *The Hive*

"With complex and intriguing characters reminiscent of their biblical namesakes, Rosey Lee's *The Gardins of Edin* provides an allegorical look at friendship, family tension, and the concept of forgiveness."

—KIMMERY MARTIN, author of *Doctors and Friends*

The
Gardins
of Edin

THE GARDINS OF EDIN

A Novel

Rosey Lee

WATERBROOK

All Scripture quotations are taken from the Holy Bible, New International Version®, NIV®. Copyright © 1973, 1978, 1984, 2011 by Biblica Inc.™ Used by permission of Zondervan. All rights reserved worldwide. (www.zondervan .com). The "NIV" and "New International Version" are trademarks registered in the United States Patent and Trademark Office by Biblica Inc.™

2024 WaterBrook Trade Paperback Original

Published in the United States by WaterBrook, an imprint of Random House, a division of Penguin Random House LLC.

WATERBROOK and colophon are registered trademarks of Penguin Random House LLC.

Library of Congress Cataloging-in-Publication Data
Names: Lee, Rosey, author.
Title: The gardins of Edin: a novel / Rosey Lee.
Description: First edition. | [Colorado Springs] : WaterBrook, 2024.
Identifiers: LCCN 2023015850 | ISBN 9780593445495 (trade paperback; acid-free paper) | ISBN 9780593445501 (ebook)
Subjects: LCSH: Christian fiction. | LCGFT: Novels.
Classification: LCC PS3612.E348529 G37 2024 |
DDC 813/.6—dc23/eng/20230725
LC record available at https://lccn.loc.gov/2023015850

Printed in the United States of America on acid-free paper

waterbrookmultnomah.com

2 4 6 8 9 7 5 3 1

Book design by Diane Hobbing

Flower illustrations based on the original image by AdobeStock/Ringele

To my teachers: my parents, who were my first teachers; my preschool teachers, who made me try spinach; my Sunday school and Vacation Bible School teachers; my summer camp art and logic teachers; my church members who taught me sewing, acting, public speaking, how to manage a meal program, and how to throw a fabulous luncheon; the teachers who believed in me and nurtured my gifts; and even the teachers who challenged me to prove them wrong when they misjudged me.

The
Gardins
of Edin

Chapter One

How have I lasted in this family so long? Ruth thought as she steered her golf cart toward Naomi's driveway. The cart bounced up and down along the old redbrick path, and Ruth wobbled along with it. She was tired of being jerked around—by the golf cart and the tensions brewing in her family. She wondered if the bumpy shortcut to her mother-in-law's cottage was symbolic of her convoluted placement in the Gardin family tree and the repercussions that came along with it.

Visitors usually parked in the small circular driveway in front of the house, where the asphalt was smooth, but Ruth rarely drove along the street to get to Naomi's cottage during the daytime. Although the women lived next door to each other on the Gardin family estate, their homes were separated by a couple of acres of deciduous trees, and the brick path connected the far end of Naomi's driveway to Ruth's backyard. It was the last original road on the estate, its bricks crafted and laid by the formerly enslaved people who settled the land and whose descendants comprised the family into which Ruth had married. Ruth treasured the path's history and convenience, but they weren't the reason she tolerated the uncomfortable commute. It was because she finally felt peaceful when she drove over the last brick, marking the spot where she and Beau had spent hours talking and stargazing when she first moved to Edin with Naomi.

After Ruth stopped the golf cart at the edge of the bricks, she took a long, deep breath, leaning into the headrest with her back slightly arched. The stretch reminded her of yoga class but did little to ease the tension in her lower back. Once a regular attendee, Ruth hadn't gone to a yoga class in a year and a half, since the morning Beau died. But she visited the spot in Naomi's driveway almost every day, most often in the middle of the night when she couldn't sleep.

Dissatisfied with her stretch, Ruth opened her eyes. She stared up at the sky, thinking of Beau. Red, orange, and bright-yellow hues reflected off the thin clouds as the sun set. She marveled at the horizon, which felt like a fiery reminder that she was about to face a task she'd dreaded all week. Instead of backing down, Ruth was emboldened. She jumped out of the cart like a Manx cat, landing flawlessly in the stiletto heels she'd worn since her 7:30 A.M. check-in meeting with the event planner she hired for the Gardin Family Enterprises Christmas party. With the gathering only a week away and this year being her first time relinquishing the party-planning duties since she married Beau, Ruth was nervous, especially given the media outlets and influencers scheduled to cover the high-profile event.

As Ruth sped up the front walk to Naomi's cottage, she smoothed the soft fabric of the black V-necked pencil dress she wore. She hardly noticed the multicolored flashing Christmas lights Naomi had placed in the bushes that afternoon. Ruth's schedule had been filled with back-to-back meetings since she took the helm of Gardin Family Enterprises after Beau's death, and it was beginning to wear on her. She was grateful when she noticed the small details she used to obsess about previously, but Ruth couldn't deal with Naomi's unauthorized holiday decisions. Though Christmas remained Ruth's favorite time of the year, she had no time to commit to her tradition of coordinating decorations at the four homes on the family estate. Without someone to rein her in, Naomi was prone to go overboard. She couldn't help it. A simple decorated bush could morph into a flood of string lights cascading from the fountain in the front yard with a sea of candy canes and inflatables spilling into the street.

Ruth slowed as she accessed the steps of the wraparound porch, digging inside her black Brandon Blackwood tote until she found a scratched heart-shaped key chain. She inserted the single key in the door lock but decided the evening might go better if she rang the doorbell instead. As she eased the key from the lock, the door opened.

"I was wondering what took you so long to come up to the house. It's too early for you to be sleeping in the driveway again," Naomi said with a sly grin. She extended her arms in a broad V shape. With her silver curls falling below her shoulders and white oversized cardigan draping her petite frame, she looked like a mischievous angel.

"When did you see me sleep in the driveway?" Ruth asked as she crept toward Naomi, extending her arms to return the greeting.

"Almost every night," Naomi replied. She wrapped her arms around Ruth and squeezed while she rubbed her back.

"Well, I wish you'd told me. I might've appreciated some company," Ruth joked, attempting to mask her shock. The visit would be emotional enough. She needed to save her energy, so she focused on the familiar aroma that had hit her as she entered the house and had then intensified as she hugged Naomi. Despite the woman's ill-timed observation, Naomi gave the best hugs. Ruth held on for another second before she let go, savoring the buttery smell with hints of cinnamon and vanilla that meant Naomi had made an impromptu batch of snickerdoodles.

"I'm too cute to sleep outside. Camping was never my cup of tea. Speaking of tea, would you like some hibiscus tea?" Naomi asked as she sauntered down the hallway leading to the kitchen.

"Yes, that sounds good," Ruth said as she followed behind Naomi. She hoped to look as good as her mother-in-law did in fitted jeans when she turned sixty-nine years old.

"By the way, I'm thinking of redecorating. I've got an appointment tomorrow with an interior designer. I think it's time for another project. I feel like I need something to do."

Ruth pretended not to be affected by the revelation that, as always, Naomi was a step ahead of her. "Okay," Ruth said, the last syllable dragging out as the muscles tightened at the nape of her neck. Before they reached the kitchen, the doorbell chimed. "I'll get it," she said, angling to buy some time to regroup. "Go ahead. They'll want some tea too."

Ruth entered the foyer and peered into the large oval mirror opposite the door. *Why didn't she tell me my hair is a mess?* Although the natural curls gathered at the top of her head were already neatly coiffed, she pulled and fluffed them while she inspected her makeup.

The doorbell rang again as she lowered her face to the peephole.

"Open up. It's us, your favorite nieces," a muffled voice said.

Even through the peephole, their flawless deep-brown skin, pouty lips, and prominent eyes made the sisters look like models in a Doublemint gum commercial.

Ruth took a deep breath and opened the door. Greeting Mary and Martha with a quick hug as they entered the foyer, Ruth marveled at how much the sisters looked more alike as they got older. Although sometimes confused for twins, the women were two years apart. They had such similar taste that they bought the same clothes even when they didn't shop together.

"Hey, Ruth. Do you know you left your golf cart running? Are you okay?" Mary asked, handing Ruth her keys.

"Oh, I was rushing to get inside. Thank you. I have a lot on my mind. I . . . I guess I'm more distracted than I realized," she said, lowering her voice to a whisper. "So, I think she suspects we're up to something. Which one of you told her? She's talking about renovating. How can we convince her to move in with me if she's planning to update the house? And she baked snicker-doodles too. She knows."

"I bet Aunt Naomi is making tea. I'm going to go help," Martha said as she scurried past Ruth.

Ruth's head swung toward Mary. "Martha told her, didn't she?" she whispered. "A lot is going on at the company right now. I need everything to be perfect for the Christmas party. I don't have time for this."

Mary shrugged and followed her sister without answering Ruth's question.

Ruth sighed. *I'm gonna have to clean up their mess, just like when they were kids.* She followed the sisters into Naomi's kitchen, like ants following the scent left behind by their leader. Ruth pointed to the dry-erase board sitting on an easel in the center of the kitchen table. "Look at this," she said as she walked closer. "'The honor of your presence is requested at high tea. Please join me in the dining room.'" Ruth shook her head. "I *told* you she's on to us."

Martha dismissively waved her hands. "I didn't tell her, but she probably figured it out because we don't get together much anymore and we asked if we could come over today even though we have the Gardin Family Enterprises board meeting at your house tomorrow. You have to admit that a bunch of family time all of a sudden *is* a little strange. She put it together and realized we were up to something."

Martha nudged her sister.

"Yeah, that makes sense," Mary said as she backed away from Martha.

"I guess," Ruth replied. "You can say it. You're busy at the hospital and don't have time for us."

"That's not true," Martha said. "I—"

"Martha, remember when Aunt Naomi used to have us over for high tea in Atlanta when we were kids?" Mary asked. "We never wanted to stop playing when she called us to dinner, but we were interested when she called us to high tea instead."

"And then we would race to see who could get to the bathroom first to wash our hands," Martha said, then laughed.

"C'mon, Martha, let's race like we used to," Mary said.

Ruth wished Mary wouldn't intrude when she tried to call Martha out, but Mary's words packed a double punch, as the high tea parties they remembered were Ruth's idea. Somehow they didn't recall *that* part. Being left out of cherished memories made Ruth feel only more insecure about her place in the family. *When will I be good enough to be included?* she wondered.

* * *

RUTH AND NAOMI had been inseparable since Ruth married Marlon, Naomi's son, after graduating from college. Naomi had lost her husband the year before, and she was elated when the newlyweds asked if Ruth could live with her in Atlanta while Marlon was deployed with the Air Force. Most daughters-in-law might have been put off by the arrangement, but Ruth loved living with Naomi. She spent all her free time with her, despite having many friends from college who stayed in Atlanta after graduation. The women were so close that Ruth felt unnatural calling Naomi *Mrs. Gardin,* so she called her *MIL* instead, turning the mother-in-law acronym into a nickname. After Marlon died while on active duty, their mutual loss drew the women even closer, so close that Ruth insisted on moving with Naomi when she decided to move onto the Gardin family estate in Edin.

Ruth had always enjoyed weekend trips to Edin, only eighty miles southwest of Atlanta. She was proud of the Gardin family's history of leadership among the formerly enslaved people who founded the town. Although she hadn't been excited about full-time rural living, she couldn't imagine life without Naomi. And once she got settled in Edin, she didn't miss the city as much as she thought she would. She also adored Naomi's preteen nieces back then, but things had changed over the years.

Mary darted through the living room toward the bathroom, with Martha following behind closely. In an attempt to cut Mary off, Martha bumped into the sofa table, which held stacks of photos Naomi had been sorting before they arrived. Ruth spread her arms and pushed her body against the table, preventing memories from cascading to the floor.

"Oh, thanks. You always have impeccable timing," Martha sneered.

"Uh-huh," Ruth said, opting to save her energy for the battle with Naomi that lay ahead. She pushed the photos back a few inches and noticed that one of them had fallen on the dark oak floor, just beyond the baby grand piano. Already frustrated with how the evening was progressing, Ruth considered leaving the photo where it landed, but curiosity caused her to linger and she flipped it over. She remembered going with Naomi to a family cookout by the lake shortly after they moved back to Edin, but she had forgotten how sad her mother-in-law was back then. She was about Ruth's age, forty-eight, in the photo. Naomi's skin glowed after a week of gardening on the estate, but Ruth recognized her forced smile and the distance in her eyes. Over the past several months, she saw the same things on her own face each time she looked in a mirror.

Minutes flew by as Ruth sat on the piano bench, staring at the photo. She startled when she heard Naomi yell her name from the dining room.

"It doesn't take that long to wash your hands. What are you doing?" Naomi continued.

"Just looking at the photos by the piano. Be there in a minute." Ruth slid the photo into the interior pocket of her tote bag. She wasn't sure what she would do with the picture, but she wanted it to be with her wherever she went.

As Ruth washed her hands in the bathroom next to the dining room, she grew more worried that the sisters weren't taking her warnings seriously. She half dried her hands and hurried to join the other women.

"Aunt Naomi made all my favorites!" Mary said as Ruth entered the dining room.

"I did, and I may have a special treat for dessert," Naomi sang.

"No! Not my favorite snickerdoodles?" Mary asked playfully.

"Yep, but I made the plant-based version you serve in the restaurant!" Naomi said, bobbing her head from side to side in a dancing motion.

Mary licked her lips. She was falling for Naomi's plan. Ruth had seen the dynamic play out many times over the years. Mary was going to support whatever strategy Naomi had concocted.

Ruth loved when Naomi baked, but she wasn't in the mood for cookies anymore. How could she think about dessert when she wasn't sure how she'd make it through dinner? She slid into her usual seat next to Naomi.

After Naomi said grace, Ruth removed the pressed linen napkin from her plate and nestled it on her lap, revealing the delicate gold floral pattern on Naomi's wedding china. Ruth usually hated avocado green, but the color gave a regal effect on the exterior of the china in contrast with the cream-colored interior and handles. Ruth couldn't remember the last time Naomi had used the plates. Instead of getting them out for family gatherings, Naomi preferred to admire them on the top shelf of the nineteenth-century stepback hutch she bought when she moved to Edin. Ruth had convinced her not to refinish the cupboard's chipped dark green and cream paint. Its contrast with the pristine china created a stunning classic-meets-modern design aesthetic and served as a visual reminder to Ruth that she belonged on the estate.

"So, what's the special occasion, MIL?" Ruth probed.

Martha and Mary didn't look at Ruth. They maintained their focus on the dishes they passed back and forth to each other and filled their plates with Caesar salad, garlic green beans, sautéed mushrooms, roasted butternut squash, and homemade dinner rolls. Ruth wasn't sure if they had come up with their own plan since she had deviated from the subtle approach the three of them had agreed to take. But Ruth didn't care. She figured the dirty work would be left to her anyway. She might as well get it over with.

"Just a nice Friday evening meal with the family," Naomi said with a smile.

Ruth exhaled. "MIL, it's been a long week. Can we make this easy? Please just tell us what's on your mind."

"Fair enough," Naomi replied, dabbing the corner of her mouth with her napkin. "Something tells me y'all are here to stage some sort of intervention, but none of that will be going on tonight." She turned to Ruth. "I'm not moving in with you. I don't want to leave my house."

Ruth ignored her hunger pains and the sweet aroma of the button mushrooms that sat in front of her on the table. "You're home all the time," she said. "That's the problem. I'm worried you're starting to isolate yourself from us. What's going on?"

"I've been going out more, but you've been so obsessed with running Gardin Family Enterprises that you haven't noticed," Naomi replied, fiddling with the sparkling diamond stud earring in her right ear.

A smirk developed on Martha's face, but Ruth pretended not to see it. She was too busy looking at Naomi's earrings, which Beau had given Naomi on his and Ruth's twentieth wedding anniversary. After he died, Naomi went from donning the two-carat studs nearly daily to wearing them only at events she said Beau wouldn't have wanted to miss. Ruth began to realize that she had grossly underestimated her mother-in-law's strategy for the gathering.

"You're right," Ruth replied. "It seems I've missed some important things. But you threw a tea party just to tell us you refuse to move in with me? Why go through all this?"

"Yeah, what can we do to make it better?" Martha asked, popping up from her seat and putting her arm around Naomi. As she rose, she knocked her fork across her plate, hurling the garden green beans and squash across the table. They landed on Ruth's empty plate.

Martha inched closer to Naomi. "Sorry, Ruth," she said with a half smile.

"No problem," Ruth replied dryly.

"I want to see y'all more often. We live on the same property— land our ancestors bought and handed down to us. We can get to one another's houses in minutes, but we barely spend any time together anymore. We've gotta do better," Naomi pleaded. "We only have each other left now."

Their family was small, and now with Beau gone and Ruth and Beau's son, M.J., away in graduate school, the only remaining Gardin family members in Edin were Naomi, Mary, and Martha. Ruth enjoyed being with Naomi, but it was hard to sacrifice her rare free time if Mary and Martha were also invited. It had become harder to manage the tension between them without Beau as a buffer. As Naomi spoke, Ruth wondered how she could spend more time with her mother-in-law without including them.

"But we just had Thanksgiving dinner together," Martha whined as she returned to her chair.

Naomi squinted. "Are you serious? You and Mary hardly ate anything at Thanksgiving, and you left early. Before that, we hadn't all been together since the breast cancer awareness luncheon at church a whole month before. And we were only there together because you were the keynote speaker. Mary couldn't even sit with us because she catered it, so the luncheon doesn't count!"

Ruth buried her head in her hands.

"Speaking of holidays, didn't we talk about rules for our Christmas decorations?" Mary asked. "Aunt Naomi, your lights are tacky, so don't be mad when you come outside tomorrow and can't find them."

"Don't touch my lights, young lady!" Naomi said, wagging her finger.

"I will make no promises," Mary said, cackling.

Ruth lifted her head. "Could we be serious and get back to the topic? Would it help if *I* moved in with *you*?" she asked.

"My goodness, child, no," Naomi responded. "You live right next door. I know it's hard being in that big house by yourself since Beau died and with M.J. away at school, but I'm used to having my own space."

Martha rested her fork on her plate and leaned forward. "Besides, Ruth, I couldn't let you do that. *I* could move in. We appreciate what you've done for our family, but you've got so much on your plate at the company." The words flew out of her mouth so melodically that it was as if she had rehearsed them for years and saved them for the perfect time.

"That's enough," Naomi said. "No, you will each stay in your own home. I think I've made my point clear. I'll see you at Ruth's tomorrow, so maybe we can figure out a plan for regular family time then."

"Fine," Martha said, lowering her eyes. She turned toward Ruth. "Please pass the tea. And what are we meeting about tomorrow, anyway?"

Still distracted by Martha's earlier comment, Ruth stared

down at the green beans and squash that Martha had flung to her plate. *They really don't want me here anymore.* She felt defeated but tried not to let it show.

"Ruth, the tea, please," Martha said. "And what are—"

"Oh," Ruth said. She grasped the delicate teapot, her hands shaking slightly. "Sorry, the pot is still a little hot," she said as she tilted it toward the matching cup Martha held. "I'd like to provide some updates and talk through plans for the company in the upcoming year." She steadied her hand, thinking of the photo she had found on the floor beside the piano. Then she forced a smile.

*   *   *

THE COUNTDOWN TIMER on the control pad of Ruth's house alarm was almost at twenty seconds. She wiped her puffy eyes and tried entering her alarm code for the third time, smudging damp mascara on the buttons. The chiming finally ended. *Thank goodness. The last thing I need is the alarm going off and Mary and Martha running over here to see what happened.* She couldn't bear for them to see her like this and know that they'd caused her to lose her composure after all.

Ruth kicked off her shoes and looked toward the staircase to yell up to Beau, but then she remembered he wasn't there. When Beau was alive, he rarely had to intervene in family arguments. Just the thought of his doing so kept the Gardin women from going too far. Ruth could never figure out how he exerted so much influence, especially since Naomi was older, but she was glad it kept her life peaceful. The women seemed afraid of disappointing Beau. They placed him on a pedestal, but her relationship with him was different. She loved and respected him too, but they functioned as partners at home and at work. As Ruth took on more responsibility at Gardin Family Enterprises, he coached her and helped her understand the nuances of relationships—the professional ones and those within the family. Now she had to figure things out on her own.

Martha's words echoed in Ruth's head, and they stung: *"We appreciate what you've done for our family."* Ruth sat on the edge of the stairs and began to cry again. *"Our" family. Like it's just "theirs." Like I'm still not part of it after twenty-six years. I mean, have I not earned a place here? What do I have to do to be accepted? I've been married to two of their cousins. I had a chance to escape, but I stuck around.*

"This is my family too!" she yelled between sobs. She cried so hard that she didn't realize she was kneeling on the stairs and gripping the rectangular cutouts on the iron spindles until her hands began to ache. She let go. Her body fell against the spindles, and she landed on her rear end.

It felt good to release the pent-up emotion she'd been carrying around, but she wondered if her tears were about more than the evening at her mother-in-law's house. She recalled that her therapist, Shari, had recommended that she ask herself two questions the next time this happened, only she couldn't remember what they were. Those types of assignments always made her uncomfortable, but she had too much at stake with the family business meeting the following day not to give it a try. She couldn't afford to have a meltdown there.

Ruth ran up the stairs to the second floor. Within seconds, she passed M.J.'s bedroom and two guest bedrooms. She paused as she touched the glass knob on the antique french door to Beau's study. She revered the space and wouldn't dishonor it by rushing and inadvertently displacing anything inside. She never spent much time in the room when Beau was alive. It was too stuffy for her contemporary taste. Despite the large windows on both sides of the desk, the office was cast in shadows. Recessed lighting accentuated the dark wood in the ornate coffered ceiling and wall-to-wall bookcases, making the study reminiscent of a castle. She referred to it as the library in conversation with other people because she didn't want to divulge that she used Beau's office regularly but hadn't yet removed any of his belongings in the year and a half since his death. Aside from her journal and a box of tissues, everything in the office was just as Beau left it, and Ruth liked it that way. In her heart, it was still his space, and she wasn't ready to do anything yet to make it her own.

Ruth flipped the light switch, and her eyes darted to the tattered therapy journal on the far-right corner of the desk. It was exactly where she'd placed it after last week's session, but she still felt relieved that it was there. She opened it to the page held by the brass monogrammed bookmark, the last gift from her beloved Beau. The questions jumped out at her as boldly as Shari had announced them verbally: *"What is the feeling? Where does it come from?"* She paused for a moment, asked them of herself over and over again, and then started writing in her journal.

> I feel very angry and hurt and disappointed right now. It hurts so much that my whole body feels light and numb, like there is a vacuum in the center of my chest and it is trying to take my breath away from me. But I'm not going to let it. I felt helpless before, but now I feel like I can take control. Like I can do something about this, even though I don't know what I can do, because I really want to run away. But why should I run? It's my family too. It is. It just is. They can't take that away from me. But more than that, I have invested years in the family. I have helped to nurture the bonds in the family AND build the company. Martha and Mary say they appreciate my efforts, but I am afraid they don't

value them now. When Martha said, "We appreciate what you've done for our family," it felt like she was talking to me like I was an employee instead of part of the family. I think Martha said the same thing to the funeral home staff when we made the arrangements for Beau's funeral. That's not something she should say to me too! The funeral home has always come through for our family during our greatest times of need over the years, but they're not in the family. Who does Martha think she is? Is she trying to tell me that even though I've invested all these years, I still don't have a family? It's like she's saying the family is only theirs and so they can take away something that even death shouldn't be able to affect. I've chosen this family twice, once through Marlon and then through Beau, but now they don't want to choose me. What more do I have to do to prove myself?

Ruth's pen froze in her right hand. The fingers of her left hand tapped on the desk. She squeezed her eyes closed as she took a deep breath. When she opened them, tears fell onto the page of her journal, and words rushed to her mind. She began to write again.

I guess I'm afraid that my relationships with Naomi, Mary, and Martha (yeah, I put Martha last on purpose) will end up like my relationship with my mother. That's it. Hold on, does this stuff work? Wait until I tell Shari this! She won't believe it! Okay, she will believe it, because she's the one who told me to do this.

Ruth fanned the teardrops on the journal page with her hand. *I'll have to leave this open to dry.* She reached for the box of tissues she'd placed on Beau's desk the week before, but it was empty. The extra-large boxes were no match for her nightly crying sessions. Her tears always fell as quickly as time flew. Ruth opened the right-middle desk drawer and lowered her head until her eyes focused on a vintage burnt-wood box. Her fingers caressed the floral carvings in the wood as she lifted the container and sat it on the desk. She forced the stubborn metal latch open and removed the handkerchief on top. She folded the upper edge and dabbed her eyes, inhaling a subtle hint of citrus and cardamom from Beau's favorite cologne left on the soft bamboo fabric. She felt almost as comforted as she would have if Beau were there to wipe her tears.

Ruth let out a big yawn. It had been a long evening. She was ready to wind down and at least try for a good night's sleep. As she stood to begin her bedtime preparation, she noticed a bright-yellow envelope in the handkerchief box. Her eyes welled up again when she saw her name on it, in Beau's handwriting. She ripped open the envelope, straying from her usual compulsion to use the letter opener a few inches from her hand. A waterfall of tears ran down her face at the sight of the gold-engraved bumblebee on the outside of the folded card. Bumblebee was Beau's nickname for her because of her persistence in bringing out the best in him and the family business. She read the note aloud.

My Dearest Bumblebee,
It has been my greatest honor to be your husband.
Thank you for choosing me and blessing me with
your love. Thank you for always believing me, even
when I doubted myself and my ability to be the part-
ner and provider you deserved. Thank you for help-
ing me learn to live each day to its fullest, especially

*during my recent health issues. I know that the busi-
ness and family may become challenging at times.
Even if they test you, remember that you are one of
us and that you have everything you need to find
your way forward. Don't give in to fear. My prayer
for you is that you will continue to be true to yourself and trust your inner voice. It led you to us, and
we are all the better because of it.*

    Forever Your Beau

There wasn't a dry spot left on the handkerchief. Ruth retrieved another one and tucked the box back in the drawer. She
clutched the note to her chest as she walked toward the lighting
panel next to the office doors, marveling that she discovered the
note on the day she needed it most. She turned off the lights before grabbing the chenille throw at the edge of the sofa and cud-
dling with the oversized pillows, the note placed a couple of
inches away near the sofa arm. She'd hated when Beau fell asleep
reading on the office sofa and ended up spending the night there.
But after her emotional evening ended on such a reassuring note,
she decided there was nowhere else she would rather be on the
night before her big meeting.

Chapter Two

The woodpecker's rhythmic drumming was no match for Martha. She tapped the utility pole in sequence with the beat and mimicked the slow, deep rolling sound she heard coming from the acres of pine trees next to the lake. She still had pent-up energy from her visit to Naomi's house the day before, and a little drumming always made her feel better. It was unseasonably warm for December, so Mary and Martha walked to Ruth's house for the family business meeting. It was quicker to cut through the wooded area between their cottages, but meeting at the fork in the road that led to the sisters' respective homes allowed them to split the distance and be closer to the main road leading to Ruth's and Naomi's homes on the estate.

"Why don't you drum anymore? You should take some classes or something," Mary said as she approached her sister.

Martha walked up beside her, and they started down the asphalt path. "I wish I could. Between my new administrative duties at work and trying to keep up my patient care hours, I can barely handle the necessities. And now we have to take time on a Saturday afternoon to talk about the company? I don't have even a moment to myself these days."

"It's one day," Mary said. "We haven't had a meeting in months, and Ruth's sudden request makes it seem like there's something important going on. I'm worried the business might be in trouble."

"Could be. It looks like this year will be the warmest one on record, and that's gotta have an impact on our peanut crops.

Beau had added some new business lines over the past several years, but peanuts are still the core of our business."

"Yeah, I'm concerned about the weather fluctuations and the crops too," Mary said. "Speaking of the weather, you know it'll be a little cooler by the time we leave Ruth's tonight. Do you want to go back for a sweater or something?"

"Tonight? I plan to be home long before dark. This is not a social gathering. It's almost two o'clock, and I'm not staying for more than an hour. But your sweatshirt could come in handy if the temperature drops before we leave. I'll gladly borrow it," Martha said with a smirk. "You wear that beat-up thing everywhere. How about I buy you a better one for Christmas?"

Martha loved teasing Mary about her favorite sweatshirt. Martha had tried on many occasions to get rid of the faded gray hoodie, but Mary clung to it, even rummaging through the dumpster at the rear of the family property after Martha said she accidentally put it out with the garbage.

"I like this one just fine, thank you very much," Mary said as she tied the sweatshirt tighter around her waist. "But did I hear you correctly a minute ago? You're talking like you've been keeping up with the company. When did you start paying attention? I didn't think you read the emails and reports Ruth sends out."

"Of course I read the reports now. I could trust Beau, but I don't know if I'll ever trust Ruth. Now that Beau isn't here to keep an eye on her, I have to. I hope you are too. We both need to watch."

"Yeah, I am. I wish one of us had studied agriculture in school, or at least paid attention while we were growing up," Mary said.

"Ruth didn't study it either, and Beau made her president of the company."

"Not automatically. Wasn't she chief operating officer first?"

"Yeah, but she still doesn't know anything about farming. Shouldn't the person who's the president *and* interim CEO have experience in the company's core business function?" Martha scoffed.

"She was a double major in college, right? Business and—"

"Psychology," Martha said, rolling her eyes. "That's how she manipulated Beau into marrying her and got control of the business."

"You really think so?"

"I'm one hundred percent sure! She had all of us fooled for a while, thinking she loved our family so much that she decided to move here. She tricked us. She only thinks about herself and what works for her special little life. That's why she has us meeting on weekends. I have other stuff to do. We just had a bunch of family time yesterday, and you see how that ended up."

"You never complained when Beau called family meetings, and they were always on Saturday afternoons. Wait a minute. Aren't you the one who asked for the meetings to be on Saturdays so you didn't have to try to get someone to cover your patient schedule during the week?"

"Oh . . . maybe you're right . . . but it was different with Beau. He was such a good guy. Everybody loved him, and you know as well as I do that Ruth took advantage of his kindness. He was old and kind and—"

"Girl, stop. He was not old. Wait, let me count. . . . He was only fifteen years older than Ruth," Mary said, laughing.

"Well, he was just happy that a tenderoni showed a little interest in him. But everybody knows Ruth only cared about Beau's money and what he could do for her. He didn't see it, and Marlon didn't either. It wasn't enough that she got Marlon's money after he died. She wanted more, so she moved here and went after Beau. And it worked. That's how she got that big house out of him. They only have one kid, and M.J.'s in grad school now. Why does she need such a big house?"

"I guess because she wanted it. I mean because *they* wanted it," Mary said. "Beau sacrificed a lot to expand the family business, and he deserved to be compensated for that. We approved his salary, and he could spend it however he wanted to."

Martha winced. "You make it sound like I'm jealous of Ruth or something."

"Well, are you? I don't care that your cottage is larger than mine. Do you hear me going on and on about that all the time like you talk about their house?"

"That's not fair," Martha said, waving her pointer finger in the air. "I came back to Edin after residency and had my pick of the two empty cottages. I chose the one that was closest to the entrance because I come home late from work sometimes."

Mary stopped abruptly and stared at Martha. "Sure—*that's* it. And your cottage just happens to have three bedrooms, and mine only has one. The size of the cottages has nothing to do with it, right?" she said, her voice dripping with sarcasm.

"So what if I like nice things?" Martha shrugged.

"No, you care too much about outward appearances. There's a difference," Mary shot back.

"Okay, so I took the nicer cottage. And when you moved back home, you had to take what was left. That's not my fault. If you don't want to be here, that's on you. Maybe you should've stayed in New York City."

"Whatever. My cottage is just fine," Mary said. "I like it, but don't get off track. Why couldn't Ruth and Beau do whatever *they* wanted with *their* money? Nobody tells us how to spend *our* money, so why should we care how they spent theirs?"

Martha lowered her aviator sunglasses to the crook of her nose and peered at her sister. Weren't they supposed to be on the same side? Had Mary forgotten who lent her money when she needed to come back home for Beau's funeral and then convinced her to stay in town? "You're only taking Ruth's side because you wasted your inheritance and you don't want to hear my opinion about it," she replied.

"That's unnecessary, Martha. You always go too far. You don't have any respect for boundaries—mine or anyone else's."

"I spent my inheritance on college. After graduation, I didn't have anyone taking care of me. I had to work to support myself while I studied to get into medical school. When I finally got in, did anyone in the family offer to pay for it? No. They didn't even ask. I had to take out loans."

Mary let out a loud sigh. "Are you ready to get off your soapbox yet? 'Cause I'm tired of hearing you whine. And that's not how it works anyway. We've always known that we'd get one disbursement from the trust. That's it. What we did with it was up to us. The trust was designed to give us a jump start, to plant a seed. You planted your seed where you wanted to plant it. Why should anyone else have to pay for your med school expenses because you chose the most expensive undergrad you could find and spent all your money on it? Everything isn't about status."

"I don't always get what I want like you and Ruth do," Martha pushed back. "I'm sorry I didn't want to go to a state school on scholarship like you and I wasn't strategic enough to marry into money twice like Ruth so I could have a cushy life. I had to figure things out on my own. I have to go to work every day to make money to take care of myself."

"So now you're complaining about how hard you have it? No ma'am. We had access to the family trust, and we can live mortgage free on the family property for as long as we want. I'm tired of hearing how privileged you think Ruth is. I know that primary care doctors like you don't make as much as specialists, but you're far from poor. And you got a raise when you became head of primary care at the hospital. Do I need to ask what you do with your money?"

Martha narrowed her eyes at her sister. "No, you'd better not," she snapped.

"Exactly, so I suggest you apply that same thinking to Ruth."

Martha didn't respond, and the sisters walked in silence. As they approached the outlet leading to Ruth's home, Mary cleared her throat.

It's about time, Martha thought, expecting Mary to apologize for not being more supportive. But she was wrong.

"I'm gonna run ahead. See you at Ruth's," Mary said. And then she jogged away.

* * *

RUTH HAD BEEN talking nonstop for almost twenty minutes. Her outfit—a black asymmetric draped blouse with tapered trousers in the same color—impressed Naomi as much as the charts and figures she displayed. But her mind wandered five minutes into the presentation. She loved having Gardin Family Enterprises board meetings in Ruth's sunroom. A few minutes before the meeting started, Naomi had suggested they sit in the rattan rocking chairs instead of at the long table in the dining room. The chairs were arranged in a circle, allowing Naomi to feel connected to her family while also providing an excuse to enjoy the soothing garden view. But she also hoped the configuration of the chairs would promote a collective mindset that could then serve as a launchpad for future meetings and family gatherings.

Although she preferred having her own space in the cottage next door, Naomi never tired of spending time in Ruth's home. It was grand but welcoming. Ruth and Beau had taken care to ensure that the large addition to the home and modern conveniences complemented the traditional elements of the original cottage's facade.

Naomi appreciated that Ruth and Beau had taken a similar

approach to their relationship. They nurtured their union while still acknowledging Ruth's first marriage. Naomi gazed across the sunroom at the row of pomegranate trees lining Ruth's backyard. The bell-shaped orange-red flowers sprinkled across the bushy plants were emblematic of the life that Ruth had built—at home and through the family business. People fixated on the fruit that resulted from the flowers, but they discounted the body of work that made it possible.

Despite being distracted by her thoughts during the meeting, Naomi stayed plugged in enough to assess how everyone got along. She was sure the squabbling at her house the day before was nothing out of the ordinary, but she remained conscientious of interactions around Gardin Family Enterprises. She took her family's long-standing commitment to collective work and responsibility and cooperative economics seriously. She felt a duty to her present-day family as well as her ancestors, whose early entrepreneurial endeavors led to the company's founding.

The tempo of the meeting picked up as the women reviewed the financial statements, and Naomi thought the meeting had reached a happy ending when the component discussions of the balance sheet, income statement, cash flow statement, and statement of shareholders' equity ended without a hitch. She glanced at her watch, hoping to run a few errands in Macon before catching the last matinee at the movie theater.

"Before we wrap up, here's the draft strategic plan that Beau wrote before he passed away," Ruth said, handing Naomi a thin stack of papers and motioning for her to pass it around the circle. Ruth took a deep breath. "I'll email the full document, but I'd like to share the executive summary and call your attention to a point for discussion at our next board meeting. I didn't want there to be any surprises, so I thought I'd let you know what to expect."

Martha rolled her eyes. She relaxed them and smiled when she noticed Naomi grimacing at her and extending the executive summary in her direction.

"As you may recall," Ruth continued, "Beau had begun succession planning. When he first outlined the strategic plan, he anticipated retiring in five to ten years. But after his health began to decline, he updated the plan so the company would be prepared to carry on. You'll see that the plan includes a recommendation that I serve as the permanent CEO of the company. Although I've served as president for the past six years and feel obligated to Beau and his legacy, I've been very thoughtful and prayerful about whether I'm the right choice for the position in Beau's absence. I believe I'm a good fit. I would like us to start thinking about the next steps to move forward. I'm not in a rush, so this isn't time sensitive. However, it benefits our staff and partners for the company to move away from the interim CEO title as quickly as we can. It helps provide a perception of stability and confidence. You can read through the full strategic plan, and we can revisit this at our next meeting."

Ruth paused, scanning the room. The other women focused their attention on the executive summary, but Naomi lifted her gaze from the page. As her eyes met with Ruth's, she smiled and nodded reassuringly.

"Oh, one more thing. Sorry, it'll be real quick. We spoke earlier about our plans to explore selling the business lines that aren't core to our agricultural portfolio, but I forgot to mention that the consultant who's been working with me and the senior leadership team on divestiture options and realignment strategies will be in town on Friday. He's planning to attend the company Christmas party that night. Okay, so that's it. Thanks so much."

Martha placed the executive summary on the table beside her and sat her pen on top of it. "Ruth, we certainly value your contributions to Gardin Family Enterprises, but I don't see why we should be in a rush to decide on a permanent CEO," she said, leaning on the armrest and rubbing her chin. "Right, Mary?" she added, turning toward her sister.

Mary looked up briefly from the executive summary. Then she returned to the document and began to rapidly underline sentences on the page.

Clenching her teeth, Naomi looked at her watch again. *Looks like I won't make it to the matinee.* As the matriarch, she assumed responsibility for the family's successes as well as its failures. But she owed a special debt to Ruth, whose move to Edin had breathed new life into the family and its business. Soon after the women arrived in town, Naomi had suggested that Ruth help Beau, Naomi's first cousin, translate the ideas he'd been talking about for years into a plan to expand Gardin Farms. While their planning sessions established the framework to turn the family's peanut-farming business into a multimillion-dollar enterprise, a romance also blossomed between them. Naomi gave her blessing, and the couple married a few months later. With the Gardin family's prominence in Edin, Ruth had raised eyebrows within the family and across town by marrying her recently deceased husband's cousin. But Naomi's opinion was the only one that mattered to the couple.

Ruth squinted at Martha. "I'll reiterate my previous comments. I'm not in a rush, so this isn't time sensitive," she said. "But again, it would benefit our staff and partners if we made a decision with little delay, particularly as we move forward with our plans to grow the company."

"Noted. I heard you the first time," Martha said. "I also suggest that we meet at the office in the future, preferably not on a weekend. What does everyone think about returning to our quarterly meeting schedule? Or maybe we should meet monthly if we need to consider what to do about the CEO position. It takes time to find a qualified candidate with experience. I mean, you know, if we decide to go in that direction."

"Meeting regularity, date, and location never seemed to be an issue when Beau was CEO," Ruth contested.

"Unfortunately, Beau's not here anymore," Martha mumbled.

Realizing the otherwise straightforward meeting had not presented her niece with any strands to unravel before this point, Naomi now understood that Martha was like a kitten who had finally found a thread. And if swallowed, it could threaten the viability of the business and the sustainability of the family. Naomi leaped from her chair. "Cadence Martha Gardin, that's enough! You were not raised to behave like this. It's one thing to disagree or raise your concerns, but you will not be disrespectful, especially not in their house."

Ruth slid to the edge of her chair, extending her arm toward Naomi. "It's fine, MIL," she said. Ruth turned to Martha. "We can meet at the office in March. I'll have Chloe send out some potential dates to see what works for everyone's schedules."

Naomi looked at Mary discreetly, hoping a glance would prompt her to speak up.

But Mary averted her eyes from her aunt's direction before she gave a conciliatory response. "Thank you, Ruth. I appreciate your leadership. I know you've been handling a lot of the business on your own. You and your staff seem to be doing a great job. Change can be difficult for everyone, but I agree it's a good idea to go back to the quarterly meeting schedule with the option to meet monthly, if needed," she said.

Naomi was disappointed but not surprised. Her nieces had covered for each other since they were kids, even when doing so got them in worse trouble. Naomi had expected them to become more independent and mature in their thinking as they aged, but they hadn't. Naomi suspected Mary was beholden to Martha because Mary hadn't had anything when she'd returned to Edin. Mary hadn't been able to afford to turn on the utilities in her cottage, so she stayed with Martha for a while. And now Martha was ready to collect. Mary had gone to Naomi for money first, but Naomi had turned her down, fearing that financial assistance would enable Mary to continue to make foolish financial decisions.

Martha held her head high and cut her eyes at Ruth. She pushed back in her rocker and let go suddenly, inadvertently initiating the chair's leg rest and automatic rocking mechanism. Her body fell backward into the chair.

Naomi chuckled. *Serves her right,* she thought. But she quickly caught herself and feigned a cough.

Ruth focused her gaze on Martha. Without turning her head, she slid the glass on the adjacent table toward Naomi.

Martha propelled herself forward and stood, forcing the leg rest down with a graceful recovery. She folded the executive summary into a small rectangle and placed it in the side pocket of her cargo pants. "Ruth, I'm looking forward to meeting the consultant. I imagine he also has experience in mergers and acquisitions?" she asked.

"Yes, he has extensive experience in mergers, acquisitions, *and* divestiture," Ruth replied.

"Excellent. I've been reading up on things since Beau died, and I understand that selling our noncore business lines could create value for the company in the event that we sell it. Is that correct?" Martha asked.

Ruth nodded as she began to speak. "That would fall under divestiture, but selling the entire company is not part of our strategic plan," she replied, her head movements transitioning to abrupt side-to-side movements as she completed her thought.

"Since we've already engaged him, I'd also like his opinion on the overall value of the business, in case we decide to explore selling the whole thing. That could create cash flow for individual family members. I imagine you hadn't thought about that perspective, but we should keep our options open, right?" Martha's tone matched the smug look on her face.

Naomi fiddled with the emerald stud earring in her right ear. She shook her head in disbelief. *How could Martha be thinking about selling the company or replacing Ruth? Other than me, the company is the only thing holding this family together.*

Mary stared out the folding glass door that opened the room to the patio.

Ruth paused as she stood. "I'd like to highlight that our strategic plan calls for us to reinvest the proceeds from any divestment activities back in the company to expand our greatest competencies. But, sure, we can keep our options open," she said, gathering her belongings from the end table.

"Well, it's getting late," Martha replied. "I have to get ready for work tomorrow. Don't worry about walking me out. I know the way. I look forward to the follow-up meeting."

* * *

RUTH SWEPT HER fingers across her eyelids and stomped into the kitchen, her bare feet smacking the hardwood with each step. "So, y'all want to stay for dinner? I can throw something together in a few minutes. Let me see what I have in the fridge," she said, her voice trailing off with the increasing distance.

Mary and Naomi followed Ruth's track from the sunroom to the place where she, only nine days prior, had prepared a six-course Thanksgiving meal for the family with painstaking care—a meal that Mary and Martha barely ate. Mary looked to her aunt with widened eyes, searching her face for the guidance her mouth wouldn't allow her to request, but Naomi turned away. She floated across the kitchen floor and pulled Ruth into a tight embrace. As they hugged, Naomi's head tilted such that Mary couldn't see if Naomi's lips were moving, but Ruth's punctuated nodding confirmed that Mary was not welcome in the brief exchange.

The seconds felt like hours as Mary surveyed the kitchen to pass the time. She liked Ruth's eclectic taste, even if Martha didn't care for it. She wondered how Ruth determined that putting a chandelier in the same space with industrial-grade appliances and a collection of red-enameled cast-iron pots would look tasteful, but it worked. Her design choices came off brave yet understated.

"Thanks for offering to cook, but I need to run some errands before it gets dark," Naomi said, letting go of Ruth.

Finally, Mary thought. A spectrum of emotions washed over her, but she didn't want to process them in Ruth's kitchen. She needed time alone. She struggled to find the right words to simultaneously make things right and create an exit. "Me too. Well, I don't have errands. But I . . . I . . . have . . . other stuff. . . . The . . . um . . . the eight-year-olds from Sunday school are coming to the restaurant for a cooking class after church tomorrow. I need to de-stress so I'm bright-eyed and bushy-tailed for them." She paused. "Look, I know Martha crosses the line sometimes. She does it to me too."

"It's okay. Yeah, it's been a stressful couple of days, hasn't it?" Ruth's words were interspersed with awkward laughter. "I thought I was the only one who felt that way—until MIL called Martha by her whole name. Then I knew I wasn't alone in being stressed about things."

Mary folded her arms, the afternoon's compounding tension finally boiling over. "Oh, okay. Our family is a mess, and you think it's funny," she said. She didn't understand how Ruth could be so poised and composed one minute and say something inappropriate the next. At least Martha was tactless all the time.

Naomi, standing equidistant between Ruth and Mary, sighed loudly.

"No, you're right. It's not funny," Ruth responded. "I was just thinking about how we should get along better. We have a lot in common. All three of us have old-fashioned names. And, like I was trying to say, we should try to think more about what we have in common. Right? . . . I'm not being very articulate at all, am I? Well, I remember in college . . . you know, when I first met Marlon. And he introduced himself to me and said I had an old-fashioned name like his little cousins. And he said he liked that about me. I didn't believe him. I thought he was trying to flirt with me. Well, he *was*. But it turns out it was still true—we have old-fashioned names. And he said I reminded him of you and Martha, and he thought we would get along well. And—"

"At least they're our middle names," Mary interrupted. "But your first name . . . never mind. I can't talk about our names right now. Look, I was embarrassed by how my sister acted, so I figured I should say something to you. But I think I should go now," she countered.

As soon as the words came out, Mary was ashamed. Her disappointment and embarrassment compounded with the anger she retained from her earlier talk with Martha, and the walls were closing in on her. She had to get out. The shock on Naomi's face didn't register until Mary was halfway to the front door, at which point she also realized she'd left without saying goodbye to her aunt. She would ordinarily hug Naomi when they parted ways, but she'd had her fill of hugs in Ruth's kitchen for the day. Mary retreated far enough back down the hallway to be within earshot. "Talk to you later, Aunt Naomi," she yelled and then jetted toward the foyer without waiting for her to respond. She didn't mean to slam the antique mahogany door, but the force she exerted to escape was the most accessible instrument she had to express herself. She knew she'd have to answer for it later, but it was worth it in the short term.

Mary paused to suck air in and out of her mouth as though she'd held her breath all day. She took a path home through the woods to make sure she didn't run into Martha. The closer she got to her cottage, the more she wished she'd left Ruth's house on better terms. But she wasn't willing to do anything about it now, and she didn't want to talk about it. She silenced her phone. She had tortured herself enough by second-guessing her actions, and she felt like she would suffocate with any additional pressure from her family members.

There was always a side to choose and someone to defend. Mary didn't want to deal with Martha's inquiries about what happened after she left. She feared her relationship with Ruth would become more strained, and Ruth's awkward attempts to connect weren't helping either. She was tired of the back-and-forth. Her primary allegiance would always be to Martha, but she felt that Ruth deserved a little loyalty too. Having her father die before she was born and a nearly nonexistent relationship with her mother as an adult, Ruth could relate to a portion of what Mary and Martha felt after their parents died. And while Ruth acknowledged the differences in their experiences, she empathized with the acuteness of their grief, having lost her first husband only a year before their parents' fatal accident. Mary didn't want the family to fall apart, but she couldn't hold it together. She had her own problems to deal with.

She untied the tattered hoodie from her waist and held it up at eye level. The letters on the front were so faint that people strained to make them out, but that didn't make them any less meaningful to Mary. She could still see them: $T.E.A.M.$ She slid the shirt over her head and ran her fingertips over the peeling letters. She didn't care about the holes around the neckline or the frayed edges of her de facto security blanket. *These letters mean something. Not that I would ever tell my family anything about it. They wouldn't understand, but Martha was right about my sweatshirt coming in handy on the walk back, even if she was being sarcastic.* It was still warm outside. Mary didn't need a sweatshirt for the weather. But after a stressful afternoon, she yearned for the comfort it brought.

Chapter Three

The sun peeked through the trees, its rays casting a shadow on the speckled grass in Ruth's backyard. It was afternoon, but it felt like morning. Exhausted from the long workweek and then the even more grueling meeting with her family the previous day, Ruth had slept in. She'd intended to wake up in time to attend the eight o'clock church service, but she'd slept in Beau's office for the second night in a row, where the dark room tricked her into thinking nighttime lasted longer than it did. When she finally pried her eyes open, the midmorning church service had already started. After spending some time in prayer and reflection, she decided not to commit the rest of the day to reviewing business projections as she'd initially planned. Instead, she opted to take a step toward reestablishing her self-care practice.

Ruth stood outside on the turquoise yoga mat with her right thigh crossed over her left one. She hooked her right foot around her left calf and swung her arms in front of her chest. As she straightened her back and tried to cross her arms, she lost her balance, landing on her left shoulder with her legs still crossed. She rolled back onto her bottom and looked up, spotting her mother-in-law walking toward her.

"Oh, I didn't hear you sneak up," Ruth said to Naomi as she sprang to her feet.

"That was like watching a twisted pretzel fall over," Naomi said, brushing the grass from Ruth's flank. "You okay?"

Ruth laughed. "Yeah, I'm fine. Thanks," she said.

"I've been calling and texting you all morning. Since you

wouldn't pick up, I decided I needed to lay eyes on you. You forget I live next door, so ignoring my calls doesn't work," Naomi said, playfully glaring upward at Ruth, who stood six inches taller in bare feet.

"Touché," Ruth replied, her previously congenial tone flattened by the validity of Naomi's declaration. The last thing she wanted right now was to be chastised.

Naomi sank on the mountain of plush pillows on the circular outdoor daybed. "We missed you in service this morning. The sermon was good. It was called 'How to Save Your Family from Ruin over Christmas.'"

Ruth pulled her yoga mat onto the porcelain patio tiles and resumed her stretch routine in the seated position. "For real?" She squinted as she angled her chin over her extended leg.

"No, I'm kidding, but that would've been helpful." Naomi sighed, adjusting the pillows.

"I planned to go, but I overslept. It was good to have some quiet time alone. Besides, I'm not sure if church was the best place to see Mary and Martha after yesterday . . . and the day before."

"Maybe that's exactly where y'all need to see each other. God is everywhere, but at least being at His house would be a good reminder that He's watching all this nonsense. But I hope they weren't the reason you didn't come to the service, especially because they skipped church today too."

"I'm sorry I missed the opportunity to have you all to myself at church," Ruth said.

Naomi drummed her fingers on the daybed mattress as an exaggerated smile spread across her face. "Yeah, that's too bad, but I'm here now. So, how are you feeling today?"

"My faith is what helps me keep trying to make everything work, but my patience is wearing thin," Ruth said. "I've told you that over the years, but it's different now. It's harder to keep my cool while trying to figure out how to cope with all this dysfunction without Beau."

"Keep trying to do the right thing. You'll figure it out," Naomi said, her harsh smile softening to the reassuring one Ruth needed.

Ruth rose and looked up at Naomi. "I hope so," she said. The meeting the previous day was the first time she considered leaving Edin. Edin was home, and she didn't know where else she would go. The uncertainty lingered as she stared at her mother-in-law, but she wasn't ready to talk about it. She squeezed her eyes tightly and took a deep breath, swallowing the words before they flew out of her mouth. As she exhaled and opened her eyes, another thought bubbled up.

"I have a question," Ruth said as she turned away from Naomi and spread her feet hip-width apart. She leaned forward until her torso met her legs. "Mary, Martha, and I have had our issues over the years, but I didn't know they had so much spite toward me—especially Martha. I just thought we didn't get along sometimes, but now I'm wondering if Beau knew how bad things really were. Did he ever talk to you about it?" she asked, reaching her hands toward the floor and letting her head hang.

Naomi sat up. "I don't want to get in the middle. This is between you girls," she said, her head shaking from side to side.

Ruth grabbed her ankles and straightened her knees. "I've been intentional about that over the years. I've always let you bring them up, because I never wanted to be accused of putting you in the middle. I used to be able to talk to Beau about their treatment toward me, but now what do I do?"

"Talk to Mary and Martha. Tell them how you feel. Listen to their side."

"That's all I've ever done, but it feels like I've wasted a lot of time with that approach. Why is it starting to feel like you're taking their side? I'm not trying to get you to side with me per se.

But I expected you to be on the side of what's right," Ruth said as she released her ankles and stood straight.

Naomi bowed her head.

Ruth didn't know if Naomi was ignoring her or praying, but the silence unnerved her. She added, "Every woman in this family has a flair for drama, including you. That's why you and I clicked from the time we first met, but we both also stand up for what's right."

Naomi lifted her head. "Beau was a wise man. He excelled at business. But let's just say he wasn't as good at figuring out family conflict as he was at growing a company. I wonder if he'd have been able to expand Gardin Family Enterprises as much as he did if he had to deal with family members poking their noses in everything like they do since he passed away. All the coaching you got from Beau over all those years—do you really think he came up with it by himself?" Naomi asked.

Naomi leaned on the arm of the daybed and rested her cheek on her hand. "Now, think about it," she said. "You weren't the only woman in this family who had his ear. Just like he talked to me before he started dating you—because he knew people would talk, including our own family members—he talked to me afterward. We worked together to manage the fallout of the two of you getting together. And that's a big part of why the family is in this situation right now."

Ruth picked up her yoga mat and shook it to release any debris it picked up from the ground. "I can't believe you and Beau kept that from me," she said as the calm she accumulated during her yoga session decreased with each shake of the mat. Ruth took a deep breath and exhaled loudly through her mouth. Then she leaned against the patio wall and rolled up her mat. "So, how do we fix it?" she asked.

The expression on Naomi's face showed empathy but not remorse. "I can't be the reason people in this family behave," she said. "I can't fix everything anymore. I took off my cape and burned it. Y'all aren't children, though I have wondered, based on some of the behavior I've witnessed this weekend. Butting in and putting my foot down is a short-term solution. Even if it worked, y'all would be right back in the same place when I leave this earth. And even though I wouldn't be there to go through it, I shudder at the thought."

"No. Don't do this. I can't think about that right now."

Naomi softened her voice. "It's inevitable, but I know you don't need me to remind you of that. I'm not worried about dying, because I know I'm going to heaven. But I want the family to stick together when it happens. We can't let this family fall apart because the person who held it together passed away."

"Okay, I get it," Ruth said. "You're right. I'm sorry we ended up at this point, but I'll do my part to repair things. I don't know what that will look like, but I'll try to come up with something." She sighed.

"Yeah, I'm sorry too. Sometimes things have to get messy to reveal the beauty underneath."

* * *

ONLY TEN MINUTES *left. If I can just get through this, I can reset and start over,* Mary thought as she put the last snickerdoodle on the tray. She imagined herself doing the breathing exercises she found online while soaking in a warm bubble bath. Her bouts of anxiety over the past couple of days had driven her to revisit the self-care promise she'd made when she first moved to Edin. Now only the last few minutes of the cooking class taking place in her restaurant's dining room were all that stood between her and her bathtub.

Mary stretched out her arms and threw her head back, feigning the relaxed state she anticipated after her bath. Carrying her make-believe act too far, she took a sudden step away from the counter and tripped. She quickly regained her footing. She'd never outgrown the clumsy stage of preadolescence, but it was always worse when she was exhausted.

I need a break. Maybe I should have a cookie. Cookies never let her down. They always seemed to make everything better. Her restaurant, Alabaster Lunch Box, specialized in healthier versions of traditional comfort food, but spending so much time around the tasty treats all day challenged Mary's willpower now that her life was so much more stressful than when she lived in New York. She wanted to work on setting better boundaries with her family and herself. Shari, the therapist she liked so much that she had recommended her to Ruth, had helped her work on her boundary issues, but Mary's busy schedule had made the bimonthly visits less of a priority since the restaurant opened. She felt less guilty eating her plant-based version of her cookies, yet she tried to remind herself that they were still a treat that required boundaries. But she wasn't successful.

What's one more cookie when you've already had eight? Mary thought as she slipped the last broken cookie into her mouth before washing her hands. She licked the crumbs from the corners of her lips and checked her reflection in the small mirror she kept over the handwashing station. There were no crumbs, but she noticed that her face seemed to get fuller by the day. Her size four body was a distant memory, which she suspected her sister secretly loved. Now they were the same size. But at least she could borrow Martha's clothes now. *Twenty pounds in eighteen months. I've got to back off of this stress eating.* She dried her hands, grabbed the tray, and darted into the restaurant dining room to resume teaching.

The children looked eager, but the parents looked skeptical. Unflustered, she started with the kids, remembering how her grandmother and namesake always leveraged her grandchildren to convince their parents to try her latest culinary experiment. "And a little child will lead them," she used to say with a soft chuckle. Mary's parents were just as reluctant to embrace her grandmother's deviations from traditional cooking, but their children convinced them every time. Mary hoped for the same outcome with her class.

A complimentary children's cooking class was a way for Mary to do the kind of outreach around healthful eating that she'd always hoped to do for the community. Alabaster Lunch Box had been open for only six months, and Mary was still working on her outreach plans. Martha had come up with the idea of teaming up with the Sunday school. She always had a million ideas for the restaurant. Every now and then, one of them made sense.

"This is the best cookie I've ever had!" exclaimed a fidgety eight-year-old girl at the first table. "Can I help you pass them out?"

"You sure can," Mary said with a cheerful smile. The little girl reminded her of herself at that age. Mary hoped to be as good a role model as her grandmother had been. "Take these napkins and give them out ahead of me. I'll be right behind you with the cookies." Mary followed her helper to the two-seater tables in the center of the restaurant and then to the long table near the front window.

"Oh, taste and see that the cookies are good," Mary said, smiling like she was a kid in her grandmother's kitchen again. She wondered if anyone caught her corny Bible reference.

"I'm glad to hear that you found a way to work in today's Sunday school verse," Naomi said from the back of the room. "Taste and see that the LORD is good; blessed is the one who takes refuge in him!"

Mary playfully hid her face. "Oh, hi, Aunt Naomi."

"And she's telling the truth about these cookies," said a mother seated at the teal sofa booth in the corner of the restaurant. "Sorry to talk with a full mouth, but are you able to accommodate an order for the choir's Christmas social next week?"

"I would be delighted to," Mary replied, beaming.

As she looked around at the heads nodding in agreement, she noticed the room was silent for the second time that afternoon, the first being when the class sampled her confetti pizza. Most kids in the class said they didn't like veggie pizza, but they were swayed when they tasted Mary's version. The dish featured colorful vegetables cut to look like confetti, and pad thai sauce with a subtle peanut base. The class was a lot of work—from making sure none of the kids had peanut allergies to ensuring the cooking demonstration was interactive and educational—but seeing children enjoy healthy food made it worth it. Mary was so pleased that she almost forgot to make her closing speech.

"Thank you for coming to Alabaster Lunch Box for your Sunday school field trip. We have cooking classes from time to time, so subscribe to our newsletter to receive notifications about future classes. And please know that you are welcome to join us for a meal during our usual business hours: eleven to two on weekdays, and noon to three for First Sunday Brunch. We love to host special events such as birthday parties, showers, and other celebratory gatherings for children and adults. Of course, we also welcome your catering orders. We pride ourselves on a menu full of food that tastes good and is also healthy. Like with today's recipes, our menu features many plant-based options in fun and imaginative ways. Please come back and see us. Thanks again."

Naomi led the applause. "I'm so proud of my niece," she gushed, her hands waving back and forth in an enthusiastic clap. The guests followed with a barrage of applause and cheers. A little girl sitting with her family stood up and yelled, "Yay!" The child's older sister and parents joined in, precipitating a standing ovation from the crowd.

Mary blushed. She was appreciative whenever she received compliments about her food or the restaurant's early success, but it was her family's validation that she craved most. When she first moved back to Edin, she wasn't sure that she could make them proud of her again, but Naomi's response this evening made her feel like she was finally on her way.

Mary said goodbye to everyone and walked the Sunday school teachers out to their cars.

When she returned, Naomi greeted her with a prideful grin. "I'll finish cleaning up here. You go to the kitchen and get started there. I'll join you in a few minutes."

"That would be lovely! Thank you." Mary smiled, still riding the wave of the praise her aunt had extolled on her in front of her church members.

The successful class and supportive response from her aunt gave Mary the boost she needed to push through her cleaning ritual, so she strutted into the kitchen. She had a system for washing dishes, and even though she was tired, this was no time to abandon it. She washed dishes in the same way that she approached her life: tackling the biggest items first so everything else could fall in line.

As the hot water and soapsuds accumulated in the sink, Mary imagined soaking in her bathtub. She plunged the commercial-grade cookie sheets and mixing bowls into the water. She washed and rinsed them carefully, trying not to splash water on the floor. *The last thing I need is to have to clean up a mess before I leave here tonight.*

As Mary lowered the mass of utensils into the sink, Martha walked into the kitchen. "Hey, sorry to track you down here, but can we talk?" she asked.

Mary sighed. *I spoke too soon about not wanting to clean up a mess tonight.*

* * *

"CAN WE DO it another time?" Mary pleaded.

"It won't take long. Just give me a few minutes. It's gonna be a busy week," Martha said.

"Not tonight, please."

Martha picked up a forgotten pizza pan on the countertop and carried it to the sink where Mary stood. "I can talk while you clean up. I can even help you," Martha replied, nearly smearing pad thai sauce on her white long-sleeved T-shirt.

Mary grabbed the pan as Martha held it over the soapy water. "No, please don't. I don't mean to be short, but I can't do this tonight. I'm drained."

Martha wasn't accustomed to getting so much pushback from her sister, and she didn't like it. The only thing she hated more was when Mary whined to get her way. "I'm on call tomorrow through Thursday. Then we have the Gardin Family Enterprises Christmas party on Friday, and—"

"It's always about what's best for you, isn't it, Martha? Oh, wait. I know what this is really about. You want to make up with me so we can be on good terms for the party. I see what's going on. You don't want to have to face Ruth on your own."

"That's not—"

Mary barged through the swinging door into the dining room, leaving a trail of soapsuds along the way. "Don't bother. Let's just get this over with," she said. The door slammed against the distressed brick wall.

Naomi jumped up from her seat. "Oh goodness!" she yelled. "What is it with you and these doors this weekend? Is everything okay?"

"Martha has something on her mind. Apparently, she won't be able to function this week unless she tells me right now."

Martha followed her sister, zigzagging to avoid getting suds on the glittery silver Brother Vellies boots she wore. Her small cobalt Telfar shopping bag swung on her wrist like the kitchen door as she ignored Mary's opposition and tried to stay focused on her goal. "I don't like the way things ended with us yesterday," she said.

"No, you seemed fine with that, judging from your behavior at Ruth's," Mary said. "You don't like that I didn't answer when you blew up my phone afterward."

"That seems to be going around today, but I'll let the two of you talk," Naomi said, rising from the highboy table near the wall.

Mary slid into the teal sofa booth in the right corner of the restaurant. She looked at her aunt and tapped the seat twice. "No, please stay. I may need a witness."

"I don't understand why you're so upset with me," Martha said. "Why didn't you tell me about the cooking class? I've been trying to get you to start classes since you opened the restaurant, but you didn't bother to let me know that you decided to do it. I happened to drive by and saw your and Aunt Naomi's cars here, so I came in. Aunt Naomi told me I just missed the cooking class. I'm really hurt, Mary."

"It's not my fault. Most of the time we talk, I can barely get a word in. You go on and on about yourself—what's going on at work, how unfair life has been to you, how much Ruth doesn't deserve the life she has. I tried to tell you about it last week, but you cut me off and went back to a story about yourself."

Naomi winced, but she kept her mouth closed.

"If that happens from time to time, I'm sorry. But it does not happen often," Martha argued.

Mary rolled her eyes while shrugging. "It happens so much that I've started to only call you when I have other stuff to do.

That way I can put the phone on speaker while I multitask. You don't seem to need me in the conversation, so I make it work for me."

Martha was shocked that Mary was being so selfish and dismissive, especially after everything she'd done for her over the years. "So, I don't add anything to your life?"

"I didn't say that. This is not about you, Martha! For once, this is not about you."

"I don't need this," Martha said as her eyes brimmed with tears. She rummaged through her tote for her keys, blinking to try to hold her tears in. But they dropped down her bronzed cheeks despite the effort.

Mary held firm. "I'm sorry your feelings are hurt, but that's too bad. I told you I didn't want to talk tonight, but you insisted on ruining my evening. I listen to you whether I want to or not, so it's my turn now. You can wait until I'm done."

Martha lowered her head, looking up at her sister with raised eyebrows like she had done when Mary stood up to her when they were kids. In keeping with the tradition of their episodic sibling rivalry, Martha didn't back down when her sister forgot her place. "And what about yesterday? What happened?"

"You mean after you left Ruth's? I'm not ready to talk about that," Mary said.

"Oh, I wasn't talking about Ruth. She'll be fine. I meant what happened between us yesterday, on the way over?"

Mary shook her head. "Look, Martha. I've had enough. We got along so much better when we lived in different cities. When I'm with you, it's the Martha Show. You don't care about how I feel or what I think about things. I don't know how much more of this I can take. I have mixed feelings about Ruth leading the company, but I hate that you force me into being so negative all the time."

Martha backed away from the tabletop. "Wait a minute. I force you? You're a grown woman. You make your own decisions."

"You're right. I'm grown, and we're two different people. But how about you try to remember that? It seems like it never occurs to you that I have my own thoughts. You project opinions on me with the expectation that I'm gonna join every battle that you decide you want to fight. I'm carrying my own baggage—a lot of it. I can't carry yours as well. It's too much."

"So, this was a waste of time," Martha said.

"A waste of time? That's how highly you regard me?" Mary said. "This is exactly what I mean. Again, I told you when you first showed up that I didn't want to talk to you, but you forced the issue. I never thought I'd have to say this to you, but I need some space."

"What? For how long?"

"I don't know. I mean, not forever or anything. But I need enough time to sort through things. We're sisters. We'll always be in each other's lives. But sometimes we act like it's just the two of us, which seems so unnecessary. We're not alone. We have Aunt Naomi and Ruth."

"I don't understand. Where is all this coming from?" Martha asked.

"I've held this in for a long time. Too long. And the past few days have shown me that I need to find a better balance between supporting you and allowing myself to be drawn into battles that aren't mine. After Mommy and Daddy died, you said it was me and you against the world. But this has gotten out of hand. You have to get over their dying early," Mary said, her voice cracking.

Naomi placed her hand atop Mary's and squeezed it gently. "You're doing great," she said.

Tears fell from Mary's eyes. "I have some things that I need to make amends for," she continued. "Beau and Ruth were good to us. Yeah, we stayed with Aunt Naomi when we came home for school breaks and weekend visits, but I remember that Ruth was there doing her part for us too, even though we weren't kind to her. She kept reaching out to me, but I kept her at arm's length. I'm not sure if she should be CEO or not, but I have to figure out how to not allow my drama with her to cloud my thinking about the business."

"But—"

"No, Martha. I can't. I just can't," Mary said, extending her left arm toward her sister, her palm flexed.

Martha pivoted to Naomi. "Clearly, I've missed something. Now I want to know what happened after I left Ruth's yesterday. Something big must've happened to turn Mary against me like this!"

"I can't be in the middle of this," Naomi replied, throwing her hands in the air.

Martha couldn't believe her ears. "So, you're taking her side, just like you take Ruth's?"

"Let me know when you're ready to act like a grown-up, Martha," Naomi replied.

"Enough about sides!" Mary yelled. "What does it take for you to realize that we should all be on the same side, Martha? You're going to drive us to the point where no one in the family wants to talk to you. Please don't let your hardheadedness break up what's left of our family."

Martha slid out of the booth and stood up, avoiding eye contact with her sister and aunt. "Fine. I'll give you all the space you want," she said coolly. But she channeled her anger to her boots' three-inch heels, clacking them across the stamped concrete floor on her way out of the restaurant.

Chapter Four

The agenda for Ruth's standing Wednesday afternoon meeting with her senior leadership team was crammed with presentations and last-minute details to prepare for the day-and-a-half-long session Ruth had arranged with Nicholas Dorsey, one of the most in-demand merger, acquisition, and divestiture experts in the country. Although their numerous one-on-one teleconferences and email dialogues in the preceding months had facilitated an exhaustive exchange of information that left Ruth feeling reassured about the business's standing, she was nervous about the in-person consultation. The visit would usher Gardin Family Enterprises into a new phase, whether it meant recommending the family stick to the plan Ruth and Beau had outlined or sell the entire business, the jarring option Martha had raised at the board meeting four days prior.

Ruth sat at the large table at the rear of her office, surrounded by her most dependable employees. The senior leadership team members agreed that the landscaping division would command top dollar, as it was highly profitable, but they couldn't reach a consensus on the balance between community impact and profit maximization. Ruth worried they weren't prepared for the consultant's arrival in two days.

"The revenue from selling both the landscaping division and peanut fundraising line could be a game changer since we can use the money to expand our peanut-shelling operation," said Nia, the director of special projects, as she concluded her report. "I'm sure Mr. Dorsey will agree with my assessment."

Fatou, the company's vice president, pursed her lips as Nia spoke. "Maybe, but we must consider all angles. The company is not experiencing any operating difficulties or financial losses. The fifty percent profit that our school and nonprofit partners make from their annual peanut fundraisers pays for youth sports leagues, libraries, and other important community programs. It is going to break their hearts if we part with the fundraising line. And mine too," she replied. Her heavy Senegalese accent emphasized just the right words, making her sound authoritative yet comforting every time she spoke.

"We can negotiate terms with a potential buyer to protect the community's interests," said LaKisha, the company's chief financial officer, as she looked up from her laptop. "I encouraged Beau to refuse some very lucrative offers for our fundraising line in the past because our community partnerships are a treasure trove for public relations. But my preliminary analysis shows we're on the cusp of a peak sales price. We'll need to move soon."

Ruth slid her right foot back and forth until it spilled out of her cozy skin-toned Kahmune mules and brushed against the area rug. Trying to be discreet, she felt around for her shoe with her foot. The tip of her toes connected with the edge of the shoe, but the mule had fallen just out of reach. Growing more frustrated by the second, Ruth suddenly ducked under the oval table and grabbed her shoe.

Nia paused midsentence and looked quizzically at Ruth.

The other women looked too until Chloe, Ruth's executive assistant, waved them back to work. *It's okay. Keep talking,* she mouthed to Nia.

"Can I get you anything, Ruth?" whispered Chloe.

"I'm good, thanks," Ruth murmured, staring at the rug's colorful floral motif as she slid her foot back into her shoe. The orange, red, yellow, and pink blossoms on the aqua background awakened a spirit of whimsy, reminding Ruth that they had worked through their break and nearly missed the company's tradition of having a peanut-based snack at staff meetings. Though they made an effort to feature healthful selections, this week's treat was more extravagant. *I really must be stressed if it slipped my mind.*

When the debate around the table fizzled out, Ruth spoke up. "Let's keep an open mind as we go into our meetings with Mr. Dorsey, and we'll see what he recommends. I've pushed y'all so hard this afternoon that I forgot about our refreshments. Chloe, do you mind?" Ruth asked, rapidly tipping her head toward the console table next to the bright-yellow accent wall decorated with hexagon trim work.

Her assistant picked up on the cue, her attention shifting to the teal cardboard box and basket of whole fruit sitting on the table.

As Chloe stood, Ruth admired her sassy double-breasted trench dress. The belt at the empire waist accentuated her growing baby bump, prompting Ruth to retrieve the goodies herself. "That's okay, Chloe. Sit and rest," she said as she rose from her chair.

"No problem. I'll do it. I've been looking forward to eating a piece of peanut butter crunch since I called Mary to place the order," Chloe said, sashaying across the room.

Ruth shrugged. She cleared a space in the middle of the green frosted table as she took her seat.

"I gathered the documents Mr. Dorsey requested. I may pull a couple of additional files based on the pros and cons Nia highlighted in her update. But otherwise, we're all set," said LaKisha.

All set? Maybe, but I'll feel better once we can get through his visit and enjoy ourselves at the Christmas party, Ruth thought. She sighed.

"We have a good team, and we are ready," said Fatou as her eyes met Ruth's in a knowing glance. "It is not lost on me that

Beau was secure enough to have so many strong women working for the company. I miss having him around."

"Me too." Ruth smiled. "Beau always said we chose the strongest candidates for the leadership team and that they happened to be women."

"That's beautiful . . . but speaking of women and men working together, I found Mr. Dorsey's photo on his company's website earlier this afternoon. Have y'all seen him?" Chloe asked in the giddy voice she used when she got excited.

Fatou and Nia shook their heads.

"Yes, Chloe. We've seen his photo," LaKisha replied, cutting her eyes.

Chloe lowered the dessert box pressed against her pregnant belly onto the table. She extended her right arm, causing the sweetgrass basket in her left hand to lean toward the floor. Ruth caught the basket, handmade by her favorite Gullah artisan in Charleston, in time to prevent the apples, pears, oranges, and kiwis from tumbling out.

"LaKisha, don't look at me like that," Chloe said, then giggled. "Beau always complimented me on my candor, so he wouldn't mind if he were here. Anyway, I don't usually think older guys are attractive. But his curly, mingled gray hair and rich-brown skin are something to see. I even like his beard. I'm leaving my husband home with the kids and bringing one of my aunties with me to the Christmas party so she can meet Mr. Dorsey."

Ruth chuckled. "We can trust Chloe to bring some levity to our meetings," she said. Ruth relied on her executive assistant for comic relief as much as for her keen observations about the happenings in the office. Chloe never hesitated to give Ruth a heads-up, even if it was something unpleasant. This had endeared Chloe to Ruth, as well as to Beau. "But seriously, Chloe, leave your aunt at home," Ruth continued. "We need everyone to be on their best behavior. Nothing can mess this up. We have no time for distractions."

"All right," Chloe said, her voice laden with disappointment. "It sounds like you need a piece of peanut butter crunch more than I do."

Aware of her boss's weakness for sweets, Chloe opened the pastry box and slid it to Ruth. A nutty caramel fragrance overpowered the sterile scent of the gel sanitizer Ruth rubbed into her hands as she peeked into the box. She grabbed one of the shiny, firm squares and lifted it to her mouth. She exhaled as she chewed, savoring the softness of nut butter with pops of crispy rice cereal and crunchy peanuts.

"Mmmm," she said. "Now, this is the way to end a meeting."

* * *

ON MOST DAYS, the Alabaster Lunch Box dining room cleared out by three o'clock, but Wednesdays were different. Not only was the crowd more robust than other days of the week, but people also socialized with each other more. That was the intention of Peanut Wednesdays, when Mary offered complimentary peanut-based desserts to her customers. Her mantra was to work smarter, not harder. She figured it would be easy to make enough of whatever dessert Gardin Family Enterprises ordered for its weekly staff meetings and also serve it in the restaurant. It felt like an extension of the hospitality her family had shown to guests for generations, and it was her special way of honoring her ancestors. The last remnant of the lunch crowd dawdled in the teal sofa booth at the left corner of the restaurant. Their roars of laughter throughout the lunch service had alerted the entire restaurant that the group was enjoying themselves. But now that they were the only remaining guests, the two couples

kept looking at Mary to see if they had overstayed their welcome.

"Stay as long as you want," Mary yelled across the restaurant.
"Would you like more peanut butter crunch?"

The gentleman seated at the far end of the booth conferred
with his wife and the other couple before he replied, "Yes, please.
We hope we aren't being too greedy."

"Of course not. It's a compliment to the chef. I'll be sure to let
her know she did a good job," Mary said playfully.

The table broke into more laughter.

Shirl, Mary's new catering manager, sat across from her in an
identical sofa booth at the right corner of the restaurant. "Let
me take care of it," Shirl said as she slid out of the booth.

"Thank you," Mary said, returning her gaze to the floor plans
of the Edin Inn, the site of the Gardin Family Enterprises Christmas party.

I can get used to this, Mary thought. She had been reluctant to
trust anyone other than herself to serve in a leadership position
at the restaurant, but her hand was forced. She recognized her
limitations, and there was no way she could provide catering services at the Christmas party unless she put more infrastructure
in place. Although Shirl was only three days into her position,
her insight was already paying off. A seasoned catering manager,
she didn't mind working for someone younger who had less experience. And Shirl had provided Mary with wise recommendations that helped her figure out the amount of food to purchase
for the party and the timeline needed to place the orders, saving
Mary money and time.

Shirl dropped off the treats to the guests and returned to her
seat opposite Mary. "Here, I thought you might be thirsty," she
said, placing a glass of fresh pineapple juice on the table.

"I am. How did you know I—"

"You've got to take better care of yourself. If you run around like this now, I hate to think what it was like before you hired me."

"You make a good point. I'm working on doing better," Mary said, trying to sound convincing.

"Good. I reviewed the revised closing checklists with the staff when I went to the kitchen. They're making excellent progress. In a few minutes, I'll transition them to the prep we need for the party."

"Perfect. We've got a little over forty-eight hours until show-time. Can you believe it?" Mary asked, her forehead wrinkling.

"Try not to worry. Everything is going according to the time-line. It'll turn out great."

Mary stared at Shirl. *Ruth. She reminds me of Ruth.* From the first time Mary had met Shirl, which was at her interview, Mary had noticed something familiar about her. Their personalities clicked, and their conversation was easy. Now Mary had figured it out. Although Shirl was several years older than Ruth, her interaction with Mary reminded her of how she imagined her relationship with Ruth would feel if it were more peaceful. Unlike her sister, Mary wanted to get along with Ruth. But every time she tried, something seemed to get in the way.

Mary was so deep in thought that she didn't hear the front door of the restaurant open.

"Smile, Mary," Shirl said through her teeth.

Mary looked up. "Mrs. Jones!" she exclaimed as the event planner responsible for the Christmas party approached her. Because of her smooth ebony skin and stoic expression, Mary referred to her as the Dora Milaje general of party planning. "Did I forget that we had a meeting?" Mary said in a panic.

"No. Calm down, child," said Mrs. Jones, pecking Mary on the cheek. "You know me. It's my job to pop in and make sure my vendors are all set."

"Got it," Mary replied. She wasn't sure she believed Mrs.

Jones made spontaneous visits to everyone, but the event planner's renown for having discerning taste told Mary she still had doubts about Mary's ability to deliver. "I'd like to introduce you to someone. This is Shirl, my catering manager."

Mrs. Jones squinted at Shirl. "Didn't you used to work at the Golden Jubilee Country Club?" she asked as they shook hands.

"Indeed." Shirl nodded. "I was the country club's assistant catering manager before I moved home to New Orleans for a few years. And then I had my own catering company there. Nice to see you again. I hate to run, but I was about to check on the staff, so I'll let y'all talk."

"Take care, Shirl. See you at the party," Mrs. Jones said.

Shirl squeezed Mary's shoulder as she headed to the kitchen.

Mrs. Jones rubbed her chin. "Impressive hire, Mary. Very impressive. A few catering companies tried to steal Shirl from the country club, but she's very loyal."

"Thanks." Mary grinned. Compliments from Mrs. Jones were scarce. The woman had lobbied for one of her tried-and-true catering partners to get the contract for the Christmas party, and it had taken her some time to adjust to having to work with a novice.

"So, I'll be brief since I see you're on top of things," Mrs. Jones said. "You should've received the final payment via direct deposit."

"Yes, it came through last week," Mary replied. With Mrs. Jones in charge of the party, Mary didn't expect to get the catering contract. But the job came through at the perfect time, as Mary was beginning to wonder if Alabaster Lunch Box was sustainable. She viewed the cash flow from the contract as an early reward for stepping out in faith to open the restaurant.

"My pleasure. I'm pleased with your work ethic so far. If things go well on Friday, I'd be happy to add you to my list of catering partners."

"That's a wonderful compliment," Mary said, her face covered in shock.

Mrs. Jones chuckled. "We'll see how it goes," she replied.

"Thank you so much," Mary said as a bashful smile broke through.

"Very well, then. Let me get on the road to my next stop," said Mrs. Jones, kissing Mary on the cheek.

As the event planner walked out, Mary scanned her restaurant, marveling at how far she'd come since returning to Edin. She'd gone from borrowing money from Martha to relying on tips from customers for gas money to now having cash reserves in her business account. But she was tired. *Shirl is right. I've got to take better care of myself.* She decided to carve out time during the holidays to follow through on her self-care goals. *No excuses this time.*

Chapter Five

Mary hurried up the stairs of the Edin Inn, her red one-shoulder jumpsuit's flutter sleeve flapping in the air. *This is not the time for my stomach to start gurgling.* She wanted to do one last walk-through with her staff before guests arrived, but she was late. She had spent the day balancing her usual lunch service at Alabaster Lunch Box and preparing for what she described as her catering debut. Although she had filled orders for small parties at the restaurant and in people's homes in the six months since it opened, it all felt like practice for tonight: her big introduction to society. The Christmas party was her first time catering a large event. She was grateful to have Shirl on hand to oversee operations at the party as well as the influx of catering orders she anticipated afterward, but she would feel less anxious if she could check in on the preparations. Mary relished the opportunity to promote her restaurant, and she didn't want to let her family down.

As a member of the host family, Mary had to look the part. She couldn't just throw on a chef's jacket, as she usually would at a client event. After orienting Shirl and assisting with setup in the hotel ballroom, Mary rushed home to get ready for the party. Now she had a mere twenty-five minutes before it started. She resolved that whatever she lacked in preparation, she aimed to make up in poise.

While her sister had called catering the event Mary's birthright, Mary recognized Ruth's generosity in taking a chance on her for such a high-profile occasion. Ruth spared no expense for the party, so the catering job was profitable. Mary still struggled to process the events of the previous weekend, and she felt guilty about the way she'd treated Ruth, especially in light of Ruth's support of her business. She also hadn't spoken to Martha since their confrontation at the restaurant. She hoped her stomach would survive the emotional trifecta.

"Hello again," Mary said to the doorman. She adjusted the dainty ring handle of her multicolored crystal sphere-shaped purse to accentuate her wrist like a bracelet.

"Oh, hi. I'm sorry I didn't recognize you. You look so different now," he said, admiring Mary's festive ensemble.

Mary's face lit up with pride. She needed a transformation if she was going to pull this off. Mary also saw this night as a personal graduation. Since her return to Edin, she was finally at a point where she felt victorious. Mary wanted a look that communicated she was ready for what life had to offer, and the doorman's reaction confirmed that the splurge on her outfit and the extra time she put into getting ready were worth it.

Hints of eucalyptus and pine wafted from the garland draped around the foyer. The fragrant decoration usually had a calming effect on Mary, but she had no time to stop and savor it. She needed to get to the ballroom as quickly as possible. Suddenly Mary remembered that she could take a shortcut behind the hotel's front desk to access the service entrance to the grand ballroom. It could save her a couple of minutes of walking to the room's main entrance, and every second counted, especially in the glittery red Jimmy Choo peep-toe pumps she chose for the evening. Mary whipped around the corner and barreled toward the front desk attendant, her heels clicking on the hand-painted porcelain floor tiles.

"Excuse me, I'm so sorry to interrupt. I—" Mary stopped abruptly when she noticed the guest checking into the hotel. "Tynan?" she asked, her voice increasing an octave.

Tynan whipped around, his eyes as wide as the smile on his face. He reached out for Mary. "Hello, love. I've missed you," he said, his voice deep and velvety like a late-night DJ.

Mary fell into his arms, sobbing into the dark brown twill sport coat that perfectly matched his skin. "You're alive! I can't believe you're alive!"

"I am. Yes, of course I am. Don't be silly," he said, lowering his head onto Mary's while he rubbed her upper back.

"What happened? Where were you? Are you allowed to tell me?" Mary fired, pulling away and holding Tynan at his upper arms. Tears streamed down her face as she looked him up and down. Mary expected him to have lost weight and maybe have some scars and bruises, but he looked as striking as she remembered: muscular build, tailored sport coat and slacks, smooth skin, and a fresh haircut.

"Yes, I promise to fill you in soon. Just not here in the lobby. I planned to surprise you tomorrow, but you always knew how to ruin a surprise," he said with a smirk.

"Ruin a surprise? Are you critiquing me already?"

"No, love. I wanted our reunion to be special, that's all. But you and I keep each other in line. That's what we do. And I can see you've deviated from your diet. You've been eating all the good Southern food your aunt likes to cook for you, huh?"

Mary's head whirled. She froze for a moment as she stared at Tynan. "Did you just call me fat? Who do you think you are, talking to me like this? And you just got back from who knows where and you're already acting like a fool! Do you think this is a game? This is my life, Tynan!"

"No, love, I didn't mean it like that."

Mary had envisioned a thousand scenarios when she would finally see Tynan again, but this was not one she had expected. "How else could you possibly mean it? Do you know what I've been through for the past eighteen months? You've commented on my weight and called me silly. Neither belongs anywhere in this conversation."

"Please don't be angry. I thought you would be happy to see me."

"I *am* happy to see you. You just—"

"Where's your ring? Have you stopped wearing it? Are you seeing someone?"

"Tynan!" she yelled. After so much time away, Mary couldn't believe Tynan had been back for two minutes and was already asking questions about her loyalty. She turned to walk away, then realized that she and Tynan weren't alone. Noticing the small crowd that had gathered, Mary gasped loudly and began to sob. Through a blurry gaze, she locked on a familiar set of eyes. Mary knew what had to be done as the eyes drew closer.

"Mary! Are you okay?" Martha asked.

"Mary, love, wait. . . . Let's talk about this," Tynan urged.

Mary didn't acknowledge either of them. She removed her heels and took off down the long corridor opposite the check-in desk. Martha scurried behind her.

*　*　*

MARY PACED BACK and forth in the restroom, pivoting before hitting the wall on each end. Her deliberate stride made her look like a model on a catwalk, but the tears still streaming down her face told a different story.

Martha leaned against the wall closest to the sink. "I'm so sorry, Mary," she said.

"Why do you keep apologizing? You didn't do anything wrong. I can imagine what people must be saying at the party," Mary said shakily. "I've made a total spectacle of myself and embarrassed the family. Aunt Naomi and Ruth must be so ashamed of me."

"It's still a little early," Martha replied. "We have a few minutes before the party starts. They may not know about—"

"*Of course* they know! How could they not know? Everyone was standing around looking at me, watching me break down as the love of my life returned out of nowhere, only to repeatedly insult me within seconds of our being reunited." Mary started sobbing.

Annoyed at her purse's incessant smacking on her leg, Mary tossed her bejeweled bag onto the bench opposite her. Martha put her arm around Mary and tried to guide her to the bench as she walked along with her, but Mary pulled away and paced faster.

"I'm sorry, Mary. I'm so sorry. It's going to be okay," Martha said, settling on the bench. "I don't think very many people saw you and Tynan arguing. It looked like the people who gathered were hotel staff. And even if they were hotel guests or people here for the party, who cares?"

"Who cares? Are you serious? You know how fast word spreads around here. Everybody at the party will be talking about me."

"And if that happens, we'll . . . we'll deal with it. Maybe it could be good for Alabaster Lunch Box. Free publicity, right?"

Mary was touched that Martha wanted to make her feel better. This version of Martha was so different from the one Mary had encountered at her restaurant the week prior. Besides, Martha was usually obsessed with the family's standing in the community. But her ability to come through when she was needed most was what endeared her to those who knew her best. Mary appreciated that her sister cared enough to prioritize her feelings at such a fragile time.

Mary groaned, wishing she could undo the entire evening. If

she hadn't been running late, she wouldn't have crossed paths with Tynan at the front desk. She would have been able to complete the final walk-through with her staff, and she would be greeting the party guests right now instead of hiding in a restroom. She blamed herself.

No matter how she strategized ahead of time to ensure that everything would go smoothly, it never did. Things always came crashing down in the worst way at the worst time. And she was tired of digging herself out of the rubble.

"Did you see anybody recording?" Mary whimpered as she paced.

"No! Do you think you're a celebrity or something?" Martha teased.

"Okay, good. Because I thought I heard 'Run Rudolph' playing in the lobby as I took off my shoes. That would've been awful had it been captured on video."

"That's exactly what was playing," Martha said, followed by a loud cackle. "It's funny thinking about it now."

Mary slowed down, and her head spun toward her sister.

"But it was not funny then," Martha added quickly.

"Martha! This is serious!" Mary yelled, speeding up again.

"Yes, I know. Mary, I'm sorry, but—"

"I don't understand why he would show up like this, without any warning. I mean, I'm obviously glad he's alive and everything, but . . ." Mary sobbed harder.

"Wait, I don't understand why you thought he was dead. I just thought y'all broke up."

Mary was so shaken that she had forgotten that Martha didn't know the whole story about her past with Tynan. She rushed to the restroom door and twisted the silver knob to the locked position.

Martha grabbed a handful of tissues from the box at the left of the faucet and handed them to her sister. Mary wiped her eyes as she took deep breaths in and out of her mouth to help orient herself.

"There's a lot I haven't talked about since I came back home," Mary said, picking up her purse from the bench to make room for them both to be seated.

"Yeah, I know. I've been asking you what—"

"Martha, let me finish."

"Sorry."

"Thank you. It made sense for me to stay in town after Beau's funeral. I pretended that you convinced me to stay, but I'd only bought a one-way ticket here. I didn't have anything to go back to in New York. I said that Tynan and I had broken up, but we hadn't. He . . . well . . ." Mary put her head in her hands. "It's a complicated story. And there's a lot even I still don't know. But I'll take that up with Tynan after the party. For now, I need to pull myself together. We have guests waiting for us, and I have a catering job that also needs my attention. I know I'm being evasive, but there's a good reason for that. I need you to be patient with me. I promise we can talk about it later."

"Okay, well . . . *I* kind of have a confession to make now. Is that okay?"

Mary cut her eyes at Martha. "Uh, that depends. Go ahead."

"Well, Tynan called me yesterday and asked if you were in town. He said he'd been trying to find you because you weren't answering your phone."

Mary gasped. "*That's* why you keep apologizing!" she yelled.

"Yes. I feel horrible. I'm so sorry."

"I . . . I had a bunch of calls from an unknown number yesterday, but I thought it was a telemarketer. He called *you*? And you didn't tell me?"

"Mary, I'm so sorry. He said he wanted to surprise you and asked me not to say anything."

"Wait a minute. So, a man who you think is my ex-boyfriend

tells you that he plans to surprise me and is coming to town on our family's biggest night of the year, a night that's also a huge deal for me professionally, and you didn't think it was a good idea to let me in on it?"

"Well, you weren't talking to me. What was I supposed to do?"

"Get over yourself—that's what you're supposed to do! This is too much for one night. It's just too much. That was an emergency, Martha! Okay, maybe not an emergency, but it was at least something urgent! You should've called me, texted me, come to my house, slipped a note under my door. You should've done whatever was necessary. You don't let somebody get ambushed like this."

Mary stood up and looked in the mirror. She marveled at the contrast between the woman staring back at her and the well-put-together version of herself she had imagined prancing around the ballroom. Under normal circumstances, she wouldn't worry so much about how she looked in public. Her family's stature in the community had meant spending a lifetime of perfecting her ability to project their best image. But a lot more was at stake since the last time she attended the company Christmas party. Mary didn't share Martha's preoccupation with status, but she acknowledged how important the evening was to her family. She pointed to her face. "Do you see my makeup? It's a mess! How am I supposed to walk into the party looking like this? All this could've been avoided if you weren't always being selfish and trying to get back at me."

"You're right. And I'm so sorry now. I knew you would want to know, but I told myself it was your problem since you weren't speaking to me. But I had no idea this would happen. I'm so sorry, Mary. But how was I supposed to know?"

"That's just it, Martha. You always think you know everything. You can't possibly imagine that you might be wrong, or maybe that you don't have all the information."

"I wish I could rewind and do things differently, but I can't," Martha said, shaking her head as she eyed Mary's face in the mirror. "Do you have makeup in the car?"

"No, I went home to change, so I didn't bring my makeup bag with me. I only have lipstick. I guess I'll have to run home."

"Oh, you can't leave looking like that. Your mascara is all over the place, and tear tracks are running through your foundation. It's a good thing we wear the same shade. I came straight from work, so my makeup bag is in the car. I'll be right back. Do not leave, okay? Promise me."

"Okay, I won't. That won't make up for everything, but it's a start. Thank you, Martha."

* * *

MARTHA WALKED INTO the ballroom with her sister beside her. Party guests waved and nodded as they entered. A few people pulled out their cameras, and the duo paused in a rehearsed pose that was designed to look natural. Martha usually scanned the room for the most popular party guests as soon as she hit the door, but she wanted to keep an eye on Mary. And she needed to see if she picked up on any behavior from guests that showed they had seen the debacle in the hotel lobby.

Some people looked at Thanksgiving as the start of the Christmas season, but the Gardin Party, as it had been known for generations, was the most important social event of that time of year. Everyone in Edin vied for an invitation to the annual celebration, and some of the most prominent people in Macon were beginning to jump on the bandwagon too.

Once the camera flashes in their direction stopped, Martha checked in with her sister. "How are you feeling?" she asked.

Mary didn't answer the question. Her attention focused on the food stations. "Everything looks magnificent. I'm so thankful," Mary said, surveying the room and raising her thumb at the attendants at each of the food stations nearby. "I know how much you and your bourgeois friends hate waiting in line, so each section of the room has its own buffet set up."

"We are not bourgeois! Okay, maybe just a little bit." Martha giggled and nudged her sister.

"Ouch!" Mary laughed. Then her face went back to business. "But seriously, I'm relieved that Ruth let me change things up instead of doing the same menu and traditional layout that's been done year after year. Check out the mashed-potato bar and salad stations and let me know what you think."

"Will do. And smile," Martha said. "Someone's always watching."

Mary complied but continued talking through her teeth. "And Shirl even remembered to use the new silver table card stands engraved with the restaurant's logo. I wasn't sure if they would make it in time, but they arrived today."

"Nice touch," Martha said.

"Now I hope my stomach will stop grumbling," Mary whispered.

"Did you eat something that upset it?"

"I don't think so. I think it's nerves. It's been happening all evening. I kind of forgot about it when Tynan popped up, but I'm starting to feel it again."

Naomi sneaked up from behind and hugged her nieces. "I've been searching all over for y'all." She looked back and forth between the women. "Ooh! Y'all look gorgeous! Did you plan your outfits?" she said with a huge smile that shone almost as much as her special diamond studs adorning her earlobes.

Mary inspected her sister from head to toe. "Martha, how did I miss that we're wearing almost the exact same thing? The only difference is your jumpsuit has a long batwing sleeve with a split, and I can't afford those," she said, pointing at the velvet Agnes

Bethel sandals on Martha's feet. Mary had fallen in love with the way the shoe's deep red hue and metallic gold trim complemented the carefree vibe of its tie-up ankle bow. She promised herself she would buy them after her catering business was on solid ground. For the party, she opted for a pair that she found on a luxury resale website.

"Yeah, I didn't want to bring it up, but I guess we both have good taste," Martha replied, lifting her sleeved arm and twirling like Diana Ross in *Mahogany*. She surprised herself by being so playful in public, but she felt she owed her sister a little compromise to lighten her mood. As Mary laughed again, Martha felt proud of herself for taking the risk and tickled that it paid off.

"It's good to see you two getting along." Naomi grinned. "But let's go. Ruth is on her way to the microphone. I'm so glad you made it in time."

"Just in time," Mary said, smiling at Martha.

The women locked hands and walked to the front of the room, with Naomi leading the way. The lights dimmed when they reached the center of the parquet dance floor, where Ruth stood. Naomi grabbed Ruth's hand, and the room erupted in applause. The women smiled graciously. As the applause tapered, Ruth cleared her throat and began to speak. "Thank you so very much for making time during this busy Christmas season to celebrate with us. We always enjoy sharing this joyous time of year with you. For me, tonight is bittersweet, as this party was my late husband Beaumont Gardin's favorite Christmas activity."

Ruth paused as a wave of murmured condolences ran through the crowd. "Family is such an important part of Christmas, and I would like to extend a special greeting on behalf of the remaining members of the Gardin family who stand with me tonight. As many of you know, our son, M.J., is studying peanut farming in Senegal this year, so he's the only member of the family who couldn't be here this evening. I'm proud to represent Beau and the Gardin family tonight. And I'm pleased to honor him every day through my service and combined roles of president and interim CEO. As you know, Georgia grows about forty-five percent of all U.S. peanuts, and Gardin Family Enterprises remains one of the top producers for the tenth straight year. We are planning to expand our technology, and we will continue to invest in our future. We look forward to M.J. enlightening us with everything he's learning in his graduate program and during his time abroad, and we also will continue our support of the Gardin Family Agricultural Scholars program, as well as our collaboration with the National Peanut Research Laboratory and many of you. I would like to offer special thanks to the Gardin Family Enterprises employees and partners who are here tonight. We'd like to ask you to stand so we can salute you."

Ruth clapped, and the audience joined in. When the applause ceased, she continued, "You mean so much to us, and we wish you and your families a very blessed Christmas and New Year. If you haven't already done so, please help yourself to this wonderful spread, which was brought to us by Alabaster Lunch Box. And if you love the food as much as I believe you will, please stop by and see Mary at the restaurant sometime. Thanks again for joining us! Enjoy the party!"

Per Gardin family tradition, the women dispersed into the crowd to greet guests while the live band played "Angels We Have Heard on High." But this year's band was different from the jazz band that had played for years. Their replacement played a soulful R&B rendition of the song that had the crowd buzzing with excitement.

Martha flashed a huge grin, but inside she was seething. *Humph . . . Well played, Ruth. . . . And the band is a nice touch too,* she thought as she walked toward her assigned area, the ballroom addition otherwise known as the overflow section. People seated in that area were still privy to a good view as well as separate food and drink stations. However, it was filled with first-time attendees, people who narrowly made the cutoff for the invitation list, media representatives, and last-minute additions. Those weren't the people Martha desired to connect with. The assignments had come in an email from Mrs. Jones, but Martha was certain Ruth had given the event planner specific instructions to send Martha to that area to get back at her. That was bad enough, but Ruth's speech also reverberated in Martha's ears: *I'm proud to represent Beau and the Gardin family tonight. And I'm pleased to honor him every day through my service and combined roles of president and interim CEO.* Over and over again, she heard, *I'm pleased to honor him every day through my service and combined roles of president and interim CEO.*

She's sending me a message, and she's trying to get everyone on her side. Although Martha fumed inside, she was careful to keep a broad smile on her face as she greeted the guests.

"Thanks so much for coming."

"Merry Christmas!"

"You look gorgeous, as usual."

"Thank you for covering the event. Don't forget to tag us when you post on social media."

"So good of you to join us."

"Of course, I'd be happy to take a photo with you."

Martha wanted to scream by the time she'd worked through her section and reached the rear of the room. The dim lights made it hard to see from afar, but her eyes landed on the chiseled face that had propelled her sister into a state of agony not an hour earlier: Tynan, the ideal target for her venom. He walked behind a couple searching for their seats, but Martha kept him in her sight until she caught up with him as he was forced to stop when the couple paused to take a photo with guests at a nearby table.

Martha's smile enlarged as she opened her mouth to speak,

but there was no mistaking the intent behind her narrowed eyes. "I don't know how you got in here, but it's very important that you leave and not make a scene. It would be catastrophic for Mary and devastating for our family's reputation. I don't want to draw any unwarranted attention, so I'd hate to have to summon security to escort you out. But I will. We've always gotten along, so you may not know I'm the loose cannon of the family. Please go away for the remainder of the evening. I promise to be in touch tomorrow. We have a lot to discuss."

Tynan chuckled as he ran his hand across his mouth. "Oh no, I've heard about you," he said. "Point taken."

"Splendid," Martha said as she watched him exit the ballroom.

Chapter Six

Naomi snapped her fingers, swaying to the beat of the band. "Yes, honey, this party is lit. Isn't that what you kids say?"

Martha leaned toward Naomi's ear. "Sure. Um, I just kicked Tynan out."

"Oh no. Mary's food is delicious. Why do you want to eat out?"

Martha leaned closer to her aunt. "No, I said, *I just kicked Tynan out.*"

Naomi's head bounced with the music. "Who?"

"Tynan."

"Huh?" Naomi asked, shimmying to the music. A photographer took candid photos at a neighboring table, and the ruby-red sequins on Naomi's ruched dress mimicked a disco ball as the camera flashed.

"Tynan Wright, Mary's ex-fiancé."

The music was still playing, but Naomi froze. "Oh dear, what's he doing here? Is he trying to get her back?"

"Wait. Come with me."

Martha broke through the sea of people streaming in and out of the ballroom. She pulled her aunt into the ballroom's busy foyer, the informal gathering spot with brighter lighting where guests went to see and be seen. Old friends from Atlanta made plans for dinner after the new year, noting that they never ran into each other at home but could always count on seeing each other at the annual party. Latecomers chatted with guests who arrived on time, getting highlights about what they'd missed. A couple posed for photos in front of the black grand piano, and a line of people waited their turn for selfies and group shots in front of the massive Christmas tree decked in red, green, and gold ornaments. The women tucked into a small hallway off the ballroom foyer so no one would interrupt.

"Okay, what's going on?" Naomi asked, her speech pressured like she'd been holding her breath.

Martha exhaled. "Well, it seems Mary and Tynan never broke up. I couldn't get any details out of Mary, so I don't know what's going on yet. But I certainly will soon."

"Mary told you this? Is she happy to see him?"

"Not exactly. I think she was happy at first, but she's mad now. Anyway, Tynan called me, and he—"

"He *called* you?"

Martha looked away from Naomi. "Be patient. Let me get the story out," she said nervously.

"Well, hurry up!"

"You know how I answer calls from unknown numbers when I'm on call, because I never want to miss any calls from my VIP patients. Not that I give preferential treatment to certain types of people or think some are more important because of who they know or what they do for a living, but some patients expect access to their—"

"That's exactly what you do," Naomi interrupted. "But we're not talking about that right now. And why are you rambling? You've done something bad, haven't you?"

"Okay, okay. So, Tynan called me after he couldn't reach Mary, and I happened to pick up. Since Mary never told us much about what happened between them, I didn't think it was a big deal."

Naomi stepped closer to her niece. "So, he told you he was coming, but you didn't tell her. And now she's not happy that he's here?"

"Right." Martha sighed.

"Oh, Martha!"

"I know, I know. But lower your voice, Aunt Naomi."

"Sorry. Go on."

"I love my sister, but you know how she's always kinda screwing things up. I still can't fathom how she went through all her money from the trust. So, why wouldn't I have wanted to help her get back together with a good catch like Tynan, who works for a billionaire financier in Manhattan? Well, now I don't think I made the right decision. He said some concerning things to Mary in the lobby, and she—"

"In the lobby? You mean *here*? Were people around? Oh, Lord have mercy!" Naomi exclaimed.

"Aunt Naomi, please keep your voice down."

"My bad. Continue."

"So she ran away from him in the middle of the lobby."

Naomi held her head in her hands.

"Yeah, it was dreadful," Martha said. "But I don't think any of our party guests saw. Somehow we got lucky. There were a bunch of people around, but I think they were all hotel staff. No one at the party has said anything to me about it, so I think we're all clear. It's kind of a miracle."

"That's good. I haven't heard anything either. No one has even hinted at it."

"Oh, there y'all are!" Ruth exclaimed, waving her arms. "I've been looking all over."

"How did she find us?" Martha muttered under her breath.

Naomi squinted at Martha. "I heard you. It's not that noisy in here."

Ruth cut in front of some photographers to join the women. "Sorry. Oh, excuse me, please," she said, smiling. Martha thought she evoked a peacock as she strutted through the foyer in red satin Aminah Abdul Jillil pumps with an oversized bow at the ankle and a matching asymmetrical pleated skirt that grazed the floor.

Concerned that Martha and Ruth had not spoken since the meeting at Ruth's home the week prior, Naomi had kept a watchful eye for the moment the women would interact at the party. She braced in the imminence of the moment. "Be nice," Naomi whispered to Martha as Ruth approached.

"Don't worry. I'm going to go check on Mary," she said before she blew an air-kiss to Naomi.

"So, what's going on?" Ruth asked.

"Great speech," Martha said to Ruth with a slight, close-lipped smile as she walked away.

* * *

RUTH FOUGHT THE urge to roll her eyes. She funneled her frustration at Martha's sarcasm into a toothy smile in case any of the guests were watching.

"It really was a great speech," Naomi said.

"Thanks, MIL. But don't try to cover for Martha. I saw her pull you out of the party. Did she bring you into this little hideaway to complain about what I said up there?"

"No, she didn't mention the speech at all. She was telling me about what happened to Mary. Walk with me so I can fill you in while we go look for her. I need to lay eyes on her to make sure she's all right. I don't have a good feeling about this at all."

As Ruth and Naomi entered the ballroom, they heard Mary's voice, sounding strong and confident over the band's rendition of "What Christmas Means to Me." They surveyed the immediate area in search of their target.

Naomi leaned close to Ruth. "There she is. I guess I was worried for nothing," she said, pointing to Mary.

They joined Mary as she stood at the right of the doorway talking with Eve Greenwald and her son, Oji, a real-estate developer and recent *Georgia Business Chronicle* "40 Under 40" honoree.

"Oh, thank you so much! I would be delighted to explore opening a second location in Macon," Mary said.

"Excuse us for barging in on your conversation," Naomi interjected, "but I like what I heard. So good to see you, Eve and Oji."

"Yes, of course! Your timing is perfect," Mary replied. "Oji just mentioned that he's working on a new development around Macon General Hospital, and he suggested that Alabaster Lunch Box would be a good fit."

Eve's dangling ruby and diamond earrings swayed as she looked Mary up and down. Ever majestic in appearance, her large bouffant bun and Salone Monet slingback sandals made her taller than her natural five-foot, seven-inch height. "There's nothing like a savvy businesswoman who can cook too. You remind me so much of my younger self," Eve said, smiling.

"Thank you," Mary said, her eyelashes batting with embarrassment.

Naomi discreetly nudged Ruth with her elbow.

Ruth chuckled. Eve had been born into one of Macon's wealthiest families, and she was known to have strong opinions about who her children dated. Ruth was tickled that Mary seemed to have Eve's approval.

Oji directed his attention at Naomi and Ruth. "The food is amazing," he said, squeezing his mother's arm without otherwise acknowledging the comment she made to Mary. "Mary explained that everything on tonight's menu was made with consideration of people who need a low-salt, low-fat, or low-sugar diet, but it doesn't taste like it."

"It sure doesn't," Eve replied, removing Oji's hand without

looking at him. She wiggled, causing the red taffeta ruffles at her shoulders to flutter against her shimmery brown skin like tissue paper atop a gift bag.

Oji playfully cut his eyes at his mother.

Ruth clasped her hands, drawing them to her chest. "That's one of the reasons we changed from our long-term caterer. It wasn't nepotism," she said excitedly. "With the rates of chronic diseases like high blood pressure, high cholesterol, diabetes, heart disease, and stroke in our family as well as in the community, we have a responsibility to help people make healthy choices while celebrating the holidays." Ruth locked eyes with Mary and smiled.

Mary blushed. "We're still perfecting the low-sugar part. People love holiday desserts, so I can't totally eliminate them. We have healthier options for those too. Even so, we hope people will exercise moderation," she said.

"I'm working on that part myself," Ruth said, then laughed.

"We're all works in progress. But everyone in Edin knows about your sweet tooth," Naomi teased, placing her arm around Ruth.

"It makes good business sense for an agricultural company to champion plant-based foods," Oji said, "but it's commendable that you're supporting people to make smart decisions for their health, even in a celebratory atmosphere. This party has been more high yield than all the meetings I've had in my office this week combined, and my meetings didn't have great food or a live band." He smiled. "And since you're such a gracious hostess, maybe you won't mind if I cut our conversation short. I see someone across the room I've been trying to meet with for two months. Mary, I'll definitely be in touch."

"Oh goodness!" Ruth beamed. "Thank you. Yes, go! Enjoy!" She loved that the party upheld its tradition of being a place where people could have a good time and also make connections that foster cooperative economics in the community. *Beau would be so proud.*

Eve shook her head at her son. "I'm going to stay here and talk with Mary. . . . And Naomi and Ruth too, of course."

"Mother, they have to tend to their other guests," Oji replied, taking Eve's hand while guiding her away.

"Fine," Eve relented. She followed her son as she waved good-bye and bobbed her head to the music.

"I can't believe it!" Mary said. "It's been a little bumpy, but this evening is turning out well after all."

"What a great opportunity for your restaurant!" Naomi exclaimed. "I'm so proud of you. Let's go enjoy the party."

It seemed natural to ask what had happened to make the evening bumpy, but Ruth already knew. Naomi had filled her in after Ruth found Naomi and Martha talking in the hallway. So, Ruth followed Naomi's lead. Although Mary and Ruth's relationship had swung like a pendulum over the years, Ruth was always protective of Mary and Martha. Ruth had watched them grow from cute preteens to women who carried on the family legacy. They had said more hurtful things to her over the years than she could remember, and she could forgive them only because she understood the root of their pain, their parents' early death. She wanted them to prosper, even when they seemed to lack the same wish for her. Ruth wanted to help Mary work through whatever splinters of pain remained in her heart, but the look of glee on Mary's face was enough to satisfy her for the time being.

Although Ruth was comfortable not asking about what had happened earlier in the evening, she wondered if the women would still meet for their usual debrief at her house after the party. But she decided not to inquire. For now, she wanted to appreciate the moment and let things proceed naturally.

"Wait a minute. I want you two to meet someone before you go," Ruth said as she grabbed Naomi's arm and waved vigorously at a gentleman walking toward the buffet. He returned the wave and joined the trio.

"This is Nicholas Dorsey, the merger, acquisition, and divestiture consultant we talked about last weekend," Ruth said. Although his dapper appearance had made half of the Gardin Family Enterprises staff swoon, Nicholas's face displayed the sternness that had kept the other half of the team on edge all week. A sharp dresser, he projected a playful vibe at the party in a red tailored suit with black Santa boots that featured a white band of fluffy cotton around the calf. Ruth hoped his wardrobe choice, albeit festive, didn't undermine her family's confidence in him.

Nicholas extended his hand to Naomi. "Happy to meet you," he said with a dashing smile.

"Yes, it's lovely to meet you, Mr. Dorsey. Now, please tell me you wore this outfit to the Gardin Family Enterprises office today when Ruth handed out the Christmas bonuses," she joked.

Nicholas chuckled. "Feel free to call me Nicholas." He turned to Mary. "How did you get here so quickly? I saw you talking to some people by the Christmas tree in the corner a minute ago, unless you have a twin. I would have introduced myself if I had known you were one of the Gardin women."

"Nice to meet you, Mr. Dorsey. We—"

"Let's not be so formal. Nicholas, please," he said.

"Okay, Nicholas," Mary said. "We're not twins, but that was my sister, Martha. My *older* sister. People always mix us up, and it doesn't help that we're wearing almost the same outfit tonight." She laughed, holding her abdomen under the draping of her jumpsuit.

"Oh, yes. I've heard about Martha," he replied.

Ruth narrowed her eyes at Nicholas. She prayed his reply hadn't let on that she and Nicholas had spoken about Martha's challenge to Ruth's position in the company. "Speaking of out-fits . . . Nicholas, I'm intrigued by your interpretation of our request that guests wear holiday-chic attire."

"This is the one time of year that I don't mind people teasing me about having a white beard and being named Nicholas. Plus, talking about my suit and Santa boots is great for awkward moments when I put my foot in my mouth," he said.

The ladies laughed.

Good save, Ruth thought. She wanted things to go well when her family met Nicholas, but there was still one person left. Ruth hoped the tension between her and Martha would subside soon. She had been increasingly conflicted about the unrest in the family while she tried to take Gardin Family Enterprises to the next level. Nicholas had a way of bringing calm into her professional life, but Ruth hadn't figured out his MO. She could bounce ideas off him like she could with Beau, yet it was different. Perhaps it was because she was in charge, or perhaps it was their nearly twenty-five-year age difference. She couldn't put her finger on it, but it felt like nothing she'd experienced before.

"Ruth has been singing your praises all week. She said you've had some very productive meetings," Naomi said.

"Yes. I'm just getting started," he said, "but it's remarkable how much the company has grown over the past several years. Ruth and Beau were forward-thinking in their planning."

"Indeed. It's an exciting time," Naomi replied. "Excuse me, but they're starting a line dance, so I need to make my way to the dance floor. I'm looking forward to hearing your recommendations for the company. It was nice to meet you, Nicholas."

"Nice meeting you too," he said with a grin. "Maybe I'll see you on the dance floor later, but first the buffet is calling my name. Ruth, you weren't kidding about the spread, were you?"

"No, I wasn't. Mary sure outdid herself," Ruth replied.

Mary smiled. "Enjoy, but remember moderation."

As Nicholas walked away, Ruth noticed Mary's hand at her abdomen. "Mary, are you okay?" Ruth asked.

"I'm not sure. My stomach has been bubbling off and on all evening, and now I'm starting to feel nauseated. I think I'd better excuse myself too. I'm sorry," Mary said, taking off toward the door. She disappeared in the group of people walking toward the main ballroom exit. Ruth followed, with the sounds of "This Christmas" trailing behind them.

* * *

MARY BARRELED THROUGH the restroom door. After she cleared the threshold, she let go of the door, causing it to fling backward. Ruth turned her head and threw her hands up, catching the door and narrowly missing the right side of her face.

"I can't do anything right today!" Mary exclaimed, rushing toward the single stall. She stopped, pivoted quickly, and tossed her purse onto the bench for the second time that evening. She scooted into the stall, slamming the door behind her.

Ruth leaned on the wall of the restroom. "No, no . . . it's okay. Don't worry about it. . . . This is a historic hotel . . . and we're in the original part of the property. I think the doors are old. . . . You know . . . compared to the addition . . . where the ballroom is located," she said.

Mary swung the stall door open. "I need help! The zipper— it's stuck! Help me get out of this. Please hurry!" she yelled. Mary raised her right arm and danced in place, squeezing her legs together. "See. It's stuck!"

Ruth trotted over to Mary. She gripped the zipper and tugged it back and forth, taking care not to rip the delicate crepe fabric. "Try to hold still. I know it's hard. . . . Wait, okay there it is," Ruth said, then sighed.

"Thank you," Mary said, shuffling back to the stall. She slammed the door again and slid the bar of the lock into the keeper. As she slipped out of her jumpsuit and flung it over the door, she thought about the uncomfortable situations Ruth had seen her through over the years, from helping her through her first menstrual period to nursing her first heartbreak, but she was wary of a stranger walking into the restroom during such a vulnerable situation. "There's a lock on the door," Mary said.

Ruth sat on the bench, scrolling through the social media posts about the party. "I don't know. I'm out here," she replied.

"No, the main door. Would you lock it, please?"

Ruth's head swiveled toward the entrance. "Oh yeah. There sure is. Smart," she said. Ruth put down her phone and leaped to the door. She turned the old silver lock before returning to the bench. "Wait a second. How did you know the hotel had a restroom with a single stall all the way down here?" she asked.

"Give me a minute," Mary said, her voice strained.

"Take your time. I'll turn on some music," Ruth replied. She selected the Silent Night station on her phone's music app as an unspoken prayer request for the rest of the evening. After three soothing songs, Mary emerged from the stall and walked to the sink.

"I feel so much better," Mary said. "Oh, you asked how I knew about this private restroom. It's a long story, but Martha and I ended up here earlier this evening . . . after I walked up on Tynan checking in at the front desk. He came to town to . . . surprise me."

"I see. . . . Yes, Martha told MIL, and MIL told me about Tynan."

"Word travels fast in this family, doesn't it?" Mary said, lathering her hands. "I mean, I'm not surprised, but I hoped that with the party going on, I could at least make it until our debrief later tonight to tell y'all about it myself."

"Martha is worried about you," Ruth said as she shifted on the bench.

"Yeah, I figured. I guess I should've expected she would say something to y'all about it."

"But she doesn't think anyone saw. MIL and I haven't picked up from any of the guests that they saw it. I can think of a few who would've hinted around to see what we would tell them. And Sister Johnson would've been one of them. She may be the pastor's wife, but she keeps up half the gossip in Edin."

Mary nodded. "True. That's a relief that even *she* doesn't know what happened."

"Are you sure you feel better? I don't want to pry, but it doesn't seem like you did much in there."

Mary dried her hands and walked to the full-length mirror. "It felt like my stomach was about to explode, but it feels a lot better now. And you've helped me through a lot worse. Remember that time I came home from college and I was supposed to take M.J. to the movies but couldn't because I was hungover from partying the night before?"

"That was horrible!" Ruth laughed.

Mary chuckled. "Ow, my stomach," she said. "Beau would've been so mad if he had been there instead of you. Did you ever tell him about that?"

"Nope. I never told him. He was still working in the peanut fields then, so he was too preoccupied to notice. That was the first time I learned that oral rehydration fluids for children work so well on adults." She laughed. "You and Martha have certainly taught me some things over the years."

"I bet, but let's focus on you for the rest of the night," Mary said, smoothing the front of her jumpsuit in the mirror. "I hope you can enjoy the party now. I know it is work for you, too, but at least try to have fun."

Mary inched closer to the mirror and inspected her face. "At least I don't have to fix my makeup on my return visit to this beautiful restroom. You should go back to the party. I'm sure the guests are looking for you. I'm gonna sit here and gather myself for a few minutes, and then I'll be right down."

"Are you sure?"

"Yes, I'm absolutely certain," Mary said, sitting next to Ruth on the bench and throwing her arm around her. "Thank you for taking care of me. I know I don't always act like it, but I appreciate you for always being there for me."

Ruth squeezed Mary with both arms. "You're so very welcome. I'm glad I could help." Ruth tilted her head back and fanned her eyes with both hands as she released Mary. "Whew! Now you're gonna make me cry. It must be something about this old bathroom." She laughed.

"Yes, that's gotta be it," Mary agreed.

* * *

MARTHA LINGERED IN the hotel gallery, admiring her favorite piece of art. She made a point of having some quiet time with the oil painting before whatever function she attended at the hotel, but the commotion at the front desk earlier in the evening had forced her to change her schedule. She was delighted that when she mentioned the hotel's collection of artwork by Black Southern artists to one of the out-of-town guests attending the party, the guest asked for a brief tour.

Before returning to the party in the neighboring wing, Martha had stayed behind for a brief moment of personal reflection, marveling at the long-suffering but proud faces of the men and women in the painting. Her sixth- and seventh-great-grandparents stood in the middle of the group, flanked by the other formerly enslaved people who'd made the treacherous trip from the Georgia coast to found Edin. As she imagined the perils they must have encountered on their journey, she heard a hushed voice.

"You always forget that you get chill bumps when you wear a cold-shoulder. That's why you need me to remind you."

"What?" she asked, pivoting like a fighter in one of those 1970s martial arts movies she used to watch with her grandfather. She swung in the air before the identity of the speaker registered in her mind. "You again? We have to get better security," she said, forcing herself to project a quieter tone than her physical response merited.

Tynan leaped back and extended his arms to block any additional unanticipated moves. "Oh, Martha . . . sorry. I thought you were Mary. You two look so much alike from the back. I never understood how people confused the two of you, but I guess I haven't seen her for a while. Was it your idea for the two of you to dress alike? Mary would never have gone for that if I was around."

What a jerk. It's not the same outfit. It's close, but not the same. And I would never dress like anybody else on purpose. She liked to point out when others were wrong, but she had no time to spend on trivial details right now. She'd become accustomed to people confusing her and her sister. It happened a lot, and wearing similar outfits at a dimly lit party had made their physical likeness a topic of conversation all evening. But this was the first time it upset her. Facing a man who she feared had hurt her sister far more deeply than she knew was different from encountering someone who thought Martha was responsible for the tasty sautéed vegetables at the buffet.

Martha raised her right arm in the air, waving her pointer finger. "*You* don't get to ask *me* any questions. Didn't I tell you to stay away from my sister?" she said with a scowl, accenting each word with a bounce of her finger. Then she looked at the cell phone in her left hand. "Yes, as a matter of fact, I did tell you that. It was about two hours ago, just down the hallway. Do I need to ask security to help me this time? Security! Security!"

"No. Please, no," Tynan replied, struggling to keep his voice down. "I got it. Please don't get me thrown out of the hotel. You don't know what I've been through the past eighteen months. I don't want to waste time or upset anyone. I'd like to make up with Mary and go back to our old life in New York."

"I don't know about going back to your old life. Mary makes her own decisions, but based on how you spoke to her earlier tonight, I wouldn't count on her returning to New York. Now, I warned you before. You don't want my trouble."

"I simply want to talk to Mary. I'm not trying to cause any problems." Tynan narrowed his eyes. "You know, this is exactly why Mary left Edin in the first place. Your family was always butting into things that weren't your concern."

"Are you listening to yourself? You sound like a psychopath. I was always rooting for you, but I get it now. You were trying to isolate my sister in New York."

"Mary always said you thought you could diagnose every-body."

Martha seethed. She didn't want to give Tynan the satisfac-tion of knowing he'd hit a sensitive spot, but she was never good at running away from a fight. She put her hands on her hips and slowly looked him up and down. "I see you. But your little mind games don't work on me. You aren't as smart as you think you are. Mary doesn't want to talk to you, okay? I don't know the full scope of what you did to her, but I'm gonna find out."

"Martha, please . . . I want us to be friends. I don't want to cause any drama for your family. Hopefully, it'll soon be *our* family."

Our family? Martha thought. She'd had enough of people

marrying into her family and spreading their issues and insecurities like an infectious disease. She was tired of cleaning up the mess.

Martha frowned. But then she recalled her grandmother's admonition about reining in your feelings and wearing what she called "your public face" outside the house. The two sisters had cast aside their public faces enough times for one evening. Though Martha was reluctant to deprive Tynan of the reprimand he deserved, she didn't want to make another scene.

Martha looked over her shoulder at the oil painting. She felt as though her ancestors were standing behind her, giving her strength to ensure she represented her family with honor. She could do it for them. She took a deep breath and relaxed her facial muscles. When she exhaled, the corners of her mouth turned up and exposed her teeth. "No, I won't do this here. I don't have anything more to say to you. I have your number. I'll make sure Mary has it. Please go to your room. And I'm going to watch you get on the elevator this time," she said, ending with a tight-lipped smile.

Chapter Seven

Martha hoped she could make it back to the ballroom without anyone stopping her to talk. With most of the attendees on the dance floor, the odds were in her favor. She wasn't being antisocial. Aside from her brief blip with Tynan, Martha was enjoying the party. She just didn't want anyone to hear her growling stomach. She had been so busy exchanging pleasantries and taking photos with guests that she hadn't had anything to eat. She'd forgotten how much energy was required to navigate the Edin social ladder.

As she approached the ballroom, Martha ran through her mental checklist of all the people she needed to talk to at the party, and she was almost done. Only one person remained—Oji Greenwald—but the CEO of Macon General Hospital had just told Martha that Oji had left the party a few minutes earlier.

Every woman in the room had wanted to talk to the handsome bachelor real-estate developer, but no one more than Martha. Unlike the other women, though, Martha was only moderately interested in seeing whether there might be a spark between them. She was far more concerned with the opportunity to work with him on his new project near the hospital. She had advocated fiercely for Oji to be invited to the party, even sacrificing one of her long-standing personal invitees to ensure that he made the cut. And now she'd have to go back to cold-calling his office—unless she could figure out an alternative way for their paths to cross.

Martha hadn't told anyone about it yet, but she had been saving her money for the past four years for a restaurant where she
could provide "community food prescriptions," event menus
that featured healthy versions of both traditional Southern food
as well as foods that people might not have tried before. She already hosted healthful-cooking classes at work, but she wanted
to extend her reach. Just as food brought families together, she
believed it could make people more comfortable with physicians
and other healthcare providers. When Martha heard about the
plans to redevelop the abandoned building near the hospital, she
was certain it was the perfect place for her high-concept restaurant. Her training in culinary medicine and primary care made
her the ideal candidate to lead her own patients, as well as the
community as a whole. But Martha's aspirations were only partially benevolent. She also anticipated that the restaurant would
enhance her social standing. To the community, Ruth was the
darling of the esteemed Gardin family. Martha was tired of being
in her shadow, and everyone loved a selfless physician who put
her community first.

Although Martha didn't think she needed Mary's permission,
she was concerned that her sister might feel she was encroaching
on her territory. While Macon General Hospital was one of the
largest hospitals in Georgia and the only top-level trauma center
in the area, it also functioned as a safety-net provider, which
meant that most of its services were provided to patients who
were uninsured, received Medicaid, or were at higher risk for
medical conditions. Martha would be the primary investor, but
she'd researched business models that would also allow her to
integrate a teaching kitchen and other grant-funded opportunities that would provide healthy and affordable food options to
people across the community instead of limiting it to only the
people who could afford it. Although Martha genuinely cared
about the socioeconomic groups that comprised most of her pa-

tient mix, she loved that the restaurant also had the potential to offer curated events for the high-society folks in the hospital's faction of VIP patients.

Martha's mouth started to water as she finally arrived at the buffet. She had stolen some glances over the course of the evening, but the food was even more impressive up close. The tri-layered buffet glowed. Mirrored shelves holding marinated olives and cheese, stuffed mushrooms, and sautéed vegetables were held up by glass vases filled with shimmering lights and holly. The staff's running back and forth all night to replenish the food stations almost as soon as they'd filled them was a testament to the fact that the party guests were pleased.

Oh, the potato bar! I'd forgotten about it, Martha thought as she spotted it out of the corner of her eye. She decided to start with soup and salad and make another trip for the potato bar and other goodies. Even though she usually ate light at the Christmas party, she was eager to enjoy every course of Mary's menu. As the band ended its set, the buffet attendant slowly ladled roasted red pepper and tomato soup into a bowl. Martha stopped next to her and loaded a hefty portion of Christmas spring mix salad onto her plate. As she reached for a mini jalapeño cheddar biscuit, a man with a deep voice yelled in the distance.

"I need a doctor. Is anybody a doctor around here? She's having chest pain!" he roared, his voice reminiscent of a cartoon hero.

Martha's head snapped up. She flung her plate and it landed in the server's half-filled soup bowl. The deep-red liquid splashed into the salad as the server clumsily connected with the plate. Martha spun 180 degrees toward the door. "Yes! I'm coming! I'm a doctor!" she shouted.

As she reached the edge of the foyer, Martha saw a man dressed in a maintenance uniform helping someone who leaned against the wall in the hallway. The man's broad torso blocked the upper body of the person he had stopped to help, but she recognized the red crepe pant legs and red sparkly peep-toe shoes as her sister's.

"Mary!" she screamed.

Martha was already walking fast, but she increased her speed for the remaining twenty feet that lay ahead. The heavy gold curtains covering the windows on both sides of the hallway turned to a blur.

Mary put her hands to her chest. She looked as though she had run a marathon without having completed a training regimen. Suddenly Martha remembered that she had passed a pair of Louis XVI–style chairs on the way from the ballroom. She kept her eyes fixed on her sister as she said, "She needs to sit. There's a chair somewhere down there. Someone get it!"

As a gentleman passerby retrieved the chair, Martha put her arm around Mary and used her free arm to check the pulse in her sister's wrist. Mary's skin was damp, but even though her pulse was a little fast, it was strong. Martha exhaled a tiny sigh of relief.

The gentleman returned in a few seconds. A small crowd of partygoers gathered as Martha and the maintenance staff person helped Mary to her chair.

"What's wrong, Mary?" Martha asked.

"My chest started hurting. . . . I tried . . . to get you . . . but I was . . . out of breath," Mary muttered.

Martha turned to the maintenance staff person, quickly reading his name tag. "Thank you for helping, Sam. My name is Martha. I'm a doctor. Can you tell me what happened?"

"I got a call to bring more electrical tape because the DJ was setting up, and I saw her on my way to the ballroom. She was creeping out of the restroom over there, and she stopped and leaned on the wall, holding her chest. I asked if she was okay, and she shook her head and said she was short of breath. That's when I yelled for help. That's all I know."

"Thank you. You gave me what I needed," Martha said.

Martha pulled out her cell phone and dialed 911. "I'm in Edin, at the Edin Inn. We need an ambulance. . . . My sister is having chest pain and shortness of breath. . . . She is stable. I'm a doctor. . . . Her pulse is strong, but she needs to go to a heart center. Please make sure you send an ambulance that can take her to the heart center at Macon General Hospital. . . . Yes, I'm going to stay with her. . . . Yes, thank you."

Martha turned to Sam. "Would you call the front desk and let them know we've called an ambulance? Tell them we'll need someone to walk the emergency personnel here to meet us?"

"Sure. I'll radio them now," Sam replied, stepping a few feet away.

"Thank you," Martha said. She turned to Mary. "You doing okay?"

Mary leaned back in the chair. "I think so," she whispered.

"Good. Let me know if anything changes."

"Martha, is she okay?" Ruth asked, her voice trembling.

"Oh, Ruth. I didn't see you walk up. She needs to go to the hospital. An ambulance is on the way. Would you find Aunt Naomi and bring her here? I don't want her to hear about this from someone else."

Ruth kissed Mary on the forehead and quickly walked back to the ballroom.

*　*　*

NAOMI STOOD AT Mary's side, her lip quivering as she tried to understand how her young niece was experiencing such concerning symptoms. Ruth stood next to her with her left arm around Naomi and her right hand rubbing the nape of her own neck.

Martha grabbed Mary's hand and turned to her aunt. "I know you're worried, Aunt Naomi, but I need you to trust me and calm down. We don't have any new information. Please stop asking Mary the same questions over and over," she said.

"I know. I'm scared. I . . ." Naomi said with tears pouring from her eyes. There had been a time when she could hold her emotions in, but it had become harder with each family member's death. Naomi was worried about her beloved niece's heart, but she also worried her own would break if she lost another loved one, especially so soon after Beau.

Ruth's arm wrapped around her so tightly that Naomi felt like if they survived this emergency, it might leave them physically connected. "I know you don't want to, but maybe we should take a walk," Ruth said.

"No, I'm not going," Naomi responded. She figured Ruth suggested they leave because she thought it would be best for Mary or maybe for Naomi, but Naomi didn't care. She couldn't bear to miss a moment of being with Mary. *What if something happened?*

After a few seconds, Naomi thought of another possibility. Perhaps the situation might be difficult for Ruth since Beau died after having a heart attack. Naomi wept harder—in part because of her own memory of the sadness and pain of Beau's passing but also for Ruth. She shook her head twice. No, she couldn't let herself feel too deeply for Ruth. At the expense of her own healing, she had put Ruth's feelings first when Beau and Marlon died. In both situations, Ruth recovered and moved forward with her life, and she failed to realize that Naomi's prolonged sadness and withdrawal were a consequence of her decision not to put herself first. Naomi wanted to empathize enough to ask Ruth if *she* needed to go for a walk, but she couldn't risk hearing an affirmative answer. For a change, Naomi needed to prioritize her own feelings. She needed to stay, and she needed Ruth to stick close by.

If Ruth decided on her own to take care of herself, that was fine—Naomi wouldn't try to stop her. But she wouldn't give her an easy way out either.

Naomi pulled Ruth closer and laid her head on her shoulder. When Naomi looked up, Nicholas approached with a Louis XVI–style chair in tow that matched the chair where Mary rested. He was sprier than she thought.

"I'm sorry to interrupt, but I heard an ambulance is on the way," Nicholas said, looking at Naomi while tapping the chair. She stared at him blankly. He inched the chair closer toward Mary. Ruth followed, pulling Naomi along begrudgingly. "Is there anything else I can do to help?" he asked.

Naomi sat in the chair. She sniffed, attempting to stifle her emotion. "Thank you," she said, nodding as she slid her fingers along the chair cushion's soft blue velvet fabric.

"Of course. You're welcome," Nicholas replied.

"Thank you, Nicholas," said Ruth. "You've already been a huge help by breaking up the crowd and encouraging people to go back to the party. I think we're okay now. We'll be fine."

The ambulance siren sounded outside. "Sounds like the ambulance is here now," Nicholas said.

"There may be something else," Martha said. "The emergency staff should be inside any minute. We can't all ride with Mary in the ambulance. I'm going to go with her, and neither Aunt Naomi nor Ruth should drive under these circumstances, and . . . well, I hope you don't mind my asking, but—"

"No problem. I can take them," Nicholas said.

"We couldn't ask you to do that," Ruth replied.

Nicholas placed his hand on Ruth's shoulder. "I'd be happy to do it. Please don't worry about it," he insisted.

"Thanks, Nicholas," Martha said. "Would you pull the car up so they can jump in? And you probably already know this, but it'll be better if you don't try to follow the ambulance. Lots of accidents happen that way. So just meet us at the emergency department."

"Don't follow the ambulance," repeated Nicholas. "Okay, I hadn't thought about that. Makes sense."

"The hospital is about thirty minutes away, though," Ruth said. "Is that okay?"

"It's in Macon, right?" Nicholas asked.

"Yes," Ruth said as Martha and Naomi nodded.

"No problem. I'll go get the car now," he said, heading toward the exit. "Ruth and Naomi, I'll meet you out front."

The women thanked him as their eyes fell upon Mary again.

* * *

MARTHA'S ATTENTION SHIFTED from Mary as the emergency medical responders approached in the distance—two pushing a stretcher and another carrying a large monitor. As they got closer, their radio transmitted a coded language that she partially understood.

"Hi, we received a call about someone with chest pain," said one of the paramedics.

"Yes, me," Mary said. "I feel a little better, but I'm still having some pressure." She looked at Martha. "My sister can tell you what happened."

The paramedic glanced at Martha. "Oh yeah," he said, focusing on Mary again. "I figured you must be sisters. Twins, right?"

"Almost," Mary and Martha said in unison.

Mary smiled slightly before looking up at her sister.

"I'm Dr. Gardin. I'm director of the primary care center at Macon General Hospital." There was a visible shift in the emergency personnel when she said those words. Pleased with the response, Martha straightened her back. "My sister developed chest pain and shortness of breath. We have a strong history of heart disease in our family, but she doesn't have any known risk factors otherwise. She's healthy. I was in the ballroom, but I came out after I heard someone calling for help, probably within about five minutes of her experiencing symptoms. Her pulse was a little fast, but it was regular. She was standing when I arrived, so we sat her down. She looks a little better now."

The paramedic scribbled notes while Martha spoke. "I thought you looked familiar. I've seen you in the primary care center when we've had calls to transfer patients to the hospital."

"Nice to see you again," Martha replied, even though she couldn't say she recognized him.

"Likewise—although I'm sorry it's under these circumstances. We'll check her out." The paramedic extended his pointer finger and flicked it quickly, indicating to the team that they should begin their process. The other two personnel lowered the stretcher to the height of the seat and supported Mary while she climbed on top. They took her blood pressure and placed a plastic tube under her nose to deliver oxygen, threading the extra length behind her ears.

"Thank you," Martha said. "Has a hospital assignment already been made? She needs to go to Macon General Hospital because there's a heart center there."

The paramedic continued his note-taking. "Yeah, dispatch told us to bring her to Roberta Medical Center. It's just down the street. You don't want to go there?" he asked without looking up from his document.

"No. Macon General Hospital. It has a heart center," Martha repeated, her voice louder this time.

"You think she's having a heart attack, Doc?" His eyes were still fixed on his document, but his voice sounded doubtful.

The encounter was all too familiar. Despite her knowledge and rapid ascent to leadership at the medical center, Martha received more challenges to her decisions than most of the resident physicians she supervised. The questions were always posed in an innocent and well-meaning way, but that didn't prevent her from noticing the frequency at which she received them. Martha looked younger than her age, and at thirty-seven, she was the youngest of the hospital's medical directors and one of a handful of women and people of color. She wasn't sure if one of these characteristics played a factor more than the others, but she suspected that their cumulative impact was to blame overall.

Though having to repeat herself was one of her greatest pet peeves, it usually solved the problems she faced on a daily basis. But when it failed to work, she resorted to a more direct approach. "No." Martha stepped closer. Her tone remained pleasant, but she placed emphasis on the last word of each sentence when she said, "I don't want to waste time. And I don't want to get into details in front of everyone. There's something else going on with her heart. So it's imperative that she go to a heart center."

The paramedic lifted his head and looked at Martha. "Got it," he said. "Let me radio our dispatcher and make it happen."

* * *

RUTH HATED RIDING in the back seat. She was always more likely to get motion sickness there. But she didn't want to leave Naomi in the rear of the car alone. They were only five minutes into the thirty-minute ride to the hospital. She tried to follow the advice Marlon had given her when she developed motion sickness while on a flight, but there weren't many stationary objects on the dark interstate highway to keep her eye on. Nighttime driving on the interstate in rural areas was dangerous. The highways often weren't lit enough to see debris or animals crossing the road until it was too late, and Ruth wondered how many people got into accidents during health emergencies because they'd rushed to the hospital in the middle of the night. She didn't understand why the state seemed to prioritize lighting interstates only in more populated areas. *Beau always used to say that we have to recognize these issues and work on them together as a community. I spoke with our state representative at the Christmas party. Why didn't I think to mention that to her?* She made a mental note to have Chloe set up a meeting.

Ruth spotted the lights of a billboard for the gas station at an upcoming exit. She'd never been more relieved to see a sign in all her life. She fixed her eyes on it, but they soon passed it. She spotted another ahead and locked her eyes on it.

"Why do you keep moving your head like that? Is it some kind of yoga move?" Naomi asked.

"No, I'm trying to get rid of motion sickness," Ruth said.

"I'm sorry. Is my Philadelphia driving bothering you?" Nicholas asked. "I'm trying to get you there as fast as I can while also getting you there safely."

"Oh no. Not at all. It's not you. I always get motion sickness when I sit in the back of a car."

"I can pull over at the next exit if you want to move up front. Is that okay?"

"Thanks, but I'd rather not. I just want to get there as fast as we can," Ruth replied. "Plus, I like holding MIL's hand."

"What do you call Naomi? Is that some sort of nickname?" Nicholas asked.

Naomi smiled.

"It's kind of a long story," Ruth said. She felt comfortable with Nicholas, but she barely knew him. It was nice working with someone from out of town who wasn't familiar with her history with the Gardin family. It was one less person she had to worry about judging her. Ruth wondered if Nicholas's helping out during the health emergency would invite him to a deeper level of scrutiny of her relationships with the women and, subsequently, her ability to lead Gardin Family Enterprises. She hoped Nicholas's access to their personal lives wouldn't undermine her upper hand in her quest for the permanent CEO role in any way. She couldn't let anything jeopardize the company.

Martha could turn the slightest vulnerability into an opportunity to get what she wanted. Ruth often wondered when she had become so calculating. Ruth had always been impressed by her strategic abilities, even when Martha was a preteen. She had gotten Ruth into a few sticky situations. The Gardins were very particular about what activities their kids did, what they wore, and the friends they made. Martha used to ask Ruth for permission to do things that her parents and everyone else knew weren't allowed, but Ruth, in her naïveté about the Gardin family ways, would always say yes. For her thirteenth birthday, Martha tricked Ruth into buying her a cell phone, even though her mother had forbidden her from having one. By the time Ruth found out, she had committed to a two-year contract and couldn't get out of it. She was surprised the family continued to allow the kids to hang out with her. Over time, she had gotten used to it, but Martha's strategic inclinations had seemed to take a malicious turn after Martha found out that Ruth and Beau were engaged.

"It's not that long of a story," Naomi said. "Ruth calls me MIL. You know, the acronym for mother-in-law. Ruth's first husband was my son. He died in military service. Ruth moved here with me and later married my cousin Beau. And although their son, M.J., is technically my cousin, I consider him to be my grandchild. It's simple, see?"

"Oh, I see. I hope I wasn't intruding by asking," Nicholas said.

"It's okay. I guess I just wasn't expecting it," Ruth said. "We're very private. But you're getting an accelerated lesson in our family life, as well as in our business. It's a good thing you signed a confidentiality agreement already." Ruth laughed.

It felt good to laugh. Ruth wasn't usually successful at making jokes to lighten the mood. She usually tried too hard. Ruth looked over at Naomi, who was laughing, too. She could feel the tension in Naomi's fingers lessen, and Naomi gradually released Ruth's hand. "I guess we both needed a laugh," Ruth said, noticing the impressions left by Naomi's fingernails.

"It's nice that you decided to stay in town for the party," Naomi said. "It seems you give all your clients very personalized attention."

He smiled. "Yes, but I don't usually stand guard and chauffeur them around. I heard one of the party guests say that the Gardins had hired a security guard who was dressed like Santa Claus. I promise I'll think about that when I wear this suit and boots to a Christmas party next year."

"Oh goodness! I hadn't thought of that," Ruth said. "But I can see how it might look that way to someone who didn't know better."

"Leave it to our family to be over-the-top, even when we don't intend to be," Naomi said.

"But to get back to your point," Nicholas said, "it just happened to work out that Ruth and I had planned for me to spend some time at Gardin Family Enterprises before the holidays, so we scheduled it so that I could attend the party. And I'm glad I did. I was born and raised in Georgia, in Statesboro. I moved to Philly after college, but I like to visit my family every chance I get. And I can tell you that I've never been to a party like yours in Statesboro. If tonight is any indication of what lies ahead, I already see that working with your family is going to be an adventure."

"Well let's hope it's a good adventure," Naomi said.

"Agreed!" Ruth added.

"Yeah." Nicholas took a smooth right turn onto Freedom Boulevard and smiled. "I have a feeling it will be."

Chapter Eight

Just when Mary thought her sister was the one with control issues, being a patient in the hospital proved that the siblings had more in common than their looks and fashion sense. "Do I really have to be hooked up to all this?" Mary asked, tapping the hard plastic device on her right index finger near the IV line on her left forearm.

"Yeah, you do. I see you're gonna be one of those whiny patients, huh?" Martha laughed.

Mary attempted to swaddle herself like a newborn with the warmed blankets the emergency department nurse had just brought her. "Believe it or not, I've been restraining myself. But you have to admit it's cold in here. I've got three blankets and I'm still cold."

"Well, you're special, because I only have two." Martha laughed again. "Do you need some help with that?"

"No, I've got it. Thanks." Mary could never understand how Martha felt comfortable in a hospital. It freaked her out. Although Martha had warned her that she would likely be hospitalized for a few days, Mary hoped her sister was wrong. She wanted to spend the night in her own bed. But before she complained about having to be admitted, she decided to wait until she had a formal evaluation by the emergency department staff and they made a definite decision. She trusted her sister's medical instincts, but she understood that Martha was making an educated guess without being able to examine her and without the assistance of blood tests and other tools available in the hospital. Mary had tried to drown out the medical jargon she'd heard when Martha talked with the paramedics and emergency department personnel. It made her nervous, and it challenged her wishful thinking that nothing was wrong with her heart.

"You look better. You really scared me, you know," Martha said. Her voice sounded sweet and reassuring.

"Thanks. It's amazing what a little oxygen can do. It's like magic or something."

"Yeah."

"And you're not scared anymore, right?" Mary said.

"I was hoping you wouldn't ask me that," Martha replied. "I should've chosen better words."

Mary didn't see this side of her sister often. Martha had been so composed during the entire ordeal that Mary assumed there was nothing serious going on with her health. Although there had been several medical emergencies in the family, her personal ordeal was her first opportunity to see her sister take charge of a medical situation. She wondered if Martha was this calm at work. Mary was proud and impressed that Martha had found a way to channel the assertiveness she had displayed since they were kids, but now Martha's response worried her. Things weren't as straightforward as Mary expected.

"So, you're not gonna answer the question?" Mary prodded. "Is that why you sent Ruth and Aunt Naomi to your office, so you could tell me bad news?"

"No, it's not that. I was honest with them, and I've been honest with you. I sent them away because there were too many people in here. I also figured they would be more comfortable in my office, and Nicholas could join them instead of having to sit in the waiting room alone. The emergency department only allows two people in a room with a patient, and it wouldn't have been a good idea to separate Aunt Naomi and Ruth." Martha sighed as she pulled the blankets up to her chin. "I'm still scared, but I think everything is going to be okay. Do you have any questions about what the doctor said?"

"She thinks my heart muscles are weak, right?"

"Exactly. I can summarize what she said, and we can talk through it. The ultrasound of your heart showed that your heart isn't pumping well, and the other results show that you haven't had a heart attack. That makes us suspect that you have a condition called stress cardiomyopathy. Does that sound familiar?"

Mary tilted her head and adjusted her upper body on the stretcher. "Yes, I remember her saying that now," she replied.

"Good. It's also called broken-heart syndrome, because it sometimes happens after people experience a major emotional stressor, like the death of a loved one. But it could also happen with extreme anger, surprise, or even fear. When this happens, the person's emotion is so strong that they develop weakening of the heart muscles very quickly and very severely. I suspect that unexpectedly seeing Tynan caused your heart muscles to weaken, and that's why you had chest pain and shortness of breath when you tried to walk."

As Mary listened to the examples Martha gave, she did her own calculation of how the evening's events led her to wear a drafty hospital gown. It wasn't adding up. "But I was happy to see him. Well, at first, anyway," she said, wrinkling her nose.

"I know it sounds weird, but stress cardiomyopathy can happen to someone after a good surprise or a bad one. There have been cases of it happening after someone found out they won the lottery."

"Wow. So, does the person have good luck for winning the lottery, or bad luck for developing a heart problem because of it?"

"Funny. I'm glad you're keeping a good sense of humor. I know this is a lot to process."

Mary shrugged. "I'm trying," she said.

"So, maybe this happened because you were happy to see

him . . . or because the conversation became so emotional. Or was it a combination of the two?" Martha asked, tilting her head and rubbing her chin.

Mary could see her sister struggling to connect the dots. She contemplated whether it was the right time to tell her the whole story about Tynan, but she wanted to get some clarity about her health situation first. "I'm not sure. What do you think?" she replied.

"Your case is also unusual because of your age. Most cases of stress cardiomyopathy happen to women in their late fifties and older, and it usually takes longer to diagnose because that age group is also more likely to have a heart attack. That's why I insisted you come to the heart center. I wanted you to get care at a facility that would provide access to the specialists and tests you need over the weekend."

"So, this is serious," Mary said.

"Yeah, it is," Martha replied, her eyes becoming glassy.

"You were so calm about everything, so I thought I might still be able to go home tonight."

Martha shook her head and wiped her eyes. "No, that's not gonna happen. It's a life-threatening condition, but it's my job to stay calm. You need to stay in the hospital, and you need some more testing to confirm the diagnosis. I think they'll be able to do it tomorrow, but—"

"Life-threatening?"

"Yeah, but you're responding well to the treatment so far. It looks like you'll be okay."

"This is worse than I thought. I guess I was in denial."

"We can talk about it again tomorrow after you've had some rest and the additional testing."

"I've been under a lot of stress in general recently. Could that have something to do with this too?"

"It could. There's some evidence that people who've experi-

enced constant anxiety may be more likely to have stress cardiomyopathy. It's good that you mentioned your history of anxiety
when the doctor asked you about your medical history. But you
didn't mention it when you told him about your recent symptoms. Has your anxiety gotten worse? What's been going on?"

Mary was silent. The question was the first time during her
medical emergency that any of the deeply personal questions she
had been asked made her pause. It was a question she had longed
for her sister to realize she needed to ask since Mary returned to
Edin, although she hadn't trusted Martha enough with her vulnerability to discuss it with her previously. But now that she was
lying in the emergency department, Mary didn't mind address-
ing it.

"If you feel more comfortable talking to someone else, it's
okay," Martha said. "I don't want to press the issue today. And I
know I'm not your doctor, so it's all right if you don't want to
talk to me about it."

"No, that's not it. You're my sister. Of course we can discuss
it. But that's why it feels so weird—because you've never asked
before."

"I always ask how you're doing," Martha said in the patron-
izing tone that never failed to unnerve Mary.

"But I don't feel like you mean it. We talked about this last
week when you came to the restaurant. . . . After my cooking
class. . . . Don't you remember? You probably weren't listening
then, either." Mary knew her words would likely upset her sister.
Under normal circumstances, they would've caused a fight. But
Mary wasn't sure how long she would be in the hospital, and she
wanted to take advantage of every second she had to get Martha
to listen to her. Between her illness and the fact that they were
sitting in the medical center where Martha worked, this was her
best chance of catching her with good behavior.

"We never talked about that," Martha said earnestly.

"We did, but I apologize for jabbing you by saying that you probably weren't listening then, either."

"I appreciate that. It *was* kind of brutal."

"I know. I'm sorry. I'm used to hitting below the belt when we have these conversations. I feel like that's what I have to do to get your attention, and sometimes I do it to protect myself because you can be so harsh with the things you say."

"Should we have this conversation later? I don't want to upset you again," Martha said, the worry returning to her voice. "Your heart is fragile."

Mary wiped a tear from her right eye. "I want us to be able to talk and be honest with each other."

Martha handed her a box of tissues. "See!" she scolded. "I don't want you getting emotional again tonight."

"This feels different. I don't feel like my emotions are inappropriate. It feels peaceful. It feels good to talk about things calmly."

"So, I need to be a better listener. Got it. I can work on that," Martha said, nodding.

Mary reached out for her sister. "Thank you. Now give me a hug."

"Okay, but keep your left arm straight. I don't want you to mess up the IV."

Mary stretched her arm as instructed. As Martha got closer, Mary said, "Oh, Martha, you're crying too! You love me after all!"

Martha wiped her eyes and laughed. "Of course I do!"

The sisters embraced in an extended hug, rocking back and forth as they used to when they were kids. "This is the best thing that's happened all night," Mary said.

"Yeah, well, other than figuring out that you're not having a heart attack."

"That's a good point. Okay, second-best thing."

Martha slowly pulled away. "I'm glad we had this talk, but you never answered the question that took us down this path. Tell me what's going on."

"I'm not sure where to start," Mary said, then took a breath. "You know I've struggled with anxiety since I was a kid, but it's gotten worse over the past couple of years. Counseling was helping, but things got busy with the restaurant and I stopped going. All the family problems over the past few months and the stress over the company have added to that. My stomach started bothering me over the past few days, but it was much worse today. The more anxious I became, the worse my stomach felt. It was horrible. Ruth had to help me out of my jumpsuit at the party."

"Ruth? At the party? She didn't tell me about it. Did she tell anyone? Something bad could've happened."

Mary realized she had gotten too comfortable in the conversation. She had let her guard down and forgotten about an important land mine, which she walked right on top of. "It didn't turn out to be anything. I mentioned the stomach symptoms when the doctor was here, and neither of you were concerned about it. So why are you getting so excited about it now? Things worked out in the restroom, and it looks like my heart will probably be okay. You said so a few minutes ago."

"Yeah. . . . That's true . . . very true," Martha said, but her shaking her head told Mary she was not convinced.

Mary felt herself getting upset. She was still figuring out how to listen to her body. There were more truths she wanted to share with her sister, and it had initially seemed that tonight might be the night when it would be safe enough to do it. But it was obvious now that Martha had reached capacity. Mary was finally learning how to recognize when her sister's window was closed. She found the first path to her recovery. She could no longer risk her vulnerability with people who couldn't handle it. "Would it be okay if I rest tonight and we talk more tomorrow?"

"Sure, but remember I'm going to stay in the hospital with you tonight. I've already asked for a rollaway bed. So let's talk later if you feel up to it. The nurse said the transport team would be here soon to take you upstairs to your room."

Mary took a couple of slow, deep breaths while she pretended to be distracted by the purring of the blood-pressure cuff, signaling that fifteen minutes had passed and she was due for another blood-pressure check. Then she spoke. "Aunt Naomi, Ruth, and Nicholas are still in your office, right?"

"Yeah, they said they would head back to Edin after you got settled in your room. I'll text them the room number so they can meet us there."

"That's okay. You don't need to stay and look after me. I could use some time alone. I'm sure the nursing staff and medical team are already on high alert that you're going to be following my progress closely. I'll be fine. And it's late. Y'all should head back home now."

Mary couldn't look at Martha. If their eyes met, Mary would feel the rejection and disappointment the change of plans had caused her sister. But she needed to close the door on prioritizing Martha's feelings over her own healing. Her weakened heart muscles had taught her to choose herself. She kept her eyes closed and focused on breathing.

* * *

MARTHA HAD SPIRALED from hero to castoff in minutes, and her dark surroundings matched her mood. She sulked as she walked through the hospital's maze of poorly lit hallways toward the adjoining primary care center. She seldom spent time at the hospital at night, but on the rare occasion she left something that she urgently needed in her office, she'd ask one of the hospital's security staff to accompany her. This time, at three in the morning, she said a prayer that she would be safe and chose time alone instead. She needed to regroup and figure out how to explain to Naomi, Ruth, and Nicholas why she wouldn't be staying at the hospital overnight and instead needed to tag along with them on the ride back to Edin.

The trek reminded her of her secret escape when she worked night shifts during residency training. During chaotic nights of juggling new admissions with calls about issues that arose with patients who were already hospitalized, Martha recharged by exploring vacant wings of the hospital. Though she could carve out only a few minutes on most nights, she discovered that doing so improved not only her attitude but also her monthly performance evaluations. She figured out that when she was more visible in the patient care area, it prompted the nursing staff and attending physicians to engage with her, usually asking her to write an order or providing negative feedback that they might have otherwise forgotten. "Visibility leads to vulnerability," Martha used to say.

The same had proven true of her interaction with Mary. Martha was upset that her sister had asked her to leave, but she was more disappointed in herself because she'd let her guard down. While tending to Mary's needs, she became distracted from protecting herself, and she was shocked by the negative feedback Mary had hurled at her. Although Martha didn't agree with it, Mary's assessment was relevant, just as constructive criticism from the nursing staff and attending physicians had been relevant during her residency. But relevance didn't make either of them more palatable.

Martha punched the code on the keypad outside the entrance of the primary care center. *Showtime,* she thought. As the double-egress doors inched open, she spotted the twinkle of Naomi's sequined dress reflecting the light from the exit sign near the stairwell.

"Oh, I guess y'all were getting antsy waiting to hear from me, huh?" Martha said as Naomi, Ruth, and Nicholas looked at her.

"I'm okay, but these two . . . well, I think you know," Nicholas said, then laughed.

Naomi shrugged. "With everything going on, we thought you were busy and forgot about us or something."

"No, I didn't. But you could've texted or called before you started wandering back to the emergency department without me. Did you remember to lock my office?" Martha asked.

"Yes," Naomi responded. "Sorry, I couldn't wait to hear from you. I wanted to see Mary again. I feel better when I can see her with my own eyes."

"But she's right," said Ruth. "We could've given her a heads-up that we were coming."

Martha was surprised to hear Ruth agree with her. "Thanks, Ruth."

Ruth smiled, but Martha pretended not to see it.

"Is Mary okay? You aren't bringing bad news, are you?" Naomi fired.

"Oh no. She's fine. The doctor recommended that Mary have a low-stimulation evening. You know, like no family for the rest of the night." She regretted the lie as soon as she said it, but it was too late. "So I'll ride home with y'all. Let's head back."

It was too dark for Martha to read the expressions on Naomi's and Ruth's faces to see if they believed her, but she wasn't interested anyway. She wanted to move things along. She started back down the hallway. Hearing only the click of her own footsteps, she stopped and turned around. Naomi, Ruth, and Nicholas were still standing in the middle of the double-egress doors.

Naomi put her hands on her hips. "That means I don't get to see Mary again tonight?"

Ruth and Nicholas lowered their heads in unison, as if they'd anticipated this moment and passed the time in Martha's office practicing a synchronized response.

"No, it's late. The daytime doctors will arrive in a few hours. I plan to check in with Mary's team after they've had a chance to see her on morning rounds," Martha said, secretly hoping that her presence would be welcome by then.

Naomi stared at her niece.

"C'mon, let's head to the car. Nicholas, you parked in the lot close to the emergency department, right?" Martha asked. She didn't wait for agreement. Instead, she just started walking. When Martha heard footsteps join hers, she presumed everyone was on board. But after a few seconds, the steps got louder, signaling that Naomi had finally joined in. Martha turned around as they passed a window. The beams from the LED light poles in the adjacent parking lot lent enough brightness to the hallway for her to see Naomi pouting. *At least she decided not to put up a fight,* she thought.

Martha was desperate to break the awkward silence as they continued on. Since she and Ruth had barely spoken since the board meeting, the late-night expedition in the dark hospital passageways probably wasn't a good time to start. There was only one remaining option. Martha looked at Nicholas. "I bet this is the most high-maintenance security detail you've ever worked, huh?"

Nicholas laughed. "You must've heard the rumor that I'm the Gardin family's new security guard."

"Well, aren't you?" Martha laughed. "Even though we managed to get Mary out of the hotel without most of the party attendees noticing, word is spreading. We've never had anyone rolled out of the Christmas party on a stretcher, so I knew the news would take off. People have been texting me to check on Mary, and a few of them mentioned that the Santa Claus security guard managed everything so professionally. A couple of them asked me to send the contact information for your security firm after everything settles down."

"I'm president of the senior usher board at my church, so I'm accustomed to managing crowds. The other ushers will get a big kick out of it when I tell them how my skills earned me a security guard title." Nicholas chuckled.

"That's funny, but all joking aside . . ." For the first time since they'd met, Martha looked Nicholas square in the eye. "It wouldn't have gone as smoothly at the hotel if you hadn't stepped in. Things could've become chaotic if people had gathered around to watch everything. It's good to have you on our team."

Ruth walked a little faster to join the conversation. "I was disappointed you weren't there to meet Nicholas when I introduced him to MIL and Mary, but it seems you two haven't missed a beat," she said.

"Nicholas's timing was perfect. I suspect the same will be true when it comes to his advice about the company," Martha said with a dampened grin.

"I see what you're doing, Martha. We've been through too much today to start talking business at this hour," Naomi scolded.

"I was—"

"That's enough, Dr. Gardin," Naomi asserted.

Martha acquiesced. But the return trip through the dark hallways had already exceeded her expectations. Ruth had expected the women to blindly trust the advice of a consultant she picked and who had limited access to the other family members, but Nicholas's extended time with the family had opened a door. And Martha intended to use it.

Chapter Nine

Mary stirred in her hospital bed. "Martha?" she mumbled.

"Yeah," Martha replied from the doorway. "Is it okay if I come in?" she asked, straining to get a look at her sister across the room.

As Mary clicked on the light over the bed, she wondered where the time had gone. It seemed she had seen Martha a few minutes ago, but hours had passed since she had booted her out of her room in the emergency department. Mary sat up in bed. "Yes. . . . Good morning. . . . Wait, the sun isn't up yet. What time is it?"

Martha gave Mary a once-over as she rested a ZAAF weekender bag at the foot of the hospital bed. "It's seven o'clock. I wanted to be here when the doctors came by on rounds. Has anyone been here yet?" Martha asked, inspecting the recliner before she sat on it.

"No, not yet."

"Perfect."

"Did you get any sleep?" Mary asked.

"No, as soon as we picked up our cars at the hotel and made it back home, it was almost time to come back. I'd have been here earlier, but I thought you could use some things from home."

"That was thoughtful. Thank you."

"You're welcome. Go back to sleep."

"How am I supposed to go back to sleep now that you've engaged me in a full conversation?"

"I brought your sleep mask."

"Why didn't you tell me it's so hard to sleep in a hospital? I'm up now. I'm gonna need a lot more than a sleep mask." Mary pulled the brown and orange bag toward her, slid the gold zipper, and pulled out the contents one by one. "Phone charger, headphones, toiletries, makeup bag, books, magazines, a robe . . . my favorite sweatshirt . . . and . . . clothes to wear home from the hospital. . . . Thank you, Martha. You did a good job."

"Happy to help," Martha said.

Mary put the sweatshirt at the bottom of the bag, her hand quivering as she touched the worn organic-cotton fabric. She stacked the other items on top of it.

Martha sat back in the tan recliner. She leaned over the left side and struggled with the handle. A moment later, the footrest extended, causing her legs to shoot up in the air.

Mary laughed, grateful for the distraction. "Didn't the same thing happen to you at Ruth's house last week? Maybe you should stay away from recliners."

"Good one," Martha said, then laughed.

"Hey, something else happened after you left last night. I'd like to know what you think of it."

Martha sat up. "Okay, go ahead."

"The medical team had a psychiatrist come by to see me, and she wants me to talk with a mental health counselor. They mentioned it in the emergency department after you left. I didn't make up my chest pain, so I'm wondering what they're thinking."

"Oh no. I'm sure that's not what they think at—"

"I thought you said that my test results showed that I have a real problem."

"They do . . . and you do. No one thinks you made up anything. The ultrasound shows that your heart isn't pumping normally."

"Right . . . exactly. So why do they want me to see a counselor? Do they think I'm crazy?"

"We don't use the word *crazy*. They want to make sure you're getting the support you need to help you cope with the things going on in your life. Remember you told me last night that you've been having a hard time dealing with your anxiety? It's all connected. And the safest thing is for you to talk with Shari about how you feel and what's been going on, especially what happened last night with Tynan."

"I can talk with Shari, my own therapist? I was willing to talk with someone else while I'm here, but I'd prefer to talk with her."

"She works here, too, as part of the coverage staff. She's usually here on weekends and Mondays. It sounds like they've already put in the referral, so we'll have to wait and find out if she's the person who comes by to see you."

"I hope so. We didn't have time to talk about it last night, but I've been feeling a lot of anxiety about seeing Tynan."

"Did you feel anxious overnight?"

Mary wrinkled her mouth. "Yeah, but I dealt with it," she said.

"Why didn't you tell the nursing staff? They could've asked your doctor to prescribe some medicine to help you feel better."

"I didn't want anybody to think I was overreacting or being weak. I watched the way you handled everything that came at you yesterday—calling the ambulance and dealing with the paramedics and making arrangements for Nicholas to help, then talking with the staff in the emergency department. You didn't flinch. How do I mention anxiety after *that*?"

Martha blew out her cheeks as she leaned back in the recliner. "I should've picked up on your anxiety and asked you more about it last night. There were so many things rushing back and forth in my head during our conversation. I didn't do a good job of balancing them all. Sorry about that."

"No, I don't blame you. No one can expect you to be the doctor and the sister every second. You have feelings too. I can't expect you to think about everything."

"I appreciate that, but you're my baby sister. I get tripped up sometimes, but I should be doing everything in my power to help you. I want you to be okay. No, I want you to be more than okay. I want you to thrive. And part of that is remembering that anxiety is as much a medical problem as chest pain. If you'd had chest pain last night, wouldn't you have pushed the button and told the nurse?"

Tears formed in Mary's eyes. She wiped them with her hands before they dropped. "Yes, of course," Mary said. She had wondered which version of her sister would show up when she returned to the hospital, and she was relieved at Martha's conciliatory tone. Her selfless temperament was just what Mary needed for the day that lay ahead.

"It's the same thing. Please don't feel ashamed. The brain is an organ in the body just like the heart is, and the connection between the brain and the heart is vital. We have to pay attention to it. So, if you start to feel anxious again, you should tell someone so we can do something about it."

Mary sniffled, nodding quickly. She turned to the overbed table positioned at the side of her bed and grabbed a box of tissues. "Can I tell you something?" she asked.

"Absolutely," Martha replied, her voice soft and sympathetic.

Mary dabbed a tissue in the corner of each eye. "That's part of the reason I asked you to leave last night. I started to feel anxious—like I could lose control. I felt like my heart rate was increasing. It didn't set off the alarm on the monitor, but . . . I started feeling conscious that my heart was beating, and it seemed faster. And I started to feel aware that I was breathing, and I had to concentrate on my breaths to stay calm so I wouldn't get short of breath."

"Oh, Mary, I had no idea you were going through that. I'm sorry I was part of making that happen. I didn't know."

"I know you didn't know. That's why I'm telling you now. And I don't want you to treat me like I'm delicate or anything. I just want you to be respectful and stop dumping your anger on me. It's like I absorb it. It feels toxic, like it suffocates me or something."

"I see. I . . . I . . . I didn't know."

"I tried to tell you the other day, but I guess I didn't know the words to use until this happened. I worried that the paramedics and emergency department staff would think I was having an anxiety attack at the party, even though I knew it was more than that. And I'm still kind of worried about it. That's why I keep asking if they think I'm crazy."

"Not *crazy*, Mary. That word—"

"Okay," Mary said. She took a deep breath and blew out through her mouth. "That's why I keep asking if they think my heart symptoms are imaginary. Even though the chest pain and shortness of breath I had at the party didn't feel like an anxiety attack, they helped me understand my anxiety attacks better. I didn't notice what was happening until it was too late. Now I think I can pick up on the feeling before it happens and try to do something to stop it. I want to talk with Shari about that too."

Martha looked up at the ceiling. Then, as her eyes filled with tears, she looked directly at Mary. "I'm proud of you. And I'm sorry about my role in hurting you. I . . . Sometimes I just get caught up in the moment. I don't want to be part of making you feel stressed or anxious or like you're about to lose control. I'm gonna work on it, but I hope that you'll feel free to tell me in the future when I'm doing that to you."

"Thank you. I will. It's going to be a process." Mary stretched out her arms toward her sister. "Hold me tight," she said, recalling their mother's old trick of distracting them from something unpleasant.

Martha lowered the legs of the recliner.

"Careful," Mary advised.

Martha laughed. She stood up and leaned over to hug her sister. "It won't be easy, but I'll do the best I can."

*   *   *

RUTH PUSHED THE large blue crate of rented plates against the exposed brick wall as sunrays beamed through the front windows of Alabaster Lunch Box.

"There's nothing for us to do here. Everything's fine. Can we please go to the hospital now?" Naomi asked as she peeked at her watch. She and Ruth had stopped by the restaurant to make sure nothing looked out of place. Mary said she trusted her staff to break everything down after the party and transport her equipment back to the restaurant, but she would be able to rest better if Naomi and Ruth confirmed that everything was okay.

Naomi had agreed, albeit reluctantly. She intentionally wore a beige cashmere sweater dress so Ruth wouldn't expect her to clean up anything at the restaurant. She didn't mind helping, but it would have to be later. She didn't want any delays getting back to Macon to check on Mary. If Naomi had her way, she would've spent the night with her at the hospital. Martha might have the medical knowledge, but she lacked the maternal instinct that Naomi believed mattered most, especially since Mary's medical workup was already under way.

"Just a second," Ruth replied. "Let me run into the kitchen and turn off the lights. Then we can go."

"All right, but hurry up. We need to get to Macon soon," Naomi said firmly. As she leaned against the wall, counting the rows of crates to kill time, she was interrupted by a knock on the door.

She squinted. She couldn't see the person through the glare, but it didn't matter who it was. Naomi didn't want to talk to anyone. Her head swung from side to side as her arms flailed like opposed-system windshield wipers. "I'm sorry. We're closed," she yelled.

The knocking persisted.

Naomi didn't move. *What if someone is trying to break in and rob us? Don't we have enough going on this weekend?* she thought.

Ruth came running from the kitchen. "Is everything okay?"

Naomi grew more irritated. "Somebody is knocking at the door, and they won't stop."

Ruth shielded her eyes from the brightness as she walked toward the door. "It's Tynan!"

"Oh goodness. We'll never get to the hospital now," Naomi fumed.

Ruth unlocked the door and pushed it open. "Hi, Tynan. Come on in," she said.

Tynan grabbed the door, sliding into the restaurant with the cockiness of someone who enjoyed being watched. "Good morning," he said, looking around. He leaned toward Ruth. "Forgive me. I'm forgetting my manners—may I?"

"Oh, sure. It's been so long since we've seen you," she said, turning the right side of her face toward Tynan. He pecked her cheek.

"Yes, it's certainly been a while," he replied. He walked toward Naomi, who stayed glued to her station on the wall. "Good morning, Tynan," she snapped.

Tynan towered over Naomi. He bent down low and leaned awkwardly to reach her cheek.

Ruth flashed a polite smile at Tynan as she locked the door. "I guess you heard about Mary. She's resting, but we don't have much of an update. The doctors are running tests today."

"Tests? No, what . . . what happened? Is she okay?" he asked, his coolness splintered like an ice cube that had crashed on the floor.

"Oh . . . you haven't heard?" Ruth asked.

"No, I don't know anyone else here. Just Mary and you all. Was there an accident or something? She's okay, right?" he pressed.

"Yes, yes . . . she's okay," Ruth said. "I figured since you were at the hotel you saw what happened or heard about it." She pulled out a chair at the long wooden table adjacent to the front window. "Have a seat."

Naomi sighed as she crossed the room to join them. *At least we'll be close to the door,* she thought.

"Mary developed chest pain and shortness of breath at the party last night, so she went to the hospital by ambulance. She's doing better now, but the doctors have restricted her visitors," Ruth said as she sat in the chair at the head of the table.

Tynan stared at Naomi and Ruth. "So, I can't see her?"

Naomi plopped into the chair opposite him. "They wouldn't let us see her before we left the hospital last night. We spent a little time with her when she first got to the emergency department, but after things settled down, they were very strict about not allowing visitors. She must stay calm. We've heard you have a way of upsetting the women in this family."

"You're not going to see her today?" Tynan asked.

I don't know who this guy thinks he is, Naomi thought. She struggled to contain herself before she replied. "Martha returned there this morning, and we're planning to go as soon as we leave here."

"Can I follow you there and visit with you?" he persisted.

"Only family is allowed," Ruth said.

"But we're engaged."

"Are you? How could Mary be engaged to someone she doesn't talk about?" Ruth asked, irritation creeping into her voice. "We haven't heard anything about you for at least a year and a half. And now isn't the time for you to drop back into her life."

"Especially if you're the reason she ended up in the hospital," Naomi retorted. She didn't understand how Ruth was so civil to Tynan, but she was relieved that her daughter-in-law hadn't totally lost sight of reality.

"MIL—now, we don't know that for certain," Ruth said.

"Wait a minute. I don't understand. . . . I didn't do anything. I didn't put my hands on her. I would never do that. And you said she had chest pain . . . and shortness of breath. . . . How did I do that? What does this have to do with me?" His eyes filled with tears. "I just want to see her. I need to know that she's okay."

Naomi ignored Ruth's admonition. "You should've thought about that before you sprang into town unannounced and talked down to her the way you did. And in public too. Is that the way to treat your alleged fiancé?"

"I—" Tynan tried to answer, but Naomi wouldn't allow it.

"I don't know what's been going on with you, or what happened between you and Mary, but she's done well since she's moved back here. Look around. This is all hers. She built this business by herself. Where were you? And things have gone downhill for her fast since you showed up. You breeze into town, and now she's in the hospital."

"Okay, but tell me what's going on," he pleaded. "It sounds like you know more than you're saying."

"We can't get into her medical condition with you, Tynan," Ruth said.

"You can't or you *won't*?"

"It's not our place to share anything else," Ruth said. "We'll have to talk to Mary about that, and it's not in her best interest to bring it up while she's recuperating."

Tynan shook his head. "I don't understand why—"

"Ruth is a lot nicer than I am," Naomi said. "Let me help you understand a little better. Go back to New York or wherever you came from. You're not welcome here. And if you don't already know, we all live on family property, so don't try to drop in to see Mary. It won't end well for you. I'm always watching."

"That sounds like a veiled threat," he said.

"Veiled? Ruth, hand me my purse," Naomi replied coolly.

Tynan stood up from his chair. "No, please. That won't be necessary. I don't want any trouble." He reached inside his jacket and pulled out a white legal-sized envelope. "Please make sure Mary gets this." He placed the envelope on the table and slid it to Ruth. "I appreciate your time. Thank you both."

Naomi and Ruth watched as Tynan unlocked the door and walked out.

Naomi sprang to her feet and reached for the envelope. "Riley & Carol, Attorneys-at-Law. I wonder what that is. Pull out your phone and look it up online."

"MIL. I don't think we should—"

"It's in New York City. Do you need me to read the address, or can you look it up with just the business name and the city?"

Ruth unlocked her phone and typed quickly. "Here, I found it. It's one of those fancy full-service firms that specialize in all areas of law, so I can't make any guesses what this is about."

Naomi drummed her fingers on the table. "Humph."

"You're not gonna open that, are you?" Ruth warned.

"You've been around me long enough to know the answer to that. Why waste your breath asking?" Naomi snickered.

Ruth sighed, then jumped to her feet and stood behind Naomi. "I hope my mail never ends up at your house by mistake," she said with a smirk as she looked over Naomi's shoulder.

Naomi chuckled as she slowly slid her finger under the envelope's flap and opened it without ripping it. *Apparently, she forgot that all our mail is delivered to the same mailbox at the front gate of the family estate and that I'm the one who's home every day to sort it and put the mail in the boxes on everyone's front porch. How does she think I got so good at this?*

Chapter Ten

Roses, tulips, and lilies filled Mary's room. They were all gorgeous, but none of the arrangements compared to the vase of multicolored daisies Naomi carried in her arms.

"Thank you. They're gorgeous! The bouquet is almost as big as you are! Why didn't you have them delivered?" Mary asked.

"She wouldn't let me help her carry the flowers up, as much as I tried," Ruth said as she stood next to Naomi at Mary's bedside.

Martha sat in a recliner next to the hospital bed. Naomi motioned for her help, pointing to a vase of stargazer lilies on the overbed table. "I wanted to see your beautiful face when you received them," Naomi said. "I bet no one else sent you daisies, huh?"

Martha rose from the recliner and placed the lilies on the windowsill as Naomi set the daisies on the overbed table and positioned the vase so it was immediately at Mary's side.

"Only my favorite aunt would bring my favorite flower." Mary smiled.

Naomi embraced her niece. "Maybe it's the sunlight, but you look so much better today."

Mary tried to let go, but Naomi gripped her tighter. The moisture from Naomi's face transferred to hers as they hugged. "It's all right, Aunt Naomi. I'm going to be okay."

Naomi finally let go.

"My test results confirmed the diagnosis. Martha was right. I have stress cardiomyopathy, but my doctor expects me to make a full recovery. She said my heart arteries look great, as she expected for someone thirty years old."

Naomi laughed. "Girl, add five years to that! You are thirty-five years old! Are you trying to tell me that the hospital has a procedure for decreasing age?" she teased. Naomi kissed Mary on the cheek. "I'm so relieved that your test went well."

Ruth leaned in to hug Mary. "Me too," she said, squeezing her with both arms.

Martha stood at the windowsill. "Hi, Ruth."

Ruth looked up from Mary's embrace. "Hi, Martha."

"Aunt Naomi, don't I get a hug?" Martha asked.

"I guess," Naomi joked. She turned around and enveloped Martha in her arms. "You've done a good job here. It looks like Mary's coming along. Thank you, Martha. Thank you so much. My heart couldn't take it if something happened to one of you. I just couldn't take it." Naomi's voice trembled as tears fell from her eyes.

"Oh, Aunt Naomi, it's okay," Mary said. "Can y'all bring the hug over here so I can join in?"

Naomi and Martha stayed connected and walked over to Mary's bed. Martha latched on to Mary, while Ruth grabbed Mary and Naomi.

"Aunt Naomi, it's okay. It's all right now. The doctor wants to keep an eye on me for one more day, but I can go home tomorrow," Mary said.

Naomi freed herself from the hug and clasped her hands together against her chest. "Praise God. I've been praying non-stop."

Martha walked back over to her spot by the window, leaving Naomi and Ruth at the bedside.

"We all have," Ruth agreed, wiping her eyes.

"Yeah, I'm happy with her progress," Martha said, leaning on the windowsill as she tapped the top of the recliner. "Aunt

Naomi, please sit here. Ruth, there's a chair in the corner. You can move the weekend bag."

Naomi nodded at Martha in gratitude as she sat down. Ruth picked up the bag and crammed it inside the small closet next to the bed.

"I thought y'all would've been here earlier," Mary said.

"Remember, we had to stop at the restaurant," her aunt replied, "and we had to stop for the flowers too."

"Thank you for doing that!" Mary said. "I meant to ask you to bring me some leftovers. Last night's party menu was heart-healthy, so I don't think the doctors would have objected to your bringing it. Plus, I have a clean bill of health."

"Now, now. Let's not get ahead of ourselves," Martha said. "You still have to recuperate, and the doctors will be following you closely to make sure your heart function returns to normal. I don't want you thinking you can start running marathons when you get home. You've got to pace yourself and take it easy."

"Don't worry. I'm going to be keeping an eye on her. Especially after what happened at the restaurant," Naomi said.

"MIL, I thought we agreed to wait until Mary was discharged to tell her," Ruth chided.

"Something happened at the restaurant, and neither of you thought to mention this to me before bringing it up in front of Mary?" Martha objected.

"What happened?" Mary asked, raising her voice.

"It was Tynan, wasn't it?" Martha said.

"Yes." Naomi rose from the recliner and sat next to Mary on the hospital bed. She held her hand. "Tynan came by the restaurant to see you, so he and I had a little talk. He wanted to come by the hospital, but we told him we didn't think it was a good idea for you to see him yet. But on second thought, it would be better for your heart to be monitored when you talk with him again."

"Aunt Naomi, that's not funny." Mary sighed.

"Oh, I don't think she was joking," Ruth said.

"No, I'm not joking at all. You look better, and I'm glad the doctors say that you can probably go home tomorrow, but I want you to be more stable before you see him or talk to him. I told him to leave Edin because you need to start working through whatever happened between the two of you on your own before you see him."

"I get it, and I agree with you. I'm planning to work through it, but let's go back to Tynan. Did he say where he was going?" Mary asked.

"No, and I didn't ask him. Should I have asked?" Naomi hesitated. "Honestly, I didn't care where he went. He just needed to get out of town."

"And this is why we should've talked about this before you brought this up in front of our hospitalized patient," Martha said with her voice taking on a singsong pattern.

"Martha, singing the words doesn't necessarily prevent conflict," Mary said, then chuckled. She looked at Naomi and Ruth. "Martha and I had a conversation earlier about how she behaves toward me."

The women looked at each other. "Oh, well, that's good," Naomi said.

"Look, I'm trying. I'm a work in progress," Martha said.

Ruth smiled.

Mary made light of the situation, but Tynan's reappearance weighed heavily on her mind. She hadn't told Martha, but thinking about him was what had prevented her from sleeping. She'd struggled to sort through her feelings. Mary had been afraid he would show up at the hospital, but she hadn't dared mention that possibility to her family, because she feared they would never leave her hospital room. She had not yet begun to think about how she was going to navigate a conversation with him,

but she was confident she could make her way through it somehow.

"So, what did he tell y'all? Did you ask him a lot of questions?
Were you nice to him?" Mary asked, looking at Naomi, who was
more likely to give specific details about what had happened. But
Ruth chimed in.

"We wanted to respect your privacy, so we didn't ask him
much. We decided to follow your lead and let things happen naturally in their own time. He seemed nervous once he found out
you're in the hospital, but we told him not to come here. I think
he feels that we blamed him for your being hospitalized."

Mary folded her arms and leaned back in bed as she tried to
decode Ruth's response.

Naomi rolled her eyes. "You're gonna find out eventually, so
I'll tell you the whole story. I told him it's his fault that you're in
here. I don't care if he's mad or uncomfortable. I care about *you,*
Mary, and how *you* feel about things. . . . But there is something
else." Naomi retrieved the envelope from her cream and cognac
Peryton tote. "He wanted you to have something. I kept it nice
and flat in my purse because I wanted it to look just like it did
when he gave it to me," she said, patting her bag as she handed
the envelope to Mary.

Ruth shook her head.

Mary placed the envelope on the overbed table.

"Aren't you gonna open it?" Naomi asked.

Martha's eyes darted between Ruth and Naomi. "Yes, Mary,
please open it. I want to know what's in it. . . . For your health,
of course."

"I bet. No, I'll just hold it here for now," Mary said, afraid
that opening the envelope in front of her family would force her
to explain details of her relationship with Tynan that she wasn't
ready to share.

* * *

RUTH PEEKED AROUND the open door to Martha's office. Martha sat behind the desk with her head down on folded arms like a sick elementary school child. Ruth considered sneaking away, but she was concerned about leaving Martha asleep with her office door ajar. Although the primary care center was closed over the weekend, Ruth had charmed a sympathetic member of the custodial staff into letting her into the center, and she wasn't sure who else might be lurking around that wing of the hospital.

Ruth tapped on the door, her knuckles grazing the wood loudly enough to ease Martha awake. "Are you okay? May I come in?"

Martha popped up. "Uh, yes. Sure. Come in." She swirled her chair to the wall behind her to check her appearance in the beveled mirror hanging over the wall of waist-high filing cabinets.

"We weren't sure why you left Mary's room, but I had a feeling I might find you here," Ruth said, walking toward the desk.

"I came back to get a phone charger, and I put my head down for a second. But I guess a second turns into thirty minutes when you've been awake for almost a day and a half."

Ruth settled into the chair across from Martha. She wondered how many of Martha's direct reports had sat in the same place for an uncomfortable conversation with her. "I imagine you're tired. I know medical issues are part of your everyday life, but I'd like to commend you on how you handled everything last night."

"Thanks." Martha shrugged. "It's not out of the ordinary, except when it's your sister. Is everything okay with Mary? Is that why you're here?"

Ruth shook her head. "Mary is still doing well. She and MIL are watching a movie. I came by because I wanted to smooth things over. You and I have been staying out of each other's way over the past week, and it feels very awkward, especially in the middle of a family emergency. I was planning to talk with you about this in the new year. But it's better if we talk about it now, so things aren't uncomfortable while we tend to Mary. Especially during the holidays."

"Don't worry about Mary. I'll look after her," Martha sneered.

Ruth's palms began to sweat. "I care about her too, and I want to help. From the way you're responding, it's almost like you don't want me around."

Martha leaned forward. "When you had a chance to look after Mary, you left her," she said, placing her elbows on her desk and steepling her fingers.

Ruth rested her hand at the base of her neck. "I don't understand. The second MIL found me at the party and told me what was going on, I went to Mary's side. I stood there with you and MIL the entire time. Then I came to the hospital, and I left at the same time you left last night. What else was I supposed to do?"

Martha shook her head. "You left Mary in the restroom when she had nausea and thought she was going to have diarrhea. She could've stumbled out of the restroom naked and in distress, or what if someone had found her stretched out on the restroom floor?"

"Stop it, Martha! Mary was fully dressed and comfortable when I left her in the restroom. I sat with her awhile. I offered to stay, but she suggested I leave. I figured she had an upset stomach because of nerves, and she told me she's had that problem off and on for a long time. I stayed until she looked better. She insisted I go back to the party. How was I supposed to know she was going to develop heart trouble and end up hospitalized?"

"You don't have to be a doctor to have compassion for people, Ruth. You were too busy trying to get back to the party to look good in front of everyone and lobby for the permanent CEO position. I heard what you said in your speech. Did you think I wouldn't catch on to what you were doing?"

Ruth sighed as she stood and picked up her purse. "Oh, Martha, are you really being petty while your sister is lying in a hospital bed? My speech was patterned after what Beau used to say. I just replaced my title with his and made a few minor changes." She headed toward the door.

"You always have an excuse, don't you? What's your rationale for letting Aunt Naomi cause more stress for Mary?" Martha said, rolling her eyes.

"What? Now you're making things up!"

"You had one job today, Ruth. One job—make sure Aunt Naomi was okay during this process. I didn't think I had to specifically ask you to make sure she didn't cause more trouble for Mary by throwing Tynan out of her restaurant but, if she did, to please make sure you tell me and get my input before you hand her some unknown legal document from a New York lawyer," Martha said, lowering her voice to sound like Ruth.

"It's not a legal—never mind. This wasn't a good idea." Ruth stood and walked toward the door. As she crossed the middle of the room, she passed a framed photo of Martha, Mary, Naomi, Beau, and M.J. on Martha's bookcase. Ruth was the only living family member missing from the photo. Ruth remembered the conversation she'd had with her mother-in-law the day after the last board meeting about how Naomi had finally realized her long-standing approach wasn't bringing the results she wanted. *All we ever do in this family is run away, and we keep ending up in the same place,* Ruth thought.

Ruth marched back over to Martha's desk and plopped down on the chair she'd left moments prior. "You know what? We're gonna finish this. My dear, you are the one who decided to cut off communication with me, and I see you've discovered there are repercussions for doing so. Mary is stable, so she can have an envelope that her fiancé, ex-fiancé, or whatever he is left for her. It's time for us to stop treating both of you like children. I've accommodated your immaturity since I first met you, and now I'm paying for it. I'm no longer going to run behind you and try to convince you to communicate with me because it's in your best interest. That made sense when you were fourteen and I was twenty-five and you were upset that I was marrying Beau. The eleven-year age difference between me and you mattered then, but it doesn't now. You're grown. We can disagree without keeping score and throwing these little tantrums. I've been going back and forth about whether I should make you an offer to buy you out of Gardin Family Enterprises. Mary's hospitalization gave me a new perspective. I came here to try to smooth things over with you, but you couldn't let that happen. So let's just get on with it," she said.

Martha groaned.

Ruth ignored the sound and continued. "Since you've already asked Nicholas to help us with a valuation of the company, it won't be difficult to figure out what your stake is worth. I'm tired of tiptoeing around you. I will not stand by and tolerate your disrespect and tyranny."

Martha stood up and looked down at Ruth. "You want to kick me out of *my* family's company?" she asked indignantly.

Ruth didn't flinch. *"Her" family. I was right.* Ruth wanted to challenge Martha about her word choice, but she remembered her promise to Naomi. Although the conversation wasn't going the way Ruth had planned, she didn't want to bicker any more than was required. She still wanted to try to have some semblance of a relationship with Martha, even if Martha was reluctant to do so. Ruth looked up at Martha. "That's not at all what I said," she replied calmly. "I have a duty to protect the company, and I'm willing to buy you out if you're interested. Perhaps that will give us an opportunity to just be a family and not let business muddle things."

"I didn't say that I want that," Martha said, her face expressionless and her tone flat.

"Oh, I understand now," Ruth said, reading between the lines. "I was trying to do the right thing by giving you the option of selling. I've struggled for more than a year with whether you saw Beau's death as an opportunity to remove me from the family and the business, but that's exactly what you'd like to do. I came here with the intention of making peace and finding a path forward, but that's the last thing you want. Regardless, the choice is yours."

Martha backed away and returned to her seat behind the desk. "Again, I didn't say—"

"Let's be honest, Martha. That's exactly what you've been trying to say, but I finally get it. Next time use your big-girl words. And now I'll put you on notice. I've invested too much in building the business and the family to just walk away from either of them. So you can figure out how to deal with it." Ruth stood again. Then she walked out of Martha's office and marched straight to her car without looking back.

Chapter Eleven

Mary expected to be discharged from the hospital in a few hours, and a single conversation with her therapist would be the ticket to freedom. She could take the easy road and cooperate enough with the session so that she would be cleared to go home, but she wanted to fully commit. She needed to finally open up about the topic she'd been running from since she left New York. Her last session with Shari had been uneventful, but that was eight months ago. Her life had changed a lot since then, especially over the past three days, and Mary didn't know where to start.

Mary had assigned herself to the bed all three days of her hospital stay, and it never occurred to her that she could use any of the other furniture in the room. It was a treat to sit in the recliner, across from Shari, but preparing to talk about the secrets that caused her life to unravel overshadowed the newness of sitting somewhere different. She had traded her solid-blue hospital gown for a black-and-white striped tie-neck blouse and cuffed slacks. It was a good thing she still wore the yellow hospital slipper socks, because her left leg jittered. The configuration in the room forced Mary to sit closer to Shari than she would have in Shari's office in Edin, making her hospital room feel like a fishbowl.

"I worried you would have trouble fitting on this side of the room in your wheelchair," Mary said.

Shari smiled. "I appreciate your thoughtfulness. The hospital rooms are small, but they were renovated a few years ago with accessibility in mind."

Mary stared at the natural curls in Shari's pixie cut. With Shari sitting so close to the window, Mary could see that the bronze highlights in Shari's hair perfectly matched her skin. "That's good. The room looks so different from here. It's nice to be out of the bed. I should've switched things up before now." Mary twirled her hair around her finger.

"Sometimes a change in location is what we need to see things differently," Shari said, removing her oversized cat-eye glasses and placing them atop her coordinating tortoiseshell notebook on the overbed table. "But tell me how you're feeling right now."

Mary admired Shari's style—her fashion sense as well as her direct approach during counseling sessions. The women were similar in age, and Shari was so relatable that Mary hadn't been able to resist telling Ruth about her when she'd mentioned she was considering therapy. "Nervous . . . I feel very nervous." Mary sighed.

"That's understandable. I spent some time looking through the medical team's notes before I came in, and it sounds like the twenty-four-hour period before your hospitalization was stressful."

Mary grimaced. "To say the least. I've been talking to my family about my feelings since I've been here, and it's worked out overall. But there's a big piece of the story that I've held back. I wanted to talk with you about it first, but I'm still a little concerned about what you're going to think," she confessed.

"Thank you for sharing that. I know it's hard to talk about private things, especially when they've been painful for you in the past, but I want to remind you that part of my job is to provide you with complete acceptance and support. That's my way of saying I'm not going to judge you."

"That's helpful," Mary replied, nodding. "I've been thinking about where I should start, but you said something about changing locations earlier when I was stalling." She chuckled.

"Yes, I noticed that you were stalling, but you came along in your own time," Shari said with a reassuring smile.

"Well, I never thought I would stay in Edin as long as I have. I figured it would only be for a little while, but a couple of months turned into a year and a half. And now I'm realizing that my outlook has changed."

"What do you mean?"

"Every decision I've made in Edin has been in anticipation of one day moving back to New York, but now I'm not sure I want to go back there."

"It sounds like something changed suddenly. Is it because of your illness and hospitalization?"

"I wish it were that simple. I think it's more about what led to my illness and hospitalization. I've been avoiding talking about the stuff I have to talk about now. I grew comfortable not talking about it. Well, I *thought* I was comfortable."

"Why do you feel like you have to talk about it now?"

"I don't want to be stubborn and cause any additional damage to my heart. I wonder if I would be hospitalized if I'd have been willing to talk about things before."

"That's hard to say. I'd like to get a sense of how anxiety has been affecting your life before the episode that led to your hospitalization."

"Of course. . . . I've been increasingly anxious over the past few months. . . . I opened a restaurant. It's been doing well, so my schedule has been busy."

"What about those issues makes you feel more anxious?"

"Even though I can tell you that I've been more anxious lately and the issues I just mentioned have taken up space in my life, I didn't feel directly stressed about them. But I guess I just didn't realize they were wearing on me. I mean, I'm tired and don't get much sleep because I work at the restaurant so much. But I enjoy it. We've had a lot more family drama over the past couple of weeks. My family gets on my nerves. I need to enforce my boundaries with them, especially my sister. I put my foot down with her the other day, but I need to keep working on it. And over the past week or so, I've also begun to recognize my contributions to the family drama."

Shari nodded as she scribbled. "Good that you've been able to start working through things. I'm keeping track of some topics for us to dig deeper into after you leave the hospital."

"Okay."

"So, tell me, what was going through your head during some of the times that you were anxious?"

"Hmm . . . anger. I've been very angry."

"About anything in particular?"

"The longer I've been here, the angrier I've become."

"Here, meaning in the hospital?"

"No, here in Edin. Away from New York. And even though my life is coming together nicely, I've still been angry about being here."

"You haven't spoken much in our sessions about why you left New York. Is it okay if we talk about that?"

Mary raised her eyebrows and shifted in her chair. "I guess."

"How are you feeling now when I ask about New York?"

"I feel anxious. I feel like someone is sitting on my chest, but not like I did when the ambulance came to pick me up and brought me here."

"Do you want to take a break?"

"No, I'm okay." Mary inhaled deeply through her nose and exhaled through her mouth. "I think I just need to say it. I think that's the problem—that I haven't been willing to talk about New York, and Tynan, my ex. Well, that's not totally accurate. He isn't my ex. We're still technically in a relationship. We never broke up. It's just been easier to refer to him as my ex because then people tend not to ask questions about him."

"Have you talked to your family or anyone else about what happened between the two of you and why you moved here?"

"No."

"Okay."

"All right, I'll say it." Mary took a deep breath. "I moved here because my fiancé disappeared and he took two hundred thousand dollars that was in my bank account. It was my disbursement from my family's trust. I had just quit my job and was planning to open a restaurant in Brooklyn. I was about to sign a lease for the space. Then my cousin died unexpectedly. I came home for the funeral and decided to stay here."

"I see. . . . Did you file charges against him?"

"No. I can't prove that he did it. The money was transferred from my account a couple of days after he disappeared. The bank said that my password was used to transfer the money to an offshore account. I shouldn't have used the same password for more than one account. I should've known better, but I used the same password for a small account that we opened together for our wedding. Tynan knew the password."

Mary felt relieved as she spoke the words. She'd imagined she might pass out once she finally heard herself say them aloud. But she didn't. She felt lighter, like she'd just had a deep tissue massage.

"So, did you report him missing?" Shari asked.

Mary was surprised by Shari's neutral tone. *I guess she wasn't kidding about this being a judgment-free space,* Mary thought.

"Mary?" Shari pressed.

"Oh, sorry. . . . No, because I didn't think he was missing."

Shari scratched her forehead. "Huh? I don't understand."

"It's complicated. Tynan's job was very private, and he told me when we first got serious that the nature of his job could cause him to go away unexpectedly and that I shouldn't involve the police. I know it sounds strange, but it was the nature of his work."

Shari reached for her eyeglasses. "So, does he work for the CIA or something like that?" she asked.

"Martha asked me the same thing when I first started dating him," Mary said, shifting in her seat. She lowered her voice to just above a whisper. "It took me a couple of years to find out that he actually worked for them before we met."

Shari's eyes widened. "Oh," she said, revealing a puncture in her usually unflappable demeanor.

"I know." Mary laughed uncomfortably. "He was recruited right out of college. He was an analyst, whatever that really means." She rolled her eyes. "Tynan always gave vague answers whenever I asked about it. I think he worked for them maybe three or four years, and then he went to law school. He planned to go back, but he took a job at a family office instead."

"A family office? Like his boss owned a small business?"

"No, it's a privately held company that oversees wealth management and investments for a family to help them transfer wealth across generations."

Shari tilted her head. "I see," she said.

"Yeah, I didn't know it was a thing either before I met Tynan. The Loughty family is very wealthy—like private-planes wealthy. After a couple of years, he became the office's chief of staff. His job was to look after the family's wealth and interests. He told me general things about work, but he never got into specifics. And I met the family and other people who worked for them, so I know it was true."

Mary crossed her legs at the knees. "We stayed in the family's properties around the world when we went on vacation. Tynan was usually traveling for something business related and quick, like picking up artwork or jewelry, and I went with him. Sometimes we had armed guards. But they were very discreet. The trips were otherwise low-key and we had fun the rest of the time. It was a good life. Tynan had unexpected work trips from time to time, but he was always back in a couple of days. He always updated me, so it was never a big deal. Sometimes I might get a call from his office, or he'd leave a note for me with his doorman. But he always had a story that checked out. He told me that if anything ever happened, I should be patient and that someone would get in touch with me."

Mary continued, "A few days after he disappeared, I went to his apartment—it's on the Upper East Side of Manhattan, not far from his office. His doorman didn't say anything or do anything unusual, but it was odd inside. Everything was neat, but he'd packed stuff you wouldn't expect. It was summer, but he took his winter coat—the casual one that I've never seen him wear. I figured either he planned to be away for a while or he was going to Iceland. And he's not the type to go to Iceland," she said, then chuckled. "Tynan's boss owns the apartment where he lives, but I never heard from him, his family, or any of the office's other employees. I called and called, but no one got back to me.

"After a couple of weeks, I saw news stories that his boss was under federal investigation. So, I figured my missing money had something to do with it, and I never called again. I didn't want to get involved with that," Mary said, waving her hands.

Shari squinted. "Did Tynan ever reach out himself or send you a message?" she asked.

"Not until Friday, the day I was admitted to the hospital. I ran into him in the lobby of the hotel where our family company has its Christmas party. He said he came to town to surprise me, but we ran into each other before that could happen. I was shocked and happy to see him at first, but then it turned into an emotional fiasco, with me running away through the halls of the hotel. It was so embarrassing!"

"And that's the emotional situation the doctors think caused the problem with your heart, right?" Shari asked.

Mary nodded. "I'm trying not to be angry with Tynan about that too, but his decisions have wreaked havoc on my life."

"Have you considered that it might be a good idea to allow yourself to feel the anger? Even as you've shared your story with me today, you seem surprisingly calm."

"I'm still figuring out how I should feel and how I should behave. Before my hospitalization, I was afraid that expressing my anger would cause me to tell my family what happened with Tynan. In some ways, that would've been better for me because then they wouldn't have assumed I squandered my money. Their judgment has been hard to bear. But I was afraid that if I told them what happened, they wouldn't accept Tynan when he came back. Now, since I've been hospitalized, I've been worried about getting upset again and injuring my heart."

"I understand," Shari said. "I'm also concerned that there's a greater risk that you would hurt your heart by not expressing how you feel. It seems that holding things in worsened your anxiety, which may have put you at higher risk when you felt a surge of emotion when Tynan returned. So expressing your anger in a constructive way may be a better decision."

Shari cleared her throat. "Now, you said earlier that the longer you stayed in Edin, the angrier you got. Was that because you were worried about Tynan?"

"A little," Mary said, her head tilting. "I've had moments where my mind wandered and played a game of what-ifs—what if he was kidnapped and being tortured, what if he's dead, or what if he was in witness protection and I would never see him or my money again? But that wasn't my overwhelming sentiment. I've just always had a feeling that he was fine. I was angry because I had to rebuild my life."

Mary paused and took a breath. "He left me for dead financially. I was devastated. Everything I was planning had to be put on hold and I had to start over," she said, her voice quivering.

"Over the past several months," Mary continued, "I've felt like my life was finally coming together again, and that's made me think about him a lot more. I mean, I already thought about him and prayed for him every day. I've been waiting for him to come back and save me from the mess he created, but instead I've had to save myself. And I get angrier and angrier about that as time goes on. And I'm angry about all the things he missed in my life—holidays, our dating anniversary, my accomplishments. Friday was a big day for me because I catered the Christmas party. He acted like he expected me to sit around and wait for him as if he'd just gone out to run an errand before picking me up to go to a fundraiser or party associated with his job. But Friday was *my* big day. It wasn't about him."

Mary balled her left hand into a fist. "Tynan knows how to make everything about him, and that infuriates me. If he had left me a bunch of money to amuse myself with while he was away, then maybe I would be sitting around waiting for him. But that wasn't the case at all. He disappeared with my money and left me to fend for myself instead."

"Interesting," Shari said, adjusting her glasses. "And from what you've said about his employer, it sounds like Tynan made a lot of money. Has that played a role in your anger about his stealing your money?"

"I wouldn't call it stealing."

"Did you give him permission to take it?"

"No."

Shari scribbled in her notebook. "Do you think you have a hard time calling what Tynan did stealing because putting that label on it would force you to experience emotions that you don't want to feel?"

"I hadn't thought about it that way." Mary lowered her head

as she covered her eyes. "Stealing makes it sound so much worse. I mean, that's breaking a commandment."

"It's also a felony. Do you ever think about *that*?"

"I know. That's one reason I didn't go to the police. I didn't want to press charges against him. But I want to understand what happened. I have so many questions. When I saw him Friday, I was just so relieved. I couldn't ask him anything. He bombarded me with questions and accusations. He actually mentioned, in the middle of the lobby, that I gained weight and asked if I was seeing anyone, because I stopped wearing my ring. It was too much to handle, so I ran off. Could you imagine if I were still wearing the ring after he disappeared? How would I have explained that to my family, especially when I hadn't even told them we were engaged? I've tried to come up with an answer for a year and a half, and I still don't have one. That's why I told them we broke up. That was easier. Now I have to explain this to them. I still don't know how to do that." Mary broke into tears. She removed a tissue from the box on the overbed table.

"You can tell your family whatever you want. You're not obligated to explain anything to them."

"That's easy to say, but it's not so easy to live out," Mary said, sniffing.

"That's fair. There are repercussions to our decisions. Sometimes they're positive, and sometimes they're not. But it's okay to make the decision that you need to in order to protect yourself. It sounds like you've made decisions to protect Tynan, although you've convinced yourself that you made those decisions for yourself. I suspect you've done that for a long time and Tynan took advantage of that in your relationship. Did you feel unsafe with him Friday or at any other point in your relationship?"

Mary shook her head. "No, and he's never been physically abusive. But the way he spoke to me Friday didn't feel respectful. But it's not new. . . . He's always spoken to me that way when he gets in a mood, but I couldn't take it on Friday. After everything I've been through and everything I've sacrificed to get where I am now, it just wasn't okay. I don't know how the way he treats me never bothered me before."

"I'm glad you listened to the voice inside you that said he wasn't treating you appropriately," Shari said. "It sounds like the relationship wasn't emotionally safe for you, and you noticed it on Friday because of the growth you've experienced since you left New York. Sometimes it's hard to recognize growth when we're going through it, but your time in Edin has shaped you more than you realized." Her voice was consoling and encouraging.

"Thank you." Mary smiled softly.

"You're welcome. One reason I think you couldn't see it was that you've been under a lot of pressure without a real outlet to process it. You have to create a safe space for yourself. Therapy is just one part of that. Supportive family and friends can also be helpful, but exercise, journaling, pursuing a hobby, and taking time for yourself are some other healthy ways to provide the support you need."

Mary had been meaning to take better care of herself, but now that doing so was part of her treatment plan, she was going to take it more seriously. "I can work on that," she said.

"Was there a reason you didn't feel comfortable being open in therapy before now? I can help you find another therapist if I'm not the right fit for you."

"No, I like talking to you. This was easier to talk about than I thought it would be. I was worried that anyone I told about Tynan would think I sounded naïve and gullible. Even after you spoke about not judging me, I was afraid you would. I really appreciate that you kept your word. Now I'm trying to figure out what to do next."

"Do you mean you're deciding if you want to talk to Tynan?"

"Kinda. I need to speak with him eventually, and I need to get ready for it. My family told him to leave and that I would reach out to him when I'm ready. I think he left town, but he brought a letter. I haven't read it yet. I wasn't sure how I would react, so I decided to save it for this session today. Is that okay?"

"Yes, of course."

Mary stood and walked to the overnight bag sitting on her bed. She slid the white envelope from the folded bag handles that held it in place.

As she walked back to the recliner, she blurted, "Would you open it and read it?"

"No, Mary. You should open it. You can do it."

Mary sat in the chair and stared at the envelope in her hands.

"Take your time," Shari said reassuringly.

"I can't do it."

"What are you thinking right now?"

Mary placed the envelope on her lap. "I have a bunch of thoughts. I'm afraid that whatever is in this envelope will determine my future with Tynan, and that makes me very uncomfortable."

"Okay, what do *you* want to happen between the two of you? If you're clear about that, you can remind yourself that you have the power to decide if the relationship continues or not. The decision is not solely Tynan's, and it's not solely based on what is communicated in the envelope. What *you* want matters."

Mary took a deep breath. "Okay," she said, her voice shaky.

"You're allowed to change your mind, but tell me what you want right now."

"I wish Tynan hadn't done this."

"Unfortunately, neither of us has the power to turn back time or to control anyone else's behavior. Let me ask the question a different way. Do you still want to be with Tynan?"

"I don't think so . . . but I need more time to think about it to be sure. Everything has happened so fast. I don't know how to tell him it's over. I don't want to talk to him until I'm certain about what I want and what I'd like to say to him."

"I agree one hundred percent. Let's have another session in a week or two to discuss what you want to accomplish in the conversation, as well as how much you want to share with him about your pain. I'd like you to go into the conversation being very clear about your boundaries and knowing how to exit the conversation if your boundaries are crossed. You can start thinking about it in the meantime, and from there we'll talk through a plan so you feel prepared for whatever you decide to do."

"That's helpful." Mary picked up the envelope. "Okay, I'm ready to open it." She slid her index finger under the sealed flap and ripped through the top of the envelope. "That felt good," she announced.

Mary removed the letter. As she opened it, a rectangular piece of paper fell to the floor. She bent over to pick it up and exclaimed, "It's a check for three hundred thousand dollars!" She jumped to her feet and stared at the check. "I wasn't sure this day would ever come. I didn't think I'd ever get my money back." She bowed her head. "Thank You! Oh, God, thank You!"

"Would you like some water?" Shari asked.

Shari reached for the water pitcher and cup on the overbed table and poured Mary some water.

As Mary accepted the cup, her hands trembled. She extended her neck and gulped the water down, squinting as a pain bolted across her temples and forehead. "Brain freeze!" she said, then laughed. "I've never been so happy to have a headache!" She attempted to fan herself with the letter, but the page flopped back and forth on the fold.

"How do you feel?" Shari asked.

"Light and free. I didn't expect to feel this way, but I feel free. I don't know what I thought it would feel like . . . probably because I haven't allowed myself to imagine it. . . . I didn't want to think about how I would feel if it never happened . . . but I feel peaceful. I feel like my life is starting over right now, just by opening this letter." She took another tissue from the box and wiped her eyes. "Oh, the letter. I have to read the letter."

Mary's voice fluttered with excitement as she read the letter aloud. "Dear Ms. Gardin, our office has been retained to assist Mr. Tynan Wright. You may be aware that his employer was involved in a federal investigation. During this time, Mr. Wright's accounts were frozen. However, both Mr. Wright and his employer have recently been cleared of any wrongdoing. Mr. Wright extends his thanks for your support during this difficult time. The enclosed check provides payment for your support, plus interest. Mr. Wright has asked that I make myself available should you have any questions regarding the investigation, Mr. Wright's involvement, or the interest calculation. I can be reached at the number below. Sincerely, Thomas Riley, Esquire."

Chapter Twelve

Ruth walked into her office after a midafternoon break. Between her long days at work and time spent keeping Naomi company as she watched over Mary, she had fallen behind on her maternal duties. Because she had missed calls from M.J. twice during the previous week, her son had scheduled a call during business hours through her assistant, Chloe. Ruth suspected M.J. was homesick, as he shared his parents' love of the Christmas season. She'd surprised him by taking the call on her cell phone and visiting with Fatou, his favorite of the Gardin Family Enterprises staff members, so they could chat about his experience visiting her home country. Both women enjoyed hearing about M.J.'s love of mafé, a spicy Senegalese stew made from ground peanuts. But now it was back to business.

Chloe sat behind Ruth's desk. She looked up from the computer screen as Ruth entered the room. "Hot Santa Claus is waiting for you on Zoom," she said.

"What?" Ruth asked, puzzled.

Chloe pressed her lips together, briefly looking away from her boss. "Hot Santa Claus. You know—Nicholas. He's hot. And he wore a red suit and Santa boots to the party last week. We all call him Hot Santa Claus now."

With Mary's emergency at the end of the party, Ruth had forgotten about Nicholas's party attire. She wished she could say the same for her staff. "The speaker had better be muted, and please stop calling him that. It's so unprofessional," Ruth whispered, using the tone she used to give M.J. if he misbehaved during church service when he was a little boy.

"Gotcha. It's muted," Chloe said, unbothered by Ruth's frustration.

As Ruth approached her desk, she saw Nicholas on the video screen, his head lowered like he was reading something next to his computer. She double-checked the speaker setting as Chloe arose from the chair. *Thank God*, she thought. Ruth and Nicholas hadn't spoken since he drove her, Naomi, and Martha back to Edin from the hospital. She had worried their first conversation might be awkward, but it would be worse if she had to apologize for what Chloe had said.

Ruth settled into her chair and unmuted the speaker. "Good afternoon, Nicholas," she said.

Nicholas raised his head. "Hi, Ruth. Happy Thursday." He smiled.

"Happy Thursday," Ruth replied, loosening up. "Thanks for making time to touch base before the holiday break."

"No problem. I'd like to proceed using the agenda I included in the meeting invitation. But first, how's Mary?"

"It's very kind of you to ask. She's doing well. She's home. I'll be going to her house after I leave the office today."

"That's good news. And Naomi? I know she took Mary's illness pretty hard."

I was afraid of this. Ruth felt the muscles across her lower back tighten. It was one thing for him to ask about Mary's well-being, but she didn't want the conversation to extend beyond that. As much as she enjoyed the camaraderie between her staff and her family, the stakes felt higher with Nicholas. "She's fine too. Everyone is coming along," she said dryly. "So, how have your follow-up meetings with our staff gone?"

"They've been great. You've got a sharp group working for

you," he replied enthusiastically. "I've had several meetings with LaKisha and a few of her finance team members. I plan to circle back with them in the new year with some questions regarding your peanut seed and farm supplies division. I've included a potential January trip to Edin as a discussion item, so when we reach that part of the agenda, we can talk through what I'd like to accomplish on the visit."

"Sounds good," Ruth replied, satisfied that it had been so easy to redirect Nicholas. She liked his easygoing attitude.

"Work slows down for me this time of year," he said. "I don't know how much of your staff will be taking vacation time during the holidays. But given the short turnaround period we have for my work with your company, I can use my extra capacity to work more closely with your team if you'd like. That way, we can make sure we complete this project on time. You seem to do a great job, but I can tell that you're stretched holding two leadership roles in the company. I hope you don't mind my saying so."

Relief spread across Ruth's face. She wasn't good at asking for help, but she needed it. She kept up a tough demeanor at the office because she didn't want to undermine her staff's confidence in her. And the tension in her family prevented her from being transparent with them about the stress she shouldered balancing her responsibilities. "No, I don't mind. You're right. I appreciate that you're comfortable saying what needs to be said. Most consultants aren't as direct as you are, especially so early in our work together."

Nicholas laughed. "I'm not known for mincing words. Sometimes it gets me into trouble, but things usually work out."

"Thank you for your generous offer. Your timing couldn't be better. My senior leadership team and I are taking very little time off during the holidays, so we're happy to have your help."

"It's my pleasure. It's far too early for me to say what I'll recommend after I complete my assessment. But if you decide not to sell the company, you should consider what additional staffing is needed to support your leadership style—a chief of staff or maybe even a chief operating officer."

Ruth rested her head in her hand. *I won't be around to make any staffing changes if Martha has her way,* she thought. But she was careful not to say anything more about her family situation. She had set a firm boundary at the start of the meeting, and she intended to keep it. "Hmm, I'll think about that. In the meantime, let's go through the discussion items you put on the agenda."

* * *

MARY NESTLED IN the bay window across from her bed, surrounded by pillows and love. Well-wishes from friends and business contacts filled her bedroom. Another dozen arrangements supplemented the flowers that brightened her hospital room, and greeting cards were scattered among the sea of blossoms. It was like sleeping in a garden.

Her biggest priority was making up for the poor slumber she'd gotten in the hospital. With the exception of drowsy trips to her bathroom, her only movements had been between her bed and window seat, where she enjoyed the substantial meals Naomi prepared for her. But before retreating to her room, she'd offered to clarify for her family the events that had defined the past eighteen months of her life. She had only one stipulation: Their questions would have to wait until she reemerged from the rest her body and mind craved. The women reluctantly agreed. Mary then explained the reason for her move to Edin, the circumstances that led to Tynan's disappearance, and that he had returned the money he took from her account. Questions lingered in the air, and the cottage buzzed with debate and assumptions loud enough to penetrate the thick piece of wood that hung at the entry of Mary's sanctuary but too light to cut into her sleep.

The automatic light on the patio came on, signaling the six o'clock hour. After three days spent mostly sleeping, Mary determined it was time to rejoin the world. She sat up and retrieved the bathrobe strewn at the distant end of the fluffy mattress. The soft fibers of the gray chenille garment caressed her arms as she pulled the hood over her head, a sufficient substitute for the comfort she'd cherished during her respite. She sauntered across the room and slid the door open.

It looked like time had paused as Mary slept. Her family members sat in the same spots they'd occupied when she had briefed the trio three days prior. Naomi lounged on the couch, her command post since Mary's return home. Martha sat next to her, while Ruth sat in the club chair in the corner. Mary expected to see Naomi, but she was surprised to find Martha and Ruth in her home at the same time. Naomi served as sole caretaker during the daytime, but she tag-teamed with Martha and Ruth on alternating evenings. Martha blamed the small size of Mary's cottage for the plan to take turns, but Mary believed there was more behind the decision. Although she gave no attention to Martha's explanation then, it made the presence of all three women at the same time ominous.

"She's back!" Naomi exclaimed as Mary appeared in the doorway. Naomi was as jubilant as the day Mary had arrived home from the hospital after shocking her family by refusing their offer to drive her home and opting instead to splurge on a luxury sedan through a rideshare company and a courier for the flowers. The solo ride provided an opportunity to transition from her counseling session with Shari and gather her thoughts in anticipation of her impending disclosure. Now that she was fully rested and her family had time for the truth to sink in, Mary was ready for their interrogation.

"Yes! I'm back," she said, then giggled. "Today is the first day I've felt like my old self. I hope you'll get back to your own lives now instead of camping out here like the Secret Service."

"Glad to hear it, but we don't mind," Ruth said. "We just wanted to be close in case you needed something." She stood up. "Here, sit in this chair. I'll take the ottoman."

Mary didn't mind sitting on the ottoman. It was her favorite seat in the quaint living room, but she knew Ruth wouldn't take no for an answer. "Thanks, Ruth. I feel horrible that I've put y'all through all this."

"For the one hundred eighty-first time, it's okay. We want to be here for you," Ruth said as she settled on the ottoman.

Mary inhaled the fresh citrus scent of the Meyer lemon tree next to the chair as she leaned into its curved back. "Okay, but I still didn't hear agreement that the three of you will go home tonight. I feel great, and I promise to call so you can run back over if anything changes."

"That's reasonable," Martha said.

Ruth nodded. "I agree too."

"Aunt Naomi, how about you?" Mary asked.

"Will you finally answer some questions first?" Naomi responded.

Mary smiled. She'd anticipated that her aunt wouldn't concede until her questions were answered. "Yeah, why not? It's convenient since all three of you are here. Wait, is that why y'all are here at the same time? Were y'all planning an intervention for me today?"

"We wouldn't call it an intervention," Ruth said, "but—"

"That's the same line you rehearsed for Aunt Naomi's intervention when you were trying to convince her to move in with you because you thought she was depressed." Mary laughed. "So now you're using it on me?"

Ruth chuckled. "That's true. I guess I should've come up with something original."

"Before we ask you anything, you deserve an apology," Naomi said. "All this time, I thought you wasted your inheritance. I feel so guilty about not lending you the money you needed to start the restaurant. Please forgive me for judging you and not being more supportive."

"I'm sorry too," Ruth said. "Beau had just died. I was so consumed with grief and taking care of things at the company. I didn't stop to think about what might be going on with you."

"And I've been worst of all," Martha said. "I looked down on you, my own sister. I misjudged you. If I had paid more attention and not been so distracted by holding it over your head that you needed me, I would've figured out that something else was going on. Now all the stuff you've said to me over the past few weeks makes much more sense. I feel terrible about how I treated you and also about the things you heard me say about other people that may have offended you."

Naomi teared up. "We failed you as a family, and your illness has shown me the extent of our dysfunction."

"Thank you. . . . Thank you so much," Mary said, wiping her eyes with her robe. "I'm sorry I didn't tell you. I was afraid you would judge me, and I was afraid that you would never forgive Tynan."

"I wish I could say that you were wrong and that we wouldn't have judged you. But you're absolutely right," Naomi said. "We're judgmental, and we need to work on that."

"So, are you going to forgive Tynan and continue a relationship with him?" Ruth asked.

Martha rolled her eyes. "Of course she's not! Why would you even suggest that?"

Ruth sighed and shook her head.

"Hold on, Martha," Naomi interjected. "You don't get to decide that. You're still missing what got us into this mess as a family."

Mary shifted her weight and rested her elbow on the arm of the chair. "I have a lot to think about. I'm working on forgiving him, but not necessarily for the sake of reestablishing our relationship. I need to forgive him so I can move on. It costs me too much to carry that kind of pain. I could've paid with my life."

Naomi nodded and blinked her eyes quickly.

You okay? Ruth mouthed to Naomi.

Yeah, Naomi mouthed back.

Mary smiled as she continued. "And now I don't know if I can imagine myself going back to Tynan after all he's done. I was still in love with him while he was away, despite knowing that he stole my money. I need to sort through how I could still feel that way about him."

"Exactly," Martha said emphatically.

Mary extended her palm toward her sister. "But I also realize now that he's *not* who I thought he was. I think maybe I was in love with the person I *thought* he was, but I can't blame all that on him. It's not just about the disrespect and selfishness that he showed by stealing my money. While that's a huge part of it, I also have to take responsibility for my role. I ignored a lot of his bad behavior along the way, like the way he constantly dismissed me and the things that were important to me. I'm not blaming myself for what he did, but I taught him that it was okay to address only his needs and not mine. He knew better, but I still allowed it."

"I'm relieved, but I'm still worried," Martha said.

"It seems mature to me. I think you just need more time," Ruth said, smiling softly at Mary.

"Yes, I suppose I'll figure it out eventually." Mary shrugged.

Naomi leaned forward and rested her elbows on her knees.

"I'm proud of you, Mary. Let us know if we can be helpful in some way."

"Thanks, Aunt Naomi. I have an appointment with Shari next week. I want to talk things through with her before I speak to Tynan." Mary turned to her sister. "And Martha is going to give me Tynan's phone number."

Martha crossed her arms.

"Right, Martha?" Mary prodded.

"Yeah, I might as well. If I don't, you'll just call the number in the letter from his lawyer. He said to call if you have any questions, so I'm sure he'd give you Tynan's number if you asked for it," Martha said flippantly.

Ruth and Naomi locked eyes.

"Martha!" Ruth yelled.

Naomi held her head in her hands, rubbing her temples.

"What?" Martha snapped.

Mary squinted, her eyes shifting among Naomi, Ruth, and Martha. She sat quietly, recounting the brief explanation she'd shared with her family when she got home from the hospital. She'd thought it was peculiar that they hadn't tried to ask a single question when she disclosed her history with Tynan, especially about his involvement in his boss's investigation. "I never mentioned anything specific about the lawyer's letter. I said that Tynan's lawyer sent me a check for the money Tynan took, plus interest. I didn't give any details."

"Oh, I guess I assumed that, then," Martha said, averting her eyes from Mary and kicking her right foot against the coffee table.

"No, your words were pretty explicit. And they were accurate, like you read the letter somehow. Did you come into my room and go through my things while I was asleep?" Mary barked.

Martha didn't respond.

"No, she didn't," Naomi said, then sighed.

"Did you do it, Aunt Naomi, or was it Ruth?" Mary asked, turning her head between them.

Ruth looked away.

"It's my fault," Naomi said. "I was being nosy, but I was also being protective. I wanted to make sure it was okay to give the envelope to you in the hospital, so I opened it. I shouldn't have done that, and I shouldn't have told anyone else what it said. There's no excuse."

Mary shook her head. "So everybody is going around breaking federal laws without consequence? Tynan steals money, and you open people's mail."

"Well, he didn't mail it. He handed it to me, so I didn't break any laws that time."

"*That* time?" Martha said. "I see I'm not the only one telling on myself today. So, how often do you read *our* mail?"

Chapter Thirteen

The Gardins observed Christmas Eve by serving the community, like the generations that preceded them. The tradition began in the early years after Edin was founded, when Gardin family members and the other founders shared each other's problems daily in an effort to build and maintain the community. As the town grew and families became more independent and successful, the Gardins pledged not to forget their humble beginnings. They became more intentional about continuing the family's legacy of service. They chose Christmas Eve as an annual day for collective service, a nod to the Nativity story and the faith that had sustained the family through ups and downs over the years.

Martha relished the opportunity to lead the family on Christmas Eve, but her motivation differed from that of her ancestors. She wasn't interested in connecting with her family members or maintaining the community. The service activity reflected her social-climbing interests. If she did a good job, the buzz would spread around town that she was the one to watch in the family. As a child, Martha admired the distinction her mother and grandmother enjoyed through their roles as full-time community volunteers. She aspired to take that status in the community to the next level. Although she enjoyed practicing medicine and took her responsibility seriously, she also viewed it as a conduit to the ranking in the family and community she believed was hers—the ranking currently occupied by Ruth. And she had no intention of allowing the challenges within her family to distract from her goals. Though Mary's health emergency had pulled Martha's focus away from Ruth, she had not forgotten the threat she believed Ruth posed. The service activity provided an unexpected opportunity to address the problem that took up so much space in her mind.

Martha had convinced the family to visit nursing home residents. The elders at Edin Family Village were enthusiastic about her theme for the afternoon: Caroling and Coloring. The nursing home was accustomed to caroling during the Christmas season, but Martha had expanded the activity to include coloring because it helped seniors with memory, positive thinking, and social skills.

She anticipated the event would go over well with the residents and staff, but she was more excited to see how her family would react to Nicholas, her surprise guest. She looked over at the center of the dining hall, where her sister directed clusters of residents in a rousing rendition of "Joy to the World." Mary sat instead of standing, so as not to overexert herself as her heart healed. But her exaggerated arm movements delighted the seniors as their voices layered like a seasoned glee club. As Mary cued the group to start the second verse, she blinked discreetly at Martha, slightly tilting her head in the direction of Naomi and Nicholas.

Martha followed Mary's gaze. Naomi giggled as she circulated the room, ensuring each table had enough adult coloring books, crayons, and coloring pencils. Nicholas followed closely behind her, with a smile as big as the crate of coloring supplies he carried. Their hands collided as Naomi pointed out which supplies should be added to the table. Martha read their lips.

"Sorry," Naomi said, blushing.

"Oh, it's my pleasure," Nicholas said, raising his eyebrows.

Their conversation was cut short by the laughter and applause erupting around the room. But as the song ended and Mary feigned exhaustion from her dramatic choral directing, Martha resumed her surveillance. Nicholas placed the box of supplies on the table near the refreshments. He said something to Naomi, but Martha couldn't make out the words. Naomi nodded as she and Nicholas exchanged grins.

Martha heard a disturbance at an adjacent table, drawing her attention back to the residents. "No you don't! That's the coloring sheet I wanted!" a woman said as she snatched an open adult coloring book from a woman sitting next to her in an identical red sweater with colorful ornaments and bells strung across it. Martha knew the Smith sisters well. Mildred, the older sister, had been Martha's middle school music teacher. Geraldine, two years younger than her sister, had taught Mary home economics when Mary was in high school. Their ancestors, also founders of Edin, were included in Martha's favorite painting at the Edin Inn, and their nieces and nephews held a variety of leadership positions across the county and state. Martha expected to hear from them if she kept their aunts happy at the service event. Ever the social climber, she would cherish having the chance for face time with the most influential people in the community.

"Ms. Geraldine, how about you let your sister have that one? We have another sheet like it. I'll get the coloring book for you," Martha said.

"You always give my sister what she wants," Geraldine said, sliding the book to her left.

"Yes, ma'am, I do, but sometimes big sisters deserve a break," Martha teased.

"You're right." Geraldine laughed.

Mildred smiled. "Thank you, Martha. That's why you're my favorite too."

Martha walked toward the bookcase at the front of the room that held the coloring supplies. Mary looked up from a neighboring table, where she sat with four residents who colored pictures of poinsettias and snowmen while they discussed which Christmas song the group should sing next. As Martha passed by, she whispered in Mary's ear, "I wonder if their ancestors squabbled like this when they settled in Edin."

"Probably," Mary said, then laughed. "That's going to be us one day."

"It sure will!" Martha said.

Martha walked over to the bookcase where Ruth thumbed through additional coloring books to bring back to her table. She watched her pick up several books and add them to the stack she cradled in her arms. As Ruth turned to head back across the room, Martha arrived at the bookcase. "Hey, Ruth, have you got a second?" Martha asked, her voice as upbeat as the tempo of the Christmas carols.

Martha noticed Ruth hesitate, inching back to the table and pulling the books toward her. "Sure," Ruth said, then smiled, but the lack of wrinkles around her eyes communicated that her expression wasn't authentic. "The seniors are getting into the holiday spirit. Nice job."

Martha enjoyed seeing the strained smile on Ruth's face. She suspected that Nicholas's presence had something to do with it. "It's about giving back during the Christmas season, right?" Martha said.

"Yes, of—"

"Sorry to cut you off," Martha said brusquely, "but I've got to rush back to my table. Ms. Geraldine threw a fit over a specific coloring sheet. You just picked up the book that has it. That one on top—do you mind if I take it?"

"No problem," Ruth said. She sat the books on the table, and Martha snatched the one she needed from the top of the stack before Ruth could hand it to her. Ruth winced.

"Thanks. It looks like Nicholas is having a good time too," Martha said with a mischievous grin.

"Indeed. . . . I still don't understand how he ended up here. Did y'all exchange phone numbers or something?" Ruth asked.

"No, but that's a good idea. I'll be sure to get his phone number before he gets back on the road. I bumped into him at Stuckey's when I ran in there for a quick snack. You know how I love their peanut rolls," Martha said, intent on dragging the story out to torture Ruth for as long as possible. "Did you know Nicholas has family in Statesboro? He flew into Atlanta this morning and stopped at the gas station to check the tire on his rental car on his way to spend Christmas with his family. I invited him to drop in and say hello. I didn't think he'd show up, but he did."

Ruth shrugged. "He's a nice guy, so it's not such a big surprise."

"I don't know. He seems to be into Aunt Naomi. I think that's why he came," Martha said, gloating.

"No. I can't imagine that."

"I sure can, but here comes Aunt Naomi. You can find out for yourself."

Martha wondered how Ruth had missed the sparks flying between Naomi and Nicholas, but she was convinced Ruth wouldn't be able to deny it once she stood face-to-face with Naomi. Though Martha had invited Nicholas to get under Ruth's skin, his interaction with Naomi was an unintended bonus.

Naomi strolled up to the bookcase, her face glowing like an LED billboard advertising a pizza sale after a sporting event. "This may be the best Christmas Eve activity we've done in years! You've done a lovely job, Martha."

"Thank you! I'm pleased you're enjoying it, maybe even more than the residents." Martha gave a hearty laugh.

"What do you mean by that?" Naomi asked, then smiled.

"I saw you making sweet eyes at Nicholas. Isn't that what y'all used to call it back in the day?" Martha said, fluttering her eyelashes.

Naomi squealed. Her shoulders rose, nearly touching her ear-lobes as she covered her face. "Stop teasing me! He's gonna look over here. I'm so embarrassed."

Ruth looked at Martha. "Oh my goodness! You're right. . . . I . . . I would've never guessed. Look at her—she's giddy."

"It's not a big deal. He's nice . . . and I like talking to him, that's all," Naomi said. She bit her lower lip in an attempt to force her facial muscles to relax, but the smile kept reappearing on her face.

"This is cute," Martha said.

Ruth folded her arms. "Umm-hmmm."

"He asked me to join him for a walk after we finish here," Naomi said, grinning.

Martha gasped. "Are you gonna go?"

"I think so." Naomi blushed.

* * *

A LATE-AFTERNOON STROLL in the Edin historic district sounded like a good idea when Nicholas asked, but ninety minutes later, Naomi wasn't so sure. The rush of adrenaline she'd experienced talking to Nicholas at the nursing home had dissipated. It would have been so much simpler if she'd gone home after the coloring activity. By this hour, she and Ruth could be watching Christmas movies and drinking hibiscus tea under their matching blankets. Instead, she was stuck on an uncomfortable date with a man who held the future of her family in his hands. Naomi wasn't sure if spending time with Nicholas was a potential conflict of interest, but she figured Ruth and her nieces would've said some-thing if they thought it was a problem. However, now Naomi was the one who felt conflicted.

Naomi expected the streets to be busy and full of excitement, like in Christmas TV movies when a couple in winter coats walk arm in arm down the sidewalk, gazing into each other's eyes. But the temperature in Edin was in the sixties, and she and Nicholas walked along an empty sidewalk with an awkwardly large space between them. She wore a lightweight sweater that transitioned well between the weather fluctuations becoming more common during Georgia winters. Its crew neck fell slightly off the shoulder, connecting to batwing sleeves that tapered at the wrist. Paired with comfortable slacks of the same color, the black sweater made her feel like she looked good even if she didn't really think she did.

Nicholas was too busy rambling to notice Naomi staring down at the sidewalk as she tried to figure a way out of the date. Only when she recounted the time they spent together at the nursing home and during Mary's health emergency did she realize they had never been alone before. Naomi hadn't accounted for that when she agreed to the outing. She had also forgotten that most people in Edin were spending time with family during a late afternoon on Christmas Eve, not wandering aimlessly around town with someone they barely knew. The historic district was usually busy, but there was only a handful of small specialty shops and toy stores open on Christmas Eve. Naomi loved to shop, but she didn't bother asking if Nicholas wanted to stop in any of the stores. He didn't strike her as the kind of guy who liked shopping.

Naomi and Nicholas turned onto Jefferson Franklin Long Avenue. She usually bubbled with pride whenever she saw the street sign with Long's name. She always appreciated that the streets of Edin were named after important figures. She loved the reminder every time she was downtown, like this street that was named for the person who made history in 1870 as Georgia's first African American congressman and the first African American member of Congress to speak on the floor of the U.S. House of Representatives. But even the notable history didn't help. She was distracted by the sense that she'd made a mistake with Nicholas. She started to question everything about the afternoon. Maybe she'd misinterpreted his intentions. What if this wasn't a date at all? And if it was a date, how could she consider long-distance dating at her age? She was almost seventy years old. What kind of relationship started off in a nursing home, especially when you were both almost old enough to be in one?

Naomi kicked a pebble on the ground. "Maybe this little outing would've been better on a different day. This part of town is usually lively, with things to see and talk about."

"Oh," Nicholas said, tilting his head and furrowing his brow. "I assume that means you aren't enjoying the conversation. . . . Now that I think about it, I've been the only one talking. I've been running my mouth nonstop. . . . I'm sorry."

She lifted her head and looked up at him. She felt guilty that she may have hurt his feelings, but it was overshadowed by self-doubt. "What is this supposed to be? I mean, what are we doing?"

"Let's start over," he said, staring into her eyes.

"Huh?" She squinted. Nicholas stood a foot above Naomi, but the sincerity in his eyes was as palpable as if they stood eye to eye.

"Look, we had a good time at the nursing home. I don't know what happened or how I messed up, but I see that it's not sitting well with you. So let's reset and try again."

"That's it? We just start over?" Naomi let out a laugh so loud that it set off an echo as they walked past the alley behind the hardware store.

"Why not?" A smile spread across Nicholas's face like he'd heard a brilliant idea that he'd been waiting for his whole life.

"What makes you think you messed up? How do you know it wasn't *my* fault?"

"Because, my dear, you have a graceful and magnetic quality

about you and a compass that leads you in the direction you're supposed to go. There's no messing up in that."

Naomi laughed even harder. "What are you talking about? Are you trying to charm me?"

"That wasn't my intention at all. Well, I probably said it in a charming way, because I'm a suave and debonair kind of guy, right?" he teased.

"Cute," Naomi said, fiddling with the gold stud earring in her right ear.

"But I was serious," Nicholas said matter-of-factly as he touched Naomi's shoulder. "I'm not trying to say things to make you feel good. That's just the way I see you."

Naomi's eyes widened and she looked away. "That's sweet, but I can't live up to that," she said, struggling to process what was happening.

"I'm not asking you to live up to anything. I want you to be yourself. I'm just telling you what I see and that I like what I see."

"I appreciate that. Thank you. . . . I suppose you have seen me at my worst."

"Your worst? You mean with Mary's illness?"

"Yes. That was scary."

"It was, but it looks like she's doing better now. Besides, you weren't paying me any attention when we were first introduced at the Christmas party, which was before Mary got sick."

Naomi grinned. "Should I have been?"

"Yes, of course!" He laughed. "No, I'm kidding. There's a time for everything. It's attractive that you were doing your own thing. You couldn't wait to get on the dance floor, and you didn't let me distract you. I love that. Like I said, you follow your compass. Speaking of which, are you feeling better now?"

"I do. I feel much better. The day slowed down and I started overthinking things. I do that sometimes. . . . There's been a lot going on. . . . In our family, you know. . . . And when things are going a hundred miles an hour, I don't always notice details. But when it slows down, I can be a little . . . uh . . ."

"Dramatic, maybe?"

Naomi planted her feet on the sidewalk. "Did you call me dramatic, Nicholas? You just met me."

He stood beside her. "I recall seeing some hints of drama, but if I thought it was a bad thing, I would be in Statesboro right now. I didn't go to the nursing home today because I wanted to color and sing Christmas carols. I wanted to see you."

The words took Naomi by surprise. "I didn't expect to hear that," she said, her voice softening. On the surface, Nicholas hadn't come across as the kind of man who would tolerate her fiery personality, much less enjoy it. But she realized that she had misjudged him. Mary's illness had allowed Nicholas to see vulnerabilities that Naomi hid from people outside the family, even lifelong friends. She didn't let many people get too close, because she feared they might see her as volatile and unpoised. But Nicholas had slipped in and fit with her family seamlessly during their most vulnerable time. He was unflustered by her outbursts, and he could already distinguish when to respond and when it was more appropriate to let it go.

She wondered if it had been so easy for him to move past the coolness she'd initially shown him because he had been protecting himself in a similar way. Was that why he'd been so chatty at the beginning of their date—because he'd become so smitten with her that she made him nervous too?

"Okey dokey. So we're good?" Nicholas smiled.

Naomi smiled too. "I think so," she said, nodding.

He touched her forearm gently, guiding her to resume the walk. "C'mon."

As they turned onto Gardin Avenue, Naomi loosened up. She entertained Nicholas with stories of her grandparents' efforts to raise four children while trying to turn their peanut farming into a profitable business and her father's insightful decision to save the historic church that now served as the company headquarters. A proficient tour guide, Naomi pointed out historical landmarks: the town's original post office, which was now a small museum, and the first school in Edin, now a community center. Nicholas was awed by the wealth of history, and Naomi gladly expounded.

"Edin was founded in 1889, after most of the white population had left to move to cities where railroad stops were being built. Previously enslaved people moved here from Savannah because they didn't get the land they were promised there. They moved more and more inland in search of work and came across some abandoned land on the outskirts of the county. They cleared it and slowly built it into a town. The founders organized themselves for the sake of protection, and that structure worked for generations. I took it for granted that I felt safe in Edin when I was a little girl. But as I got older, I noticed the differences when we traveled out of town. And I learned about so many more dangers other Black children faced every day growing up in Georgia and across the South. It's a different time now, but the strong bonds in our community remain and help keep us safe. We still look out for one another. We have to."

"That helps me to understand your family business so much better," Nicholas said. "There's a strong complement between the history of Edin and the company's principles of collective work and responsibility, unity, and cooperative economics."

"Good!" Naomi said. "Those are key to our company's survival, as well as to our family's. But we're still working on them on a personal level. We have to get it right, especially since our family is so small now."

"Understanding your history can reveal a lot about your future," Nicholas asserted.

"So true." She wondered about his past, but she didn't know how to ask about it. "There's something I want to know, but I don't want to offend you."

"I'm not easily offended. Go for it."

"Okay. What's your story? Your work takes you from city to city. You must have a string of women across the country waiting for you to come back to their town."

"Oh no. I used to be that type of guy a long time ago, but I asked myself some tough questions about who I wanted to be. Then I settled down and got closer to God. My wife, Virginia, traveled with me until she died three years ago. We were married forty-five years. We never had kids, but I'm close to my nieces and nephews in Statesboro." Nicholas put his hands in his pockets. "And . . . I wasn't going to say anything, but this is my first date since she passed away." He blushed.

"Is it? It's my first date too! But it's been longer than three years for me."

"How long?"

"I'm too embarrassed to say," Naomi protested.

"Don't try to act shy now. It's way too late for that." He laughed.

Naomi laughed too, pinching his arm playfully. "Okay . . . twenty-seven years," she said, burying her face in her hands.

"Twenty-seven years," Nicholas said, wrinkling his forehead. "I'd never have guessed that, but I'm glad you shared it with me. It makes sense now. No wonder you're a little freaked out. I'm honored you feel comfortable spending time with me."

"Well, I'm honored you asked me out." Naomi smiled. She looked at Nicholas and then averted her eyes, pretending to look at the Christmas window display as they walked past the pharmacy. "It's gonna get cool soon. Do you want to grab coffee or tea before we head back?"

"Hot chocolate would be nice. If I didn't have to head to

Statesboro tonight, I would try to convince you to watch Christmas movies with me. That's what you're supposed to do on Christmas Eve—drink hot chocolate and watch Christmas movies."

Naomi giggled. "There's a coffee shop a few blocks away, around this corner. It should still be open."

As they turned the corner onto Savannah Lane, Nicholas wrapped his hand around Naomi's. Her hand fit neatly inside his. With Nicholas around, Naomi felt as though Gardin Family Enterprises would be in good hands—and that she would be too. She wasn't sure how long it would last, but she decided she wanted to enjoy it for as long as she could.

Chapter Fourteen

Naomi finished typing the last few characters of her text message and hit send. *I'm not worried. Everyone will behave. Christmas is a day of reverence,* her message said. She appreciated Nicholas's concern, but nothing was going to ruin her high. She'd waited all year to experience the joy of Christmas morning, and this year her mood had gotten an extra boost from her delightful Christmas Eve date.

Naomi treasured the family's tradition of meeting for brunch at her cottage after Christmas morning church service. She cooked the same thing every year: french toast, vegetable frittata, roasted potatoes, cheese grits, and sweet potato pie. Although the meal looked laborious spread across the dining room table, it was easy to prepare. She liked it that way. The harder it appeared she'd worked on a meal, the more her family would appreciate it. But one date with Nicholas had offered Naomi a different lens through which she could see her life. He made her wonder if she should take a more laid-back approach. Every time Nicholas was around, her life felt less complicated. She liked that too.

As she eyed the timer, Naomi recalled how Nicholas had walked her back to her car the evening before. She couldn't stop replaying their interactions in her head, from their first meeting to the last second of their date. As soon as she got inside her car, she called Ruth to get her perspective, but Ruth didn't pick up. And she never returned the call. Naomi had resisted the urge to call again or drop by Ruth's house. She wondered what would happen if, for the first time in years, she didn't pull Ruth into her relationships with others.

Ruth's avoidance was already turning out to be a gift. In a family where everyone expected to know everything about each other's lives, it was refreshing to keep something important to herself. Naomi wanted to savor every moment, because once the can was opened, she wouldn't be able to stuff its contents back inside. Even though her eyes had been closed for eight hours the night before, she felt as though she'd been awake analyzing the possibilities of her new relationship all night. She was sure she would crash after her carbohydrate-rich meal, but for now she was a ball of energy.

Naomi removed the last piece of french toast from the stove and placed it atop the shiny white platter, completing a carefully crafted ring. She tucked strawberries and fresh mint around the decadent baguette slices to create an illusion of a Christmas wreath. *It's Christmas Day. A splurge is okay,* she thought as she added a finishing sprinkle of powdered sugar to finish her platter of perfection. She liked her french toast on the darker side, and Ruth teased that it meant she liked it burnt, but Naomi had perfected her recipe over the years so that the bread achieved just the right amount of crunch on the outside without drying out internally. Ruth could needle her all she wanted. Naomi paid no attention because Ruth never left a morsel of the toast on her plate, and neither did Mary or Martha.

"The food is ready!" Naomi yelled, walking down the hallway to the dining room. As she entered the room, she noticed an identical red gift bag on each of the dining chairs. *This is gonna be interesting,* she thought, placing the platter between the roasted red potatoes and vegetable frittata. Then she grabbed the present at her spot, put it under her chair, and took her seat.

Ruth, Mary, and Martha filed into the room moments later. Mary rubbed her palms together as she crossed the threshold.

"Ooh! I can never get enough of the sweet smell of the cara-
melized sugar. I've been thinking about your french toast all
week!"

"Me too!" Martha exclaimed as she settled into her seat. "I
can't wait to dig in. And gifts, too? Aunt Naomi, you're too good
to us! But didn't we agree that we weren't going to exchange gifts
this year?"

"I can only claim responsibility for the food," Naomi said,
smiling, "but I put all my love into it."

"Oh, I can tell you did. The food looks delicious!" Martha
turned to face her sister. "Aww, Mary, I hope you didn't spend all
your big payday on us. You didn't need to do anything."

Mary shook her head. "They're not from me. I planned to
treat y'all to a spa day, but I didn't go shopping. Aside from going
to the nursing home yesterday, I've been resting all week. Doctor's orders, remember?"

"They're from me. It's just a little something," Ruth said with
a joyous grin. She lowered her head and avoided looking across
the table at Martha. "But we should eat before the food gets
cold. Who's saying grace?"

"I will, of course," Naomi said. She joined hands with Martha and Ruth as she closed her eyes and bowed her head. "Dear
God, we thank You for the opportunity to come together to celebrate the majesty of this day. We ask for Your grace and mercy
as we endeavor to represent You in all our actions." She squeezed
Martha's and Ruth's hands tightly. "And we pray that You will
bless this food so that our bodies will be nourished and our souls
uplifted. Amen."

"Amen," echoed Mary and Ruth.

"Amen," Martha mumbled. She released Naomi's and Mary's
hands and grabbed the frittata dish.

Mary put three slices of french toast on her plate and drizzled
them with warm maple syrup. "It's good you only make this once

a year, because I would eat it every day if I could. I need boundaries."

"The version of it you serve in the restaurant is so good, but mine may have a few more calories." Naomi smiled as she reached for one of the bowls stacked next to the tureen of cheese grits.

"A few?" Mary teased as she added potatoes to her plate. "You're just being nice. Even when I use your original recipe, your version is still better than mine. But you're in a peachy mood today, Aunt Naomi. Is there anything you'd like to tell us?" she prodded.

Naomi recognized her cue to dish about her date, but she deflected. "It's Christmas. I'm always happy on Christmas Day."

Martha perked up. "Yes! Tell us about your date with jolly old Saint Nicholas," she joked. She unfolded her arms and reached for some french toast.

"Fine, fine." Naomi giggled, remembering her plan to be direct and brief. "It was rough at first. We were both nervous, but we adjusted and ended up having a good time. We just walked around and then went for hot chocolate. . . . Well, he had hot chocolate, and I had hibiscus tea. . . . It was nice."

"So, do you think he's gonna call you today?" Martha asked, leaning into the table.

"He already did, and we texted too," Naomi replied, scooping a heap of frittata onto her plate.

"Really? How are you gonna handle it the next time he comes for a consulting visit?" Martha pried.

"I don't understand what you mean. He'll do his work. I suppose we'll go out or something before he leaves town, if his schedule allows. But I'm not thinking that far ahead. We're taking it slow." Naomi promised herself she would be less obvious the next time she grilled Martha for information on her romantic life.

Ruth shot Naomi a look that she couldn't ignore and said, "Wait a second. Taking it slow? So this is a thing between the two of you?"

Naomi stared back at Ruth. "We're just enjoying each other's company. Is that a problem?"

Ruth straightened her back in the chair. "I wouldn't call it a problem, but I'm not comfortable with it. We discourage workplace romances at the company."

"Is that a new rule, or was it in place when you first moved here? You know, when Aunt Naomi got you a consulting contract at the company and then you started dating Beau?" Martha snickered.

Ruth slammed the serving spoon into the potatoes.

Mary swallowed a mouthful of food. "Martha, it's Christmas. Baby Jesus is still in the manger. At least wait until tomorrow for this," she said with edge in her voice.

Martha tipped the carafe of orange juice and filled her glass to the brim. She lowered her head and sipped until the liquid was low enough not to spill when she raised the glass. "It's a fair question. I just want to make sure I understand the workplace policies."

Naomi froze. Her efforts to step away from her family's drama and do something for herself had somehow landed her in the center of a new storm. *I just can't get a break,* she thought. Her euphoria had initially blinded her to Martha's seemingly innocuous question about Nicholas's next consulting visit. But now she recognized the covert attack on Ruth and her own subsequent status as an unintended casualty. Martha was an arsonist who blended in so well when she set a fire that no one noticed—she simply faded into the background and watched it burn like a Yule log. Though Martha had been the instigator, Naomi wouldn't allow Ruth's friendly fire to go unchecked.

"I don't work at Gardin Family Enterprises," Naomi said. "I

never have, so the policies don't apply to me. But, Ruth, if you had an issue with this, I wish you'd have spoken up sooner."

"When was I supposed to do that?" Ruth asked.

Naomi rubbed her chin. "That's a reasonable question. I didn't realize what was happening. Everything went pretty fast."

"Well, thanks for admitting—"

"Admitting what? I didn't do anything wrong," Naomi declared.

"You just admitted the relationship is happening fast, but a second ago you said y'all are gonna take it slow. So which is it, MIL?" Ruth asked.

"You can call it whatever you want. Nicholas and I had fun together, and he's coming back for New Year's Eve. So if you can't handle it, don't come to watch-night service. We'll be there, and we may stay for the party that follows." She never missed the service commemorating the night before the Emancipation Proclamation went into effect. In keeping with the tradition started by free Blacks and enslaved people on New Year's Eve in 1863, Naomi looked forward to gathering with her church to pray from shortly before midnight until just afterward. And she could already tell that she was going to need special prayers for the upcoming year.

"Aww! You two are going to ring in the new year together! How adorable!" Mary cooed.

Ruth cut her eyes at Mary as she shuffled the potatoes on her plate.

"C'mon, Ruth. You have to admit it's cute," Mary said.

We are cute. Since it's out on the table now, why shouldn't I enjoy it? "Yeah, I'm excited about seeing Nicholas again," Naomi gushed. "He was planning to stay in Statesboro until New Year's Day, but now he'll drive here on New Year's Eve and then go to Atlanta to catch his flight back to Philadelphia the next day."

"And where is he staying when he comes back to town?" Ruth asked.

"Excuse me? He's staying the same place he stays when he comes to town for work—the Edin Inn. But I don't like where you're trying to go with this," Naomi warned.

Ruth recoiled. "I didn't mean to offend you, MIL."

"I'm trying to hold on to my Christmas joy, but the two of you are pushing me," Naomi said, pointing back and forth between Ruth and Martha. "I don't understand why we can't have a peaceful gathering, especially on Christmas."

"I've barely said anything during this entire conversation. I'm trying to get along with everyone," Martha said, feigning innocence. "I was just trying to get clarity on Ruth's understanding of company rules and whether they apply to *her*. It's important that people respect the norms that are agreed upon—company rules, decisions about buying each other Christmas gifts. . . . You know, things like that. I'm just trying to get a clear understanding for the future, that's all." But the politeness of her tone couldn't mask the bite of her words.

"I've had enough," Naomi snapped, popping up from her seat. She snatched the platter of french toast from the center of the table, sending the three remaining slices to the opposite end of the dish as she headed for the doorway.

Martha looked down at her plate, pouting like a toddler who was sent to the corner for a time-out.

Mary rolled her eyes at her sister.

Ruth picked up her and Naomi's half-eaten plates, grabbed their silverware, and followed her mother-in-law. "Good job, Martha. You have to learn when to stop," Ruth sneered while walking past her.

As Naomi made a break for the kitchen, she wondered what was going through Ruth's mind. But she didn't feel the usual internal pull to defend her daughter-in-law. She wasn't sure when it had dissipated, but it was gone. And she didn't feel guilty about it. It had been a long time since she'd spent time with a man she liked. *Why should I let my family mess this up?* she thought.

* * *

MARY GLARED AT Martha. After their breakthrough at the hospital, she'd believed her sister would behave differently. But now Mary felt as though she'd been tricked. She refused to tuck away her anger. She had come too far to let Martha cause an emotional or physical setback. "I can't believe you've carried on like this. You saw a chasm developing between Aunt Naomi and Ruth, and you just couldn't help yourself. And on Christmas Day too!"

"Why are you blaming me for their issues?" Martha asked coyly.

"You drove Aunt Naomi and Ruth out of the room and you're not fazed."

Martha leaned back in her chair. "I was just trying to help you and Aunt Naomi see Ruth for who she is," she said without remorse.

"What are you doing to our family?" Mary asked, squinting her eyes as her voice cracked under the weight of disappointment.

"Don't look at me like that," Martha said, lowering her head.

"You're coming to see Shari with me on Monday. I'm not accepting any excuses. And since you ruined our meal, I'm taking your share of the sweet potato pie home with me. Aunt Naomi is not going to bring it out here, and I'm not letting you go into the kitchen since you're acting like a fool."

"But—"

"No, Martha. This is serious."

"Fine," Martha replied, reaching for the gift bag she had

tucked under her seat. "Let me see what kind of bribe Ruth came up with."

Mary shot her another look. "With all the arguing, I forgot about opening the present. Yours is probably a lump of coal. That's what I'd have given you if I were Ruth," she said, reaching under the table for her bag.

Martha rested the bag on the table and pulled out a black satin drawstring pouch. She loosened the top and peeked inside. "A gold picture frame. How thoughtful," she said sarcastically. She closed the pouch without giving it a second look.

Mary mirrored her sister's initial actions, but she opened the top of the satin pouch and placed the picture frame on the table. "There's a photo inside. It's of the four of us at the Christmas Party, holding hands. What a lovely gift!"

"You're always so gullible. Don't fall for Ruth's trickery," Martha said, tossing the pouch into the gift bag.

Mary took a breath. "I've been trying to stay out of the mess between you and Ruth, but keeping quiet about the things weighing on me is a big part of how I ended up hospitalized. It shouldn't be this difficult to spend time with one's family. Today was another example of why I leave all our family gatherings early, and it's why I moved to New York." Her words came out faster than she intended, but it felt good to release something she'd held in for so long.

"You're blaming me for your decision to move to New York?"

"I'll just say that I didn't have to deal with your constant selfishness and negativity as much when we lived in different zip codes."

"Then go back to New York. You have money now, so what's holding you here?" Martha snapped.

Instead of letting Martha's bitterness force her to lash out, Mary tried to be practical in communicating with her sister. "I'm still thinking about what I'm going to do about Tynan, but I'm not necessarily thinking about going to New York. I need to weigh my options. Maybe I'll move to Macon. You and I haven't discussed it yet, but I've been talking to Oji Greenwald about opening a restaurant in the new medical complex."

Fury spread across Martha's face. "Oji Greenwald? I invited him to the Christmas party because I have an idea for a restaurant in his development. How dare you try to steal this opportunity from me!"

Mary's jaw dropped. She had wanted to make the decision about opening a new restaurant on her own, without Martha trying to influence her. Because Martha had begun offering healthful-cooking classes through the hospital's primary care center, Mary expected her to be upset that she hadn't told her about the restaurant being on her turf, but Mary hadn't considered that Martha could be interested in the opportunity for herself.

"So, I see I'm not the only one who's keeping secrets," Mary said. Her sister's admission showed Mary that their problems were deeper than she'd realized. While Mary had never looked at her sister as competition, it was obvious that Martha must not see their relationship the same way. The judgment and entitlement Mary suffered at the hands of her sister suddenly took on a different hue. "I didn't steal anything from you. I didn't know Oji before meeting him at the party, and I didn't know about the development until he mentioned it. I'm not calculating like you, Martha. You've never mentioned anything about opening a restaurant. How was I supposed to know? If you'd told me, I wouldn't have entertained any discussion about it, but now it's too late."

"Too late? So it's already decided? It's not fair! I'm a better cook than you are, and you don't employ the strategy that I do. You just show up and everything you want falls into your lap," Martha said haughtily.

"I'm just lucky? You think it's that simple, huh? Nothing falls into my lap. Sure, your culinary medicine certification is fancier than the cooking workshops I've taken, and I don't know anyone more skillful than you are at getting what they want. You're better than I am at lots of stuff, but you don't connect with people. You're motivated by the wrong things—power, getting attention, accomplishments. Nobody likes you. You don't even like yourself. I work hard, and I connect with people. That's how I get ahead."

"Wow, Mary! This is how you treat me after everything I've done for you?"

"This is exactly what I mean. Why do you have to remind people of what you've done? Ruth has done a lot for us, and she never throws it in our faces, even when we deserve it. I paid back the money you lent me when I first moved here, and now I'm about to pay off my loan for the restaurant. I hope you can finally see that I'm not the loser that you've made me out to be."

Martha gasped. "I never said you were a loser."

"Don't play games with me, Martha. Your actions and snide remarks over the years have communicated exactly how you feel about me. Just because I didn't call it out doesn't mean I didn't notice. I hoped that you would one day see that I am just as successful as you are."

"That's what I was trying to say. I—"

Mary shook her head and frowned. "No, Martha. After my health issues and the promise you made to do better, I wouldn't have guessed you would act like this on Christmas Day. You are so selfish."

Martha's forehead scrunched. "But I—"

"Let me speak. I've held this in for long enough. I should've said it after I got out of the hospital, but I let it go. It's time I got it out. Did you ever take a second to process the fact that Tynan stole my entire allotment from the trust? I didn't waste it, like you thought I did. I saved it. I had a plan for it." Mary scowled.

"Just because you aren't aware of my plans doesn't mean they don't exist. I started Alabaster Lunch Box because it was my dream—a dream I was about to make a reality in Brooklyn on my own. I had to regain my footing when I came back home, but I did it. I dusted myself off and made some revisions to my plan for the restaurant to make it appropriate for Edin. You didn't lend me the money to open up the restaurant. You didn't even offer. I got a loan on my own, and look at me now. Somehow you've convinced yourself that you're responsible for my success, but you're not. I built my restaurant on my ideas and my sweat."

Mary rested her elbows on the table and stretched her arms up in the air. "Why do you feel like you have to tear me down to build yourself up? I pity you. That's why I put up with the way you've treated me. You needed to feel worthwhile, so I let you beat me up. But how can you object to Tynan tearing me down, when you do the same thing?" Mary slammed her open hand on the table. She could feel the wood reverberate against it. "I'm done, Martha."

Martha stood up. She avoided making eye contact with Mary as she reached for the serving tray closest to her.

Silence. I guess I struck a chord, Mary thought. There was only one thing left to do. "No," she said coolly as she stood. "I'll clear the table. You need to go. I'm going to try to smooth things over with Ruth and Aunt Naomi, and it would be better if you weren't here."

Martha raised an eyebrow at her sister. "You can't throw me out. This isn't your house," she said defiantly.

Mary leaned across the table and looked Martha square in the eye. "Martha, I'm asking you nicely."

Martha slid her plate toward the center of the table and pushed her chair in. "Fine." She slipped out through the french doors leading to Naomi's backyard and left her Christmas present from Ruth on the dining room table.

Chapter Fifteen

Mary enjoyed the peace of being home alone on Christmas afternoon. After arriving at her cottage, she ate another slice of sweet potato pie and then took a nap. She felt lighter since her exchange with Martha, and she wanted more of that feeling. Although Mary had been reluctant to restart counseling before her hospitalization, her ability to be transparent with her sister a few hours earlier made her more grateful for her last counseling session than she'd felt on the day she left the hospital. The session had prepared her for the unexpected spat, and she was proud of the way she'd handled her sister. Now she was primed to face Tynan.

Mary had texted Tynan as soon as she pulled her golf cart into her driveway. *When you've been running from drama and then someone else's mess splashes on you, you might as well clean up the chaos in your own life, because you're already dirty,* she had thought as she waited for his response.

Tynan replied within a few minutes and agreed to a Skype call. That didn't surprise Mary. For as long as they had been together, he was ambivalent about the holidays. They were a time to catch up on work and sleep while everyone else celebrated. Mary wondered if that had changed over the time they'd spent apart, but she didn't intend to ask him about that. Other things were far more important.

After her post-hospitalization retreat, Mary had conducted an exhaustive internet search and talked to Tynan's lawyer. He explained why Tynan had disappeared, and Mary made some assumptions about her ex-fiancé's decision not to endanger his safety or hers by informing her of the investigation before he left. But he still needed to account for his actions.

Mary scrolled through the note saved on her cell phone. The list of questions she had prepared during her last therapy session was longer than she'd remembered. She was determined to make it through all of them regardless of the tricks Tynan tried. She wasn't interested in sharing her thoughts with him. She just wanted answers.

Mary felt calm as she sat at the desk of the makeshift office in her sunroom, contemplating the best way to proceed with the call. She walked across the room and rummaged through the plastic storage boxes in the corner until she found an old composition notebook that she'd used as a journal when she first moved back to Edin. There was a legal pad in the top drawer of her small writing desk, but she felt compelled to record the next chapter of her story in the same notebook where she'd written her thoughts at the start of her journey.

Mary flipped past weeks of daily musings and drawings until she reached an empty page. She turned to the previous page to find her last journal entry, a poem. As she read it aloud, her legs jittered from the pressure the words carried.

An empty apartment
Partial conversations
Running through my mind
Fragments of a sentence
A complex one
A clause
Missing its conjunction
You left me with nothing
And memories
Are all that remain
Of this unfinished love

Mary's heart raced. Despite the excitement she had experienced at brunch, this was the first time she felt anxious the entire day. *I guess it's not a good time to read this.* She closed her eyes and took three deep breaths. As she inhaled and exhaled, she bowed her head and responded aloud to the fears that popped into her mind. "I have control of this situation. I can end the call whenever I feel like it. I can end the call if he crosses the boundaries I set."

Then she prayed silently. *Dear God, thank You for allowing me to see the progress I've made. Thank You for the peace that lies on the other side of the call I'm about to make. I pray for Your guidance, and I ask that the small morsel of courage I feel right now grows and remains greater than any fear that may arise. In Jesus's name, amen.*

Mary opened her eyes. She removed the piece of tape covering her laptop's webcam and initiated the call.

"Hi, Mary," Tynan said. Never shy in front of a camera, he looked as good on Mary's laptop screen as he did in person. His mastery of which angles suited his chiseled face took Mary back to their frequent FaceTime calls during their early courtship. She had believed him when he'd said that he wanted to see her enchanting smile, but when she showed up early at his job one day to meet him for lunch, she'd caught him explaining to one of his direct reports that looking good on video calls at the beginning of a relationship helps endear the person to you long term.

Butterflies whirled in her stomach. She kicked herself for failing to prepare for Tynan's charming demeanor, but her need to see his face and hear him explain his life-changing choices overrode the attraction she still felt toward him.

"Hi, Ty. Thanks for being willing to take my call today. I wasn't sure if you had plans."

He shrugged. "I was just working. I have so much to catch up on since coming back."

I've really missed him. . . . But I have to pull myself together, Mary thought. She forced herself to focus on what he was saying.

"I'm relieved to hear from you. I didn't expect you to reach out on Christmas. I know how important this day is to you and your family. I worried you might not reach out at all, so I . . . I'm very thankful." Tynan paused, seeming to search for something to say. "I tried your sister a few times, but—"

"She blocked you."

"I thought she'd come around, but I guess I was wrong. Do you know your family blames me for your being hospitalized? I told them I didn't do anything. Oh, but you're okay, right? You look great now. What happened? How are you feeling?"

Mary wished he had asked how she was doing *before* he tried to clear his name, but the sincerity in his voice pulled at her heartstrings. She stayed strong. "I'm doing much better, thanks. I don't want to talk about myself, but I'd like to ask *you* some questions. There are things I need to know to be sure of what I want. Is that okay with you?"

A haughty smile crept onto Tynan's face. "Are you kidding?"

Deep down, Mary still found his arrogance attractive. *Don't do it. Don't fall for it. That's how he gets you.* She took a breath. "No, I'm very serious."

His smile disappeared. "This sounds like a deposition," he said brashly.

Okay, now we're back on track. Tynan's conceit always eventually went too far. Mary was grateful it helped her regain her footing. She stared blankly at him, channeling the look she used to give him when they played chess.

"That's cute and all, but you realize I'm a lawyer, right? You have no legal training, and you want to depose *me*?"

Mary didn't flinch. "According to my conversation with your lawyer, you've had multiple depositions during the investigation, so my questions shouldn't be difficult for you. But I hope that you will be honest. . . . What do you have to lose?"

Tynan grimaced. "What has happened to you since you've been back in Edin?"

Mary wanted to tell him that *he* was what happened. She wanted to say that her questions directly resulted from his behavior and that it had nothing to do with Edin. But she didn't. She couldn't risk an unproductive confrontation that would still leave her without answers. So she doubled down. "I can only continue this call if you're amenable to my requirements. I'd like to reiterate that I am not at liberty to answer questions at this time. I will continue to only ask questions."

Tynan sighed and shook his head. "Fine. Go ahead. Ask whatever you want."

"Where did you go when you left New York?"

"Custer, South Dakota."

Mary laughed. *He used to complain the entire winter in New York. He only tolerates it because he makes a lot of money there,* she thought. "Why South Dakota?"

"Yes, I despise the cold. I was miserable there from October through May. The Loughtys have some business there, and it's a perfect place to hide—money and people," he said, referencing the state's reputation for sprawling prairies, toppling mountains, and serving as a tax haven for the uber-rich. "I rented a cabin near the national forest. It was an economical place to have round-the-clock security."

"You needed security?"

"Yes, I had someone from a private security firm with me from the day I left New York until the day before I came to Edin. There's a lot that hasn't made it to the media about the investigation, but it was more dangerous than I can discuss."

"Why didn't you take me with you?"

"It was hard to guess how long I would be away, and I was

afraid you would change your mind and want to leave. I couldn't take that risk. I didn't tell anyone I was taking off. And you wouldn't have been able to tell anyone either. I didn't think you'd be willing to do that to your family, and I was afraid they would go to the police and file a missing-persons report. Then we would've had to figure out how to maneuver through that. And I didn't want to put you in jeopardy by telling you what was going on. I had no idea how bad things would get or who might be involved. I didn't want anyone finding out that you had information."

To anyone else, Tynan's explanation might have seemed farfetched, but Mary could imagine him alone for eighteen months without contacting anyone in his small circle of friends. *He probably didn't even talk to the security staff*, she thought.

When they first met, Mary didn't believe that Tynan liked her. He barely spoke to her on their dates. Yet at the end of each one, he would ask her out again. She accepted only because the dates were meticulously planned and he always had access to the best restaurants and events.

After a few months, Mary got bored and tried to break things off. She explained that he was emotionally distant and their relationship unfulfilling. Only then did he open up. He explained that he'd grown up in an abusive home. His mother had died when he was a teenager, and he had a strained relationship with his father, whom he hadn't seen since the day he left for college on his own. He'd excelled throughout college but never made close friends. Because his family had let him down, he'd never believed he could depend on someone he just met. After the confession, Mary felt like she could finally see the real Tynan. She understood what it was like to be without parents, but she still had Martha, Naomi, and Ruth. She couldn't imagine feeling truly alone in the world.

"Why did you steal my money?"

"I assumed you would know I was the one who took it and you would be okay with it. I figured your family would take care of you and that the missing money wouldn't have a big impact on your life. I had money in my accounts, but the investigators froze them. I had some money stashed in an offshore account, but I realized too late that it wouldn't be enough to sustain me if I was away for more than six months. So I used your money."

Mary's eyebrows lifted and her eyes widened. "But why didn't you just tell me?" she asked sternly.

"I didn't know I would need it before I left New York. And even if I had realized it, I didn't want to put you in danger by telling you anything—not before I got to South Dakota. Trust me, I've learned that I need to put more money offshore," Tynan replied, his voice stoic.

He's so cold, Mary thought. *The reasoning makes sense, but where is the apology? Where is the empathy? But that's fine. I know how to get him.* "That's what you learned? Do you realize it was illegal to steal my money and that I could press charges against you?"

Tynan leaned forward. "Are you recording this?"

Mary refused to deviate from her plan. His question offended her, she repeated the one she had already asked, her voice becoming icier with each word. "Do you realize it was illegal to steal my money and that I could press charges against you?"

Tynan didn't respond, so Mary repeated the question a third time. "Do you realize it was illegal to steal my money"—she raised her voice—"and that I could press charges against you?"

"Yes . . . but we're in this together. You're the only person I have in the world."

Mary thought she heard his voice break a little at the end of the sentence, but with the wave of emotion overtaking her, she wasn't sure.

Tynan continued, his voice stronger, like he got a second

wind. "We're a team. Remember the sweatshirt? $T.E.A.M.$—
Together Even Across Miles? You wouldn't press charges, would
you?"

The mention of her favorite sweatshirt brought tears to her
eyes. On their first dating anniversary, Tynan had two identical
sweatshirts made—one for Mary and one for him—so they
would still feel close to each other when he traveled for work.
Mary didn't know how she could've survived without it when
Tynan disappeared, but she hadn't thought about the hoodie
since she'd returned home from the hospital. Tears gushed from
her eyes, but she didn't wipe them. She wasn't willing to answer
his questions, and she wasn't ready to tell him how much he'd
hurt her. Instead, she let her tears speak on her behalf.

"Have you . . . have you had . . ." Mary sniffled. She paused,
then started again. "Have you had a relationship with anyone
else?"

"No," Tynan said, shaking his head.

Tears streamed down Mary's cheeks. "To be clear, I mean
from the time you left me in New York until today."

"No, it's only been you. I've never cheated on you, and I never
will," he said, brushing his eyes with the palms of his hands.

Mary wiped her eyes too. She pressed through with her last
question. "Are you still working for the Loughty family?"

Tynan cleared his throat. "Yes. We have a lot of restructuring
to do. It's so busy that Mr. Loughty didn't join the family in the
Caymans for the holidays. If he doesn't get a vacation, I don't get
one. He asked about you, and he said I should do whatever it
takes to get you—"

"That's enough, Ty. Please give Mr. and Mrs. Loughty my
best. . . . Okay. I have no more questions, so I'm gonna go now."

"Wait! Aren't you going to respond to anything I said?"

"No. I told you. I need time to process everything. I'll let you
know when I'm ready to talk."

"But, Mary, you haven't even given me a chance to apologize. I want to tell you how sorry I—"

"Thanks."

"Mary . . . Mary—"

She ended the call.

*　*　*

IT WAS ALMOST midnight. The sky looked darker than usual, and it matched Ruth's mood. Although she and Naomi had been cordial to each other the day before as they did the dishes with Mary after Christmas brunch and had talked by phone a couple of times since, they were still at an impasse. The coolness between them had unnerved Ruth, exacerbating her chronic insomnia that had already worsened every night since Christmas Eve. After two sleepless nights, Ruth had grown desperate. She missed staring at the stars from Naomi's driveway—the habitual cure for her problem—and her need for sleep made the risk of encountering Naomi worthwhile.

Instead of adhering to her usual method, Ruth decided to be more inconspicuous. It was nighttime, so she still took the street route, but she didn't pull up in the driveway. She left her golf cart on the street and walked the rest of the way. As she approached her usual spot, Ruth's mood mellowed with the alternating splashes coming from the fountain at the center of the circular driveway. The water danced joyfully, shooting twenty feet in the air. Beau had installed the solar-powered fountain as a special gift to Naomi when he and Ruth married. Thanks to Ruth's public relations savviness, the redesigned front yard—complete with fruit trees, shrubs, and flowers—had landed the Gardin family estate on the cover of *Georgia Home and Garden Magazine*. The coverage had helped establish the Gardin Family Enterprises' landscape division as leaders in the field, solidifying the family's financial status.

As Ruth settled onto the ground in the middle of the driveway, she recalled Naomi's confession the week before the Christmas party about her secret conversations with Beau. It still bothered her that Beau had never mentioned them, and it made her question her relationship with her mother-in-law too. Once a safe space that Ruth could count on, the relationship didn't feel that way anymore. She wondered what other secrets Naomi kept from her and if she would share them with Nicholas.

A nearby voice interrupted Ruth's thoughts as the fountain grew quiet. "That little track jacket isn't enough to keep you warm in the middle of the night. You're gonna get pneumonia sitting out here in the cold," Naomi said.

Ruth jumped. She'd been so deep in thought that she hadn't heard her mother-in-law walk up. "Oh my goodness, MIL! You scared me!"

"Sorry. I called your name as I was walking up. I thought you were ignoring me. I brought you a blanket," Naomi explained, wrapping it around Ruth. "I've had enough of hospitals, and I have no plans of going back anytime soon."

"Thanks," Ruth said, pulling the outdoor blanket higher on her shoulders. It wasn't as soft as her luxury throws at home, but the maroon and orange polyester fabric matched her tracksuit.

Naomi settled next to Ruth on the ground. "You could at least sit on the front steps instead of always being in the middle of the driveway."

"No . . . it's not the same."

"Whatever works for you."

"You know, people don't get pneumonia from the cold," Ruth said. "That's an old wives' tale. Pneumonia is caused by a virus or bacteria. Either way, it's not that cold out here. I like crisp air."

"True, but being out in cold weather can affect the immune system and make you more likely to get pneumonia. I watched a documentary about it. But we didn't come out here in the middle of the night to talk about infectious diseases."

I didn't come out in the middle of the night to talk to anybody. Ruth couldn't say it out loud, but sitting in the driveway with Naomi felt wrong. In Ruth's heart, the driveway was a space reserved for her and Beau, even after his death. Until now, she had struggled to define her problem with Naomi and Nicholas's relationship, but her mother-in-law's presence in the driveway helped her understand it. The problem was bigger than the potential impact of Nicholas's loss of objectivity. Ruth wanted privacy. And Naomi's involvement with him challenged the likelihood that Ruth would obtain it within the family during the company's transition. If she didn't negotiate it now, it would never happen.

Ruth turned to face Naomi. "I wish you and I had talked before brunch yesterday. I'm sorry I didn't pick up when you called, and I'm sorry I ruined Christmas."

"I wanted to talk things over with you first," Naomi said, "but I have to admit that it was a relief not to hear anything negative about me and Nicholas right away. It was nice to enjoy it and keep it safe for a little while before it was open for everyone's comments. It was pretty easy coaching you through introducing your relationship with Beau to the family, but it feels harder being in the situation myself."

"I wish I could be supportive of you and Nicholas, but I can't."

"But why? I thought you would be happy for me. Why wouldn't you think I'd want a partner? Because you think I'm old? I supported your relationship with Beau, because that's what I would've wanted someone to do for me. After Marlon's father passed away, I went from grieving his death to grieving Marlon's death to grieving my brother- and sister-in-law's deaths and raising their teenagers. I got used to not having a partner. But why is that okay? I happened to connect with Nicholas, and now I want to see where it goes. After everything I've been through, I deserve to be happy on my terms."

Ruth hesitated to explain. Naomi had done so much for her, and she didn't want to sound selfish. "I . . . I . . . want you to be happy. I just wish you'd find someone else," she said, looking over at the fountain as the splashing restarted.

Naomi tried to make eye contact, but Ruth wouldn't connect. "Did you see how few men were in the nursing home the other day, compared to all the women?" Naomi asked. "Maybe you haven't noticed, but women far outnumber men as we get older. I don't have the option of being picky about where I meet someone. I don't see what the big deal is. We've been on one date and I don't work for the company. I doubt it's going to affect Nicholas's ability to do his job. I know I said I was staying out of this mess between you and Martha, but I'll handle her if she tries anything shady after Nicholas makes his recommendations about the company."

Ruth turned toward Naomi. "Really? So this thing with Nicholas means that much to you?"

"I'm just saying that I want to see what happens. I've adapted to all the complicated decisions other people in this family have made, and I want *my* turn now. Maybe that means I'm being a little selfish. But if we're honest, we're both being selfish."

Ruth didn't want to tell Naomi that their relationship also highlighted her insecurities about her place in the family. In addition to whatever recommendations Nicholas made about the business, he would have Naomi's ear about the family dynamic. Ruth also feared she would one day lose her place as Naomi's confidant. There had always been secrets in the family that Ruth didn't know, and now Nicholas and Naomi would have their own secrets. In the back of her mind, she had always worried she would never be good enough for the Gardins. But now her apprehension had moved front and center. When she first met Marlon, she was nervous that his family wouldn't accept her because she didn't come from money and lacked a strong family structure. That worked itself out over time, but then she faced rejection again after marrying Beau.

Ruth looked Naomi in the eyes. "You're right. I'm being selfish too, and it has nothing to do with company policies," she conceded. "At first, I was uneasy about Nicholas getting too close to our family and knowing more about us than I wanted him to. I was concerned that our working relationship would be damaged if things didn't work out between the two of you. But now I've realized that I'm stressed about what will happen if it *does* lead to something serious."

Naomi tilted her head and fiddled with the ruby stud earring in her right ear. "We can worry about that if it happens. Right now we're just enjoying each other's company. That's it."

"You sound like Beau. He didn't like to think about what could happen down the road. If I'd left it up to him, the company wouldn't have made it through the recession. *I* forced him to plan for those types of things. Beau worked hard. He was a visionary, but he didn't analyze and prepare like I did. The company has grown as much as it has because of our combined efforts, but my instincts made his vision a reality."

Ruth searched Naomi's face for a sign that she understood her concern, but all she saw was unfounded optimism. She continued, "You can say that you're just enjoying Nicholas's company, but my gut says it's more than that. I know what I saw when I looked across the room at you and him on Christmas Eve. I'd be a fool if I didn't plan accordingly. I just wish I'd handled my reaction better. Again, that was Beau's area of expertise. I still have some growing to do."

Naomi stared at the ground. "So, what do we do now?"

"I have to figure out where I fit into everything. I'm not sure I belong here anymore—in the family or the business."

"Ruth, we've only been on one date! Don't be so presumptuous!" Naomi said, her eyes pleading as she looked back up at Ruth.

"No, it's not just about Nicholas. I'm starting to wonder if it's healthy for our lives to be as connected as they are. This goes back to when Marlon and I first got married. I wonder if you and I would have become so close as quickly as we did if I'd had a better relationship with my mother. You and your family were the picture of stability compared to my home life. After Marlon died, you and I needed each other, but maybe our lives blended too much. We've become too co-dependent. Space might be good for us."

Naomi grabbed Ruth by both shoulders. "What is all this talk about space in this family? People say they need space when they're thinking of breaking up with someone. You can't have space from me. . . . We're family. . . . We can't break up."

Ruth wriggled away and took a step back. "You and I will always be in each other's lives. I'm just saying that it's time we re-examine what that looks like. We're both showing signs that we need to. We just don't want to admit it to ourselves."

"I was hoping you might come over and say hello to Nicholas next week. He's coming up for New Year's Eve, and I'm going to show him around the estate."

Ruth sighed loudly. "Did you hear anything I just said?"

"I heard you. I suppose that means you're not going to stop by, huh?"

Ruth closed her eyes and squeezed them tightly. "Nah, I'll pass."

Chapter Sixteen

After getting kicked out of Christmas brunch, Martha was leery of attending Mary's therapy appointment. The sisters hadn't spoken in the five days since the holiday meal, so Martha was surprised when she received Mary's text message earlier that morning reminding her to attend the second half of her counseling session.

After Mary's latest emotional explosion, Martha was curious about what her sister discussed in the sessions, and she wondered how many times her name came up. But that wasn't her only motivation. There was also something in it for her. Martha expected the experience to help with her patient care and administrative activities at the hospital. She was an avid proponent of mental health counseling—at least she was when it came to someone else having a seat on a therapist's couch.

Martha regularly referred her patients to counselors, and she hoped to make mental health services available in the primary care center. She loved the idea of patients being able to walk into a primary care office without anyone knowing if they were there to see a mental health counselor or a primary care doctor. Research showed that the privacy increased the likelihood of patients following through with mental health appointments, and Martha was counting on this to boost the primary care center's quality improvement ratings. The hospital leadership was supportive, and Martha planned to work closely with the psychiatry department in the new year to coordinate the initiative. She hoped it would lay the groundwork for another promotion soon. In the meantime, she wanted to look good in front of Shari since the therapist also worked in the hospital's psychiatry department. She hoped Mary wouldn't embarrass her.

Shari's office in Edin was unlike anything Martha had experienced before. Although it appeared to be a typical patient exam room from the outside, it was just the opposite. It felt like she'd walked into a living room, and the space was larger than it seemed from the outside. The purple color scheme paired with the lavender-gray-striped accent wall and deep purple love seat and armchairs provided a relaxing but chic vibe. It looked more like a photo spread in an interior design magazine than a space inside a doctor's office.

The longer Martha sat on the plump tufted love seat, the more she wanted to kick off her shoes and take a nap. But she fought to stay focused on Shari's words.

"Mary, why was it important to you to bring Martha here today?" Shari asked.

"I feel like I've hit a wall in our relationship, and I don't know how else to get through to her. We've tried talking on our own, but it usually ends up either in an argument or with someone walking out," Mary said.

"Or getting kicked out," Martha replied. "That would be Mary kicking me out of our aunt's house on Christmas because I told the truth."

Mary put her head down and rubbed her forehead.

"I see. And, Martha, how do you feel about what Mary just said?" Shari asked.

When Mary first demanded that Martha attend the counseling session, Martha had interpreted it as her sister's way of telling her that she needed therapy. As far as Martha was concerned, nothing could be further from the truth. But Martha also loved being right. She was confident that the session would help Mary see her perspective, and she hoped it would help her sister cope with the realities of life in the Gardin family.

"I didn't understand how much Mary had a problem with me until she was hospitalized," Martha said, "so I feel like our relationship is in new territory. I'm trying to figure it out. I've been open to her feedback, and I've worked hard to listen to her and treat her better, so I don't understand the urgency for my being here. But if it helps Mary, that's what is most important to me."

Mary looked perplexed. "When I was hospitalized, you promised to do better, but you continue to revert to the same bad behavior. It's not enough that you're destroying our relationship and you've launched an attack on Ruth. But you've started coming between Ruth and Aunt Naomi too. And when your behavior upset Aunt Naomi at Christmas brunch, that was the last straw for me. You need to get yourself together, because you're about to lose everyone."

"When you say she's about to lose everyone, what do you mean?" Shari asked, scribbling notes while adjusting the round copper eyeglasses that adorned her face.

"Martha has already made it clear that she's not interested in having a relationship with Ruth, but she's also alienating me and Aunt Naomi. Historically, our family has not called each other out on inappropriate behavior. We just turn our heads and hope it gets better, but now we're down to a handful of us. And we need each other."

"I respect your opinion, Mary, and I agree with you," Martha said. "That's why I've been calling Ruth out on her bad behavior. I don't understand why you can't see that." Martha searched Shari's face for a reaction, but she offered none. Martha had hoped to win her over early in the session, but Shari's facial expressions displayed neutrality. *She'd make a great Spades partner.*

"I didn't ask you to come here to talk about Ruth," Mary said.

"We're not going to agree on that, but my goal is for you to see how toxic you've become. You lashed out at me during brunch because you thought I pursued Oji Greenwald about opening a restaurant in his new development. You said some venomous things to me."

Martha struggled to hold on to her calm facade. "I was just angry in the moment. I'm sorry about that. I should've articulated myself better, but the restaurant is a better fit for *me*."

"Oji reached out to *me* about the new restaurant. I didn't go after *him*," Mary said. "But how is it you've never mentioned to me that you want a restaurant? Aunt Naomi suggested that you and I team up for cooking classes at Alabaster Lunch Box. I thought it was a great idea, but you wouldn't commit. I thought you wanted to focus on your work at the hospital."

Martha didn't want to say that she was never good at sharing and that she couldn't imagine having to compromise her vision for the cooking classes for the sake of keeping the peace with her sister. And she didn't want to say that she was looking forward to putting her energy into herself for a change. Martha glanced at Shari's face. Again, nothing. So Martha did what she always did. "I didn't want to hurt your feelings. Why should I keep giving you my advice for free when you always ignore it anyway?"

Mary turned to Shari. "Do you see what I mean? She never takes responsibility for anything. She always turns it back on me."

"That's not true," Martha said with her nose in the air. "I envisioned a physician-approved restaurant. A place where patients—"

"Stop posturing," Mary interrupted. "You could've still had that if we had worked together. Be honest. You want a Martha-centered restaurant. You don't want to share the spotlight with me."

"I don't think we can solve the issue of who should have the restaurant. Let's try to focus on communicating about your relationship instead," Shari advised.

"I knew it," Martha huffed, ignoring Shari's guidance. "You brought me here to attack me. I came here to help you, and you're turning the tables on me. What a nice way to say thank you for all I've done for you."

"There it is again," Mary said. "I keep feeling like we're going around in circles. Every conversation we have ends up in the same place."

Shari rested her hands in her lap. "We've only spent a few minutes together in this first session. I would recommend that we continue to meet and work on your communication, and we can talk more about the restaurant too. Martha, I would suggest that you could also benefit from individual counseling. I can make some recommendations about a counselor who might be a good—"

"Thank you, but that won't be necessary," Martha interjected, straightening her posture. "I don't need individual counseling. If Mary thinks it's helpful for her healing process, I'll return. Otherwise, I think she and I can figure it out. We always have. This is just a bump in the road, but things will settle. And sometimes a little competition is healthy. We'll see who comes out on top for the restaurant."

"Mary, what are your thoughts about what Martha just said?" Shari asked.

"This is not how I hoped the session would end, but I'll deal with that," Mary said, discreetly wiping the corner of her eye.

"Okay, I'll let you two touch base outside the session whenever you're ready," Shari said.

* * *

"Why do I feel like we're sneaking around when we're riding out in the open?" Naomi asked as she turned her golf cart onto the main road of the family estate. Nicholas sat in the passenger seat. Naomi had just pointed out Ruth's house without being seen, and she hoped to do the same at Mary's and Martha's cottages.

Nicholas laughed. "This must be triggering some memories from your teenage years."

"Perhaps, but we didn't have golf carts back then." Naomi giggled. She anticipated feeling nervous seeing Nicholas again, but she was surprised that she was enjoying it so much. She liked that she could let her guard down with him, but it made her a little uneasy driving him around the estate. Doing so meant opening a door to her world that she wouldn't be able to close. The Gardin family was private, and new people were rarely invited onto the estate. Naomi was never sure how to present their situation, and people either overestimated their wealth or underestimated it because of this.

But Nicholas felt safer than other outsiders. He already knew details about the family business that allowed him to infer Naomi's wealth. But she imagined that might bring its own complications. Although she had no recent dating experience of her own, she doubted most people shared personal financial details on their second dates.

"The estate looks similar to what it did when I was growing up," Naomi said. "All four of the homes on the property still have the original buildings from the 1930s, but we've renovated them. Mary's cottage is the only one that maintains its original footprint. All the others have additions but to different extents. And you saw the peanut fields on the way here, right?"

"Yes. Ruth took me on a driving tour of the fields on my first visit, but I had no idea your family lived so close to them. It's amazing to have such intimate reminders of your family history."

"Thank you. It is, and it's a blessing to be able to live together on family property. But it has its drawbacks."

Naomi turned onto the outlet that led to her nieces' homes.

"It's funny how Mary and Martha live on this side of the estate, and Ruth and I live on the other side. It wasn't always that way. That's just how it worked out now. I've lived in all the houses on the property, except for Ruth's. I grew up in Mary's cottage. Mary and Martha grew up in the cottage where Martha lives. When their parents died, Ruth and I were living in my current home, so I moved in with the girls to give them some stability at home for a few months. Then they eventually moved into my cottage until they were able to handle a place on their own."

Naomi veered left at the fork in the road. She pointed at the quaint sage-colored wooden bungalow with a dark green roof.

"It's classic, but there's something sweet about it," Nicholas said. "It looks like somewhere Mary would live."

"Yep. This is Mary's place." Naomi smiled as she looked at the cottage again. She made a U-turn in the street and zoomed back down the road.

"Ruth told me Martha has some questions about the business. It's amazing your family can get along living so close together and also work through differing opinions about the business."

Naomi chuckled. "Things aren't always what they seem from the outside," she said as she turned left to hook around to the other side of the forked road. "Martha's cottage is up ahead," she said, pointing to the tan L-shaped cottage with double dormers.

"It reminds me of Martha—it looks like Mary's, but the addition shows there is more to it than meets the eye."

"You've got that right. I've never thought about it, but that's a perfect description." Naomi liked that Nicholas was so perceptive. His keen sense allowed her to recognize things that should be obvious but that her closeness to them prevented her from seeing. "Mary and Martha can cut through the trees and grassy areas to reach each other's homes. And they can access the lake through their backyards too, but we'll drive around to it."

"There's a lake on the property?" Nicholas asked, sounding impressed.

"Yeah, it's my favorite place. I'm looking forward to showing it to you."

Naomi turned in to Martha's driveway and quickly put the cart in reverse. Then she sped off, nearly clipping the shrubs that lined the street.

"You weren't kidding about not wanting to run into Mary and Martha, were you?" Nicholas laughed. "They know we went out last week, so what's the problem?"

"I'll explain later. For now, let's just enjoy the drive to the lake. There isn't much else to see. Aside from our houses, the property is surrounded by wooded areas."

Naomi had a two-fold reason for bringing Nicholas to the last stop on the tour. All the family's outdoor gatherings happened at the pavilion beside the lake, from weddings to marshmallow roasts to the annual Juneteenth celebration, but it was also the place Naomi went to reflect. She visited the lake almost daily, and she had saved today's visit to share with Nicholas. Ruth, Mary, and Martha didn't spend time at the lake unless they were required to show up for an event, so Naomi wasn't worried about running into them there.

Naomi pulled off the road and parked the golf cart on the gravel.

"Wait a minute," Nicholas said. He exited the vehicle, walked around to Naomi's side, and extended his hand. Naomi clasped it as he supported her while she stepped to the ground.

Naomi smiled. *I could get used to this.*

They paused beside the cart as Nicholas took in the landscape. Patches of full green trees comprised the wooded areas in the distance and along the periphery, with a mix of shedding and bare trees scattered along the paved path to the lake. "This is gorgeous," he said.

"Thank you. It's why I came back to Edin. I needed to be close to it again. I still think about playing with my brother and cousins here when we were kids. They've all passed away, but I think of them every time I come here. Mary and Martha were more interested in boys by the time I moved back, but I had good times here with M.J. And I hope to one day spend time here with any children he, Martha, and Mary have too."

Hand in hand, Naomi and Nicholas walked down the slight incline to the open-air pavilion and sat on the stone benches overlooking the lake. The water was still and peaceful. A gaggle of geese lifted off from the ground and formed a V formation over the water, serenading the couple with honking. Naomi regretted that she had to tarnish the scene with a story she'd been holding in. "I didn't tell you everything about Christmas brunch. Mary and Martha are supportive, but Ruth's not happy we're seeing each other. They know we're planning to go to watchnight service together, and it's probably easier if we all see one another in a more controlled environment, like church, instead of here."

Nicholas leaned back on the bench. "I didn't think Ruth would've had a problem with our seeing each other. Should I have talked to her about it before I asked you out?" he asked contemplatively.

"No," Naomi said as she stared at the water and fiddled with the blue sapphire stud earring in her right ear. She fought to keep her composure. "That would've been too much like asking her permission, and we don't need that. Our family is going through a crisis. So much of what she's feeling doesn't have anything to do with you. But you deserved advanced warning, because I don't want you to get caught in the cross fire."

"Is there anything I can do to help?"

"No, I don't think so. But I'm starting to rethink whether we should go to the watch-night service and celebration. I don't want to do anything that could make things worse."

Nicholas nodded and rubbed her shoulder. "If things are as bad as you make them seem, church might be exactly where we need to be."

* * *

THE LAST TIME Mary stood in Ruth's kitchen, her meltdown had begun a catastrophic domino of emotion that ended in her hospitalization. *Hindsight makes everything so clear,* she thought. But this visit had to be different. She couldn't allow that kind of drama on New Year's Day. It would be a horrible way to start off the year, plus she had a secret weapon this time.

"Sit," Ruth said, extending her hand toward a stool on the opposite side of the large island. "I won't be able to wait to eat this later. I hope you don't mind if I have it now."

"I would be honored," Mary said, blushing. She took her job of feeding Ruth's sweet tooth seriously, even when their relationship was strained. Mary looked at the empty stovetop. "I would've brought lunch, too, but I figured you cooked your own black-eyed peas, cabbage, and cornbread."

"Nah, I've been too busy working, so I ate a salad," Ruth said, looking effortlessly chic in a loose-fitting knit top with oversized buttons and matching camel-colored pants.

"A salad?" Mary asked, her eyes bulging. She internally questioned whether she'd made a mistake by not calling first. A brief phone conversation would've provided a heads-up that Ruth hadn't cooked, but she had worried Ruth would decline the visit if it had been announced. She skipped the call, knowing that showing up on Ruth's doorstep with any dessert was a guaranteed invitation inside. When Mary arrived and disclosed that she'd brought along icebox cake, a Gardin family New Year's Day tradition, Ruth opened the door with a smile so big that Mary could see all her teeth.

"No worries. I'm glad I saved my calories," Ruth said, her eyes lighting up as she unsnapped the plastic lid of the glass container. She moved so quickly that Mary didn't see her retrieve a fork from a drawer in the island. Ruth closed her eyes as her lips wrapped around the fork, assuring Mary that the smooth elixir of coconut cream and condensed milk had energized Ruth's taste buds.

"Do you need a second alone?" Mary said, then laughed.

Ruth smiled, but the expression faded quickly. "Funny. But speaking of being alone, I'm glad you came over. The house feels so empty. It doesn't feel like a holiday. I guess it's been tougher than I thought it would be to not have Beau or M.J. here," she said before taking another bite of cake.

With all the family discord, Mary had forgotten it was only the second Christmas season without Beau. She hadn't considered how hard it must have been for Ruth. "I thought you might want some time to yourself after you sacrificed so many hours at the hospital and then at my house after I was discharged. And the fiasco at Christmas only made it worse. I'm sorry about that."

"Don't worry about it. I'm happy you're getting better. . . . And you're not responsible for Martha's actions. That's on her."

"I appreciate that, but I want to make it up to you. Is there. . . . Is there anything I can do to smooth things over between you and Aunt Naomi?" Mary asked nervously.

Ruth shook her head as she took another bite of the cake.

If I don't go for it now, I don't know when I'll get another chance, Mary thought. "I sat with Nicholas and Aunt Naomi last night at church. They look so happy together. It's cute. . . .

All the single women were looking at Nicholas, and that made Aunt Naomi smile even more." Mary feigned a chuckle as she braced for the fallout.

"Humph," Ruth said, shrugging.

Mary stared at her as Ruth lifted another forkful of cake into her mouth.

"What?" Ruth asked, covering the lower part of her face to mask her full mouth.

Mary kept her gaze fixed on Ruth. She tilted her head for a few seconds before she responded. "It's weird, but thinking about Nicholas and Aunt Naomi just now made me think about me and Tynan."

"Now you've got my attention," Ruth said, looking up from the crumbs left in the glass dish. "Do you miss him?"

"I used to miss him all the time, but then I didn't for two weeks—the time between seeing him at the company party and Christmas Day, when we Skyped," Mary said, her voice softening.

"Ooh, so how'd that go?" Ruth asked as she dashed around the island with the glass dish in hand. She hopped onto the stool next to Mary.

"I got upset a few times on the call. He was dismissive at first, but he soon realized I wasn't playing around."

"Dismissive? I would think he would be eager to have your attention," Ruth scoffed.

"Well, he was, but I wouldn't let him ask questions."

Ruth cackled. "Well, that explains it. That approach didn't go over easily with us, so I know Tynan didn't take it well. Serves him right, though. . . . I'm sorry. I should've kept that last part to myself."

Mary leaned forward, sliding her elbows on the cool marble and resting her head in both hands. "I get it. I have mixed feelings about him. I hate to admit that I miss him now, but I do. Seeing Naomi and Nicholas together has me wondering what it would be like to be in a relationship with Tynan again."

"So, are y'all broken up?" Ruth asked.

"Oh, Ruth. I still don't know what we are," Mary said, shaking her hands in the air. She returned her elbows to the countertop and placed her fingertips on her temples. "Maybe I should give him another chance, but what would I do with the life I've built for myself here? What if I give up everything I've worked for, only to go back to New York and lose myself in Tynan's life again? I don't know if he's changed, but I hope he has. Why does everything always have to be so complicated?"

"Girl, I wish I knew. I really wish I knew," Ruth said. She sat the glass dish on the countertop and placed her hand on Mary's back. "You'll figure it out. Just give yourself some more time."

Mary sighed as she lifted her head. She didn't know when she would have answers, but it felt good to share her feelings with Ruth. For now, she focused on things that were easier to fix. "All right, I'm gonna run home real quick. I'll be back in a few minutes with leftovers."

"And some more cake?" Ruth asked before scraping together the tiny remnants in the dish and hurling them into her mouth.

"For sure. I didn't think you'd let me back in without it," Mary teased. It was starting to be like old times. Mary felt like there was more she still needed to say to Ruth, but she wasn't sure how to say it. She hoped her gift of food would be enough for now.

Chapter Seventeen

"Thanks for your flexibility with rescheduling our meeting at the last minute," Ruth said as she wrapped up her meeting with Nicholas in the Gardin Family Enterprises conference room.

"I was happy to oblige, but how could I put up a fuss when it's because a national news program asked to interview you for a series on women making waves in the agricultural industry? I hope you don't mind if I say that I'm proud of you," Nicholas said with a soft smile. "Plus, it only pushed our meeting back a few minutes, and we still finished on time."

"Thank you," Ruth replied, looking down at her notepad. "Most of all, I appreciate that I'm back on schedule, because my afternoon is slammed. I should've listened to Chloe and kept my meetings light today, but the Friday before the Martin Luther King, Jr., holiday is always tough on my calendar because I feel like I'm just getting back in the swing of things after Christmas and the New Year."

"You've got a good team, Ruth. You should listen to them," Nicholas said.

She shifted her weight in her seat. "You're right," she said reluctantly. She assumed Nicholas meant well, but his grin when discussing her interview and advice about her team felt a little paternal, an early warning that Nicholas's relationship with Naomi might be spilling over into the workplace. It was two weeks into the new year, and Ruth had stuck to her resolution of keeping the family's issues at home. She'd been so close to sailing through Nicholas's visit without a hiccup, and he was about to blow it for her. She would not let that happen. "Do you need anything else to work on the cash-flow projections and other documents we discussed?" Ruth asked firmly, looking Nicholas in the eye.

He picked up the stack of papers in front of him with both hands and tapped the bottom of the pages on the table. "No, I have everything I need from you. I'm meeting with a few members of your staff this afternoon, and I'll be able to give you an update on our videoconference next week. But before I go, can we do a temperature check on a personal matter?" he asked, his tone unflinching.

"Everything is fine," Ruth replied. "I'm pleased with your progress, and we're on track for the March board meeting. As far as I'm concerned, there's nothing to discuss, okay? Excuse me while I ask Chloe to follow up on the other action items we discussed."

"Okey dokey. You've made yourself clear," Nicholas said, gathering the other papers scattered before him on the conference table.

Ruth picked up the phone and dialed her assistant. The phone rang and rang, but the call went unanswered. As she hung up, there was a tap at the cracked door before it inched wider open. Chloe stuck her head through the opening.

"Excuse me, Ruth, may I see you in the hallway, please?" Chloe asked, urgency teeming in her voice.

"Would you like me to step outside and give you some privacy?" Nicholas asked.

"No, don't worry about it," said Ruth. "You're on your way out, so go ahead and gather your things. I don't want to hold you up."

As Ruth pushed her chair back from the conference room table, Chloe stepped back into the hallway. Despite her reservations about his relationship with her mother-in-law, Nicholas had proven to be a trusted professional ally. He fit in so well with the team that some of the newer employees had to be reminded he wasn't part of the full-time staff. Almost overnight, he had become part of the Gardin Family Enterprises inner circle. Ruth didn't mind if he overheard her sort through whatever pressing housekeeping issue within the company required her attention. Her personal matters, however, were a different story.

As Ruth reached the door, she gripped the doorframe and tilted her upper body into the hallway in time to see a woman making a sharp turn from the reception area in a pink Christopher John Rogers jacket and matching mid-rise tapered trousers that also hung in Ruth's closet. Her hair was pulled into a tight bun, highlighting high cheekbones that were similar to Ruth's. "Mama!" Ruth exclaimed. "What are you doing here?"

Nicholas spun his chair toward the door as Chloe, nearing her ninth month of pregnancy, swayed down the hallway to her desk.

Ruth was aghast. Employees filtered into the hallway, craning their necks for a glimpse of Ruth's elder doppelgänger. "Hi, Nikki," her mother said with the enthusiasm usually reserved for the guest of honor at a surprise party.

She really does look like me in twenty years, Ruth thought. Hearing her childhood nickname in her place of business forced Ruth to back herself into the conference room. Her mother followed her so closely that the block heel of her Kendall Miles pumps came within inches of stepping on the stiletto Kendall Miles pumps that Ruth wore. As her mother planted a soft kiss on Ruth's cheek, her medium-brown complexion and diamond hoop earrings glistened under the energy-efficient halogen lighting.

Ruth gripped the door handle, transferring her fury to a lever that would not return the emotion, and slammed the door closed.

Nicholas sprang to his feet. He shut his laptop and stuffed it into his computer bag, looking at Ruth's mother, back at Ruth, and then at her mother again.

"Yes, we have strong genes," Ruth said. "Nicholas . . . this is my mother, Linda."

Nicholas extended his hand toward Linda. "Nice to uh—"

"Likewise," Linda interrupted. She shook Nicholas's hand but didn't look at him as she spoke. She was more concerned with inspecting the conference room, from the view of the historic district through the window wall to the curated artwork, by mid-century African American artists, that adorned the rest of the space. "I'm Linda. You'll have to pardon me. This is my first time at the Gardin Family Enterprises office. Ruth likes to keep me hidden in Houston, but I see she has done very well for herself here."

Ruth considered responding, but she held her tongue. Not doing so would only make matters worse. Having spent her childhood and adolescence as her mother's naïve sidekick, she was unprepared for their bond to implode when she married Marlon. The one-sided nature of their relationship required Ruth to constantly appease her mother growing up, causing her to wonder all the more what would've become of their relationship if her father hadn't died when her mother was pregnant. Ruth discovered there was nothing she could do to make her mother happy once Marlon was in the picture. Despite her best efforts, a stable mother-daughter relationship had evaded her.

Nicholas grabbed his bag and inched toward the door. "I'm going to head out to an early lunch. I'll check in with you this afternoon, Ruth. Maybe, uh . . . maybe between your meetings."

Ruth recalled the photo she found on the floor of Naomi's cottage near the piano weeks before Christmas. She feigned a smile like Naomi had in the picture. "Thank you, Nicholas, and I'm sorry about the interruption," she said, grateful for the reset the memory offered.

"No problem," he replied, opening the door only enough to permit him to slide out. The employees gossiping in the hallway scattered back into their offices.

Linda walked around the opposite end of the custom black walnut live-edge conference table, nodding approvingly as she slid her hand along the grain of the wood. "Is it too much for a mother to expect a return call from her only child?"

The question fanned the intense anger growing inside Ruth. Her mother's gaslighting never failed to bring out the worst in her, but responding to her antics took Ruth days to recover. She couldn't afford to be emotionally incapacitated at such a crucial point in her work. Ruth had last seen her mother at Beau's funeral. Because Ruth had cut off most communication with her shortly after M.J. was born—and her mother had long burned bridges with the select cohort of family members and friends with whom Ruth still maintained contact—Ruth was convinced her mother had set up Google Alerts with her and Beau's names and became aware of his passing through the obituary. She still wondered who she had scammed to pay for the last-minute flight from Houston back then, but she was relieved she wasn't asked to reimburse the travel expense. It wouldn't have been the first time her mother's selfishness overruled a sense of decency.

"What can I do for you, Mama?" Ruth asked, then sighed.

"You're too busy to ask how I'm doing? I raised you better than that."

"I apologize. You look as beautiful as ever, Mama. Pink has always suited you well," Ruth said, having learned during her teen years that complimenting her mother made her more bearable.

"Thank you, darling. The designer calls it flamingo," Linda cooed. "But listen, I've fallen into a bit of a bind, and I was wondering if you would lend me some change."

"How much?" Ruth asked, bracing herself for the figure.

Linda smiled and fluttered her long natural eyelashes, covered in a mountain of mascara. "Twenty thousand would work nicely. Twenty-five if you'd like me to forgive you for ignoring my calls and texts over the past week."

"Twenty thousand dollars is not pocket change, Mama!" The amount exceeded the request Ruth usually got once a year, and the timing was earlier than expected. Ruth wondered what predicament her mother had gotten herself into, but she dared not ask. The less she knew, the less likely she would be called to testify. Ruth had learned that lesson the hard way shortly after she and Marlon married. While under investigation for fraud, Linda had named Ruth as her accomplice. Begrudgingly, Ruth sought her mother-in-law's advice. Naomi had not only supported an embarrassed Ruth without judgment but also paid for the best legal representation in Houston. The entire episode solidified Ruth's connection to Naomi, but it also led to the painful discovery that her mother had been using Ruth's Social Security number to open accounts at retail stores and mortgage companies. It took Ruth five years to untangle the identity theft that had taken place at escalating levels all her life.

For years, Ruth vacillated between the desire to sever ties with her mother and the self-imposed obligation to help the woman who'd given her life. The situation was such a source of conflict in both of her marriages that Ruth maintained a separate account funded from her discretionary funds to keep peace in her household. Her mother then rewarded her by making an unreasonable monetary appeal within two years of each husband's death. "I'll wire you five thousand, but that's it. No more."

"And my travel expenses from Houston?"

"Five thousand, Mama. That's it."

Linda kissed Ruth on the cheek. "Same account as usual. I'll always keep it open for you. Thank you, darling. I'll let you get back to your day," she said, grinning.

* * *

THE FRONT DOOR of the Gardin Family Enterprises office opened, and Linda slipped out as though she had just returned from a leisurely lunch. She scrolled through text messages on her phone, oblivious to Nicholas sitting on a bench outside the entrance. She walked down the stairs and turned on the sidewalk toward the parking lot.

Nicholas followed her to the white Mercedes E-Class in the rear of the parking lot, covered in a layer of dirt from her interstate trek.

"Lindy?" he asked.

Linda spun around. After looking Nicholas up and down, she recognized his sport coat and slacks as ones belonging to the man who was meeting with her daughter before she entered the conference room. She had not paid attention to the man's face then, but now it didn't matter what he looked like. Only one person called her by that name.

"Nicky? I can't believe it's you. . . . How did you find her?" Linda asked, her voice reminiscent of a schoolteacher reprimanding the class clown. She usually made up for the sympathy she lacked with charm, but her repository ran empty as she unexpectedly faced a man she hadn't seen in forty-nine years.

Nicholas held his right hand at the side of his head. "What are you talking about? Wait . . . no. . . . It can't be," he said, his nose and forehead scrunched up.

He's emotional just like Ruth. That's right. That's why we didn't work out, Linda thought. She scanned the vicinity and sighed, relieved that none of Ruth's employees lingered in the area. "Let's talk in the car."

Linda opened the front passenger door and hurled the collection of fast-food bags and magazines into the back seat, atop a small carry-on suitcase. She left the door ajar and scurried to the driver's side. Nicholas stood next to the car door, his mouth agape.

Linda slid into the driver's seat. "Nicky, get in," she commanded.

Nicholas dropped into the passenger's seat. "You called her Nikki too, didn't you?" he asked as he shut the car door.

"Yes. Nicole is her middle name. She never let anyone call her by her first name growing up. She hated it until Marlon told her he liked it. Now she goes by Ruth, but I still call her Nikki."

Nicholas's eyes filled with tears. "So, she's my . . . my daughter?"

"Yes, but we will have to do this quickly. I'm going to Vegas for the long weekend. I don't want to miss my flight." Linda wasn't known for having a delicate nature, a characteristic that had doomed relationships with both her daughter and love interests. There was a time long ago when she cared, but she had grown ambivalent as the years went by. She started the car and looked at the clock. "What do you want to know?"

Nicholas huffed. "This isn't the kind of conversation that can be rushed."

"This is why we didn't work. Live in the moment, Nicky."

"I've always wanted kids. . . . I . . . I would have done things differently if I had known about her. Are you sure?"

"I was never a saint, but I know what I did, when I did it, and with whom I did it," Linda said bluntly. "And if there was ever a time to lie, it would benefit me most to deny the truth now. But I'm getting too old for that."

"Do you have to be so callous about it? This doesn't just affect you. What about Ruth? What about me?"

Linda adjusted the rearview mirror and checked her reflection. "Look, it's been a long time, and I wasn't prepared to have this conversation today . . . or ever, for that matter. Any tears I may have wanted to cry about this left when you told me you were getting married."

"Don't try to play me, Lindy. I married someone else because you said I didn't make enough money for you. Who does Ruth think is her father?"

Linda exhaled, with her eyes shifting quickly from side to side. "I told her he died while I was pregnant with her. She's always been sensitive about it. I thought she would outgrow it, but she never did. She called one of my boyfriends her 'stepfather' for a while. He was good to her. Though we never married, he left her some money for college after he died. She's resilient. Things turned out fine for her, didn't they?"

Nicholas groaned and buried his face in his hands. "We have to tell her."

Linda pulled Nicholas's left hand away from his face. "No! Not now! You are not going to mess things up for me. I had to raise her alone."

"Mess what up? You raised her alone because of your own decisions. You should've told me. I would have been there for her. I would've stayed in Houston."

"I don't need you to mess up my arrangement with Ruth. And it's easy to say now that you would've hung around, isn't it, Nicky?"

"I lived a different life back then, but I'd never have forsaken my child," he said. "You know that."

"Life is a gamble. Sometimes you win, sometimes you don't. What can I say?"

Nicholas let out an exasperated sigh. "I am so glad Ruth didn't turn out like you, Lindy."

She pursed her lips and tilted her head as she looked at him. "Now, that's not a kind thing to say," she replied. She turned on the heater without looking at it. Instead, she looked closely at

Nicholas. He'd turned out so much better than she'd expected. *That's one I probably should've kept instead of throwing away. No, I can't go there.* "So, do you live here? I forgot your family is from Georgia. Augusta, right?"

"Statesboro. You would think that would've crossed your mind when you moved Ruth back and forth to Atlanta for college? Or during her graduation. Or her wedding. Or maybe visiting your grandchild?"

An avid poker player, Linda had learned early on that when you fold on a hand, you've got to move on. If not, you can't focus on the next hand you're dealt. "No, I didn't think of you. That's not something I do."

"Well, you should've at least thought of Ruth. I have nephews who went to college in Atlanta at the same time she was there. What if she had dated one of them?"

"But she didn't."

"Thank goodness. . . . You know, we need to talk about telling Ruth the truth."

"No. Why can't you leave this alone? I'm not telling her."

Nicholas pulled on the door handle, but the door didn't open. "I'm giving you twenty-four hours. Unlock the door, please."

Linda turned away from him as she hit the unlock button on the driver's-side door.

Nicholas opened the door and extended his right leg and started to get out of the car. He stopped as Linda began talking again.

"One more thing. If you didn't know that Nikki is your daughter, what are you doing here?"

"She's my client, Lindy. . . . My client. You've created a mess for me," Nicholas said, his body straddling the door sill. He completed his exit and slammed the door so hard that the car wobbled like a roly-poly toy.

"Sorry," Linda said, shrugging. She shifted the car in reverse and drove out of the parking lot.

*　*　*

NAOMI LAY STRETCHED out on her living room couch, absorbing Nicholas's confession. She stared at the ceiling, but she could see him out of the corner of her eye, sitting a few feet away on the bench of the baby grand piano. He leaned over with his elbows resting on his knees, and with every word that fell from his lips, it looked like he would teeter onto the floor.

A part of Naomi wished he would. She felt crushed by the weight of the turmoil his announcement would cause. She couldn't bear to sit up straight, and she didn't understand where Nicholas was finding the strength to hold himself up. *I'm too old for this,* she thought.

Nicholas spoke nonstop for twenty minutes in painstaking detail, the way some men do when they think they'll earn extra credit for not holding anything back. But those were always the rare times when women wished they would. Naomi said nothing. She'd known the blissful newness of their relationship would wear off soon, but she hadn't expected the circumstances to be so grave. Given their age, she'd predicted they would drift into the relaxed state of coupledom where there were no surprises and where boredom was the greatest risk. They had both talked about their deceased partners with ease, but Naomi never thought she'd have to endure an explanation about an ex-girlfriend.

I should've known he was trouble when he waltzed into the Christmas party looking like one of those men on social media that the young girls call 'Mr. Steal Your Grandma.' She had never admitted to anyone, not even Nicholas, that she had noticed him that night. She pretended to be oblivious, but she had picked him out the way you recognize a police car in a speed trap. She later gave in because he seemed safe, but now she was sure he would be the trouble she initially feared.

Naomi heard Nicholas say lots of words, but few of them registered until he said, "So if you and I got married, Ruth would be your daughter-in-law, cousin-in-law, *and* stepdaughter."

Naomi suddenly sat up on the sofa. "Hush! Be careful what you say! It's way too early to say things like that."

Nicholas froze. "I didn't mean to alarm you. I was just thinking out loud. I know we've only been seeing each other a few weeks, but I think we've got something special here. Don't you?"

"Sure I do, but we don't need to rush into anything. Ruth doesn't acknowledge our relationship, and now she has to figure out how to cope with you being her long-lost father. I don't know where that will leave me with her." Naomi didn't want to admit it to Nicholas, but he was becoming a liability. The Gardin family had enough drama, and she didn't want to be responsible for adding to it.

"We've both experienced enough life and enough death to know that tomorrow is not promised. I don't believe in wasting time. That's why I feel an urgency to tell Ruth I'm her father."

Although he made a valid point, Naomi was in no rush to see Ruth's world turned inside out, and she wanted more time to prepare herself for the consequences and aftershock. "Wait a minute. Are you planning to tell her this weekend?"

"Of course. This isn't something that should be delayed. I'm not scheduled to come back until March, and I wouldn't want to spring it on her when I'm in town for the board meeting."

"She's gonna relive the trauma every Martin Luther King, Jr., weekend from now on. Why ruin such a precious holiday?"

"Do you always think the worst? Maybe she will relive the weekend with joy."

Though Naomi had tolerated Nicholas's nervous rambling in the past, she lacked the capacity to absorb his speculative musings during such a tenuous conversation. "I know you thought you saw me at my worst when Mary was rushed to the hospital, but this is my new worst."

Confusion spread across Nicholas's face. "I don't think it's that bad, Naomi. This isn't going to kill anyone. Ruth and I both gain a family member, arguably during a time when we need it most. Isn't that what's most important?"

Always practical and cerebral, Nicholas had identified some truths in his statement. But he was naïve. While Ruth was usually one to help Naomi keep the peace in the family, she should not be underestimated. "Don't be fooled by Ruth's agreeable nature. She can be as temperamental as the rest of the women in the family. There's a reason she's lasted so long with us."

* * *

RUTH NEVER CLOSED the office early, but after the day she'd had, she decided it was a perfect time to make an exception. She asked Chloe to reschedule her afternoon meetings due to a family emergency. At first she felt guilty for making up an excuse, but then she realized that it was the most appropriate description. If having your mother barge into your company and make a scene in front of your employees and the consultant who held the future of your business in his hands wasn't a family emergency, she didn't know what else to call it. The employees were so happy about having the afternoon before a holiday weekend off that Ruth doubted anyone was talking about the events of the morning.

Ruth planned to sleep the trauma away, but she had too much on her mind. She lay on a chaise lounge in her backyard, bundled under a plush velvet blanket and staring at the flames dancing atop the gas fire pit. The flames reminded her of freedom. She wondered what it felt like to be that free—to move around, unencumbered by anyone else's expectations or perhaps even her own. She wondered if her mother felt free like that. Linda had always done whatever she wanted, regardless of the cost, and Ruth decided at an early age that she didn't want to be that way. She waffled between feeling grateful for her place in the Gardin family and company and wondering if she was willing to pay the price of sacrificing M.J.'s birthright to free herself from them. But she didn't want to become like her mother. She never wanted to take advantage of her child in the way that her mother had taken advantage of her.

When it came to her son, Ruth was the opposite of her mother. With the change in her relationship with Naomi, the only person Ruth felt obligated to was M.J., and he was almost on his own. She and Beau had always planned for him to take over the company one day, but she was starting to wonder if working in the family business would be an ideal life for her son. She didn't want M.J. to have to struggle with the family as she had, and she wanted him to have opportunities that had not been available to her. M.J.'s path was already off to a bright start. Ruth and Beau had decided to cover the cost of his education, so his allotment from the trust safely accrued interest while he studied. If they decided to sell Gardin Family Enterprises, as Martha suggested, M.J. would inherit a portion of the proceeds. And Ruth liked the idea of his being free to do whatever he wanted.

Over the years, Ruth had been strategic about her life, but there were times when she let her guard down and followed her heart. That's what had brought her to Edin and to Beau. She didn't regret that part, but she wondered where her life might be if she had planned more for her future.

As Ruth looked up from the flame, Naomi approached on her golf cart. She parked at the end of the brick path that connected their homes. Then she got out of the cart and walked around to the other side, removing a large rectangular glass container. One hand held the handle on top of the lid while the other supported the bottom of the container.

Ruth smiled. "You made me treats!"

"Yep, your favorite mini lemon pound cakes." Naomi placed the container on the end table between the lounge and the circular outdoor daybed.

Ruth sprang to her feet and threw her arms around Naomi, comforted by the warmth of Naomi's embrace and the light, buttery aroma that lingered on her clothing. "Thank you so much. I needed this today." Ruth leaned her head on her mother-in-law's shoulder. As she rested in the hug, tears fell from her eyes. She missed the closeness the women shared and the way Naomi always knew what she needed. "I guess you heard that we closed the office early today," Ruth said.

"Yeah, Nicholas and I were talking when he received the text message."

Ruth dried her eyes as she returned to the chair. She unlocked the lid and lifted it from the container. "Oh, I hadn't thought about how shutting down would affect his work," she said, realizing that she and Nicholas had spent most of the morning working together. With the office closed during the afternoon, he wouldn't be able to hold the essential meetings that made the trip necessary. "What a wasted trip!"

"Things happen for a reason. . . . I'm sure he'll be fine," Naomi said. "So how are you doing with everything? Nicholas told me your mother came in while the two of you were meeting."

"That was the last thing I expected today. She always shows up at the worst times. It's like she has a built-in sensor or something." Ruth took a nibble of the daisy-shaped pound cake. Still slightly warm, it was a balm to her soul. The burst of lemon-flavored sweetness perked her up immediately.

"It's a shame she didn't stop by to have tea with me. I'd have loved to spend some quality time with her," Naomi teased.

Ruth let out a loud belly laugh, covering her mouth, which still contained a piece of the soft cake. She finished chewing, then took a big swallow. "Thank you. I needed that laugh. I think you're still the only person on heaven and earth who my mother fears. From the first time the two of you met, it was obvious. I still can't figure it out."

"There's nothing to figure out. I'll say it like the old folks around Edin used to say—'The devil in her fears the God in me.'"

"Makes sense."

"So how much did she want?" Naomi asked. "It must've been more than usual if she needed to see you in person."

"Twenty thousand."

"Wow, the nerve of that woman. She might as well have asked for a kidney or some bone marrow."

"I'd rather give her the money," Ruth said, then laughed. "I didn't tell her, but I plan to transfer the full amount. Only I can't bring myself to do it yet. I don't know why. I guess I want her to squirm a little. I can always blame it on the holiday weekend."

Chapter Eighteen

"You're getting paint everywhere," Naomi said and then laughed, looking over at Nicholas's canvas. She couldn't remember the last time she had this much fun. Her New Year's Eve prayer was already working. She wanted to be open to new experiences, and it was paying off.

"This is part of my artistic process," he said, nudging Naomi.

"You're gonna make me mess up," she said in between giggles.

Naomi and Nicholas had agreed to take turns planning their date weekends, and Naomi had relished the opportunity to plan both reverence and fun for the Martin Luther King, Jr., weekend. She'd worried about how Nicholas's discovery that Ruth was his daughter would affect the trip, but she remained hopeful for his sake. They would find out soon enough, as they planned to invite Ruth over for a talk the following day after church.

Naomi had always been comforted by being in church whenever there was trouble in her life. They'd started the day with a late-morning activity in the sanctuary—a listening session of Dr. King's "I've Been to the Mountaintop" speech, followed by a community discussion. Attendees of all ages shared their reflections of the speech, from its impact on their lives to what was needed to overcome human rights injustices in the United States and across the world. Following the dialogue, the group convened in the church basement for a painting class, where an instructor from a nearby art studio taught participants to paint a landscape of the Georgia mountains. Naomi and Nicholas agreed to swap paintings so that they would have each other's as a reminder of their first King weekend together.

"Looks like we need some more paint," Naomi said as she lifted the shared palette that rested on the table between them. She walked to the end of the table and refilled the white, black, blue, red, and yellow areas on the board.

"How long have you two been married?" asked Imani, the instructor, as she made a beeline from a neighboring table to talk with Naomi.

"Oh, no. We're not married. He's my . . . friend. . . . I mean, we're dating. We've only been seeing each other for a little while. Almost a month," she said bashfully.

"Really? It looks like you've been together for years. There's a comfort between the two of you, but your love seems fresh too. It reminds me of my grandparents, and they'll have been married fifty-three years in August."

"Thank you," Naomi said, blushing. She had brushed off comments from Mary and Martha about how cute she and Nicholas were together, because she thought they were just teasing her. But hearing it from a stranger gave her pause.

Love? Naomi thought as she walked away. Her face was still a light shade of red when she returned to her easel. Nicholas smoothed the edges of the peaks in the center of his canvas, blending the borders to create a hazy effect. He stepped back and surveyed the result before looking over his shoulder at Naomi.

"You okay?" he asked.

She nodded. "Yes, everything's fine. I was talking to the instructor, that's all," she said reluctantly.

Nicholas took the palette from Naomi and slid it onto the table. "Did she say something troubling?"

"No, it wasn't troubling. Just surprising. She thinks we look like an old married couple."

Nicholas chuckled. He dabbed his paintbrush into the black

paint and turned back toward his canvas. "She has two of the three correct. I'm working on the third. She just needs to give me some time," he said, positioning his brush to place birds next to the mountains.

Naomi grew more uncomfortable by the second, but she could blame only herself for bringing the topic up. "You're serious, aren't you? This is the second time you've said as much in less than twenty-four hours."

"I don't joke about things like this, Naomi. Are you sure you want to talk about it now?" Nicholas asked, surveying the room. The teenagers who'd been sharing the table with them had long abandoned their stations, but they stood a few feet away, talking with Imani.

"You're right," she retreated. "We can talk about it after we leave. There's no rush."

Imani raised her hand to make an announcement. "May I have your attention? For those of you who are interested, we're going to take a quick snack break in the fellowship hall while I go around the room and dry your canvases before the next step."

The neighboring tables cleared as the other novice painters flocked out of the room into the adjoining fellowship hall.

"Perfect timing!" Naomi laughed nervously. "So, where were we?"

"You were going to say that you like the idea of our being together and that you can't imagine why you were saying such insensitive things a minute ago," Nicholas said with a playful grin.

Naomi spoke slowly. She chose her words as if it were her first time processing the notion, even if she'd already contemplated the future of her relationship with Nicholas after their first date. "I do like the idea of our being together, but this is all so new. I want to get used to it, and I can't imagine making any major changes in my life anytime soon."

"So, what do you want to happen when my contract with Gardin Family Enterprises ends? Have you thought that far?"

"I have, and I think we should wait and see what happens," she said firmly.

Nicholas put down his paintbrush and wiped his hands on the maroon apron draped over his jeans. He stepped closer to her but leaned on the wall behind them. "I don't live my life that way, Naomi. If you don't see a future with me, I hope you'll let me know soon. I'm not asking you to marry me right now, but I plan to at some point. I'm getting too old to run back and forth across the country every week for work. I didn't mind it so much when I was younger and had a wife to enjoy traveling with. But I'm ready to slow down and have fun. I want to spend the rest of my life with someone I enjoy, and someone who enjoys me. We have fun together, and we care about each other."

Naomi chewed her lip and blinked her eyes rapidly. "But you live in Philadelphia. I don't want to live there."

"Who said you had to live there?"

"You would move here? I . . . I like living alone . . . and having my own space. Having things the way I want them to be. . . . I don't know about sharing my space with anyone."

"I'm not fussy. You can put things anywhere you want. You can have as much space as you want. Do you want me to build a house down the street? Next door? Whatever you want. As long as I'm in the same city as you, I'll be happy. We can work out the details."

"I . . . I just don't know," Naomi said, her hands fanning her face.

"Seeing you one weekend a month isn't good enough for me. That's all I'm saying. We don't have to make any decisions right now, but you should start figuring out what you want. My contract with the company is up in two and a half months. I don't plan to renew it. But depending on how things go with Ruth tomorrow, I might not be around that long."

* * *

As RUTH PUT the key into Naomi's door lock, the heart-shaped key chain rattled against the lock's metal base. Her visits there had decreased so much since her mother-in-law had started seeing Nicholas that Ruth had nearly forgotten how annoying the clashing of the two metals could be. For years, she had thought about replacing the small ring that connected the scratched metal heart to the chain, but she'd always been afraid that any endeavor to fix it would cause further breakage. Ruth had used the key chain as a latchkey kid and again intermittently during her high school years, but she later tossed it into an old jewelry box, where she rediscovered it during college. When she moved into Naomi's house after her honeymoon, she found it again. It was the only key chain Ruth had ever used to hold a key to Naomi's home—first the house in Atlanta, and then her cottage in Edin. Ruth hadn't been able to bring herself to throw it out. It had become a visual reminder of the place Naomi held in her heart.

"I'm here," Ruth announced. The smell of pasta sauce hit her as soon as she crossed the threshold. She locked the door and nervously clutched the key chain in her hand as she walked into the foyer.

"In the living room," Naomi said. Her voice sounded heavy and quivered slightly.

Ruth's nervousness multiplied with each step she took. Having avoided church that morning so she didn't have to see Naomi and Nicholas together, she felt overwhelmed with the possible reasons for Naomi's impromptu request that she come over. She hoped her mother-in-law wasn't trying to force her into extending Nicholas's consulting contract. And she hoped the invitation wasn't an attempt to encourage them to bond as a family. She didn't need to spend time with Nicholas outside the office to help her see that he was a nice guy. She already knew that. She might consider warming up to him after their work was completed, but she wanted clear parameters in the meantime. They had found a nice balance in the office, and there was no need to disturb it.

On the way over, Ruth had begrudgingly prepared herself to deliver an apology to her mother-in-law. When Naomi had called to ask her to come over, Ruth snapped at her for refusing to respect the boundaries she'd set regarding her mother-in-law's relationship with her consultant. Naomi had remained gracious but undeterred, insisting that Ruth stop by for a few minutes. Ruth hoped she was still in a good mood.

"Are you alone? I was afraid you were setting me up for some type of intervention with Mary and Martha. Well, not Mary so much, because we're getting along well these days, but definitely Martha," Ruth chattered, trying to deflect from her real concerns.

Ruth's countenance changed once she entered the living room, where Nicholas sat on the sofa next to Naomi. Suddenly another potential reason for the meetup popped into her mind. "Are you two getting married? Please, no. I just can't deal with this right now."

"No, absolutely not!" Naomi yelled.

Nicholas placed his hand on Naomi's shoulder. "Everybody, calm down," he said. "No, we're not getting married. I'd like to talk to you about something, and it's not about Naomi."

Naomi reached across her chest and gripped Nicholas's hand. "I'm sorry," she whispered. "This is harder than I thought."

"I know. I know," he replied. "I appreciate you. I know this is hard for you too."

Naomi nodded.

"Please, someone tell me what's going on," Ruth said, but she stared at Naomi.

"Have a seat," Nicholas said.

"I hate when people tell me to have a seat," Ruth replied without moving.

Naomi stood and began walking away from the couch. "I'll leave the two of you to talk. I'll be in the kitchen if you need me," she said, holding on to Nicholas's hand until the distance between them forced her to let go. As she reached Ruth, she extended her arms and wrapped them around her. She rocked gently, but the resistance from Ruth slowed her movement. "Please have a seat, Ruth," Naomi said.

Ruth walked to the sapphire-blue swivel chair across from the sofa where Nicholas sat. She settled into the chair and placed her purse and key chain on the plush velvet chair cushion. "Okay, go for it," she said, folding her arms and fixing her gaze on him.

Nicholas began to speak, his tone as solemn as his words were measured. "When your mother came to the office on Friday, I thought I recognized her as someone I used to know, but I wasn't certain. And then she called you Nikki. It caught my attention, because she used to call me Nicky. I never let anyone else call me that, except her," he said. His face drooped as if he'd been awake all night.

Ruth swallowed a lump in her throat. "What are you saying, Nicholas?"

"And . . . and I didn't know that Nicole was your middle name until your mother told me later. I needed to talk to her to find out if I was correct, but I didn't know if—"

No . . . no . . . I mean. . . . But . . . no . . . Ruth's eyes filled with tears. She twisted her body, causing the swivel chair to follow her direction, and then planted her feet on the floor and looked down at them.

"And I couldn't be sure until I spoke with her afterward. . . . You have to understand that we were both pretty young the last time we saw each other. . . . So, I waited for her outside, and we talked in her car. I want you to understand that it was in the car, so no one heard us. I . . . I know privacy is important, and I—"

"No!" Ruth whimpered.

Nicholas rushed over to Ruth, with outstretched arms, but she pushed him away. "Get away from me! You can't do this to me! Do you know what I've been through? All . . . these . . . years! All . . . these . . . years!" she sobbed.

Tears streamed down Nicholas's face. "I'm sorry, Ruth. I didn't know. I'm so sorry."

"I don't want to hear any more of this. Nothing! Not a single word! Not another word, do you understand me? No more!"

"Okay, okay—"

"Stop! I don't want to hear your voice at all! Not another word!" Ruth said, gasping for air as her body drew into the fetal position and leaned to the left side of the chair.

Nicholas sat on the piano bench, holding his head in his hands.

The father and daughter wept, seated a few feet apart but separated by an impenetrable distance.

Naomi walked into the living room carrying two glasses of ice water. Nicholas sat up when Naomi rubbed his back. She handed him the glass of water and pointed to the kitchen.

* * *

As Ruth's breaths slowed to a normal rate, her mind settled enough to sort through the jumbled questions that ran through her mind.

Naomi moved the piano bench close enough to put her arm around her. "Ruth, sweetie, drink this water," Naomi said, extending the glass toward her daughter-in-law.

"Thanks," Ruth said. She accepted the glass, but its coldness against her hand barely registered in her brain. She placed the glass on the end table on the other side of her chair. "When did you find out?"

"Huh?"

"When, MIL?"

"Friday. Nicholas came over after he spoke with your mother."

A rush of emotions bubbled up within Ruth. She stared at Naomi, tears cascading down her cheeks. "So, you knew when you brought me the cakes?"

"Yes. I wanted to do something nice for you."

"Well, I would've preferred that you told me instead of baking for me. I worried you would keep secrets from me and that you would share them with Nicholas instead, but this . . . this is worse than I could've imagined."

"I wanted to tell you, but it wasn't my place. You deserved to hear it from your parents. Nicholas gave your mother time to tell you. But when you hadn't said anything by this morning, we figured you had no idea."

"I don't want to hear all this 'we' talk. You and I used to be 'we'! But now Nicholas is your 'we.' I told you in your driveway that I was worried about this, but you couldn't understand. It makes it so much harder that the very thing I worried about has come true. I'm jealous of a man who's my . . . my fa . . . I can't even say it," Ruth sobbed. "And wait until Martha finds out about this. I just don't know which way to turn."

Naomi leaned toward the chair to put her arm around Ruth, but she ducked and stood up. "No, please don't. Please don't touch me."

"I'm sorry, Ruth. I couldn't tell you," Naomi said.

"Why? Because you didn't want to hurt Nicholas or make him upset? What about *me*? There was a time when you looked out for *my* feelings, but what happened to that? I've been used by my mother whenever it was convenient for her and then pushed aside when a man came around. And now you're doing the same thing too."

"No, Ruth, I would never. You're the main reason I'm taking things so slowly with Nicholas. He wants to talk about the future, but I want you to be comfortable with things first. I can't imagine things going further if you're not on board with it."

"Well, I don't have anything reassuring to say about that. You picked the wrong time to bring that up, but on second thought, how can I blame you? There will never be a good time to bring it up with me, because I'll never be okay with it."

"Ruth, you're just angry right now."

"You're right. I'm angry. The more I think about it, the angrier I get. You can't see your selfishness, but I can. You were going to let me give my mother twenty thousand dollars, knowing the whole time what she had done? Does Nicholas know that she came to ask me for money? Does he know what kind of woman he left me with?"

"I didn't tell him why she came to town. I wanted to maintain your privacy."

"I'd like to believe you. I want to believe that I have somebody on my side, but you seem to only be looking out for him and yourself."

"No, that's not true," Naomi said, her voice cracking as tears formed in her eyes.

"You don't realize how caught up you are with Nicholas. You didn't even encourage me to wait to give my mother the money she asked for or even hint that I shouldn't give it to her at all. You've never held your tongue about her before. Why start now?"

Ruth watched Naomi's face wrinkle and relax, as if she doubted what Ruth said but then slowly discovered evidence within herself that it was true. That was enough for Ruth. "I never treated you that way, not with Marlon and not with Beau. So, yeah, this hurts. It's too much hurt at one time. I expect my mother to be selfish, but with you, I didn't see this coming."

Naomi lowered her body into the swivel chair and whimpered, "I'm sorry. I'm so sorry, Ruth. You're right."

It pained Ruth to watch Naomi cry, but she stood for a second and took it in, struggling to interpret the myriad of emotions she felt. It was clear to Ruth that she did not want to see Naomi in pain. But as their relationship transitioned to a place it had never been before, something inside Ruth told her to remember this moment, if for no other reason than to make sure it never happened again.

Ruth picked up her purse and the key to Naomi's home. She dropped the key into Naomi's lap without removing it from the key chain. "I don't need this anymore," she said, tears streaming down her face. "I'm not clear on where we go from here or how much time I need to figure out what I want to happen next, but I want you to know that you've meant the world to me. You have held me up when I didn't have the strength to hold myself up. But now I see that it's time for me to figure out how to do that on my own."

Ruth put her palms over her eyes and wiped them. She walked toward the hallway and continued to the front door. Then she turned back and yelled, "Nicholas, she needs you. And don't forget to lock the door."

* * *

"GIVE ME A minute. I'm going to need another handkerchief," Ruth said, sniffling. It was her first time out of the house since Nicholas's revelation two days prior. She'd called Shari first thing that morning, with the hope that she might have an opening at some point during the week, but she was relieved the therapist had a last-minute cancellation and could accommodate her on a hectic Tuesday afternoon after a long weekend.

"I feel better getting it all out," Ruth said, dabbing her eyes with one of Beau's handkerchiefs. She had missed him more than usual over the past two days, but his handkerchiefs brought comfort through her incessant crying.

"Good. So, do you have an idea of what you'd like to do going forward?" Shari asked.

"No. I keep going over things in my head, but I haven't made any decisions. I'd like to terminate Nicholas's contract, but it only has about a couple of months left. I'd hate to lose all the progress we've made and have to start over with someone else, but I fear Martha will question his recommendations once she finds out he's my father. I don't want the business conflict to escalate."

"For the sake of working through your feelings, what if Martha weren't an issue? Would there be any way to salvage your working relationship with Nicholas?"

"I can't stand to be in the same room with him," Ruth said flatly.

Shari removed her large black geometric eyeglasses and dangled them by the side of her mouth. "Let's talk more about that. What has he done to make you feel that way?"

Ruth paused to think as she watched Shari slide the glasses back onto her face. "He didn't do anything directly to me, but I've always had some resentment toward whoever my father was because he procreated with my mother. She's such a terrible person. How could someone be attracted to her? I keep asking myself that over and over again."

"Doesn't she look a lot like you?"

Ruth paused. "Yeah . . . but people should be able to see beyond her beauty."

"But when you're young and immature, it's not unusual to place an inappropriate amount of emphasis on physical looks. Why do you think so many people have conflict with their child's other parent? Often it's because they based the relationship on looks or other superficial things, only to realize too late that there were other factors they should've been considering."

"That's true, but give me a minute to get my journal so I can write this down," Ruth said, reaching toward the coffee table. She flipped open her tattered journal and dug into her purse for a pen.

"I'm glad to hear that resonated with you. Try to keep it in mind as you continue to process your experience with Nicholas and decide what you want from him," Shari said, writing in the notebook on her lap.

Where does she get this stuff? This is good, Ruth thought as she scribbled. "I can do that," she said aloud.

Shari smiled softly. When Ruth lifted her head from her journal and made eye contact, Shari continued. "I'd like to ask a more general question. Aside from finding out that Nicholas is your father, how do you feel hearing that your father is alive?"

Ruth wrung the handkerchief through her fingers. "I'm angry about the wasted time. I'm hurt that my mother would rob me of having a father. Nicholas is an enjoyable guy. He probably would've been fun to have around. And he's very wise. It breaks my heart that I missed out on all that." Ruth began to sob. She clumsily folded the handkerchief and held it against her eyes as her body heaved.

"I know this is hard. Do you want to take a break?"

"No . . . thank . . . you," she said as she cried. "I'm fine."

"Take a few deep breaths and then start again when you're ready."

Ruth closed her eyes and leaned back on the sofa. She took three deep breaths and then opened her eyes. "Thank you. So, I was saying that I'm angry with my mother. I don't think there's anything salvageable there. Just like everything else with her, I'll have to come to terms with it myself. At least I can talk through it here. And I'll also pray and work on forgiving her."

"That seems reasonable, given what you've told me about your mother in the past. But do you want to attempt to talk with her about it?"

"Probably not. Nicholas said she was supposed to call me and tell me herself, but she didn't. She didn't call about the money when she didn't receive it, so she's assumed that Nicholas dropped the news. I'm sure she doesn't want to talk about it. Otherwise, I'd have heard from her. And part of me is grateful she's made that choice. It's probably spared me a ton of emotional damage."

"It would be good to figure out if you want to just leave things like that and wait to hear from her, or if you're interested in seeing how she'd respond if you asked her about it."

"I'm not sure I want to ask her," Ruth said. "Her previous behavior tells me that she won't accept any responsibility. I'm not ready to hear that from her. She's so cold and callous when confronted, and she'll turn it back on me and somehow make it my fault, even though I didn't ask to be conceived."

"That makes sense. Well, if you decide that you want to talk with her about it, you should think about what you hope to accomplish in the conversation, whether it's an apology or just acceptance of responsibility. It seems that either of those would be progress, but in the event that neither happens, would you be okay with just being heard?"

"I'm not sure it would be a productive conversation, but let me write this down just in case." Ruth paused as she stared at the chicken scratch in her journal. "So, are these the same questions I should ask myself before I have a conversation with Nicholas and Naomi?"

"Yes, exactly. Remember, therapy is about giving you the tools you need to deal with the tough things you've encountered. And you can apply the tools and lessons you learn to a variety of relationships."

"Got it. Okay, what else?"

"Do you want your mother to know you're hurt?" Shari asked. "If so, how much of it feels safe to share with her? You should also decide if there are any lines that you don't want her to cross. And communicate those boundaries to her. Also, have an exit plan ahead of time, in case the conversation goes in a direction that's hurtful to you."

Ruth nodded, jotting the questions and statements Shari fired off.

"And if you want to have another session or talk through things by phone before that time, I'm happy to do so."

"Thank you," Ruth said, her tone lighter than it was when she started the session.

"So, are you ready to talk about those questions as they relate to Nicholas and your mother-in-law?"

"I don't know yet what I want to do. It would be so much easier if they weren't dating each other. That adds another layer of discomfort."

"What makes it uncomfortable for you? When we talked about it in previous sessions, you said their dating complicated things because of privacy. Now that you know that Nicholas is your father, he's already in the family. So, it seems like privacy isn't so much a factor—at least, not in the same way you were worried about it before. Do you have other privacy concerns, or is something else bothering you?"

"I hadn't thought about that. But I guess not," Ruth said, her voice soft and robotic.

"Have you ever considered that their relationship could give you the things that you've always wanted? Perhaps the problem is that it doesn't look like what you expected, so you didn't recognize it."

Ruth looked at Shari with doubt enveloping her face. "That one is going to take some time to sort through."

Chapter Nineteen

Frequenting the heart center for follow-up appointments was starting to pay off for Mary. When Oji Greenwald asked her to meet him in the east lobby, she knew exactly where to go. She parked in the same garage she used for her cardiology appointments but used the entrance opposite the atrium where the Heart Month blood drive was held each February.

As she navigated through the rows of white partitions checkered with red paper hearts, she spotted Oji sitting in a section of café tables on the other side of the people snacking on bagels and orange juice after their blood donations.

"Hey, Mary," he said, waving her over to his small table. "I've got to go," he said into the phone that was glued to his ear. "My ten o'clock is here. . . . Yes . . . yes . . . okay . . . I have to go. . . . Love you too. Bye."

"How sweet," Mary said, extending her hand.

"Thanks," Oji said, shaking her hand. "And that was my mother, by the way. I can't have you telling everyone around town that I'm in a relationship. That'll totally ruin my reputation."

Mary laughed as she took the seat across from Oji, who still held his cell phone in his hand. "Good to know," she said, feigning interest. He wasn't her type, but she could see how women were suckered by his vibe. He seemed like the kind of guy who hid his intelligence from his teammates on the football team in high school, pledged a fraternity in college while holding down a 3.8 GPA, and then used his charisma, good looks, and family connections after graduation to secure a high-earning position.

But Oji had left his first job after two years to get into real estate, and Mary suspected he was wildly successful at it for the same reasons women were drawn to him.

"Speaking of my reputation, I've received a bunch of calls from your sister," Oji said. "She hasn't come up during any of our discussions, but are you planning to work with her on the restaurant?"

The question took Mary aback. She'd assumed that Martha would've met with Oji and talked with him about her interests on her own time. She didn't want to be responsible for representing her sister in any way. "No, this will be a solo venture, just like Alabaster Lunch Box. I hope that's okay."

Oji smiled. "It's perfect. I don't mix business with pleasure, so I hoped you'd say that."

Mary tilted her head and looked at him from the corner of her eye. "I don't know what to make of you."

"Most people say that, but I'm very loyal to those I choose to establish a relationship with, be it business or personal," Oji said fervently.

His response reminded Mary of a candidate on a job interview, but she needed to let him know that she was not the hiring manager. "I'll keep that in mind, but I'm staying out of whatever you might be planning with my sister. I think that's what you're getting at, and I'd like to focus on the restaurant." She gave him a closed-lip smile. *Besides, I have my hands full trying to figure out what I'm going to do with Tynan.*

"Perfect again! You're two for two! I hoped you wouldn't mind. This meeting is off to a promising start," Oji said jubilantly.

Mary laughed and shook her head.

He slid his cell phone into the pocket of his sport coat. "So, I bet you're wondering why I asked you to meet here. I've received word that I have preliminary approval for the development from the City of Macon Planning Commission. That's why I was talking to my mom. This project has the potential to get national attention, and she was the first person I wanted to tell."

While they got along in the few minutes they spoke at the Christmas party, Oji had been a little like a snake-oil salesman at their first meeting about the new real-estate development. But after numerous phone calls and a handful of in-person meetings, he was starting to get comfortable with Mary and starting to show his cards. She was certain it wasn't by accident. He was as strategic as Martha—the phone call with his mother, mentioning his reputation, and bringing up Martha, when he'd never brought her up before. Today's meeting seemed to be an excuse for Oji to see how Mary felt about his making a move on her sister.

In Mary's eyes, they would either be a perfect match or as flammable as powdered sugar on a birthday cake. But it would be entertaining regardless.

She decided to play along. "That's great news! Congratulations!"

"And congratulations to you too. All the preliminary feedback I've received suggests that your restaurant proposal sealed the deal. They love your ideas for community outreach and incorporating a teaching kitchen. The current plans call for the restaurant to be a 4,400-square-foot space that seats two hundred, with ninety-five additional seats in the teaching kitchen, which could be converted into a dining area. And the hospital has also expressed interest in having you partner with the primary care center for some of the classes, if that's okay with you. Since so many medical conditions are affected by what people eat, they want to be part of this. You know, to give their patients more opportunities to learn about healthy eating and cooking. So, what do you think?" Oji asked, looking pleased with his delivery.

Mary wasn't sure if she should give him more credit for play-

ing her or if she should blame Martha for a backhanded attempt
to sneak into her project, but she intended to find out before the
deal was finalized. "We talked about me teaching the classes. I'm
already doing some at my restaurant in Edin," Mary said, speaking firmly and looking Oji in the eye.

"Certainly, and that was part of what the planning commission likes about you. You check several boxes for them. But you
know how things can get political." He shrugged. "The restaurant will be on the corner, just over there," he said pointing out
the window. "And with it being so close to the hospital, they
want in."

Mary chose her words carefully. "Let me give it some thought
and get back to you."

"Sounds like a plan." Oji smiled.

* * *

"Who is it?" Naomi said, nervously peeking through the peephole at the stranger on the other side of her door. She'd been
expecting Nicholas to buzz at the front gate of the estate when
he arrived, but she hadn't heard from him since he texted to let
her know he'd landed in Atlanta and was on the way to Edin.
And she hadn't buzzed this person in either.

"I'm with Nicholas, ma'am," the man responded.

Already on edge after going back and forth about whether she
should proceed with the date, now Naomi was leery about trust-
ing the unexpected person standing on her porch. She texted
Nicholas to confirm he had sent someone to pick her up. When
he quickly replied that he had done so, she cracked the door open
and peered outside.

"Good evening, ma'am. I'm Gabriel. I'll be your driver for the
evening," the gentleman responded.

Naomi looked past Gabriel to a black sedan parked in her

driveway. The car's floodlights beamed like a spotlight. Nicholas stood next to the vehicle, holding a bouquet of flowers and looking like a bachelor on a reality TV dating show.

Naomi sighed with relief. She stepped out onto the porch, locked the door, and set her house alarm.

Impressive. Maybe it's good I didn't cancel the visit after all, she thought as she walked to the driveway. She forced a smile, trying to get on board with the romantic gesture. Still frustrated about the cold shoulder Ruth had given her and Nicholas and worried about how her nieces would react when they learned the paternity news, Naomi was considering a breakup . . . even on Valentine's Day. As much as she cared for Nicholas, she didn't want to sacrifice her family for him. Although he had been diligent in trying to address her discomfort, a chasm had developed between them in the nearly four weeks that had passed since his last visit. And it had grown bigger than any distance she expected the miles between Philadelphia and Edin to create.

As Naomi reached the car, Gabriel opened the door. Nicholas kissed Naomi on the cheek and handed her a bouquet of stargazer lilies and light pink roses similar to the hand-embroidered flowers on the shawl she wore over her fuchsia midi dress. "You look lovely," he whispered.

"Thank you." She blushed. "You look nice too."

Naomi slid into the back seat of the car and buckled her seatbelt. She picked at her freshly manicured nails and fidgeted as Nicholas chatted about his commute from Philadelphia.

"Are you okay?" he asked.

"I've just got a lot on my mind," she said, trying to throw him off and also convince herself to enjoy the evening.

Nicholas picked up her hand and touched it lightly as the car turned onto the main road of the estate.

"I'm curious about where we're going. Will you give me a

hint?" Naomi asked, fiddling with the pink sapphire stud earring in her right ear.

"By the time you guess once, we'll be there," he responded.

She tried a little harder to get in the mood. "Oh, that's not fair," she said coyly. "Come on. Just one hint."

"That *was* your hint." Nicholas smiled.

Naomi paused, noticing that instead of waiting for the gate at the main entrance of the estate to open, the driver had turned left. Rather than exiting, the car was still on the property, traveling along the road to the east side of the grounds. "We're going to drive by the lake? It's too dark and chilly to do anything more than stand outside for longer than a second, but it would've been an ideal place to spend Valentine's Day. I wish you had told me you wanted to go there. I could've prepared some food, and we could've bundled up and had a nice evening," she said, her voice full of sadness.

Nicholas held Naomi's right hand between his hands. "That's a good point. I'll plan better next time."

She looked down at the sandwich their hands formed and smiled softly. She wasn't convinced she could give Nicholas up. *I'll just enjoy tonight and see how I feel tomorrow.* As the car came to a slow stop, she lifted her head and looked outside the window. Candles lined the path to the lake, and string lights adorned the lake pavilion, forming a constellation on land in the darkness wrapped around the lake.

Naomi started to take shallow breaths. "Oh, Nicholas! You're not going to—"

"Oh no. We're just gonna have a nice evening. I promise."

"Okay . . . good," Naomi said, simmering down.

"I thought about warning you, but I hoped the surprise would be worth the risk of alarming you for a few seconds." He smiled.

"But how did you do this?" she asked, pulling him into a hug.

"I'm resourceful if nothing else," he said, then laughed. "I'm glad you like it so far. I wanted to do a little something to let you know how much you mean to me. Wait here for a second."

Gabriel opened the door. Nicholas stepped out of the car and got into a black golf cart that Naomi recognized as Mary's.

"Okay, ma'am. Your turn," Gabriel said, assisting Naomi and her flowers with the transfer from the car to the golf cart.

Naomi sat next to Nicholas in the cart, bundled in her shawl. It was her heaviest shawl, the one she wore when she wanted to prevent her clothes from becoming wrinkled under a coat. She worried it wouldn't keep her warm enough by the chilly lake, but she decided not to be as presumptuous as she had been in the car. She savored the quiet beauty of the moment as Nicholas drove down the hill. As they neared the pavilion, she could see that its two-story stone fireplace was lit, and patio heaters were scattered along the periphery of the open-air structure.

Mary greeted the couple as they parked at the foot of the pavilion. "Happy Valentine's Day! As I anticipated, you are right on time, Nicholas."

He acknowledged the compliment with a wink. Then he walked around the golf cart to assist Naomi.

Naomi's eyes danced with excitement as they met Mary's. "Thanks so much for your help!" Naomi exclaimed.

"You deserve to enjoy every second of the evening," Mary said. "Nicholas has designed a delicious menu for you. Please let me take those. I've got a vase ready for them."

Naomi handed Mary the flowers, and a broad smile spread across Naomi's face as she noticed a table set for two in front of the fireplace. She held on to Nicholas's hand and stepped to the ground, maintaining her grasp as she laid her head against his shoulder and paused to take in the scene. "This is breathtaking. It's like you read my mind. Thank you," she whispered.

"Anything for you," he said, beaming.

* * *

"I STILL CAN'T believe you convinced me to go hiking," Naomi said, dragging out the last word. "This isn't my thing, but it's beautiful out here," she continued as she scanned the landscape of grass, mounds, and trees surrounding the path she walked in the Ocmulgee Mounds National Historical Park in Macon.

Nicholas chuckled and shook his head. "Naomi, a hike is just a long walk. You grew up in the country with woods all around your family's estate. You've hiked most of your life. You just didn't use that word. If I hadn't called it hiking, it wouldn't have bothered you. I should've just said we were going on a sightseeing walk."

Naomi stared at Nicholas as his words sunk in. "I never looked at it that way, but you're right. I wouldn't have complained one bit," she said. She had delighted in the lakeside dinner the night before, so it was only fair that she went along with the rest of his plans for the weekend. Although she was apprehensive about what lay ahead for their relationship, the evening had also gone a long way to remind her that she had a strong feelings for Nicholas.

Despite the thirty-minute drive from her home, Naomi had never once visited the park, which was on sacred Native American tribal land. Some parts of the area reminded her of a very hilly stretch that could be anywhere in a rural area, but the mounds were more meaningful than that. The layers of earth and plant matter were used as religious structures and burial mounds, and the land was the ancestral homeland of the Muscogee (Creek) Nation, who were forcibly removed from the land in the 1800s and marched about a thousand miles from Georgia to Oklahoma along the Trail of Tears.

The solemnness of the space weighed on Naomi. She struggled to reconcile herself with its beauty and its place in American history, on top of the personal heaviness that she carried with her on the hike. One minute the serenity of her surroundings took the edge off her feelings, but the next minute it made her miss a key figure in her life.

"I want to bring Ruth here. I—" She caught herself. "I'm sorry. I've been trying not to bring her up during your visit."

"She's all we've talked about for the past month, so it wasn't hard to notice that you've avoided speaking about her this weekend. But it's okay. She's important to both of us. We can't pretend she doesn't exist."

"But that's what she's done to us." Naomi sighed. She zipped her purple windbreaker all the way up until it covered her chin. Then she quickly lowered it a couple of inches and then raised it again.

"I know that's what it feels like, but we don't know if that's what she's doing. We only know that she's taken some time away. I doubt she just stopped thinking about us. We're probably on her mind a lot and she's trying to figure out how to deal with everything."

"You two are so much alike. I never noticed how much until she stopped talking to me," Naomi said as she lowered her zipper to her collarbone.

Nicholas smiled softly. "She'll come around. She just needs time. I'd love for her to have someone to help her through this, and I feel guilty that she's giving you the silent treatment."

"It's not your fault. I was trying not to talk about it, but I have to be honest with you. I've been wondering if we should take a break," Naomi said, crossing the second of the two boundaries she'd set for the weekend.

Nicholas stopped in the middle of the path and looked at her. "I wondered about that too."

"You did?" she asked, stopping beside him.

"Yeah. I love you, but I don't want to come between you and

Ruth. As a father, I want the best for my daughter. She's already lost so much. It's obvious that you've brought her stability and a type of love that she'd never experienced before you came into her life. I don't want to take that away from her. Even if she never speaks to me again, she's still my daughter. She's the child I've always wanted, and I'd do anything for her," he said, wiping his eyes.

Naomi couldn't get past the first part of what Nicholas had uttered. She was sure he said lots of important things, and she wanted to address them. But she was stuck. She needed to rewind.

"Did you just say that you . . ."

He exhaled deeply and his eyes widened. "Oh, that slipped out. . . . I didn't mean to make you uncomfortable. Did I?"

Naomi chewed her lip and fixed her gaze on Nicholas as she struggled to process what she'd just heard. She wanted him to take it back. She didn't understand how he could feel that way already. She stumbled over her words, trying not to let on that she wasn't certain she felt the same way. "I . . . uh . . . I just . . . I just wasn't expecting this. . . . How can you be sure?"

"Let's not talk about it, okay?" he said.

Jolted by the sudden shutdown of the conversation, Naomi restarted on the trail. "Okay. Let's get back to our walk," she said, fiddling with the purple sapphire stud earring in her right ear. She cared about Nicholas, and she didn't want to hurt him. As much as she wanted to act like she didn't hear his extroverted confession, she'd shared her feelings, honoring the transparency they prioritized in their relationship. Now it just made her want to talk even more, so she walked faster to avoid doing so.

Naomi stopped when she noticed that Nicholas wasn't walking alongside her. She turned around to find him bent over in the middle of the path, several feet away. He looked like he was about to fall over, barely supporting himself by placing his left arm on his thigh as he rubbed his left jaw with his right hand. "Give me . . . a minute," he said slowly, taking a breath between the words.

She rushed over to him. "What's wrong? What's happening?"

"I don't know. . . . It felt like . . . indigestion . . . when we first . . . started walking. . . . I thought it was from . . . eating late . . . last night. . . . But my jaw . . . hurts and . . . my arms feel funny . . . kinda numb."

There were no chairs nearby, so Naomi did the next best thing. "Let's take a break. We can sit on the ground." She held Nicholas's arm and supported him as he lowered his body to the ground. He leaned slightly toward the right, but she pressed her body against his and guided him so he didn't fall. She felt the dampness of his sweat on her skin, even though the temperature was in the low sixties.

Nicholas closed his eyes slowly and then opened them quickly. "Sorry. . . . I thought . . . I was . . . gonna throw up," he said.

Naomi reviewed Nicholas's symptoms in her head. *Jaw pain, arms feeling funny, nausea, sweating—all symptoms of a heart attack.* Recalling the training she'd learned at one of her senior citizen meetings at church, she helped him bend his legs at the knees to relieve any strain that his heart might be experiencing.

"Try to rest," she said, clutching his hand. "I'm gonna call for help."

She pulled out her phone and called 911.

* * *

THE GARDIN FAMILY gathered in the Macon General Hospital emergency department for the second time in two months. But this time, Ruth was missing. Naomi had called and texted her several times but had not heard back. She worried Ruth would regret it if she didn't make it there soon, whether for not being at the hospital as Nicholas's life hung by a thread or for missing out on a familial relationship with him if he passed away. But Naomi was also concerned about what Ruth would face if she arrived while Nicholas was having his heart procedure. She would have to reconcile herself with having wasted precious time not speaking to him after she learned their connection, and she would also relive her experience waiting for the outcome of Beau's heart surgery, which didn't have a happy ending.

Naomi, Mary, and Martha gathered around Nicholas as he lay on the stretcher in the emergency department, their spirits stifled by the beeps of the heart monitors and machines to dispense medications. He awaited transfer to the cardiac catheterization lab, where a cardiologist could perform a test to diagnose a blockage in his heart arteries and perform a nonsurgical procedure to restore blood flow to the affected portion of his heart. Nicholas had arrived at the hospital twenty minutes after the onset of the chest pressure, well within the thirty minutes recommended in the clinical guidelines. But he looked older as he lay on the stretcher, aged by the cocktail of pain, sweat, and fear.

"Did you call Ruth?" Nicholas asked, his voice faint and mind groggy from the pain medicine administered for his worsening chest pressure.

"Yes," Naomi said. She hoped he wouldn't say much more about Ruth, as Mary and Martha were still unaware of Nicholas and Ruth's biological connection. Naomi couldn't bear to add an inadvertent disclosure to the mounting pile of conflict that already plagued the family. She resolved that she would blame the medication if he let it slip, and she prayed silently that God would forgive her for the double infraction of telling a lie and planning it ahead of time. She also thanked God for His mercy and offered thanks in advance that her prayers for Nicholas's healing would still be heard.

"I hope she will get here soon. I want to see her. . . . Make sure she knows . . ." Nicholas mumbled weakly. Naomi's jaw tightened with anxiety as he continued on, his eyelids fluttering. "All my paperwork is in order . . . in case I don't make it. . . . You know, if she wants what I have . . . I want . . . to leave everything for her . . . to make up for what I . . . couldn't do before."

Tears ran down Naomi's face. "Okay, I'll tell her. . . . Now hush. . . . And rest. You need to rest."

Mary put her arm around Naomi. "We're staying positive, Nicholas. You're gonna be fine," she said. "He's so committed to his work with the company that he's worried about Ruth getting his reports. He's such a good guy."

Naomi looked up at Mary. "Yes, he is. Thank you, Mary," Naomi said, relieved at her niece's interpretation and appreciative of the hug.

Martha examined the monitor, noting that Nicholas's blood pressure and heart rate had improved since he first arrived. "Your numbers are looking much better, and you're in good hands. The cardiologist who's assigned to your case did a special presentation last week for the hospital's Heart Month festivities, and she talked about her experience with the procedure you're having. The fact that you got here so quickly makes me very optimistic."

The emergency department staff had moved without delay when Nicholas and Naomi arrived by ambulance. They lauded Naomi for recognizing the heart attack symptoms onsite, calling for emergency assistance, and proactively alerting the park service staff so they could coordinate with the emergency responders to get the ambulance to their precise location in the park. Her quick thinking saved time, virtually ensuring that Nicholas would make it to the hospital within the window required for him to receive lifesaving heart testing and intervention.

The door to Nicholas's room crept open.

Naomi craned her neck. "Ruth?" she whispered.

But it wasn't Ruth. Nicholas's nurse entered the room. "Okay, they're ready for you in the cardiac cath lab, Mr. Dorsey. The transport team is here."

While the nurse disconnected Nicholas from the monitor and closed his intravenous connections, Naomi inched toward him. Mary lowered her arm, and she and Martha stepped back toward the monitors.

Naomi kissed Nicholas on the cheek, stroking his opposite cheek with her hand. "I'll see you when you get out," she said, stepping back to the wall behind the stretcher, where Mary and Martha stood.

The nurse connected Nicholas to a portable monitor. He slowly turned his head toward Naomi and said, "Thank you. . . . You . . . have brought . . . a light . . . a light to my life . . . that I never . . . thought I . . . would see . . . again."

"Oh," Naomi said as tears streamed. She pulled her hands to her face and wiped her eyes, but more tears fell. Mary and Martha placed their arms around her, each wiping their own tears with a mass of crumpled tissues from the small box that sat near the sink.

The nurse and transport team wheeled Nicholas out of the room.

Naomi leaned back on the wall, her sobs growing louder by the second. She slid a couple of inches down the wall before Mary grabbed her and held her up while Martha dragged a nearby chair into place. Naomi's windbreaker nearly fell off the chair with the rapid movement. Mary guided Naomi to the seated position while Martha held the jacket in place.

"What have I done that God has made life so bitter for me?" Naomi sobbed. "I love him, and I didn't tell him. I couldn't say it. I don't know why it wouldn't come out. But what if he doesn't make it through the procedure?"

Mary squatted next to Naomi, and her aunt fell into her arms.

"It's okay," Mary said. "I believe he's going to make it. You'll be able to tell him later."

Martha grabbed the box, removing the last two tissues as Naomi's phone rang.

Naomi lifted her head enough that it cleared Mary's shoulder, her puffy eyes becoming redder with each tear she shed. "It's in my jacket," she said, her words barely intelligible.

Martha handed Mary the tissues. Then she dipped her hand deep into the windbreaker's pockets. In the third pocket, she touched a hard plastic case. Martha pulled it out and glanced at the phone, immediately recognizing the group photo that had thrown Christmas into a downward spiral. She slid her finger across the screen to answer the call.

"Hello, Ruth. This is Martha."

* * *

RUTH KNOCKED ON Martha's office door. The last time she found herself there, she had hoped the olive branch she carried would be well received. But her offer had backfired, and their relationship became more brittle with every subsequent interaction. Now, as Ruth stood at the entry, her vulnerability took her to a place that didn't allow her to give the previous encounter or her other sour experiences with Martha any weight in her heart. She let them all go. Ruth didn't care about their conflict. She had only one goal, and if Martha wouldn't give her the information she needed, she would find someone else who could.

"Ruth? Come in," Martha said.

Ruth pushed the door open and walked in.

Naomi jumped up from the small sofa near the door and hugged Ruth tightly. "I wasn't sure if you were gonna come. Thank you for being here," Naomi sobbed.

Ruth's eyes were glassy and pink, remnants of the emotions

she'd experienced on her quick commute to the hospital. "I'm sorry I didn't answer when you called. I was at a retreat, one of those semi-silent ones where you're not allowed to talk or use your phone most of the time. Luckily, it wasn't too far from here."

Mary rose from the sofa and took a couple of steps to meet Ruth. She gave her a partial hug, as Naomi clung to the other side of Ruth's body. "I'm glad you were able to make it," Mary said. "Aunt Naomi needs all the love she can get right now."

"Thank you," Ruth replied, motioning for Mary to switch places with her.

"Sit on the sofa with Mary. I'll be right back," Ruth said to Naomi.

Ruth walked across the room to where Martha sat behind her desk. "Thank you," she said, extending her arms for a hug and putting Martha on notice that Ruth was not to be dismissed.

Martha stood and gave in, though her movements were stiff with a quick double pat on the back.

Ruth returned to the other side of the room. She sat on the sofa, squeezing in next to Naomi and placing her purse on her lap. Naomi held Ruth's hand as Ruth began to speak, rotating her head between the sisters. "There's no easy way to say it, especially under these circumstances. I'm just going to put it out there so we're all on the same page." Her tone sounded professional, but her voice wavered like she was about to announce downsizing at the office. "It's recently come to my attention that Nicholas is my father."

The sisters gasped in unison.

Ruth read the questions on their faces. "Yeah, I know," she said, her pent-up emotion escaping from the corners of her eyes. "Obviously, this isn't the time to talk about Gardin Family Enterprises, but Nicholas has not been back to the office or performed any work for us since we both found out."

Naomi closed her eyes and gripped Mary's and Ruth's hands, alternating her hand movements for stress relief as though their limbs were made of pliable foam rubber instead of flesh and bone.

The sisters' raised eyebrows conveyed their need for more information.

"He found out a couple of days before he told me," Ruth continued. "You probably understand now why I was at a semi-silent retreat for the past three days. I've had a lot of thinking to do."

"Wow," Martha said.

"Right. So, is Nicholas getting the same medical treatment that Beau had?" Ruth asked, her voice becoming stronger.

Martha leaned in. "Yes and no," she said, tilting her head from side to side. "When Beau first had the heart attack, he had a test to examine the blood flow through his heart arteries and then a procedure to open them up. Nicholas is going through the same thing right now. But Beau later had bypass surgery, which required taking a blood vessel from his leg and placing it in his heart to create another route for the blood to flow around the blockage. Nicholas doesn't seem to need surgery right now, as far as we know."

Ruth squeezed her eyelids together and dabbed the corners of her eyes as she spoke. "Okay. That's a relief. . . . How long has he been in there?"

"It usually lasts anywhere from thirty minutes to two hours," Martha said, "and Nicholas has been in for about an hour. The nurse said she'd call me when it's finished so we can head over and be waiting when the cardiologist is ready to talk to us." She handed Ruth a tissue.

"Thank you, Martha," Ruth said.

Chapter Twenty

Ruth and Naomi sat in the heart center's family consultation room. During Nicholas's procedure, they'd quickly figured out how to interact with each other while other people were around. But now that they were alone for the first time in a month, the silence between them was thick. The small consultation room was minimally furnished with a rectangular table and six chairs. The size was perfect for the family meeting with the doctor. But now with only Ruth and Naomi remaining, the room seemed so much smaller. After the cardiologist's debriefing, the sisters scattered. Mary set out for Edin, while Martha returned to her office to gather her things so she'd be ready to go with Naomi to see Nicholas once he was moved to a room.

The procedure had been successful overall, but an unexpected complication had caused it to last more than two hours. Although the doctor expected him to do well, Nicholas would need to stay in the cardiovascular intensive care unit for close observation overnight, with strict visiting hours enforced.

Ruth and Naomi's relationship also needed specialized care. The women looked the same, but the events over the past month—and their reactions to them—had changed them both in ways that could not be undone.

Ruth sat across from Naomi with her arms folded. "This feels weird. It's like we don't know each other anymore," she said.

"I don't know if I would go that far," Naomi replied, her shoulders slightly slumped.

"How else would you explain it?"

Naomi didn't know the answer to the question but was glad she and Ruth were talking. "We're just going through a phase," Naomi said. "All families go through difficult times. That's how you grow."

"See, that's what I mean. You're being so positive."

Hearing the feedback from Ruth was like getting a passing grade on a pop quiz. Naomi appreciated the pat on the back, even if it wasn't intentional. She'd made an effort to be more positive, but she felt as though she'd failed at it the entire day. "Isn't that a good thing?" she asked.

"Maybe, but it could also be denial. I don't know." Ruth shrugged. "I guess I need more time to work through it. I'm trying, MIL. I just don't know what's going on."

"I understand that. And you've taken some time for yourself to try to figure it out."

"That sounds like something Nicholas would say."

Ruth was right. Naomi was echoing the words that Nicholas had spoken to her in so many conversations over the past month. It was like he had taken over her mind while he was in the procedure.

Such things had never come out of Naomi's mouth before. Nicholas had been confident in their relationship since the beginning, and it was obvious that he was making space for her in his life and speech. But Naomi had thought it was weird. Now that Ruth had pointed it out, it was a badge Naomi wanted to wear proudly, an accolade for surviving Nicholas's heart attack. "I guess I do sound like him. . . . It seems we both have a lot to think about, but let's not rush things between us. As long as our hearts are in the right place, things will work themselves out naturally. And we'll be forced to see each other now that Nicholas is in the hospital."

"I'm still working through what that means for me," Ruth said. "This has all happened so quickly. I'm relieved that it looks like Nicholas will be okay, but I'm not some sort of plug-and-play daughter. I care about him as a person. We had a good working relationship, and—"

"Working relationship? That would crush him if he heard that."

"That's what it was, MIL."

"But you didn't have to say it that way," Naomi protested.

"See, this is why we haven't talked in a month. You keep trying to force me into things I'm not ready for. I just can't do this right now. There's too much at stake with the company."

"Well, when will you have time to do it? Because it's happening now, whether you like it or not. You've never been one to run from inconvenient things before."

"And that proves my original point. We've changed, and we don't know each other so well anymore. But we don't have to figure it all out now." Ruth picked up her purse and stood up. "I'm gonna go, but I'm sure we'll be in touch."

Naomi watched in disbelief as Ruth walked out the door. For the second time that day, she fiddled with the purple sapphire stud earring in her right ear. Her wide eyes stayed fixed on the door as it closed. She thought Ruth would come back, but she didn't. *How can someone who wants a family so much run from it?*

* * *

RUTH HAD LOST track of time. She expected it to still be light out, but the windows of the waiting area outside the cardiac catheterization lab told another story. The sky was dark and the streetlights were on. The sunset she had planned to watch at the retreat center had passed, and the whirring of a dozen simultaneous conversations in the waiting area was a poor substitute for the silence she'd planned to enjoy with her evening meal. Her conversation with Naomi had left her feeling jumpy. She contemplated going back to the retreat center, but she didn't want her family emergency to intrude on the other attendees' experience.

As Ruth turned the corner to go to the elevator, an illuminated wall of colorful stained-glass windows caught her eye. The bright primary colors and playful patterns offered a diversion from the cloud that hung over her head. She entered the corridor, which had no light aside from the illuminated wall. The balance of circular and leaflike patterns on the stained panels and the otherwise dark environment in the hallway created an experience that awakened the senses yet invoked peace.

A chapel sat at the end of the corridor. As Ruth walked inside, she heard a voice call out from behind her. "Excuse me, ma'am?"

Ruth turned around, anticipating that perhaps she'd forgotten something in the family consultation room. A perky young woman with wavy shoulder-length hair and pale-pink lipstick stood behind her. *She must work here,* Ruth thought, slightly annoyed by the woman's pleasant demeanor.

"Hi, I'm Ruth. I'm one of the hospital chaplains," the woman said, waving a hand in the air as she caught up. "I was trying to catch you when you left the family consultation room, but it turns out we ended up at the same place anyway."

"Oh, I didn't see you. I've got a lot on my mind. . . . And my name is Ruth too. I'm Ruth Gardin."

"Nice to meet you, Ruth Gardin. I'm Ruth Finkelstein." She smiled. "I was trying to catch you to introduce myself and check in with you. A big part of my job as a hospital chaplain is to lend support, so let me know if you'd like to talk."

Ruth felt guilty for her irritability. "Thank you. I'm just gonna sit in here and think for a little while," she said with a polite smile.

Ruth rarely met women who shared her name, but it resonated

with her on a night when she had spent so much time thinking about her parentage. It reminded her of the reason her mother said she'd chosen her name, one of the few redeeming memories she had from her childhood. *Ruth means "companion, friend." I named you Ruth because I wanted you,* her mother said once after Ruth asked about her father. Now Ruth wondered if *that* was a lie too.

The lighting was ideal, dim but with enough light to see a podium in front of several rows of chairs. Ruth took a seat at the end of the second-to-last row. Although the neutral colors were a departure from the whimsical designs in the hallway, Ruth felt a continued peace in the chapel. She sat for several minutes, reflecting on the day and the past month. She also expressed thanks to God for Nicholas's well-being and prayed for guidance about her conflicted feelings about him, Naomi, and her mother.

After she transitioned out of her time of prayer, Ruth was so relaxed that she drifted in and out of sleep. She began to think about the colorful stained-glass images in the corridor. They reminded her of the playfulness of childhood, which had always seemed just beyond her reach while she was growing up. Ruth had yearned for a normal family instead of a mother who always said she wanted a daughter for a companion and friend but was more preoccupied with her boyfriends and what they could buy for her. Because her mother refused her requests for information about her father, Ruth daydreamed about what he must have been like and made up stories about him. The heaviness of his absence overshadowed most of her childhood memories. And though Ruth had made peace with it when she left her mother's home, it had all come back with Nicholas's revelation.

Ruth awakened fully, feeling slightly refreshed but no closer to knowing what her next steps should be. As she picked up her purse and stood to leave the chapel, she heard a thud at the rear of the room. She looked around. She was still the only person in the chapel, aside from the chaplain, who had just knocked a large vase of water to the floor. Ruth ran to help.

The chaplain put her hand against the edge of the table to prevent the water on the table from dripping to the floor. Ruth picked up the vase and held it against the edge of the table.

"I'm sorry. I didn't mean to disturb you," the chaplain said, lifting her hand and sweeping water into the vase.

"No worries," Ruth replied. "I was just getting ready to leave. I'm just not sure where I'm going yet."

The chaplain smiled. "You'll end up exactly where you're supposed to be. Whoever you're here to visit is blessed to have you in their life. Everyone needs someone who isn't afraid to jump in to help when the time comes."

As Ruth exited the chapel, she replayed the chaplain's words in her head. *Am I afraid to jump in? Is that what's going on?* She walked back down the hallway past the illuminated wall of colorful stained-glass windows. The playfulness of the images caught her attention again. It gnawed at her, bringing up memories of the stories she'd made up about her father. And it touched the piece of her heart where she had tucked away a new source of pain: She still hadn't spoken with her mother since learning that Nicholas was her father. Before his heart attack, she was content not knowing when she would speak to her mother again. But in the game of chicken that she and her mother played with their emotions, Ruth decided it was okay this time if she was the first to swerve.

Ruth removed her phone from the pocket of her Ankara bomber jacket and dialed as she sat on a bench in the hallway.

"Hello," her mother said, her inflection making the statement sound more like a question.

"Hi, Mama."

"How are you, Nikki?" Linda asked, her voice melodic.

It was just like her mother to pretend like everything was normal, but Ruth wasn't in the mood for it. "I'm at the hospital. Nicholas had a heart attack. He told me about . . . about the two of you, so I thought you might want to know."

Linda's voice grew sweeter. "Oh, darling, that was a long time ago."

The dismissiveness of her mother's tone stung. She'd hurt Ruth so much over the years, but she was still her mother. She had clothed her and provided for her, even if she didn't meet her emotional needs. Ruth felt convicted that her mother should have the opportunity to finally do the right thing, not because her mother deserved it but because Ruth felt that she owed it to herself. "Right, but don't you care?"

Linda paused. "Is he okay?" she blurted as if something she'd forgotten to add to her grocery list had popped into her mind.

"Yes, it seems so."

"Well, good, then. I'm glad that worked out."

Ruth sighed. "Why didn't you tell him about me? Did you ever love him?"

"Love is a peculiar thing, Nikki. I wanted to provide the best life for you. Nicholas wasn't prepared to do that. And then I met someone who could, so I went with the better option. But that only lasted for a year, plus or minus, so you know . . . I made the decisions necessary to take care of you myself."

Ruth shook her head, unconvinced by the picture of selflessness her mother painted. "So why lie to me all these years?"

"I didn't want to upset you, Nikki. You know how you can get so caught up on things. It's like you can't move on. Sometimes you just have to move on."

Ruth closed her eyes tightly and softly knocked her head repeatedly on the wall behind her. "I see," she said, finally accepting the fact that her mother, not Nicholas, was the reason she grew up without a father. "Okay, well, I gotta go."

"Wait, Nikki. What about the money we talked about when I came to see you?"

Ruth wasn't sure where the conversation left her relationship with her mother, but she was certain that the Bank of Ruth was closed. She wanted to scream and yell, but she came up with a better idea. She channeled her mother's usual icy demeanor and added sarcasm through her mother's own words. "Oh, Mama. You know how you can get so caught up on things. It's like you can't move on. Sometimes you just have to move on. I have to go. Take care."

Ruth hung up the phone and placed it in her purse. She slid her hand back and forth across the top of the bag, her fingers riding the gathers formed by the purse's drawstrings like imaginary waves while her mother's words replayed in her head. *Sometimes you just have to move on.* Then she remembered the photo of Naomi she put in there on the day of the tea party. She slid her fingers into the interior pocket and hit the top of the photo. She pulled out the picture and looked at it. Her gaze was again drawn to Naomi's forced smile and the distance in her eyes. *But I don't want to live like this anymore.*

Ruth recalled the moments she had felt at odds with herself over the past several months. Although she had a strong sense of obligation to the company, she'd briefly considered leaving it—and the family—when the conflict among the Gardin women took the fun out of her work. She imagined a life with less restraint. *But what if it's not about needing to cut myself off from the company and the family to release my burden? Maybe I've been yearning to feel free within myself, to be free from the pain I've held on to since childhood.* She wasn't sure if it was possible to bridge the brokenness from her childhood into a father-daughter relationship with Nicholas, but they had built a friendship during his time with the company. She wondered if it could form the foundation for a new version of their relationship.

Maybe Shari was right. I need to open my heart to the love I've always wanted.

Ruth turned her head quickly with the epiphany, and one of the colorful circular patterns in the stained-glass windows seemed to spin like a pinwheel. *As the saying goes, what if I'm not too old to have a happy childhood now?*

*   *   *

It was the middle of the last visiting hour of the day in the cardiovascular intensive care unit. Ruth spotted Nicholas's room number on the silver doorframe as she approached. But the glass door was closed, and so were the curtains inside. Her heart started to beat fast. *No, it can't be. Not again,* she thought, overcome by the eerie similarity of the scene to the one she'd been met with shortly after she'd received the call that Beau had died unexpectedly after his bypass surgery. Ruth charged past the nurse's station.

"Ma'am, are you okay? Slow down," said a nurse peering around a computer.

Ruth ignored the directive. She was too determined to find out if Nicholas had suffered the same fate as her late husband.

The nurse bounced to her feet. "Ma'am, may I help you?" she asked. But Ruth continued to Nicholas's room and banged on the glass door. Instead of waiting for a response, she slid the door open and yanked back the curtain.

A startled Naomi and a living, breathing Nicholas stared back at her.

Nicholas leaned forward slightly in bed and squinted at Ruth.

"What are you doing?" Naomi asked, seated at Nicholas's bedside.

"Oh, thank *God* you're all right," Ruth said, her hand clutching the middle of the curtain.

The nurse rushed up behind her. "Ma'am, you can't barge into a room like that." She looked at Naomi and Nicholas. "Do you know this woman?"

Nicholas sighed as he leaned back in bed and tried to regain a comfortable position. "That's my . . . uh . . . daughter."

Daughter. Hearing Nicholas use the word felt like putting medicine on a cut. It stung a little at first, but then came relief. Ruth released the curtain. "I'm sorry. I didn't mean to be disruptive. When I saw the door and curtains closed, I thought . . . I thought something . . . bad happened to you . . . like with Beau," Ruth said, bursting into tears midsentence.

Naomi rushed over to Ruth and wrapped her arms around her. "Oh, sweetie! You poor thing," she said. Ruth fell into Naomi's arms, her back heaving up and down with each sob. She cried the tears that she'd been holding in that evening.

"I'm sorry for your family's loss," the nurse said, her voice overflowing with empathy. "Thankfully, Mr. Dorsey is doing pretty well. Is there anything I can do for y'all?"

Naomi shook her head and mouthed a thank-you as she rubbed Ruth's back.

"Thank you for your concern," Nicholas said.

"You're welcome. You've got about thirty minutes left for the visit. Enjoy your time together," the nurse said. She closed the curtains and the door as she exited the room.

"I feel so horrible about scaring you, Nicholas, especially in your condition," Ruth said, emerging from Naomi's embrace.

"You were worried. There's no need to apologize. I appreciate that you cared. And that you came back," he said, wiping his eyes. "Sit, please."

"Thank you," Ruth said. She turned toward the chair in the corner of the room, next to the television.

"No, sit in the one next to the bed," Naomi said, reaching for Ruth's hand. She squeezed it and smiled. "It's okay. I don't mind."

Nicholas lifted a small tissue box from the overbed table and extended it toward Ruth. She grabbed a couple of tissues but avoided making eye contact with him. "Thank you," she said, sitting in the seat her mother-in-law left. Naomi settled into the chair across the room.

"How are you feeling?" Ruth asked, finally working up the courage to look at Nicholas.

"Tired and sore," he replied. "And a little groggy, but they said that's normal. I can rest better with the curtains and door closed. Martha came for a few minutes, but she went back to her office. I didn't think anyone else was coming, so she closed them on her way out."

"That makes sense. MIL, you can ride home with me. Do you want to text Martha so she knows she doesn't have to wait for you?"

"Oh, that's a good idea," Naomi said.

"How long do they expect you to stay in the hospital?" Ruth asked.

"Two days if all goes according to plan," Nicholas replied.

Ruth had toyed with an idea on the walk over from the chapel. She had talked herself out of it by the time she reached the sign-in desk at the front of the cardiovascular intensive care unit, but her emotional reaction to entering Nicholas's room told her that she needed to go through with it. She was apprehensive about how he would react, but working with him had taught her that she would have to appeal to his practical side to get his buy-in. "Have you started thinking about what you plan to do after you're discharged?"

"We were talking about that right before you came in," Naomi said. "There's no one to take care of him in Philadelphia, so I suggested he stay here."

"No, I don't want to be a burden. I can arrange for help when I get home," Nicholas insisted.

"It wouldn't be a burden," Ruth blurted out. Then she slowed down so that he would hear the sincerity in her voice. "I imagine it's not such a good idea for you to fly back home immediately. And even if it were, you couldn't fly back by yourself. Plus, we wouldn't allow MIL to fly back alone with you. It's just too much. One of us would have to go too, so it's easier if you stay here for a while."

"Ruth is right. And the doctor mentioned that you'll need physical therapy for your heart. What do they call it again?" Naomi asked.

"Cardiac rehabilitation," Ruth replied.

"You can do that here too. I can drive you to your cardiac rehabilitation sessions and follow-up doctor's appointments," Naomi said.

Nicholas closed his eyes and ran his hand across his forehead. "You two make a valid argument," he said, rubbing his chin.

"And I'd like to invite you to stay at my house," Ruth said. "I have a guest bedroom suite on the first floor. I've read that it's typically okay to take the stairs after a heart attack as soon as you can walk at your usual pace, but it'll be easier for you to live in a place where you don't have to bother with stairs. You know, in case you forget something and have to go back and forth to your room." She focused her eyes on Nicholas even though she anticipated a reaction from her mother-in-law.

"Oh, I hadn't thought about that," Naomi said. "I assumed he would stay with me, but I guess you make a good point about the stairs. All my bedrooms are upstairs."

"I don't know about all this," he said, shifting in bed.

"What's the big deal? I've got tons of space, MIL is next door, and you'll have a physician *and* a chef at your beck and call. Who would turn that down?"

Nicholas flicked the monitor on his finger. "Please don't feel obligated to help me. I don't want things to be awkward between us. If I can be direct, you said you weren't going to come see me after my procedure, and now you want me to stay in your home—a home I've driven past multiple times when I came to see Naomi but was never invited to visit. I hope you understand my uneasiness." His voice was charged with a mixture of grogginess, angst, and hurt.

Ruth nodded. "I understand where you're coming from. It's going to take a little getting used to, but it's the right thing to do—for both of us." She reached for his hand and interlocked her fingers with his. "I've had a lot of loss in my life. I'd like to do whatever I can to keep you around for as long as possible," she said, tearing up again. "You know a lot about me and my family because I had to trust you for the sake of Gardin Family Enterprises. That's a big part of why I had so much difficulty with the two of you being in a relationship."

Ruth glanced across the room at her mother-in-law. Naomi looked at her proudly, with tears falling from her eyes as they met Ruth's.

Ruth turned back to Nicholas. "It felt like a violation of our working relationship. Then I struggled with what our relationship should be like now since we're related, but I realized this evening that it doesn't have to be complicated. We have an existing relationship, and that's a good starting point for whatever growth may happen between us in the future. I'm not going to overthink it. Does that make sense?"

His eyes filled with tears. "Yeah, it does. Thank you. You don't know how much that means to me."

Ruth picked up the tissue box from the overbed table. She removed a couple of tissues and wiped her eyes. Then she pointed the box toward Nicholas. He grabbed a tissue and followed suit.

Naomi held out her hand. "I'm going to need some of those too."

* * *

RUTH NESTLED IN front of the roaring fireplace as Nicholas slowly walked around the first floor of her home with Naomi in tow. His face lit up as he walked toward the sunroom.

"So, that's where Martha almost fell out of her chair during the board meeting, right?" he asked.

Naomi looked at Ruth nervously.

"It's okay," Ruth said, then laughed. "He was bound to connect the dots from the stories you told him. I'm glad he's enjoying the tour."

Ruth appreciated the comic relief as she watched from the couch, adjusting to the new normal in her once quiet house. She and Nicholas had been home from the hospital only an hour and she was already feeling the pressure of their new relationship. Nicholas was on a quest to make up for the years he'd lost with her, and Naomi's help gave Ruth a chance to recover from the car ride. With the commute being the first opportunity to have Ruth to himself since they'd discovered their biological connection, Nicholas had forced Ruth to update him on the recent developments at Gardin Family Enterprises. Aside from Ruth's pushing pause on Nicholas's valuation and divestiture work, it was business as usual at the company overall.

The staff was still oblivious about Ruth and Nicholas's relationship, and she wanted to keep it that way. But his absence had allowed her to discover the extent to which he had assisted with the day-to-day operations at the company and how much her staff relied on him. For the past month, Ruth had received the emails and phone calls that would have otherwise gone to Nicholas. He had proven himself to be more than a consultant. Her staff viewed him as a core member of the team.

The sweet smell of roasted yams whirled through the air,

tantalizing Ruth. She and Naomi had agreed to share duties in caring for Nicholas, which would test their newly rekindled relationship. And Naomi already had a head start. She and Mary had planned a heart-healthy dinner. Nicholas had requested something light, so Mary had tried a new soup recipe. As Mary put the finishing touches on the mustard green and roasted yam soup, Nicholas filled up on details of Ruth's family life. He was captivated as Naomi led him on a show-and-tell excursion through the family photos interspersed around the living and dining rooms. He took notes in his phone, entering birth dates and anniversaries in his calendar.

After Naomi finished correlating photos from M.J.'s school years with stories she'd previously told Nicholas, they joined Ruth in the living room.

"You have a beautiful home. I'll be very comfortable here," Nicholas said, his eyes beaming with paternal pride.

"Thank you," Ruth said, then smiled. Although she didn't make a big deal about it, the sincerity of the compliment was not lost on her. His work had taken him around the world, and he was accustomed to luxurious accommodations.

"I almost forgot—I've got something for you," Naomi said as she and Nicholas walked to the sofa across from the one where Ruth rested.

Veering left toward Ruth, Naomi reached into her pocket. When she removed her hand, her fist was closed, concealing something inside. She extended her arm and released her fingers over an empty section of the sofa beside Ruth.

Ruth looked down at the sofa. "Oh, my key to your house," she said, picking up the old heart-shaped key chain that held the key.

"I hope you're ready to take it back," Naomi said, walking quickly to the sofa where Nicholas sat.

Ruth chuckled. "Yeah, that's a good idea. But you don't need to try to run from me. I could get up and hand it back to you if I wanted to."

"You'd have to catch me first." Naomi laughed.

Nicholas extended his neck. "Hold on. May I see that?" he asked.

"Sure," Ruth said, shrugging.

Nicholas picked up the key chain as he stared at it. Then he closed his eyes and rubbed his fingers over the scratches on the puffy metal heart, some superficial and others deep. When he opened his eyes, they began to water.

"Are you okay?" Ruth asked, remembering that people were often emotional after a heart attack.

"The silver has held up well," he said, his voice cracking. "It's sterling silver. . . . It was made in Italy."

"No. . . . You?" Ruth said, choking up.

Nicholas nodded. "I gave it to your mother. . . . And you had it with you all this time, through all the stages of your life that I missed."

"This means so much to me. . . . And we can make up for lost time," Ruth said, weeping. She stood up and carefully pulled Nicholas into a hug. *After all the years of daydreaming about what my father was like, I'm so grateful for the chance to get to know him.* The father and daughter stood in the middle of the living room with their arms wrapped around each other while Naomi looked on.

"Wow . . . just wow," Naomi said, wiping her eyes.

Mary entered with a tray containing a pitcher of cold water and drinking glasses. "Awww, how sweet!" she said as she placed the tray on the large marble coffee table.

As Ruth and Nicholas let go and went to their respective sofas, Ruth noticed that there were only three glasses on the tray. "How thoughtful, Mary. Thank you. Won't you sit and join us?" Ruth asked.

"Oh, no thank you," Mary replied. "The soup is almost done. I'm going to finish it and set the table while Nicholas rests for a bit. Then we can eat." She exchanged glances with Naomi as she poured the water and distributed the glasses. Ruth wondered what conversations had transpired between them before she and Nicholas had arrived.

"Are there any rules of the house I should know about?" Nicholas asked.

"Not really. As long as you pick up after yourself, we'll be fine."

"Of course," he said. "That's easy enough."

"I'm going to be around to help him. So, he won't need to do much for himself, at least for the first week or two," Naomi said.

"You two take such good care of me," Nicholas said.

"The first week or two? You live next door. Are you planning to move off the estate after the first couple of weeks? Or is Nicholas chasing you away?" Ruth laughed. She looked up at Mary. Their eyes made contact, and Mary chuckled before rushing off to the kitchen.

"Nicholas doesn't know his way around here, so I figured I'd stay over and help," Naomi said.

Ruth shook her head. "Wait a minute. You never mentioned anything about moving in too."

"A few months ago, you tried to convince me to live with you, remember? So now your wish has come true. I've already unpacked my bag in the upstairs guest room." Naomi smiled. "Things have a way of working out, don't they?"

Chapter Twenty-one

Mary inspected the dining room at Alabaster Lunch Box before she left for the day. The tables were spotless, and the chairs at the long wooden table near the front window were lined up twenty-four inches apart—a number that allowed diners elbow room but didn't compromise space in the dining area. To the naked eye, things looked the same, but they weren't. So much had changed in three months.

The early March days were getting longer, and Mary was able to enjoy her free time outside the restaurant. With less than a week remaining in her catering manager's ninety-day trial period, Mary was pleased with her impact. Shirl had taken on additional responsibility after Mary's health crisis. The staff had adjusted well to the leadership transition, and having someone to share the day-to-day duties with had substantially improved Mary's quality of life after she returned to work. Her follow-up testing had revealed that her heart was back to normal, and she was making progress with getting her personal life back on track. She still didn't like waking up early to get to work, but she loved that on most days, she left the restaurant during the afternoon rather than staying into the early evening, which she'd done every day before Shirl came on board.

A loud knock at the front door interrupted Mary as she turned off the lights in the dining room. A courier peered through the glass door, holding a medium-sized cardboard box. Mary ran through her mental to-do list and confirmed she wasn't expecting a delivery.

She opened the door and held it open with her backside as she signed for the package. "I've never seen your company around here. Is it new?" she asked the courier.

"No, but we're based in Atlanta. I'd never heard of Edin, Georgia, before I received the assignment this morning. I assumed you ordered this, but I guess somebody wanted you to have a nice present. We do a lot of work for the antique store where I picked this up. They have some nice stuff in there. Enjoy," she said, smiling as she handed Mary the box.

"Thank you. Safe travels back to Atlanta," Mary said, looking down at the package. She estimated that it weighed about five pounds. But when she shook it gently, there was little movement.

Mary locked the door behind her and placed the package on the wooden table near the door. Then she carefully ran the door key along the tape stretched across the center of the package. She pulled open the flaps, revealing a rectangular teal velvet box tied closed with a satin ribbon.

Mary looked across the room at the splashes of teal in the restaurant: the sofa booth in the corner of the restaurant, the shutters around the windows, the base of the counter. *I can't stand that he still knows me so well,* she thought, recognizing the special delivery as Tynan's handiwork.

"No," she said aloud. She closed the flaps and slid the box away from her.

But she couldn't fight her curiosity. Within seconds, she pulled it toward her and flipped up the flaps. She untied the ribbon and raised the top of the velvet box. She reached inside and carefully removed an oblong box that looked similar to the cream-colored marble cutting board she had in her kitchen at home, but this box was softer. It took Mary a moment to realize that it was made of alabaster—a tribute to the name of her restaurant.

Her heartbeat quickened as she lifted the top off the alabaster box and found a piece of paper rolled up inside. She sat the lid on the table and unrolled the page. Instead of the expected material and typeface used in package inserts, Mary found archival-quality bamboo paper with Tynan's handwriting. *Of course. Nice touch,* she thought, recalling his close relationships with numerous antique dealers on behalf of his boss.

> *Dear Mary,*
> *I'm sorry for the pain I have caused you. I still struggle with selfishness. Perhaps my writing this is a reflection that I still care too much about my own feelings, but I thought I would have heard from you by now. I've tried to be patient, but I miss you. Please talk to me. I'm outside in the parking lot. Come to the door if you're willing to talk.*
> > *Ty*

As Mary dropped the note onto the table, her indecisiveness about Tynan fell away with it. She was more surprised by the certainty she instantly felt than by the gift or note. It was characteristic of Tynan to try to bribe her with an extravagant gift, but it was also typical of him to ignore her request to wait to hear from her. She was exasperated by his selfishness, and she wanted to tell him so. But she wasn't sure if she was comfortable with the idea of talking to him right then. She didn't want her anger to get the best of her. She needed a second to be sure. She wanted to be confident in her actions so there would be no second-guessing herself later.

Mary rested her forehead in the palm of her right hand and tapped at her hairline. She prayed for guidance. Then she squeezed her eyes tightly at the realization that she possessed the strength to move forward with her first instinct.

She lifted her head and opened her eyes. Tynan stood at the door, staring at her.

Mary sighed as she walked slowly to the door, allowing herself space for any last-minute revelations. But there weren't any, so she stuck with her gut and unlocked the door. When she swung it open, she looked in Tynan's direction, but she avoided making eye contact. Instead, her eyes landed on the gray sweatshirt he wore. It was identical to hers, with *T.E.A.M.* across the chest in black writing, but his sweatshirt still looked new. Its letters weren't faded and peeling like the one that had become Mary's lifeline during Tynan's disappearance.

"Thank you for letting me in," he said.

"Yeah. Have a seat," she replied with a matter-of-fact tone.

Tynan walked over to the table and sat next to the one that Mary had used when she'd opened the package. He looked back and noticed her standing at the edge of the table with her arms crossed. "Don't you want to sit too?" he asked.

Just because he thinks he's in control doesn't mean he is. He's not going to come to my restaurant and tell me what to do. She looked him in the eye. "No, I'm fine here, but thank you for the thoughtful gift. It looks like it set you back a bit."

Tynan picked up his chair and turned it toward Mary. "It wasn't too bad, but I wanted you to know that I'm sorry," he said, his chest sticking out like a peacock's.

"I appreciate your apology, Ty. But it's hard to believe that it's heartfelt when you're still only thinking about what's best for you."

"Don't say that. I think about you all the time. That's why I'm here."

"All the time? Sure, you do. When's the last time you wore that sweatshirt?"

Tynan looked down at the shirt. Then he looked blankly at Mary.

"Have you worn it since you gave mine to me?"

He shook his head.

A mixture of contempt and disappointment spread across Mary's face. "Exactly. And I'm sure you didn't miss it while you were in South Dakota either. Just like when you gave me that hoodie, wearing it today is about making yourself look good. That's what everything's about, even that beautiful alabaster box. Your selfishness almost took away my dream of opening my own restaurant. How dare you co-opt a symbol of my success for your own needs."

Tynan didn't flinch. He said softly, "But, love, that's not—"

"Don't call me that," Mary snapped. "This isn't something I'm making up. You acknowledged your selfishness in your note. And I asked you to wait until I reached out to you . . . yet here you are. You couldn't even be patient enough for me to come to the door. You always make decisions based on what *you* want," she said, pointing at him. "There's no room for me in your world, and I don't want to be with someone who thinks of me as an accessory in the life he's carved out for himself. That's not a partnership."

"But I came all the way here for you," he whined.

"No, you did that for yourself. If you were thinking about me, you'd have waited, as I asked."

"Would your answer have been any different if I had waited?"

"No, I doubt it."

"Well, it sounds like I made a good decision to come here, then. I only wish I'd done it sooner," Tynan said dismissively.

Mary shook her head. "Do what you gotta do, right, Ty?" When they first started dating four years prior, Tynan explained that the saying was his guiding principle. Mary initially regarded the statement as a reflection of his work ethic, but she eventually came to view it as a representation of his need to overcompensate for his abusive childhood by working too hard and refusing to establish real connection with anyone. It was what had always motivated him to survive and succeed, but it was also the foundation of his decision to mistreat her.

"Of course," Tynan said. "Why are you shaking your head at me? I'm just being honest."

Don't give foolery the benefit of the doubt. Don't even give it the benefit of consideration, Mary thought, recalling her grandmother's advice growing up. She wished she'd listened earlier. "It makes me sad, Ty. I hope things work out for you someday."

He sighed. "They always do. I hope the same for you." He stood up and walked toward Mary. "Reach out if I can ever be helpful to you." He bent down and gently kissed her forehead. Then he walked out the door.

* * *

NAOMI SWAYED ALONG with the jazz riffs that Nicholas played on her piano as she sipped hibiscus tea and chatted with Martha, who had stopped by for a visit after work.

"You look great, Nicholas," Martha said when he finished playing. "I'm impressed with how committed you've been to your healthful diet and cardiac rehabilitation program."

Nicholas swung his legs around the piano bench so he could face the two women. "Thank you. But how could I not take this seriously? The heart attack was a wake-up call when it came to my poor eating habits. All those years of traveling and eating junk finally caught up with me," he said, patting the center of his chest. "But I'm doing better. I used to tease Naomi about how different her food choices were compared to mine, but now I see why your family eats mainly plant-based foods. Thanks for being patient with me. I'm getting used to eating healthier."

"We're happy to help," Martha said. "Beau's death was a big lesson for us. We all improved our diets after that. I have patients who have reversed their heart blockage by changing to a totally plant-based diet, but even doing it part-time can make a huge difference. And exercising is vital too."

"Yes, I walked a half mile this morning," he said. "I plan to be jogging around here before you know it."

Naomi looked at Martha as she patted Nicholas's leg. "Yeah, he's doing well. I can't believe it's been three weeks already. The days are going by quickly."

"Do you miss each other now that you've come back to your house?" Martha asked.

Naomi and Nicholas laughed.

"How could we?" Naomi said. "It's only been two days since I've been back here, but we still spend nearly the same amount of time together."

"So, Nicholas, how are things going for you at Ruth's?" Martha pried.

"Fine, just fine. It's thoughtful of you to ask, Martha. And I'm planning to return to Gardin Family Enterprises next week. I'm working from home this week so everything will be on track for the board meeting." He smiled.

"Oh, I didn't expect you to be back at work so soon," Martha said, leaning forward.

"I could've gone back after two weeks, but I wanted to give myself some time to relax and spend time with Ruth and Naomi. It's important to me that the transition goes smoothly for everyone. . . . And I trust that if you had any reservations with my continuing in my consulting role, you would've spoken up about them before now, right?" Nicholas asked, his tone shifting to the one he usually used in the office.

Martha cracked her knuckles. "Right. . . . Yes, absolutely."

"Good. I hoped you would agree," Naomi said with a smile, her eyes squinting.

Martha laughed nervously. "Have you two thought about

what you'll do after your consulting contract is over? You're not trying to take our aunt back to Philadelphia, are you?"

"Well, that will be up to your aunt, won't it, Naomi?"

Naomi blushed.

Martha leaned forward and stared at Nicholas. "Okay, seriously. If I may ask, what are your intentions, Nicholas?"

He turned to Naomi. "Is it okay if I answer?"

"Sure," Naomi replied. She lifted her cup of tea to her lips.

"I've been very clear with Naomi that I see a future with her, but I don't want to rush things. I want her to be comfortable."

"Good," Martha said, leaning back in her chair. "And we will want to be sure that she is protected financially. We will not allow anyone to try to take advantage of her."

"That's understandable," Nicholas said coolly.

Naomi took another sip of her tea before she spoke. "Please don't be so arrogant, Martha. I wouldn't ordinarily discuss such a personal matter, but you've already opened the door." Then she looked over at Nicholas. "May I?"

"Sure, it's fine. We're all family, right, Martha?" He winked.

"Nicholas's net worth far exceeds mine, by several times," Naomi said.

"I invested well." Nicholas smiled. "But I'm happy to sign whatever agreement your aunt might want to protect her assets should she decide that she would like things to move forward in our relationship."

Naomi laughed. "That's only if my niece doesn't chase you away."

Martha lowered her head. "I'm sorry. I didn't mean to offend you, Nicholas." She wouldn't dare say it out loud, but she was kicking herself for not realizing his wealth. She believed that Ruth had schemed her way into the family fortune and that Mary was lucky with Tynan before his financial situation took an unexpected turn at her expense, albeit temporarily. Now even her aunt was astute at choosing a man with means. Martha couldn't understand how the trait had somehow skipped over her. *I need to do something different.*

"Maybe you mean well, Martha," Nicholas said, raising an eyebrow, "but it would help if you got to know me instead of jumping to conclusions. That seems to be a recurring theme with you, whether it involves relationships in the family or how Gardin Family Enterprises is run."

Naomi nodded.

He leaned forward and continued. "As a physician, you're accustomed to having to make a quick assessment when taking care of patients, but what happens if your assessment is wrong? Could your mistake cause a patient to become sicker? Or could they die? What if something similar is happening with your assessments of family situations? How would it feel to cause the Gardin family to topple before it became the empire it was destined to be?" he asked with the vocal inflection of a seasoned attorney on cross-examination.

Martha looked at Nicholas intently. She had always been careful to listen to patients and manage her ego as she did her clinical work, but she'd never believed the same approach was needed with her family or that her failure to do so could prevent her dreams from coming to fruition. She was starting to second-guess her perspective, even if it was just because she admired Nicholas's success.

* * *

THE HOSPITAL CAFETERIA was busier at lunchtime than Martha had remembered. Hospital employees and visitors filled all the tables. A line stretched along the hot-food bar and salad bar, converging into a sea of people near the cash registers. Martha usually brought her lunch and ate in her office, but she had forgotten her food at home. Grabbing lunch in the cafeteria made sense because she'd soon be heading to a meeting in the conference room just down the hallway.

As Martha took the last bite of her salad and answered emails on her phone, she was interrupted by a smooth baritone voice. "Excuse me, Dr. Gardin. Is it okay if I join you?"

It had taken Martha five minutes to find the empty table in the rear corner of the cafeteria. She had hoped no one would see the extra seat, but it seemed her luck had run out. She had only a few minutes before her meeting, and the last thing she wanted to do was engage in idle talk with someone she didn't know.

Martha looked up from her cell phone and found herself face-to-face with Oji Greenwald. Despite her efforts to reach him and discuss her desire to work with him to bring her restaurant idea to life, he had remained elusive. Yet when she had finally given up, here he was. The shawl collar and elbow patches on his cardigan added a conservative spin to his business-casual attire, but the smile on his face revealed a more playful interest.

Months of pent-up frustration over Oji's evasiveness collapsed as he stood before her. She had dressed that morning in a fuchsia wrap dress so that she would feel confident in her afternoon meeting with the hospital's other center directors, but she hadn't expected that she would need a boost of fortitude as she hovered over a bowl of lettuce. "Oh, Mr. Greenwald. Yes, of course. Please have a seat," she said, fighting the urge to grin like a schoolgirl who'd found out that the cool guy all the girls wanted to date knew her name.

"Thank you. Please call me Oji," he said, lowering his tray of nearly finished food to the table and sitting in the empty chair across from Martha.

"I've been trying to get a meeting with you for months."

"I apologize for giving you the runaround. At first my schedule was all over the place. I fell behind with returning messages.

Then we made a decision about the restaurant, and I was trying to figure out how to best proceed with you."

Martha wrinkled her forehead. "Yeah, I was disappointed to hear that you'd already made a decision." She appreciated Oji's explanation, but it did little to assuage the rejection she felt. She didn't understand the purpose of his intrusion during her few moments of free time, but she maintained a professional disposition in hopes that she might somehow be presented with another opportunity to work with him.

"So, it sounds like you've talked to your sister," he said, leaning toward the table as his voice deepened slightly.

"She mentioned that the two of you have been speaking about the restaurant. Why do you ask? Is there something I can do for you?"

"We had already made the decision to work with Mary by the time I realized why you were calling me, so I hope you won't hold that against me. But I've been admiring you from a distance for a while now, and I'm wondering if I could take you to dinner this weekend."

Martha's eyes widened. Her mouth flew open in shock, getting wider when she laughed awkwardly. "That wasn't what I was expecting at all."

Oji blushed. "I hope that doesn't mean you're turning me down. I excused myself from a lunch meeting with the hospital's marketing director so I could ask you out. She wasn't happy with me for bailing on her, so it would be horrible if this didn't turn out well."

"Perhaps that's what you deserve for ignoring my calls. All you had to do was tell me you were seeing someone else—I mean, that you decided to work with someone else, even if it was my sister."

"I like that Freudian slip, and I heard you were the type who didn't hesitate to put someone in their place." He smiled.

Martha was embarrassed by her verbal mix-up, but she decided to use it to her advantage. She rested her head on her hand
and lightly fluttered her eyelashes. "Well, I guess you've got me
all figured out, huh?"

Oji chuckled. "So, dinner?"

"That's the least you could do," she said, then smiled.

"I like a challenge," he said, bobbing his head. "I'm looking
forward to it."

Martha looked at her cell phone. "Well, I've got to head to
a meeting and I'm going to be late if I don't get moving. Do
you need my number?" she asked, lifting her lunch tray as she
stood up.

Oji reached for the tray. He brushed Martha's hand as their
eyes met. "I'll take your tray as I leave. And I've got your number.
The messages, remember?" He grinned.

"Oh yeah." Martha giggled, her hand lingering before she released the tray. "Thanks. I look forward to hearing from you."
She would've preferred getting her restaurant, but hanging out
with a handsome rich guy who enjoyed making power moves as
much as she did was a suitable consolation prize.

* * *

MARY HADN'T BEEN to her sister's home since Christmas morning, when she'd picked up Martha on her way to Naomi's cottage for brunch. The sisters had spoken little since their joint
counseling session. Their interaction had been limited to coordinating support for Naomi and Nicholas in the wake of his heart
attack. Martha had made sure Nicholas understood the direc-
tions from the doctors and followed through with them, and
Mary had taught him some of her favorite heart-healthy recipes,
supporting his desire to eat a largely plant-based diet without
totally giving up meat. So, when Mary received a call from Mar-

tha asking for her help, she was leery. But she couldn't turn her down. Her sister's voice sounded light and airy, and that was enough to pique Mary's interest.

Not much had changed in Martha's cottage in two and a half months. It was spotless, and everything was in its place. A stack of coffee table books in the living room was placed at an angle such that the spines could be read and the vase of camellia blooms sitting atop could be appreciated from any position on the sofa or love seat. The jackets and scarves on the mudroom hooks were arranged by color, as meticulously as the clothes in Martha's bedroom closet.

But something about Martha had changed. As Mary rummaged through her sister's bedroom closet, Martha didn't complain that she was making a mess. She hummed a familiar tune that Mary couldn't name, ambivalent that Mary didn't follow her rule of keeping all the hangers a half inch apart.

Mary was intrigued by her sister's pleasant mood, but she grew frustrated that she knew so little about what had caused it. She had followed Martha's lead and tried to oblige her vague request to help her find the perfect outfit to make a good impression, but she needed more information. "What kind of event are you going to?" Mary asked. "I can't make a recommendation if you aren't willing to share details."

"There's a good reason for that." Martha sighed. "I've been trying to figure out how to apologize."

Mary paused and replayed the sentence in her head. Martha rarely apologized, and when she did, the apologies never started with her being in a good mood. They were usually forced and took place when Martha was backed into a corner, which caused her to be defensive and snarky.

Mary abandoned her post in the walk-in closet and joined Martha in the bedroom. "I'm gonna need to get comfortable for this," Mary chirped as she settled into her favorite spot in the cottage—a dark gray balloon-back porter's chair placed next to a wall-high window that spilled into a skylight. She rested her arms on the hand-carved mahogany chair frame like a queen sitting on her throne.

Martha added a lime-green asymmetric pleated skirt to the clothing options draped over her sleigh bed. Then she sat on the floor, looking up at Mary. "I want to apologize, but I feel like I've said 'I'm sorry' so many times over the years that it may not mean anything to hear me say it now. But I am sorry for being so arrogant and disrespectful."

"Hmm," Mary said. "I appreciate that, but where is this coming from all of a sudden?"

"Something Nicholas said to me the other day clicked in my head. It's like I was able to see myself the way he saw me. I didn't like what I saw. Then I ran into Oji Greenwald yesterday, and I felt sick afterward thinking about how it must've looked for me to be competing against my sister for a business opportunity."

Mary was grateful for Martha's newly found self-reflection, but she wasn't sure how much she could trust it long term. Besides, Martha still seemed to be focused on what others thought of her. But Mary tried not to let that discount that her sister was experiencing a long-overdue breakthrough. She could accept Martha for who she was. That would allow her to maintain the sisterhood they shared, even if she wasn't sure they were suited to be friends. They could at least try to have a healthy sibling relationship. "That's a start in the right direction," she said.

Martha looked relieved. "Thank you."

"So, *you* weren't behind the request for me to partner with the primary care center on some of the cooking classes at the new restaurant?" Mary asked.

"No, this is the first I've heard of it," Martha replied. "My boss asked to meet with me next week about a new opportunity in the community. He hasn't told me anything else about it yet, but I bet he's behind this. Would it be okay with you if it turns out to be about the restaurant?"

"I need to sit with it for a while, but I think we can make it work," Mary said.

"Well, the day is full of surprises! And to get back to your question. . . . I have some news . . . Oji asked me out and we're going to dinner Saturday night."

"Oh, so *that's* why you're so giddy! I don't think I've ever seen you like this."

"It feels weird! I'm excited but so nervous. And worried too. I wasn't expecting it at all."

"Well, you're both very strategic. I don't think you have anything to be worried about. It'll be fine. Just focus on having fun."

"Thank you! I'm gonna try. But speaking of strategy, I need one more favor. There's somewhere I'd like you to come with me tomorrow."

Chapter Twenty-two

Ruth stared at the calendar on her computer screen, trying to figure out the purpose of her five o'clock appointment and with whom she would be meeting. The event name said "GardinSis." She assumed it was some sort of typographical error. With Chloe on maternity leave and the fill-in assistant from the temporary employment agency out sick during her first week in the office, Ruth had no choice but to wait and see who showed up.

As she freshened up her nude lip gloss, there was a knock at her office door. She rubbed her lips together and blew herself a kiss before she tucked her compact mirror and gloss in her desk. "Come in," she said.

Nicholas opened the door. "It's five o'clock and the entire office has cleared out," he said from the doorway. "You shouldn't work late on a Friday. It's officially the weekend. You can work from home if you insist on it."

Ruth smiled. She and Nicholas had found a nice rhythm. Although she had worried they would get in each other's way at home or at work, that hadn't been the case. Their friendship was solid, and she didn't mind when he became a little paternal from time to time. "I can't leave yet, but I'm glad you stopped in. I've got a five o'clock meeting. I hoped you might have some idea what it's about."

"I don't know, but I can't see why Chloe would've scheduled that."

"I don't think she did. It was probably scheduled earlier this week."

"Will you make it in time for dinner? It's veggie pizza night. Naomi actually makes that plant-based cheese taste pretty good."

"I love when you admit I'm right," Ruth teased. "Her house or mine?"

"Yours, of course. You've got a pizza oven in your backyard. That's enough to convince me to stay at your house for a while." Nicholas laughed.

"I like having you around. By the way, your contract will be up next month. Have you and Naomi—"

Before Ruth could complete her thought, Nicholas heard the front door open. As he turned to look into the hallway, he heard familiar voices in the distance. "Mystery solved! I know who you're meeting with. It's Mary and Martha!" He waved down the hallway to get the sisters' attention.

"Mary and Martha? That's odd," Ruth said.

"Indeed. I don't know why I'm always around when you have these surprise family meetups at the office, but I'm not staying for this one. I've got a date with a pizza!"

"I imagine that whatever this is won't take that long. Are you sure you don't want to stay?" She smirked.

"I will if you want me to. I shouldn't abandon you just because I've got pizza on my mind."

Ruth laughed. "I'm just kidding. It'll be fine," she said, standing when she heard Mary's and Martha's footsteps in the hallway.

Mary hugged Nicholas. "Hi! It's fun to see you in work mode. Are you headed out?"

"Yes, I don't do five o'clock meetings," he said, laughing and hugging Martha as Mary inched into Ruth's office.

"That's my fault," Martha said. "I had a meeting at the hospital, so I wasn't able to get here earlier. I hope it's okay, Ruth?"

"No problem," Ruth said, equally confused about the nature

of the surprise meeting and by Martha's pleasant disposition. "Make yourselves comfortable." She extended her hand toward the chairs on the opposite side of her desk. She considered the friendlier environment offered by the table at the rear of her office but opted to sit at her desk in case she needed the positioning to establish the power differential during the conversation.

"Have a good evening, ladies. See you at home, Ruth," Nicholas said. "I'll lock the front door on my way out."

"Okay. Thank you," Ruth replied.

"Bye," Mary and Martha said in unison.

"So, what brings you here this evening?" Ruth asked.

Martha cracked her knuckles. "This is harder than I expected," she said, her voice shaking slightly. "I've been horrible to you for a long time, even before Beau died. I've blamed you for things that weren't your fault . . . since I was a kid. And even after I was old enough to understand, I carried a grudge anyway. I'm not saying I agree with everything you've done, but you don't deserve the treatment I've given you. I shouldn't treat anyone like that, especially not a family member. I'm . . . I'm sorry I hurt you."

"I've not been much better, so I want to apologize too," Mary said, wiping her eyes. "I've betrayed the relationship we had. This is going to sound silly for a grown woman to say, but it needs to be said. I've finally figured out that I can love both you and Martha. I don't have to choose. Thank you for your unwavering support throughout my illness. Even though things have been better between us for the past couple of months, I still need to apologize to you and also acknowledge how hard it must've been for you to go through my illness so soon after Beau's heart problems . . . and then to go through it again with Nicholas. You've been the backbone of our family, quietly holding everything together, while we were only thinking of ourselves."

Tears flowed down Ruth's face. She'd waited so long for recognition and apologies that she no longer expected to receive them. "Thank you. This is a big surprise. I thought you were coming to present some type of legal document to throw me out of Gardin Family Enterprises, and I'm relieved that's not the case."

"No, my biggest misstep was questioning your place within the family, but kicking you out of the company would've been catastrophic too," said Martha. "I've spent some time talking with Aunt Naomi and Nicholas, and I understand how much you've contributed to the company. I can't think of a better person to serve as the permanent CEO."

"That means a lot to me," Ruth said, dabbing her face with tissue.

"Maybe we could get some help with navigating between the family relationships and professional issues so we're less likely to cross the lines in the future," Mary said.

"That's a great idea," Ruth said. Although she was able to reset with Nicholas fairly easily, Ruth's history with Mary and Martha was more complicated. She made a note to ask Nicholas to recommend an organizational psychologist who could consult with the family. The process would be challenging, but Ruth felt as though her success with working out her relationship with Nicholas and Naomi would help her to establish a new path with the sisters.

"I agree with that," Martha said, nodding. "We'd like you to have whatever support you need."

The unexpected meeting was a new starting point, prompting Ruth to move forward with something she'd been mulling over. "I have another idea that I'd like to discuss with the two of you and Aunt Naomi in preparation for our board meeting next week."

* * *

Naomi sat erect in the chair, her eyes focused on the figure that Nicholas used to explain the last potential divestment scenario. There was little space for her mind to wander during the fast-paced Gardin Family Enterprises board meeting. The new meeting location in the company conference room made for a more rigid environment. She also wanted to support Nicholas and show him that she took her stewardship of the company seriously. The past few months had been filled with many firsts for their relationship, and this was their first Gardin Family Enterprises board meeting together. But as Nicholas's contract with the company ended in two weeks and his cardiac rehabilitation program ended in another month, questions hung in the air.

As Nicholas finished his presentation and turned on the lights, Naomi scanned the room. Ruth, Mary, and Martha jotted down action items and reviewed notes, but Naomi couldn't help thinking about what it was like when Ruth and her parents had converged there in that same space. As much as the past few months had raised the question of family connectedness and its place in the company, Naomi had never been more grateful for the bonds and the restoration she witnessed throughout the board meeting. She was proud that the family had finally come to a place of balance without much intervention on her part. But she was still nervous about what lay ahead for the rest of the meeting.

"You've asked lots of questions throughout the presentation, but there's still plenty of time for more," Nicholas said. "I want to make sure you're clear on my recommendations, as well as the potential next steps. Obviously, I will still be accessible after my contract is over." He smiled at Naomi. "But it's easier if you ask them now. Then I can use the next week to make sure you have the information you need to move forward."

As Ruth stood up, she looked at Mary, Martha, and Naomi. "Any questions from the three of you?" she asked.

The women shook their heads.

"We'd like to formally express our gratitude so that it's on record for the minutes of the board meeting," Ruth said, looking at Nicholas. "We're very thankful for the way you've taken on your work with us. Even before our personal connection emerged, you extended yourself to me and my staff in a way that I have never experienced with anyone outside the Gardin family. I'm happy to share that we've talked among ourselves and, based on the preliminary reports you provided to us prior to this meeting, we've decided not to sell the company. As you recommended, and in keeping with our initial plan, we will consider the divestment options you've presented and likely be prepared to move forward with a plan later this year to sell some of our business lines. That's going to be a heavy lift."

Ruth smiled ear to ear. "I'm also happy to share that I will move to the permanent president and CEO position. I'm going to need some help, so the board has authorized me to inquire about your interest in working with us long term as chief operating officer. We understand that you had plans to retire after this project, so we would be happy to have you work with us even on a part-time basis. We're hopeful that the flexibility of the position is enough to entice you to seriously consider our offer."

Nicholas laughed loudly. "I didn't see this coming." He turned to Naomi. "Did you know about this?"

She grinned. "Yes, of course! Your favorite questions are the ones that you already know the answer to," she teased.

"And you didn't say a word. I'm impressed!" he said. Then he turned back to Ruth. "Congratulations! I'm very proud of you. I've enjoyed getting to know the nuts and bolts of this company and this family. There's no one better to run the company. I had no inkling you were thinking about asking me to stay on, but I'm intrigued by your offer. Let's talk about it and see what we can work out."

* * *

EASTER MORNING WAS quiet in downtown Edin, except one place. The crowd had disbanded after the sunrise church service, and the Gardin family gathered around a dining room table at Alabaster Lunch Box for breakfast, where there were seemingly endless quantities of laughter and Mary's lemon-blueberry scones. The family couldn't get enough of the pastry's sweet tartness, prompting Mary to return to the kitchen twice to refill the basket, even as they feasted on omelets, grits, sweet potato hash browns, and a fruit salad made of strawberries, kiwi, mango, pineapple, papaya, satsuma, and star fruit.

Easter Sunday always felt full of possibility and hope for Ruth, and her mood was buoyed by the feeling of new beginnings in the air. The centerpiece, a rose gold and rhinestone-encrusted egg atop a bed of eucalyptus leaves surrounded by an array of pastel alabaster eggs, added to her joy. She had offered to host breakfast at her house, but Mary overruled her by insisting on hosting it at the restaurant. Ruth relented in support of Mary starting her own traditions in Edin, especially because she had decided not to return to New York. With the restaurant closed for the holiday and Mary's cottage too small to host everyone, the restaurant was the perfect breakfast location. It served as a reminder of Mary's recent accomplishment of finalizing the agreement to open a second location of Alabaster Lunch Box in Macon—a feat that also made Easter Sunday an ideal occasion for Oji Greenwald, who was now dating Martha exclusively, to have his first meal with the Gardins.

"Mary, I could eat these scones all day. We may have to start talking about mass production," Ruth said.

"Thank you, but I don't think so. I'm gonna have my hands full with two restaurants!" Mary replied. "But since Martha will be working with me on the teaching kitchen and the community-outreach activities, I may have more free time than I initially expected." She glanced sideways at her sister. "As long as Martha remembers that I'm the boss."

Ruth was pleased to hear that Mary and Martha had found a compromise regarding the new restaurant. Although Oji had largely been quiet during the meal, Ruth liked the influence he'd had on Martha so far. Between their relationship and Martha's eventual involvement in the new restaurant, Ruth expected to be the prime beneficiary of Martha being distracted from Gardin Family Enterprises. Ruth would be Oji's cheerleader, as long as he stayed loyal to Martha. Ruth also was amused that Mary's suggestion of an organizational psychologist the previous month was likely motivated by her realization that she would need one to deal with her new working relationship with her sister. *It's never a dull moment in this family.*

"Don't worry. I got it. You're the boss. Oji will remind me in case I forget," Martha said.

"Oh no! I'm staying out of that." Oji laughed.

"You're a smart man," Nicholas said, rising to his feet. "If it's okay with everyone, I'd like to say something. Easter is a day for counting our blessings. It's a day for celebrating renewal. When Ruth reached out to me about the opportunity to consult with Gardin Family Enterprises, I almost declined it. I wasn't sure I should take on another project, because I was thinking about retiring.

"But I felt like I was being led here. I'm so thankful that I listened. You have trusted me with your business, first as a consultant and now as chief operating officer of Gardin Family Enterprises. I'm excited about this new adventure. However, I'm most touched that you have trusted me with your hearts. You have helped heal my heart, and you have given me my heart's desire—a daughter I've always wanted and a partner I never knew I needed. I am thankful for this family." Nicholas paused long enough to look at Naomi, then Ruth, Martha, and Mary.

He removed a handkerchief from his back pocket and wiped his eyes. Ruth dabbed her eyes too, fighting to hold back a barrage of tears. She looked at Mary and Martha, who also wiped their eyes.

"I'd like to share something with you," Nicholas continued. "It's a token that I hope will serve as a reminder of this day of new beginnings." He reached across the table and pulled the rhinestone-encrusted egg that sat in the center of the table toward him. He flipped open the top of it. Then he removed four gold chains, from which hung identical egg-shaped Fabergé pendants covered in diamonds, rubies, emeralds, and sapphires.

The women collectively gasped.

He turned to Ruth, who was seated at his left. "Thank you," he said as he hugged her and handed her a necklace. Tears streamed down Naomi's face, but she kept her eyes fixed on Nicholas as he moved around the table, having a similar moment with Mary and then Martha.

He held the remaining necklace in his hand. "Is it okay if I put this on?" he asked as he approached Naomi.

"Yes," she said, her eyes twinkling as she arose from the chair.

"Please sit," Nicholas said.

"But I can't see you."

"It's okay. Give me a minute," he said as he wiped his eyes and fastened the necklace around Naomi's neck. He walked around the chair. "See me now?" He smiled.

The table erupted in laughter, and Naomi blushed.

Nicholas continued to speak. "It's important that I'm able to see you for what I have to say next. There's a reason I chose the necklace that I've given to you, Ruth, Mary, and Martha. You inspired my choice. The bold, colorful jewels remind me of the intense love you show to those dear to you, and I'm honored to count myself among those who benefit from your love." He looked around the table at the women. "Each of you is a force in this family, and you have also each become a force in my life. The past three, almost four, months have been a whirlwind. I'm not usually a whirlwind kind of guy, but you have challenged me to ask myself what's important in life. There's no place I'd rather be than here in Edin with you and this family."

Nicholas stared into Naomi's eyes. "I love you, and I love your family. So, Naomi, it's time that I ask you a very important question."

He reached into his pocket as he bent down on one knee. "Will you marry me?" he asked, holding an eternity band that matched the bejeweled necklace that he had placed around Naomi's neck.

Tears poured from Naomi's eyes as she looked down at him. "Yes!" she yelled. "Absolutely, yes!"

Nicholas placed the band on her finger, and Naomi locked her arms around him, rocking back and forth.

Applause and sobs broke out around the table. The women jumped up and gathered the couple in a group hug.

As the embrace disbanded and the women marveled at Naomi's ring, Oji walked over to Nicholas.

Mary nudged Martha, not wanting her to miss the dialogue between the two men.

"Well done, Nicholas," Oji said, patting him on the back. "And, of course, I don't feel any pressure at all." Oji laughed. "None at all."

The men chuckled as they shook hands.

Martha nodded approvingly. She leaned close to her sister. "I've learned a lot watching Ruth maneuver to get what she wants, so I'm finally using it to my advantage," she whispered.

Mary stared at Martha. Then she squinted while tilting her head.

"I'm just kidding," Martha said.

"Are you?" Mary asked.

"Of course I am," Martha said, then grinned.

Mary slowly returned the smile. "Okay . . . good," she said hesitantly.

Naomi looked around the room at the smiling faces, her own filled with delight.

"You were right, MIL. It's beautiful," Ruth said.

"My ring?" Naomi asked, gleefully extending her hand toward Ruth.

"Your ring is gorgeous, but I was talking about the family. You once said things had to get messy to reveal the beauty underneath."

Naomi winked. "We're not a perfect family, but we're making it work."

"Yes! And I got the family I always wanted," Ruth said, beaming.

Readers Guide

1. The town of Edin plays an important role in the Gardin family's history. What connection do you have to your hometown or a place that is important in your family's history? How has that connection influenced your life?

2. *The Gardins of Edin* raises the question of what it means to belong in a family, as well as what rights, privileges, and responsibilities a person has when they are part of one. How do you feel about these concepts?

3. Discuss the lessons *The Gardins of Edin* offers about navigating family conflict. What do you think of Naomi's hands-off approach to dealing with conflict in the family? Was it fair for her to change her approach after Beau died? What would you have done differently, if anything, if you were Naomi?

4. How do the characters' personalities and behavior line up with any previous knowledge you have of the women from the Bible who loosely inspire them?

5. What do you think of Martha's interaction with the emergency responders at the Christmas party? Have you ever been in a similar situation? How would you have handled it if you were in Martha's place?

6. What is your opinion of Ruth's reasons for objecting to Naomi and Nicholas's relationship? Whose side were you on—Ruth's or Naomi's?

7. How did Ruth's experience growing up with her mother influence the relationship she built with Naomi? Discuss how Ruth's approach to setting boundaries with her mother and holding her accountable differed from the way she did so with Naomi.

8. What are your thoughts on how Ruth and Nicholas's relationship evolved over the course of the story?

9. Mary saw red flags about Tynan when she first met him. What traits do you notice about Mary that may have led her to brush away her concerns and tolerate Tynan's behavior throughout their relationship?

10. What does Mary's final interaction with Tynan show about her growth and what she learned about herself in Edin?

11. How did *The Gardins of Edin* influence your perception of heart health? Why might the author have chosen to feature the most common type of heart disease and a less common one in the same book?

12. The connection between physical health and mental health is prominent in this book. Discuss how this played out with Mary and what impact it had on her and the family.

13. How did *The Gardins of Edin* influence your perception of mental health?

Acknowledgments

I am indebted to those who sowed into me over the years to help make the vision I had for this book a reality.

Many thanks to my developmental editor, Jamie Lapeyrolerie. You were meant to edit *The Gardins of Edin*. I don't believe in coincidences. We are our Louisiana ancestors' wildest dreams. They would be proud of our partnership to share the Gardin women with the world. I also extend tremendous thanks to the other members of the WaterBrook team who worked on my book: Helen Macdonald, Cara Iverson, JoLeigh Buchanan, Mollie Turbeville, Diane Hobbing, Luverta Reames, Ngozi Onike, Shauna Carlos, Jessica Kastner Keene, Elizabeth Groening, Joseph Perez, Jaya Miceli, Kristopher Orr, Ginia Hairston Croker, Beverly Rykerd, and Laura Barker.

To my fantastic agent, Amy Elizabeth Bishop, thank you for your insight, candor, and conviction. I knew you were special when you replied to my query by your stated deadline. And during a pandemic too! You make it all look easy, but I know your preparation takes lots of skill.

Lauren Cerand, my publicist extraordinaire: You are a stabilizing force and an answer to my prayers.

Asharee Peters and Zakiya N. Jamal: I am so honored that you made time to share your savvy with me. Very special thanks to you!

I am grateful to Zakiya Dalila Harris and Tom Colgan for editorial feedback that bolstered both early versions of the manuscript and my confidence as I navigated the grueling querying and submission processes. Such a godsend!

Many thanks to Don Pape for championing my manuscript.

I am very thankful to *The Gardins of Edin* launch team. I appreciate your advocacy, enthusiasm, and commitment. You are invaluable!

Thank you to the members of my Facebook group—The Petal Garden. You always brighten my day. Your feedback, likes, and overall support make social media fun. We are a joyful bunch, aren't we?

A million thanks to Dr. Preston Wigfall, my secret weapon.

I owe deep gratitude to JaNeen Molborn, LPC, MAMFT, the best mental health sensitivity reader and a true conduit of healing.

I don't know how I could have weaved some of the most intricate details of this story together without the expertise and kindness of Carol Riley and Kent Lindner. Thank you for your patience with my countless questions and potential scenarios. You are heroes in more ways than one!

I am especially thankful to Shari Oliver for inviting me to your office Christmas party in December 2019, which inspired the setting of the Gardin Family Enterprises Christmas party and catapulted me from the planning stages of this book to actually writing it.

Everyone needs writer friends like Jen Gilroy and Jayna

Breigh, who always make time to help while juggling their writing schedules and busy lives.

Condace Pressley, Melanie C. Duncan, and Terri Wiggins: I am so appreciative of your sage advice. You're absolute treasures!

Big thanks to the women who cheered me on, served as de facto stylists for me and my characters, provided comic relief on tough days, and so much more: Leslie Abbott, Kelly Burton, Chris Chanyasulkit, Rixney Reed Crockett, Tristane Darensburg, Felecia Emery, Wilsan Louidor, Janel Lowman, Dee McLeod, Patrice Tyson, Jan Buckner Walker, Josie White, and Keisha Williams.

I offer heartfelt thanks to Valerie Berry, the consummate encourager of my writing and the best beta reader *ever.* Your energy is a blessing!

My new aunty, Shilpa Gandhi: I appreciate you so much for looking out for me and treating me like family. You are the best!

Shivani Goswami: Thank you for *everything*! I could never have imagined the possibilities that you made a reality for me. I am indebted to you and Saumya Gandhi.

I owe deep gratitude to Hope Ferdowsian for your friendship, sharp insight, and thoughtful advice. I've learned so much from you.

Mrs. Sarah Laster, thank you for always encouraging me and believing in me. Your faith and wisdom are a gift.

A huge thanks to my parents, who made me look up everything in the encyclopedia as a kid but now seem shocked at how quickly I google things mid-conversation. Thank you for being my first writing teachers and editors.

I am grateful to Aurie and Ravie, Jr.—my siblings, advisors, and built-in accountability partners. Thank you for always reminding me who I am and what's expected of me. And thank you for sharing your talents with me.

CJ, Lundi, and Dilly, you inspire me to keep going. Thank you for always keeping me on my toes.

Lastly, this book is in honor of the women who lent me their names. May your love live on through every word I write.

About the Author

ROSEY LEE writes hopeful stories about complicated families and complex friendships.

As a native of the Westbank of New Orleans, Louisiana, who lives in Atlanta, Georgia, Rosey writes about the people, traditions, and food that anchor her to the South. She enjoys cooking, listening to live music, and occasional bursts of fanatical bargain shopping.

The Gardins of Edin is her debut novel.

About the Type

THIS BOOK was set in Sabon, a typeface designed by the well-known German typographer Jan Tschichold (1902–74). Sabon's design is based upon the original letter forms of sixteenth-century French type designer Claude Garamond and was created specifically to be used for three sources: foundry type for hand composition, Linotype, and Monotype. Tschichold named his typeface for the famous Frankfurt typefounder Jacques Sabon (c. 1520–80).